THE KING'S
FROG HUNTER

For Ellen &

D1474750

Trust in Bubo,
and believe in the Prophecy!

KINGDOM

The

Stones of
Anset

Stone Hills

Barrier

WESTERN

Marbala

Barrunda

BUSHY PLAIN

Castle
Ambermal

Dried
Bogs

Escat
Marshes

Cold Canyon

Bevie

Tamra

MIDDLE

Laundo

South
Ford

LAUNDO

Camotop

EAST
The High

ii

of AMERAM

Great Water

Land of the Insurphs
Forest

HILLS
Safedor

North Ford

Table Run

ELLO

GREAT PLAIN

Table Tops

Byron Marsh

Dudoon Bog

Dudoon

Dudoon Run

Wilderness of Touion

The Barrens

Sol Tingen River

HILLS

Ponds and Marsh

J G
A R
R A
8 T

Rainland

HILLS

W

River

S

N

RANGE

Plains of Joubar

E

THE KING'S FROG HUNTER

KEN YOUNG

North Point Publishing
Paradise, California

Requests for permission to make copies of any part of the work
Should be mailed to the following address:
Permissions Department,
North Point Publishing Company,
P.O. Box 157, Paradise, CA 95967

For information about the book and the author
visit: www.kingsfroghunter.com

ISBN 978-0-9903488-0-1

Map by Ken Young, Illustrated by Steve Ferchaud
Cover Design by C. Young & Cedar Graphis
Illustrations by Steve Ferchaud
Text design: Dan O'Brien

Printed in the United States of America

First U.S. edition

For my amazing daughter, Heather,
who continues to inspire me.

Acknowledgements

There are so many people to thank who have helped me with this book. First and foremost are Cindy and Heather, my wife and daughter, who have lived with this story for many years, yet continued to help and encourage me. Thank you for your endurance and faith in me. Much gratitude goes to my book shepherd, Dan O'Brien, who was able to corral my words and guide me forward through the publishing process; Steve Ferchaud, who did the beautiful illustrations and book cover: you took our ideas and brought them to life; to Cedar Graphics' Carole Montgomery, Elizabeth Quivey and Adrienne Glatz for their formatting magic. The volunteer "friend editors," who not only caught my mistakes, but asked the right questions: Claudia Olson, Alison Watson, Vicki Bertaina, and Wayne Stai. The readers who encouraged me and helped hone the narrative: Marilyn Stai, Ryan and Julie Van Roekel Vern, Judie and Brenna Hall, Josh Kerney, Bob Young, and Diane Carter. A huge, Thunder-sized, thank you to my youthful readers, whose comments and suggestions helped and encouraged me more than they can know: Aeon (who did a book report for her class on the unpublished manuscript), Xavier, and the ones who read the Frog Hunter on their summer vacations across the country—Kayla, Aiden and Olivia.

Author's Note

At the back of the book are profiles of the characters, animals, and locations in the story. I hope this will help you with pronunciation of the names, and provide additional information about the people, creatures, and places in the Kingdom of Ameram. The map, in the front of the book, should be a good visual aide as you follow the events taking place in the narrative. My wish is that you will enjoy the adventure, for there is much to be discovered in the world of the King's Frog Hunter.

You know the difference between what is right and what is wrong, but with no urgency to decide you let time pass. Days drift by like so many leaves in the wind; memories fade and you become indifferent. Yet the moment will come, usually unexpected, when you must choose which life to live.

–Larma

Chapter One
The Stone Truth

King Ahmbin stood on the portico to the Great Hall looking down the waterfall of stone steps at a crowd of people and a low-slung wooden cart being pushed into the plaza by several struggling workers. Riding on the cart was Veracitas, the sculptor, his daughter, Boschina, and a new statue of the king. The man-sized sculpture was covered with a tarp that shook as the wheels thumped over the cobblestones of the street.

"Help us. Help us push!" the workers called to the onlookers.

And as was tradition, commoners, courtiers, and merchants joined in the task of pushing the cart with the heavy statue forward to the base of the steps. So many people wanted to be part of the effort that they had to take turns squeezing together to press their shoulders against the wagon and grunt with all their strength.

King Ahmbin was dressed in his royal colors of maroon, gray, and blue and wore a full length cape draped over his shoulders. His Council of Learned Men in their colorful hats and robes gathered behind him, watching with worried anticipation. Among the Learned Men stood the tall and blonde Lord Baldoff with his arms folded and a smug look on his face. Off to the side, leaning on one of the massive, carved stone columns to the Great Hall, was the magician, Metro. His black hair coiled about his face and his menacing green eyes glared down at the sculptor who was smiling with joy. The king waited anxiously with one leg forward supporting his wide girth and his hands on his hips. He scanned the throng of people, turned, searched his entourage on the large stone porch of the portico, and finally focused on his uncle and advisor, Lord Rundall, who stood a step behind him. "Where is Ekala?"

"The princess is not here, Your Majesty," the tired-looking Lord Rundall answered. "If you remember, sire—"

"She's gallivanting again," Lord Baldoff said, interrupting the old advisor. "She is not dependable, sire."

"That is not true," Lord Rundall replied.

"No? Tell me where she is then," Lord Baldoff snapped. "Does anyone know where she goes or what she does?"

Lord Rundall stared at Baldoff. "Where the princess goes or what she does is not your concern."

"Stop!" the king said in an angry, high pitched, voice. He looked at the magician standing alone against the column. "Metro, can you tell me where she is?"

The magician turned to the king, his dark glare transforming into a smile. "I am afraid your daughter is a mystery, Your Majesty. All I can tell is that she chooses not to be here by your side at this moment."

"Where could she be?" King Ahmbin muttered. He looked at Lord Rundall. "She had better not be hunting frogs with Thalmus. It is much too dangerous."

"I'm sure she's not," Lord Rundall assured him.

Frustrated, the king turned back to the event taking place in the plaza. "I wish she was here," he mumbled to himself.

Veracitas kept glancing up at the king as he steadied the statue from the bumping and surging of the pushers and the uneven cobbled street. He was nervous. This was his big opportunity to finally be recognized for his skill—his art. Veracitas or Stone Cutter, as he was often called, loved to carve the stone and he had worked hard for many years. The earnings, though, had always been meager. He often created statues for free because he wanted to make a statement or honor someone he respected. Then, he was chosen to make a statue of the king for the new courtyard. Determined to make the most accurate depiction of the king, he studied the monarch's physique, posture, and peculiarities.

The sculptor chose a blue gray marble from his home quarry of Marbala to fit the king. When the drawings where approved by Lord Rundall, he worked frantically to carve the new image. Lord Rundall had ordered that no one could see the statue until it was unveiled. Veracitas worked alone, with the exception of his daughter, Boschina, who always helped him. Despite Lord Rundall's orders, Metro would occasionally appear in the dusty shop and watch him at work. This made Veracitas quite nervous, as the magician would goad him to change the statue, to make it false—to make an untrue image of the king. "You would better serve His Majesty if you made the statue thinner and taller," the dark voice would say. Or, "If you want to please the king, make him look younger—stronger." Metro's glaring eyes threatened him constantly.

When Veracitas complained to Lord Rundall, the frustrated counselor told him the king had given Metro permission to view the statue. "Ignore the magician," the kind Rundall advised. "It is important that you create the image as you see the king. It must be accurate and truthful."

When the procession reached the steps and came to a stop, the crowd quieted and waited for the king. Now, the sculptor's creation would be revealed.

"Your Majesty," Lord Rundall said quietly, encouragingly. "Your newest statue awaits your inspection."

"Of course," the king replied and started carefully down the steps.

Currad, the king's honored soldier, came quickly alongside to assist him. Lord Rundall stayed just behind the king in case he needed help. The Learned Men and others followed in a semi-circle group. Reaching the fifth step above the plaza, the king stopped and put his hands on his hips. The burly Currad stopped three meters away—still close enough to protect or help his king.

"What is your name?" King Ahmbin asked the sculptor.

Both Veracitas and Boschina bowed, each kneeling on a knee. "I am Veracitas of Marbala. This is my daughter, Boschina. And this, Your Majesty," he gestured to the covered statue, "is my homage to you."

The king smiled. "I have been waiting anxiously to see your work and your image of me, for I have heard wonderful reports of your skill."

"I'm glad to hear that, Your Majesty."

"Delay no longer, please. Unveil the statue," the king ordered, his voice pitching a little higher.

Veracitas and Boschina rose and together lifted the tarp over the statue and pulled it aside. There was a collective awe from the crowd and then the people began to applaud. Even the Learned Men joined in, nodding their heads and clapping. The statue was the exact image of the king. His long gray hair, wrinkled face, hunched shoulders, large chest and belly, thin legs with one foot forward, hands on hips: the stance that he was known for.

The polished marble gleamed in the morning sun.

Everyone was smiling and clapping, except a few. Lord Baldoff smirked, shaking his head. Metro scowled with his arms crossed.

King Ahmbin looked stunned. As the people saw the king's reaction, they stopped cheering and fell silent. Normally, the king would continue down the steps to admire the work and congratulate the artist. Instead, the king was frozen with an awful look on his face.

"That is not me," the king said, almost to himself.

Metro moved forward.

"You are right, Your Majesty. That does not look like you."

"That *is* you," Lord Rundall said quickly, countering Metro. "The statue is your exact image."

The king slowly shook his head.

"That cannot be me. I do not look like that, do I?"

Rundall moved closer to the king, blocking Metro.

"The image is true, Your Majesty."

"What a mockery," Metro bellowed. "Do you not see the insult by this...deceiver?"

Turning to Metro the king pushed Rundall aside.

"He is mocking me?"

"What would you call this shameful depiction of you, my lord?"

Veracitas was stunned. "I have only carved the truth," he protested. "There is no false character in this stone."

Now, Lord Baldoff pointed at Veracitas. "You're the false character." Still pointing at Veracitas, he turned to the king. "He's a trickster and insulter, Your Majesty."

"Not true," Lord Rundall exclaimed. "He has carved the king's image as he truthfully sees him."

Metro sneered. "If this is how he views our king, then he truly is a counterfeit sculptor."

King Ahmbin was confused. He looked at his faithful advisor. "That cannot be me, Rundall. I know that I am old, but I do not look like that."

"You never have looked like that," Metro spoke quickly before Rundall could answer. He focused his penetrating green eyes on the king's worn face. "And with my help, Your Majesty, you never will look like that stone because you will remain youthful and strong."

"How can that be?" Lord Rundall questioned the magician. He turned to the king. "No one has that power. Don't listen to—"

"This is criminal," Baldoff exclaimed, cutting off Lord Rundall. "The stone cutter should be punished and the statue destroyed!"

The king looked at the statue and began shaking his head slowly. "No...no, that is not me." He glared at Veracitas. "Yes, he has insulted me." Turning and pulling his cape around himself, he shouted: "Cover that thing. I do not want to see it!"

Currad stepped toward the king to protest. "Your Majesty, the statue—"

"Get it away from me, Currad. Break it into pieces and throw it into Cold Canyon! The stone cutter too! Throw them all into the canyon!"

The King's Guards rushed to the wagon as the people scattered out of the way. Two soldiers covered the statue while others grabbed Veracitas, yanked him to the ground, and pushed him to the steps.

"Father," Boschina cried, jumping to help him.

The soldiers shoved her back.

Lord Rundall grasped the king's arm. Hoping to save Veracitas, he pleaded: "Let me deal with him. I will see he suffers."

"Take him to the cells then," the king replied. "He can die there. The statue I want destroyed."

"I will see to it," Currad said, taking charge. He turned to the wagon. "Guards, push the cart to the canyon wall. Take the stone cutter to the cells."

Veracitas pleaded with the king. "I've done nothing but carve a statue of you. Can you not see its beauty?"

"Beauty?" the magician scoffed. "You think it beautiful to insult your king? You *are* deranged."

"Remove him," the king shouted. "I do not want to see or hear of him except to be told that he no longer lives!"

The guards lifted Veracitas by his arms and dragged him from the plaza and through the streets to the north end of the walled city. Confused and surprised at what was happening to him, Veracitas struggled little against his captors. He kept trying to look back for his daughter to see that she was not injured.

Boschina trailed behind the rough guards. She was powerless to help her father, but pleaded for his safety. "Don't hurt him. He didn't do anything wrong. Let go of him!"

Upon reaching the lane with the row of prison cells, the guards turned on her. "Go away! Get out of here or we'll stuff you into a cell!" When she hesitated, several of the soldiers chased her back down the street. "Run for your life, Stone Daughter," they yelled as they threw rocks at her.

The prison cell guards swung open a heavy wood door with iron lacing and forced Veracitas into the small dark chamber. He crumpled to the ground as they slammed the thick door shut and locked the latch.

And there, in that damp, dark, filthy cell, Veracitas was kept, fed garbage, and tortured. Pots of smoldering refuse burned constantly. Guards came and went, keeping him awake by throwing cold water on him or poking and slapping him with sticks and whips. In Veracitas' most vulnerable and confused state, Metro would appear questioning him with a slithery voice. "Do you love the king?" When he answered *yes*, he was beaten. When he said *no* to avoid the beating, he was beaten. "Do you want to make another statue?" Metro asked, his eyes glowing at him in the dark. Veracitas lifted his head and tried to focus on the magician's face. "I'll always carve stone no matter what you do to me." Metro laughed and hissed. "You will never speak in stone again. You are going to rot on the rocks at the bottom of Cold Canyon."

The continuous harassment came to a sudden stop on the seventh night when a violent thunderstorm erupted over Ambermal. Rain poured down and lightning flashed through the black clouds, striking the ground with shattering explosions and shaking the buildings. The scared guards and people of the town stayed in their rooms for protection. It was then that Veracitas' cell door opened and a dark figure entered. He came not with a bucket of water or a stick or whip as Veracitas expected, but with open hands. The stranger helped the stone cutter from the floor and onto his feet.

"You must come with me," the man said in a hurry, putting a blanket around him.

Veracitas was suspicious. "Why? Who are you?"

The man was covered with a black cape and hood. He wore gloves and a sword hung at his side. "You're leaving this castle," the man said, his voice rough and insistent. "Come, the guards are hunkered down, afraid to come out."

He grasped Veracitas' arm, placed a hat on his head, and pulled him out into the rain. Swinging the heavy door shut, his gloved hands closed the hasp and locked it. Veracitas was wobbly on his feet and confused. The man put his arm around the sculptor's waist and hurried him away from the cell, through the deserted streets that were flooded with rain water, and splashed their way to the small West Gate of the castle wall. A saddled horse waited there—tied to anchors in the archway. Extra bags were strapped onto the horse's flanks.

"There's several days' food here," the man told him.

"You're letting me go?" Veracitas stammered.

"You're an innocent victim," the man said from under the hood. "I can't let the evil here kill you." He tried to help Veracitas onto the horse.

Veracitas resisted. "What about my daughter?"

"There's no time. You must get as far away as you can before the storm passes and they find you're gone."

"I can't leave her here."

"She will find you."

"How? I don't even know where I'm going."

"She'll get help," the man insisted. "You must leave before someone sees us."

Veracitas tried to look into the man's hood.

"Let me see your face. I want to know who saved me."

"No! No one must know. It is too dangerous." He pushed Veracitas to the horse. "You must go – now!" He grabbed Veracitas' leg and foot in his hands and lifted him onto the back of the horse.

Lightning suddenly flashed above and thunder boomed around them. The startled horse jerked at his tether and reared. The man reached up to grab the reins and head of the animal to calm him. Veracitas saw the up-turned face of his rescuer in that quick burst of light.

"I won't forget you," the stone cutter said.

The man turned away, pulling at his hood. "You must go."

He untied the leather reins from the iron ring on the wall and handed the straps to Veracitas.

"Stay away from the villages—away from people. Hide where they can't find you."

The hooded man pushed open one side of the heavy double doors, and Veracitas rode out into the storm and away from the castle.

Three months later

Thalmus swung open the rose wood door of his cabin and stepped out into a bright morning. His friend and hunting companion, Thunder, the giant shell creature, was waiting for him.

"You are up early," Thalmus said, rubbing the rough skin of the tortoise's head. "Are we going somewhere?"

Thunder clicked his jaws and pushed into Thalmus' chest.

Thalmus had not slept well for several nights. Something was troubling him. He had a feeling of foreboding, but did know why. Now Thunder was telling him that he felt it too. Thalmus looked across the shining, running water of the creek by his cabin to the meadow where Dallion grazed in the tall, green grass. The big Paint stallion's head was up, looking at him. Thalmus held his open hand up toward the horse. Dallion nodded and looked around the meadow, sniffing the air, before dropping his head to continue eating. *He senses it as well,* Thalmus thought.

Thunder clicked his jaws, grunted and started plodding toward the creek. Thalmus scanned the line of tall rose trees that ringed the meadow. He felt the weight of the long knife sheathed on his right hip where he always wore it and thought about going back inside for his sword or one of his frog hunting spears. No, he decided. This was not a feeling of immediate danger. It was more a sense of a warning or something about to break.

Thalmus stretched, arms reaching over his head, and then he rubbed his face and short, sandy brown hair with both hands. He searched the trees again and glanced at the sun over his shoulder before running after Thunder and bounding onto the tortoise's broad shell just as he splashed into the creek. Thunder grunted and continued across the shallow water and climbed out on the other side.

Thalmus sat down on his friend's back and patted his shell. "A morning swim it is, then," he said, as Thunder continued on toward a second stream in the middle of the meadow.

That's when they saw her; a strange girl that they did not know. She had been hidden by the tall grass. She was lying on her back with her bare feet in the water and her head resting on a pack. There was something familiar about her. Even though she was lying down, Thalmus could tell that she was tall. Her long brown hair, tied into a ponytail with a worn leather strap, splayed out from under a straw hat pulled down over her face. She was asleep. Not wanting to disturb her rest, he directed Thunder to cross the stream and head off through the meadow to a deep pond where they both liked to swim.

Boschina awoke, feeling a disturbance in the ground. She had come through the nearby village of Tamra the night before and walked as far as this meadow before exhaustion and darkness laid her to sleep. Rubbing her eyes to clear the fog and nightmares, she saw a man riding on a giant shell creature plodding out of sight through the trees at the end of the meadow. Jumping up, she pulled on her boots, grabbed her pack and followed the trail in the grass.

Thalmus was lying on the bank of a pond while Thunder floated in the water. He felt something nearby and heard Dallion whinny from across the field. Sitting up, he turned and saw the girl watching Thunder.

"Hello," Thalmus said.

"Does he ever bite you?" she asked.

"No, we are friends."

She watched Thunder swim across the pond, the water rippling in his wake. "He's big and beautiful."

That impressed Thalmus. "I am glad you think so. Most people do not find him attractive." He glanced at his friend in the water. "He is the largest shell creature I have known. His name is Thunder."

"It suits him," the girl replied and chuckled. "I felt the ground shake when you passed by me."

"I am sorry we startled you," Thalmus said, smiling. "I hope you won't hold it against us."

"Oh, no," she said. "To be shaken from my sleep to see a man riding a shell creature was quite surprising. I thought I was dreaming. Then, I realized who you were and I was happy."

Thalmus looked at her curiously. "And who am I?"

"Why, the great Thalmus, the King's Frog Hunter," she said respectfully.

Thalmus smiled. "I am not great, as you can see for yourself." He held his hand over his head to indicate his short stature.

"Well, perhaps not in height, but certainly in deeds," she replied as she sat down on the bank several meters from him. She was wearing workman's clothes and boots. Lanky and tan, she was in that awkward age beyond being a girl, but not yet a woman.

"You are kind and well spoken," Thalmus said. "Who are you, and from which village do you hail?"

"My name's Boschina. I come from Marbala."

"I know the village. It is the home of stone cutters, of masons and sculptors who turn rock and stone into beautiful images. Why have you traveled so far and alone?"

"In search of you," she said, as if he should know.

"Me? What do you want with a frog hunter?"

"You're more than just a hunter, aren't you?" Boschina said carefully. "It's said that you have great influence upon the king."

"To that I cannot attest, for I only do his hunting," Thalmus replied. "I do not care about the matters of his court."

Boschina looked a little surprised. "But it's well known that the king would grant anything you desired."

"I am truly in his favor, Boschina, to what extent I have never measured," Thalmus answered, wondering where this was heading. "Why are you asking me about the king?"

"For my father, Veracitas."

"You are the daughter of Veracitas?" Suddenly, forgotten faces and ancient predictions poured from his memory. Had that much time passed? He looked closely at her face. Yes, he saw the resemblance: the cheek bones and lines of the chin; the calm, confident voice; and the eyes of Veracitas.

No wonder she had seemed familiar to him.

Can this be? He wondered.

Words from out of the past echoed in his mind: "When the king's only child is a woman and the daughter of the stone cutter searches the land...." *And here she is,* Thalmus realized, *the stone cutter's daughter, looking at me.*

"Why did your father send you?"

"He didn't."

Thalmus smiled. "You are a riddle."

"You haven't heard of my father?"

"Oh, I know of Veracitas," Thalmus answered. "He is a stone sculptor, like his father before him, whom I also knew. I have not seen your father since he was young. Though, I have discovered some of his work."

"Then you know about the statue of the king?"

"There are many statues of the kings. Of which one do you speak?"

"The new one, the one my father made of King Ahmbin."

"Veracitas is the sculptor condemned to the cells?" Thalmus asked, surprised. "I have not been to the castle for some time. Though, I heard the villagers talk of a stone cutter being jailed for insulting the king."

"It was not meant as an insult. My father is an honest man. It's important to him that his statues are honest, too."

"Of course," Thalmus said, nodding. "But his honesty got him in trouble."

"Well, as you know, the king doesn't have what one would call a handsome figure, and he's not nearly as attractive as most men."

Thalmus smiled as he thought of the king. "I would say that is an honest observation."

"Well, that's how my father made the statue, just as the king looks to you and me or anyone in the land. It was a beautiful statue and looked exactly like his majesty. It was honest. And for that, the king ordered Father thrown into prison for the rest of his life."

Boschina's eyes were red and moist, but she did not cry.

"You have come then to ask me to speak to the king about your father," Thalmus said gently, trying to clarify her request. "You want me to ask the king to release Veracitas?"

Boschina shook her head. "No."

"No? Why not?"

"Because," she said, looking at him, "he has disappeared."

Thalmus looked into her sad eyes, sensing her bewilderment. "This is mysterious," he said softly. "How did he manage to disappear?"

"No one knows."

"Someone must know," Thalmus replied. "The castle cells are solid stone with unbreakable doors. You don't escape from their hold by yourself. Are you sure he is not hiding in the castle?"

"I've looked everywhere I can think of for him. No one has seen him. Every place I go the king's soldiers have been there before me. Why would they be looking for him if he were still at the castle?" She looked at Thunder, who was emerging from the water, then back at Thalmus. "So, I've come to ask you, Thalmus, the King's Frog Hunter, to help me find my father and to convince the king to let him return home."

Thalmus had been watching two soldiers who had appeared from the direction of the village and were riding slowly toward them through the meadow. Dallion, who had been grazing on the far side of the meadow with two other horses, was also keeping a wary eye on them. His head was up and his body tense. Thunder, water dripping from his shell, plodded up the bank to be close to Thalmus. The giant shell creature was eyeing the soldiers as well and placing himself in position to attack if necessary.

"I have never requested anything of the king," Thalmus replied, looking past Boschina at the two riders. "It is true that he has offered me rewards, but I have never accepted."

"Thalmus," she pleaded, "of anyone in the kingdom, he's most likely to grant a wish to you."

The soldiers were wearing maroon and gray uniforms with blue crossed swords on their chests, the emblem of King Ahmbin. When Boschina saw the soldiers, she stopped talking and looked away. The two men dismounted ten meters from them. Leaving their long swords on the horses, and keeping a wary distance from Thunder, they walked to where Thalmus and Boschina sat. Both men were muscular and had bushy beards—one black, one brown—with shoulder length hair. Thalmus noted the extra bags on the horses and the dusty state of their clothes, which indicated they had been traveling for a while.

He knew them both.

"Greetings, Thalmus," the two men said in a courteous manor.

"Greetings, Currad and Dysaan," Thalmus replied, but stayed seated.

The soldiers looked at Boschina, who did not speak but acknowledged them with a nod. Thalmus watched this and waited for the soldiers to explain their presence.

Dysaan, with the black beard, squatted down and fingered one of Thunder's tracks in the ground. "I'm glad we found you," he said.

"Where else would I be but around my home?" Thalmus answered.

"Hunting," Currad, with the brown beard, said. "We thought you might be hunting." Then, showing respect, he knelt beside Dysaan to be at eye level with Thalmus.

"No," Thalmus replied. "It appears you two have been doing some traveling."

"We've been on a hunt, looking for a man," Dysaan said. "I see, though, that you must know this." He looked again at Boschina. "I'm sorry for your father. We're just following the king's orders."

"You do not agree with the king?" Thalmus asked.

"We are loyal soldiers, Thalmus. You know that," Currad said. "That doesn't mean we have to like his every command."

Thalmus caught a hint of secrecy in Currad's answer; something hidden in his eyes.

"There are many troops committed to this hunt. Most of 'em will not be kind if they find him," Dysaan warned. "It'd be best for Veracitas if we get to him first. We'll see that no harm comes to him, for he is a good man. If you'd help us, Thalmus, you'd be helping this girl and her father."

"I have no doubt that you would be kind, for that is how you both are," Thalmus said. "As for helping, I have not seen Veracitas nor have I heard of his story until today. Besides, you know that I do not hunt men."

Currad and Dysaan accepted this answer with quiet nods. Then, Currad said: "We thought because his daughter is here you might be involved."

Dysaan stood up to leave. "Others will come to you. Just be cautious of whom you help, Thalmus, for this has more meaning, more importance, than it appears."

"Yes, so it does," Thalmus replied. "Thank you for your concern."

"The warning is for your safety, and hers," Currad added, pointing at Boschina. He stood, looked at Thunder, and then at Dallion—who were both watching him. Currad scanned the trees in the distance, as if looking for something. "On second thought," he said thoughtfully. "Who are we, a couple of soldiers, to be telling you, the King's Frog Hunter, what to do? You certainly know how to take care of yourself."

Dysaan nodded in agreement and put his open right hand over his heart, over the king's emblem of crossed swords on his chest. "Until we meet again, Thalmus."

"Until we meet again," Thalmus replied.

The two men mounted up and rode back across the meadow.

Boschina did not speak. Thalmus watched the soldiers until they were out of sight. Then, he looked at Dallion, who had gone back to grazing with the mares, and at Thunder, who had relaxed—resting near him on the bank.

Something was not right.

Yes, the king could be vain, but he had never been unjust. Ahmbin had always been a fair and thoughtful ruler, a smart and valiant general in battle—ever protecting and caring for his kingdom. He was well liked and respected by the people; so why this strange behavior? Veracitas had only been honest, creating with his hands what he saw with his eyes; yet, he was being punished as if he had committed a crime.

Even the soldiers were aware of that.

Now, the man was being hunted like an animal. This puzzled Thalmus and he felt himself being drawn into a world he had not traveled in many years, a world he thought he had left behind. The ancient ancestral phrase, "a decision, once made, is a commitment," rang in his head. He looked at Boschina, who was sitting with her arms wrapped around her folded legs.

A decision, once made, is a commitment. The words stabbed at his heart. Memories of past decisions flooded his thoughts. *How long do commitments last?* he wondered. He knew the answer to that question and would not ask again, for he had agreed long ago to accept this call.

Thalmus watched Boschina and saw before him the journey about to unfold. Generations had passed, the commitment had not. The time had come.

"My friends and I will help you search for your father," he said.

Boschina looked up. "You will?"

"Yes. As for convincing the king to forgive Veracitas, I can promise nothing, for I am not good at talking and the king can be uncommonly stubborn."

"But, you will try?"

"Yes, Boschina, I will try to change the king's mind."

"Oh Thalmus, thank you. When can we start?"

"We must not delay," he answered, standing up and looking at Dallion, then Thunder, who were both watching him. *They already know and are waiting for me*, Thalmus thought. He turned and smiled at Boschina. "We shall leave today for Ambermal."

Chapter Two
On The Road

Thalmus packed supplies, clothing and food, and strapped them on Thunder's shell. The giant tortoise knew the process and stood patiently while his friend spread the items in the satchels on his back. The last things Thalmus loaded, so they were on top of the bundles, were his sword, a bow, and spears. Sheathed at his side was the large knife that he usually wore. Boschina looked at the weapons and felt the points and edges of the steel. These "tools," as Thalmus called them, looked old, well-used, but were clean and sharp. Carved in the shafts of the spears were words from a language that Boschina did not recognize or understand.

The letters looked ancient and drew her attention.

She reached out and fingered the strange figures cut into the hard wood and started to ask Thalmus the meaning of the words, when the spear suddenly began vibrating—shocking her with danger and a silver flash of flight. Startled, she quickly withdrew her hand and stared at the weapon now lying still. The force of the warning was surprising, and though she wanted to ask Thalmus about it, something convinced her that she wasn't ready to know.

She would have to let it be a mystery, for now.

While tying a knot in the packing rope, Thalmus noticed her reaction to the spear. "These tools were made for me by an old friend. Over the years, and through many conflicts, they have endeared themselves to me." He cinched the knot. "Do you know how to use any of these tools?"

"No," she answered. "Father kept a sword, but he said he wasn't skilled—that it was just for defense against bad people and wild animals. He rarely brought it out."

Interesting, Thalmus thought. He knew that Veracitas not only was adept at many weapons, but was quite good with all of them. Why had he not taught his daughter? Her life could depend on the ability to defend herself. Thalmus realized that this was part of the commitment he had made. He was to be her teacher in the skill of the tools and the knowledge of their power. He finished tying the gear to Thunder. "I think this journey will require you to develop your own skills with weapons."

Boschina looked surprised. "Do you think I need to?"

"Yes." Thalmus nodded. "I am sure of it."

Dallion, who had been watching from a distance, well aware that his friend was preparing to travel, now sauntered over to them, followed by another horse. Thalmus smiled at him and turned to Boschina.

"Have you met Dallion?" he asked her.

She looked up at the striking brown and white horse. Dallion stood sixteen hands tall with muscular shoulders and hind legs. His head was dark brown with a white star between his blue eyes. All four legs were white. The rear leg socks stopped above the knees, while the white on the front legs extended up—covering the shoulders and spreading across the back of the neck; this created the appearance of a brown shield on his chest. There were oval white spots on his dark flanks and belly. His mane and tail were yellow-gold with brown streaks. Boschina stared with admiration at the horse's exquisite white pattern over the dark brown coat that gleamed in the sunlight.

Dallion—keeping a short distance—eyed her, sniffed her scent, and snorted. Boschina knew not to approach a strange animal, especially one who had the reputation of this horse. She stood waiting for Dallion to make the first move.

"I'm Boschina," she said softly.

The stallion's blue eyes glanced at Thalmus, and then returned to the girl. He sniffed again and snorted lightly before stepping toward her, bumping her with his nose. She smiled and slowly reached up and stroked his head.

"I think you're going to get along fine," Thalmus said. "But today, I want you to ride Salas. This gray horse will be comfortable with you and you with her."

Salas had watched Dallion's acceptance of this new person and because she appeared to be a friend of Thalmus, the bay mare trusted her as well. She went to Thalmus as he motioned to her and let Boschina rub and pat her neck.

Thalmus helped Boschina onto Salas, and then turned and jumped onto Dallion's back. Dallion let out a soft, rolling, snort—repeated by Salas—and the travelers headed for the castle with Thunder plodding along behind.

Thalmus did not take the road that went through the village of Tamra, but instead chose the lesser-known trail that climbed into the hills and went above and around the small community. It was much more pleasant and less dusty because it was used by so few people. There was even an occasional view of the lower, sloping lands through gaps in the rose trees.

However, the main reason Thalmus had decided on this route was to avoid the king's soldiers.

Dallion, who was a strong and agile horse, took to the road with a brisk, but smooth, walk. Some might say he was high-spirited or untamed, though all knew of his intelligence and loyalty to Thalmus, which is what mattered. Thalmus had never broken him, as they say, or tethered him or fenced him in. That was because Thalmus did not think that he owned Dallion, like most men feel that they do with horses.

They were friends.

Dallion was as free as the day they had met on the west shore of the Laundo Pond. The wild stallion had ventured too far into the bog and become mired in the mud—a very dire situation. Thalmus and Thunder, who had been hunting frogs, pulled him from the muck and released him to run free. Dallion could do whatever or go wherever he pleased: he chose to be with his friend, Thalmus.

When the trail curved into a shady fold and dropped slightly to cross a creek, they stopped to eat and to let Thunder catch up with them.

"How long will he be?" Boschina asked, dismounting from Salas.

Thalmus looked up at the sun. "A little while," he said and swung his leg over Dallion's back and dropped to the ground.

Boschina looked for Thunder on the trail.

"I didn't know he was so slow."

"He has a different pace," Thalmus replied and smiled. "You will get used to it."

Boschina frowned. "I hope so." She was anxious to get to the castle as soon as possible so Thalmus could speak with the king about her father.

"Thunder's speed has its advantages," Thalmus said as he pulled some food from a bag strapped across his shoulder.

After their snack, Thalmus rubbed Salas' nose, thanked her, and told her to return home, for he knew that they were getting too far away for her comfort. Boschina stroked the mare's neck and thanked her. Then, Salas rubbed necks with Dallion and started trotting back down the trail. Thalmus watched her go, then found a comfortable spot and laid back for a nap. Dallion, who had accepted the tempo of his friends, drank from the stream and grazed on the fresh grass sprouts along its bank. Boschina paced impatiently near Dallion and talked to him while she watched the water rush over the rocks in the creek.

When Thunder arrived, Thalmus checked the straps on the bags and patted the tortoise's bald leathery head. They started off again, this time walking. At this slower pace, Thunder had no problem keeping up; in fact, he stayed right behind Thalmus and Boschina.

Dallion trotted ahead, stretching his legs and scouting the trail.

Boschina was happy to be moving again.

She walked with a bounce in her stride and talked of her father, his statues, and her childhood. She did not have an easy life, but it had been good and full of love. It showed in her openness and in her caring for people and animals. Thalmus listened and asked few questions, for he already knew most of her story.

Veracitas had created many statues and sculptures throughout the land. As Boschina talked of them, Thalmus remembered the ones he had seen. There was one in particular that was quite meaningful to Thalmus. It stood at the western edge of the Escat Marsh. It was actually four separate statues that created a scene and told a story. These four carved stones depicted three men in combat with a frog. The expressions and attitudes of the men appeared real to Thalmus. Veracitas had shown the fierceness, as well as the fear, in each man as they fought the giant frog. It was a true rendering of reality. Veracitas had carved these statues in honor of the three men, who had not returned from the marsh—and perhaps as a warning to other men who might be entering there to hunt the frogs.

There was another statue in the village of Moxfet that Thalmus liked very much. It was of a kneeling woman holding a baby in front of her, while four children of various sizes were crowded around staring at the infant. The woman cradled the baby carefully in her outstretched palms and forearms. She was looking down at the baby with affection in her face. All the children had looks of wonder and amazement on their faces. The smallest child was reaching out with his forefinger and was just about to touch the baby on its cheek.

Yes, Veracitas brought stone to life and stirred emotions and thoughts, so how could he have offended the king so badly as to be imprisoned? That injustice could not come from the king that Thalmus knew. More puzzling still: how did the sculptor escape the castle cells? And, where could he be now?

Thalmus knew that a man like Veracitas could not stop doing his craft—that he could not stop making his statements in stone. He had to be someplace where he could still work, where he could still express his feelings. What about his daughter, his only child? If he loved her as much as she loved him, why had he not tried to contact her?

Surely, he would not abandon her.

Thalmus knew that the answer to these questions lay in a much larger question that was driven by the power of time and the agony of change. Thalmus looked at Boschina's youthful face. *She has no idea what trials lie before her*, Thalmus thought, *nor at this moment could she understand that the fate of her father and herself were an intricate part of a destiny that they could not escape.*

"Did you work with your father?" Thalmus asked.

"Oh, yes," Boschina said. "Sometimes he'd have me buff and polish with him. I would clean up and help him with his tools." She smiled. "He always asked me questions about the statues."

"What kind of questions?"

"Oh, 'do you think he looks mad? Are the hands too big? How does it make you feel? If she could speak, what do you think she'd say?' Those sorts of questions," she answered. "We spent so much time with the statues that they became our family—the good ones and the bad ones."

"Why do you not speak of your mother?" Thalmus asked.

Boschina shrugged. "I never knew her."

"You do not remember her at all?"

She shook her head. "No. It's always been just my father and me. When I was younger, I used to ask him about her. He would just say that she'd gone away and wouldn't be back. As I got older, I stopped asking because he would get sad and be quiet for a long time."

Even though she appeared resigned to not knowing about her mother, Thalmus could see that she was troubled by the mystery of her absence.

They walked for a while in silence, pacing Thunder as he plodded along, until Thalmus wanted to know more about Veracitas' work. "Did you help your father with the statues at the Escat Marsh?"

"Escat Marsh?" Boschina looked at Thalmus with a fearful recognition of the name and place. "The one with the men and the frog? I'll never forget them. They were very difficult to place. Father wanted them partially in the water and the ground was too soft for the wagon wheels. A carpenter from the village built a sled to pull the statues across the mud and some of the people there helped us to set them. It took many days to get them placed just how Father wanted them. I didn't like it there. It was a scary place. I was afraid, and the statues scared me, too. I was glad when they were done and we left."

"Was that the worst place he had worked?"

"Yes, except at the castle when it became bad," Boschina replied, kicking a small stone and then picking up another one and throwing it at a rose tree.

High on a grassy hillside to the right of the trail stood two massive oak trees. These giants stood about twenty yards apart, but the arches of their branches intertwined with one another—forming one huge umbrella. The sun was dropping behind the tops of these oaks and their branches were splitting the sun's rays into hundreds of angular sparkling shafts of light. As the branches and leaves moved in the breeze, it appeared as if the bright beams emanated from the trees themselves and were alive with a bright, dancing spirit.

"What a beautiful sight," Boschina said.

"We will stay beneath those trees tonight," Thalmus said. "There's good water there and a view of the land."

They turned off the trail and headed up through ankle-high grass toward the grand oaks. When they reached the trees and stood in their light, they turned and looked back at the terrain. The trail they had been on was just below them. It was lined with rose trees. Beyond that row of foliage was a series of rounded ridges in which the land appeared to be rolled up into many loaves of bread and laid side by side. Below these orderly rolls was a long narrow forest, but its trees were so evenly spaced that it looked more like an orchard. The main road wound its way through this neat band of trees, running north and south. Toward the south, the direction in which they were heading, smoke from the evening fires of a village hovered above the tree tops. Thalmus' home and village was to the north and out of sight around the curve of the hills. Beyond the forest, the land leveled out into bushy plains that stretched as far as the eye could see. In the distance small, puffy, white clouds—like cotton—floated above the green plains.

"There used to be swamps out there in the flats," Thalmus said, thoughtfully. "There were many frogs; big frogs. It was good hunting. But the ponds kept getting smaller and smaller." He sighed. "They are dried up now...have been for a long time."

Boschina looked curiously at Thalmus as he gazed at the view. She could see that he was reliving a memory. "What's it like, hunting frogs?"

Thalmus did not hear her. He was already in another time, staring at the dry swamp and remembering it on a cold, wet day, full of water with scattered clumps of thick foliage. Lying camouflaged in his frog skin coat on Thunder's shell, his spear at the ready, the two hunters had worked slowly and carefully through the gray rain along the mucky, shallow edge of the bog in search of their prey. Several times Thunder had come close, but the green monsters had spooked and jumped away, splashing into the deeper water. Usually the frogs paid little attention to shell creatures for they did not see them as a threat, nor as an appetizing meal. That is why Thalmus was able to get close enough to spear them before they could lash him with a tongue or spring out of his reach. On this day, though, with a steady rain splattering down, the frogs were alert and seemed to sense his presence. It was a bit un-nerving. Still, he had had good luck on similar wet days, so they kept on, patiently moving further into the bog. Then Thunder left the bank and swam into deeper water, a risky move, for he was less stable than when fighting on firm ground. The two of them had managed this tactic twice in the past, surprising their prey before the advantage turned against them.

"Careful, Thunder," Thalmus cautioned. "It can be deep out here."

Thunder was as determined as Thalmus, and like his friend, he embraced the challenge. The tortoise swam slowly until coming upon a large brown frog with black spots. The creature was sitting on a muddy island that was barely large enough for its size. From the webbed toes to its nose it was well over three meters tall. This was the biggest, and most vicious-looking frog Thalmus had seen in a long time; and never before in this pond. It was a breed from the Laundo Ponds, and Thalmus wondered what it was doing here.

The beast appeared confident and seemed relaxed with its eyes half closed, but Thalmus knew that demeanor could change in an instant. As they approached, Thalmus gripped tighter on the shaft of the spear, preparing to thrust, and focused his full attention on the motionless monster. What he had not heard or seen because of the rain was another frog submerged in the water. Just its bulging black eyes showed above the scummy green surface. Those intense spheres had been watching the hunters approach.

Thunder slowly floated next to the little island and Thalmus leapt up to spear the brown frog. The black eyed frog sprang from hiding and hit him with a tongue that was so quick that Thalmus felt the hard slap on his body before he saw it. Jolted, he almost lost his grip on the spear. The beast's tongue had him by the waist. With just a second to save himself, Thalmus turned the spear's sharp point, and drove it into the throat of the creature as it pulled him into its mouth. The frog let out a horrible loud croak and closed its jaws on the spear, breaking it in half and releasing Thalmus into the cold, muddy water. But just as quick, he was struck again. The brown frog had seen his escape and lashed out to get him. The blow knocked him sideways and under the surface. Thalmus regained his footing and rose up spitting out a mouth full of foul water. Standing chest deep in the slime, he pulled his sword just in time to slash the red tongue with a back hand stroke as it snapped at him again. The beast roared in pain and jumped at Thalmus, trying to grab him in its jaws. Thalmus quickly ducked under the water. The plunging mouth missed. But now the frog was on top of him, smashing his body into the soft muddy bottom. His hand with the sword was pinned underneath him. Blinded in the murky water, and feeling numb from the cold and blows, he struggled to free his arm and sword. Squirming side to side, he finally rolled his shoulder enough to pull his hand and the blade out through the mud to stab the beast's soft underbelly. It was to no avail. Under the weight of the frog he could not get enough leverage to penetrate its skin. He was stuck. His lungs ached. He was out of air, when suddenly the frog was off him. Thalmus pushed from the bottom and burst through the surface gasping for air and his sword pointed up at the ready. Head and shoulders above the water he quickly looked about, expecting another assault. Instead, he saw Thunder with his jaws clamped onto the frog's throat. The creature's mouth was open and its legs were frantically kicking in an attempt to free itself. Relieved, Thalmus took some deep breaths and turned around, checking for more frogs. The one with his spear in its throat was dead and lay flat in the water. The brown one, in the vice grip of Thunder's jaws, would soon be dead also.

The frog hunter rested for a moment, catching his breath and feeling grateful for his friend. Then he set to work with his long knife, carving off the creature's large rear legs and roping them to Thunder, who hauled them out through the muck. They gave two frog legs to the people of the nearby village who were thankful because the brown frog had been threatening them for some time. Then Thalmus and Thunder traveled to the castle and gave the other two legs to King Ahmbin, who praised his hunter. However, the profits to Thalmus were the lessons he had learned that day: friends are invaluable, and a careless hunter can become someone else's meal in the blink of an eye—or the snap of a tongue. The near-fatal hunt had occurred a long time ago, before they had met Dallion, before Lady Ahmbin had died, and before the Promise. Yet, the memory was as clear as if it had happened yesterday.

"Thalmus?" Boschina asked again.

She had not received an answer to her question about hunting frogs and watching him now, she wondered if he had heard her. Boschina thought about swamps and frogs in a valley that was now dry—and that Thalmus had known her grandfather and fought in ancient battles. Although she knew it wasn't right, she could not stop from asking: "How old are you, Thalmus?"

Returning from his reverie, the frog hunter answered. "Much older than I appear." He smiled at her and added: "And much younger than I am."

"I don't understand," she said.

Thalmus did not answer. As they stood under the oaks looking out over the land, they were bathed in the sun's rays breaking through the branches and encircling them with a warm glow. Dallion had returned along the trail and was now climbing the hill toward them. Thunder had nestled himself down beside a spring that bubbled up between the two oaks and started to flow as a small creek for about four meters, then suddenly changed its mind and disappeared into the ground again.

They knelt down and drank from the spring. The water was cold and clear and tasted slightly of vanilla. Thalmus filled his cupped hands and splashed his face over and over again.

Boschina rested on the soft grass and looked up at the crooked branches of the oaks looming out over them. "This is such a beautiful place," she said. "I feel so relaxed, so safe here."

Thalmus started untying the straps on Thunder. "It is said that the great King Ahmbin the First was born here."

"King Ahmbin's grandfather? Born here?"

"Yes, in the time his family was in hiding from the Pawndors. The stories say he came back here many times by himself, even after he was king, and stayed for days and no one dared bother him. People say the oaks protected him—that he was safe here from his enemies."

"I can feel it," Boschina said. "My worries and fears have dropped away like the chiseled stone from my father's statues."

"I camp here whenever I travel this trail," Thalmus said. "I have stayed here many times; yet, I am always surprised by this good feeling, by this confidence that grows within."

They removed the bags from Thunder, gathered dead wood that the oaks had shed, and built a small fire to cook an evening meal. The sun set, and its glow faded into darkness. A breeze came from the distant night and whispered through the oak leaves. Thalmus and Boschina sat quietly by the fire, mesmerized by the flames and lost in their own thoughts. Suddenly, a soft rush blew over them like something passing in the night.

"Did you feel that?" Boschina asked, startled.

"What?" Thalmus said, still lost in his thoughts.

"That movement, I felt...."

Then it was there again, passing over their heads. This time Boschina, looking up, saw something briefly in the fire's light, something brownish and large.

"There! You see it, Thalmus? What is it?"

Thalmus did not look up. He poked the fire with a stick and spoke to the darkness: "So, you have joined us, Bubo."

Chapter Three
Ekala

From the darkness came the sound of claws on tree bark and shifting, fluttering wings. Boschina stared at Thalmus, holding her breath, waiting. He looked up from the fire and smiled at her. "Do not be afraid, Boschina. It is my friend, Owl."

"Owl? But you called it Bubo."

"Yes, I did. I also call him Owl."

A low guttural call came from the unseen bird, "Who–whoo–who."

And Thalmus answered, "Whoo."

Boschina turned and looked into the darkness toward where Owl was perched. "He must be very large, he scared me so. I wish I could see him."

"He won't come near the fire," Thalmus said. "He will sleep in the tree tonight, and in the morning you shall see him."

"He wasn't at your home."

"No. Bubo has been gone for several days. I was beginning to worry about him. But all is well now."

Boschina lay back on her blankets and was quiet for a while.

Then she asked, "How'd he know where to find you?"

"The birds along our route told him, I'm sure."

"They talk?"

"Oh yes, to each other and, once in a while, to us—if we know how to listen."

She thought about this for a moment, this revelation of birds talking to humans. "Do you know how to listen, Thalmus?"

"I'm learning. I'm always learning."

"Will you teach me?"

Thalmus smiled at Boschina. "We shall try."

"Thank you, Thalmus. Thank you for helping me."

She settled into her blankets and slowly faded into sleep.

Thalmus watched the fire for a while and thought of what had happened with the king, Veracitas and Boschina. Their actions were the beginning of the prophecy. Still, there was a lot to be done and so much was unknown. Their journey would be dangerous and success was not guaranteed. The continuation of the prophecy depended on this girl. She had completed the first step by finding him, but could she endure the coming hardship? And would the others recognize their roles and accomplish their tasks to complete the long chain of events required to be successful?

It could all collapse in failure so easily.

But that's why he was here, to step forward, to guide—to lead them through to the end. This is what he had been waiting for, what he had been called to do. He felt good. He settled comfortably into sleep and slept soundly all night.

When the sun rose across the valley, bringing light to the new day, Boschina awoke to see Thunder and Dallion grazing nearby. Thalmus was standing near the fire, cooking their morning meal, and Bubo sat perched in the oak—watching her. She walked slowly over to get a better look at him. He had pale yellow tufts around his ears with streaks of brown that stood up like small horns. His wings and tail were a darker reddish brown and dappled with white spots. His piercing black pupils and yellow eyes were set in ivory discs with dark ruff at the sides and there was a fluffy white locket about his throat. He had a chest and belly colored yellow-orange, boldly striped, and with fine dark brown feathers that cascaded down his legs and covered his feet. His sharp beak was black, as were his large claws that gripped the bark tightly.

"Hello, Owl," Boschina said politely. "You scared me last night. But now that I see you, I'm not afraid."

Owl just stared back at her.

"You are very beautiful, and I am sure very strong, too."

Owl glared down at Boschina for a moment, and then, without moving his body, he pivoted his head, and faced away from her.

Thalmus smiled at Boschina's attempt to communicate with Owl. "It takes Bubo a while to get to know people," Thalmus said from the fire. "Come and eat. We have a long road ahead of us."

Thunder, who had been munching grass, suddenly clicked his jaws several times and emitted a loud warning hiss. Thalmus looked at him as Dallion raised his head high and perked up his ears to listen.

Thalmus stopped his cooking and stepped away from the fire to listen to the distance.

"What's the matter?" Boschina asked.

"Shhhh. Listen."

She waited and listened, but could hear nothing unusual—even though her friends waited intently. "What is it?" she whispered.

"Something is approaching."

"I can't hear anything."

"You will soon. Look at Thunder."

Thunder was turning to face the east, the direction of the road which they were to travel.

"How does he know?"

"He is close with the earth," Thalmus said softly. "He feels its movements and those of man or beast upon it."

A faint rumbling became audible.

Dallion threw his head to one side, pawing and stamping his hoof.

"I can hear something," Boschina said.

"It is a horse in full gallop," Thalmus said, identifying the sound.

Owl spread his wings and sprang from the oak branch. He rose above them and headed for the road, gaining in height as he went.

They all watched the road where the dusty track first appeared to them as it snaked around the curve of the hill. The rumble was now easily recognizable as rapid hooves pounding the earth. There was something unsettling in their rhythm, an urgency that violated the calm of the morning.

Thalmus looked up at Owl, drifting now above the road, and then went back to his cooking. Dallion and Thunder stayed intent on the road. Boschina looked at Thalmus calmly tending the cooking pot. He looked at her and smiled. "Don't want to burn our breakfast," he said and took a taste with the stirring spoon.

Dallion grunted and Boschina turned in time to see a black horse with its rider bent forward, crouched close to the neck, come galloping into sight on the road. This beautiful animal ran with long, smooth strides that deceived one as to the speed at which it traveled. Before Boschina realized it, the rider and horse were on the road below them. At which point the rider sat up and pulled the horse to a sudden stop, turned toward the oaks, and looked up at Boschina and Thalmus.

The air had become still.

No one made a sound.

No one moved as both parties studied one another.

From what Boschina could see, the rider wore the colors of the Royal House of Ahmbin and was armed—but was not in a soldier's uniform. The horse, breathing heavily and sweating, wore no refinement or insignias. The rider abruptly waved his arm in an arch—–stopping it momentarily at the top with his arm straight up and the hand open in greeting—then slowly brought it down, completing the circle to gently slap the horse's flank, urging it up the hill toward them.

Boschina backed up, but Thalmus stepped forward toward the approaching rider. Dallion let out a whinny, as if in greeting, and also moved forward. Only Thunder did not move and Boschina noticed Thalmus was smiling. Bubo suddenly appeared from the sky, glided close by the stranger's head, then on up to the tree where he perched.

"You are just in time to eat," Thalmus said as the rider dismounted and walked the remaining distance to him.

"I could not refuse a meal from you, Thalmus, even if I hadn't been riding before the sun."

Boschina was surprised to hear a woman's voice and even more surprised to recognize its imposing owner. It was the king's daughter, Ekala!

Princess Ekala was well-known for her horsemanship and unladylike behavior. However, this was the first time that Boschina had seen her outside of the castle. The princess did not possess dainty, pretty features. Dressed as she was, in pants and a hat covering her head, she could pass as a man for she was broad shouldered and solid at the waist. The lack of an escort, the large knife that she wore at her side, and the sword sheathed alongside the saddle proved that Ekala was not a genteel princess.

Ekala slapped Thalmus on the shoulder, and then hugged him strongly with both arms. She was a head taller than Thalmus yet regarded him with obvious respect and affection. She greeted Dallion by nuzzling nose to nose with him. "Dallion, Dallion, yes, me too," she mumbled and stroked his neck and patted him. She walked over and stood before Thunder. "Hello, Thunder, you beautiful creature. Still not moving any more than you have to, huh?"

Thunder clicked his jaws.

"No frog legs for me, Thunder? I'm disappointed."

She glanced at Owl in the tree. "Thanks for the greeting, Bubo."

Finally, she looked at Boschina as she pulled the leather-brimmed hat from her head and rubbed her hair. "You look surprised, Stone Daughter."

"I...I am," Boschina replied. Then remembering her place, she bowed on one knee before Ekala.

"Don't do that," the princess said quickly.

"But you're the princess."

"Bowing is only necessary at the castle where my father insists it be done."

The princess had dark brown eyes, shoulder-length brown hair, a square chin with a strong, straight nose, thin lips, and tanned skin. It was not at all what one would expect of a king's daughter; yet, there was a handsome beauty to her face.

Ekala's horse, Shadahn, was bobbing and rubbing her head with Dallion. Ekala removed the saddle from Shadahn's wet back and began brushing her down.

"You had me stumped, Thalmus, I couldn't figure who was with you. That's why I hesitated on the road. And you didn't even wave."

"I knew you would come to see," Thalmus said, smiling.

"So I did."

"And now you know."

"Yes, I would never have guessed," Ekala said glancing at Boschina. "I was on my way to visit you, Thalmus. But when I saw Bubo flying overhead, I knew you must be nearby. Are you returning or on your way out?"

"We are on our way to the castle," Thalmus said.

"Will you be hunting?"

"No, not for frogs, anyway."

"We're going to look for my father," Boschina blurted out, then quickly added, "With the king's permission, of course."

Ekala was surprised. She stopped brushing Shadahn and looked first at Boschina and then at Thalmus. Setting the brush down she said, "Thalmus, it's good that you will help this girl, for she needs someone and I can think of no one better." Ekala paused, looked up at Bubo, and back at Thalmus. "There's danger in this."

"I am not afraid."

"No, you wouldn't be. There is no one as fearless as you, nor as honest. But this is different, Thalmus. There are forces at work in this matter that are controlling my father's wisdom. He has changed much since you last saw him."

"He must have, to imprison a man like Veracitas for his stone truth."

"There is behavior at the castle I don't like. Never have," Ekala said. "People with constant influences and maneuvering; lately, it has grown worse. In his old age, father has become desperate. He'll not listen to me and rarely to old Rundall, who, like you, fought at his side and was once his closest companion."

"Who then advises him?"

"Besides the Council of Learned Men? Mainly Baldoff, a devious dandy who has wormed his way into my father's confidence. And worse, Thalmus, he's given credence to a supposed man of magic named Metro."

"The king was never one to believe in magic," Thalmus said.

"He does now."

Thalmus looked up at the oaks—at Bubo perched on a branch. The owl's large eyes were watching him. *It is happening as predicted*, Thalmus thought. He recalled the old words: "When the Stone Cutter's daughter searches the land and magic fogs the royal eyes...."

"I must speak with him," Thalmus said.

"If he were to listen to anyone, it would be you, Thalmus. But, it's no good. Even if you were to get his approval, Baldoff would fight you. He already has the soldiers hunting for Veracitas and if you were to find him first, they may attack you." Ekala paused. "And I wouldn't like that."

"I would not like that either," Thalmus said with a grin and dished up breakfast and served it to them. They sat without speaking, spooning stew from warm bowls. Shadahn wandered up the hill with Dallion. Thunder moved over to get a better look at what Thalmus was eating, and Bubo appeared to sleep.

Boschina was upset about what the princess had said of the soldiers attacking them and her father. As soon as she emptied her bowl, she ran up the hill to be with Dallion and Shadahn—to get away from anymore such talk. Thalmus put out the fire, cleaned the utensils, and packed up. Ekala was quiet, looking out over the land. Thalmus glanced at her as he worked. He knew there was something more she wanted to say.

Finally, he asked, "What brings you riding so hard to see me?"

"It's been a while since you've been to the castle. I thought you might be ready for a hunt."

"Did the king request one?"

"No," she said, turning and looking at him. "I am requesting it."

"For the king?" Thalmus asked, knowing the answer.

"Yes. But more for me because I want to hunt with you."

"You know you cannot. We have talked of this before, Ekala; your father would not allow it."

"My father does not think I am capable."

"That's not the reason. You are his only child. He does not want to lose you."

"If I were a man, I would be expected to hunt."

"True, but you are not a man."

"How well my father knows that," she said angrily and stood and looked up at Bubo, who was watching and listening. She wagged her finger at him. "I must prove myself to him, Bubo."

Bubo clicked his beak as Thalmus said, "Ekala, you are respected throughout the land."

"That's not enough. I must show him that I can lead. That I am not weak—that I can rule his kingdom as strong as any man."

"Ahh," Thalmus said. "Now, we have come to it. Now, we speak of the true problem, and the question that is being asked throughout King Ahmbin's realm."

"Yes, I know," Ekala replied, as she took the knife from her belt and ran her fingers along the blade. "This land has never been ruled by a woman. Everyone wonders, including my father, if it's possible because we will be considered weak and therefore, attacked. Yes, Thalmus, I know the doubt that lives."

"Are there rumors of war?" Thalmus asked, watching her handling the knife.

Ekala nodded. "We've been told by friends that Platnock of Pawndor is secretly enlarging his army and that Toulon has issued orders for more armaments."

Thalmus shook his head in disgust. "Neither of those kingdoms has battled us since your grandfather was king. We have been at peace with them all this time."

Princess Ekala said nothing as she balanced the weight of the knife between her thumb and forefinger. With one motion of her arm, she snapped her wrist—flipping the blade end over end— and stuck the steel point into a log by the fire five meters away.

Thalmus smiled. "I suppose the matchmaking continues unsuccessfully?"

Ekala gave him a look of disgusted frustration. "It's relentless."

She stepped to the log and removed her knife from the wood. "Everyone has a candidate: a son, a brother, a nephew, a cousin, an uncle. I'm supposed to be thrilled with each possibility. Most of them don't care a whit about me. It's the position and power they want." She tossed the knife, once again sticking it in the same spot on the log. "I know Father is worried and irritated with me. But, I'll choose a husband when and where I want. It won't make me or the kingdom any stronger to have a husband who is there in name only. No, I need to prove my strength first."

"You are strong, Ekala," Thalmus said, "but in different ways than your father. You would not rule the same. You will be better."

"You think so, Thalmus, but he doesn't. I must prove myself to him—and the people."

"And you think hunting the frogs would do that?"

"It's a start," Ekala said, shrugging her shoulders.

Thalmus sighed and looked at the clouds drifting over the land, and then at Boschina who was talking with Thunder, Dallion, and Shadahn as they grazed. They had a long day ahead of them and needed to be on the road.

"Come with us to the castle," Thalmus suggested.

"No, I've had enough of it." She slid the knife into its sheath on her belt. "I'm going to see some friends. I have duties there to which I must attend."

Thalmus took her hand. "Do not try to hunt the frogs."

"I'm not a fool, Thalmus. I'll wait for you."

He looked at her closely. She did not know what had begun— that her destiny was intertwined in the journey of this girl talking to the horses. Yet, this was not the time or the place to tell her, nor was he the one to do so. That knowledge would be imparted by one greater than he.

"When I am done with this, we will hunt together," Thalmus said.

Ekala smiled. "I'm looking forward to it."

She slapped him on the shoulder and whistled for Shadahn.

Chapter Four
Castle Ambermal

Alll that day they walked along the high trail overlooking the low lands until the path led them down near the village of Bevie where they stopped near a creek and camped for the night. The families of Bevie were excited to see Thalmus and his friends again. They brought fruit and fresh vegetables from their gardens and the children sat on Thunder's shell while he ate. That night, many of them slept around the fire with Thalmus and Boschina while Bubo hunted and dined alone on his prey as he perched in a tree in the distant darkness. Rising early, the travelers got back on the road without cooking breakfast because they had been amply supplied with food from the villagers.

For Thalmus, this was a trip he had made many times with pack horses carrying the frog legs that the king was anxiously awaiting. Now, he came empty-handed to ask for a favor of the king instead of bringing him something he desired. Thalmus considered himself independent yet loyal to this country of Ameram, for he was not only a hunter, but had fought to defend the kingdom from invaders and false rulers. Still, he felt a foreboding that was compounded by Ekala's warning and the apparent beginning of the prophecy. In what state of mind would he find the king? How would he be received once his request was known? *At least*, Thalmus thought, *I shall see if the king is truly as grateful to me as he claims to be.*

For Boschina, the trip could not be fast enough. She was sure Thalmus would change the king's mind about her father. Then, they could solve the mystery of his whereabouts. With Thalmus on the hunt, it would take no time at all to find him and return home—or so she thought.

In the afternoon, Dallion—who had been gone for several hours— —trotted up behind Thalmus and Boschina as they walked in front of Thunder. He moved in between them, walked at their pace, eyed each one with his blue eyes, and then bobbed his head. Thalmus smiled and stroked the Paint's neck and patted his shoulder. Dallion turned his head and bumped Boschina's shoulder with his nose.

"Hey," she said with surprise and took a step away from the horse.

Dallion lowered his head and rubbed his nose against her again, this time less aggressively but still strong enough to push her.

"Dallion." She put her hand up for defense. "What's with him?"

"He wants to give you a ride," Thalmus replied. "Here, I'll give you a hand."

"Really?" She looked up at the blue eyes looking at her. "He'll let me ride him?"

"Yes, that's what he's saying. Put your foot in my hands and I'll lift you up."

And so she did, throwing a leg over and sitting carefully onto the stallion's brown back, her feet dangling by the white spots on his sides.

"Hold onto his mane, gently," Thalmus told her. "He won't throw you."

Dallion walked on, letting them both get a feel for one another. He then started a slow trot, settling into an easy rhythm, and a new friendship. Boschina rode Dallion as he explored the terrain ahead of them. The stallion quickly became comfortable with her on his back because she was relaxed and trusted him. He trotted into the fields, circling farther out from Thalmus, searching and watching for any sign of danger. Occasionally stopping, and standing still, he listened, raised his nose, and sniffed the breeze. Boschina would imitate him, inhaling deeply and proclaiming that the air smelled good. He would turn his head to look at her and snort as if he were disgusted. She laughed and patted his neck. Continuing on, they scouted until Dallion was satisfied and finally returned to walk beside Thalmus and Thunder on the road.

When the great walls and towers of Castle Ambermal were in sight, Bubo flew down and landed on Thalmus' shoulder. He perched there uneasily, fidgeting and fluttering his wings and pulling Thalmus' hair in his beak.

Boschina laughed, thinking that Bubo was just being playful. She did not understand what he was saying.

"Yes, yes I know, my friend," Thalmus said softly to Bubo. "Go. I will return soon."

The great brown owl sprang from Thalmus' shoulder, and with a beating of wings, flew off to the tree tops of the forest.

"Where's he going? And what is it that you know?" Boschina asked.

"That he does not like the castle," Thalmus replied. Seeing Boschina's concern, he said, "Bubo will wait out here for us, until we return."

Castle Ambermal was a walled city named after the king who started its construction many generations before King Ahmbin. Due to constant additions by subsequent rulers to accommodate a growing population, it had become a maze of narrow cobbled streets through tall, gray-brown stone buildings that housed the nobility and the thriving business of commerce. The protective outer walls with their towers grew in height and length accordingly. It was known as the most secure castle and city because its thick stone walls were over fifteen meters high and its massive double wooden and iron gates, when closed, were indestructible.

The community contained its own water system from two clear springs that bubbled into several large fountains and then spilled into aqueducts that ran like blood vessels throughout the town. The sprawling castle stood in an open plain, but its south side was built on the very edge of a cliff that dropped two hundred fifty meters into Cold Canyon. Aptly named, it was known for the cold air that rose up from its depths and actually helped to cool the castle chambers in the summer heat. This impassable gorge had proved to be a natural obstacle to attacks by invaders from the wild southern countries.

As they approached Ambermal, the soldiers at the gate recognized Thalmus and greeted him warmly. Word spread rapidly of his arrival and many people came out to wave and say hello to him. Children walked along with him as they hung onto Thunder's shell. Thalmus sat the smaller ones on Thunder's back to ride until they reached the Great Hall. Waiting there, at the foot of the grand stairs, was the royal cook: a plump, red-haired, red-faced man named Culinary who liked eating, only second to cooking. He thought Thalmus was bringing frog legs for him to cook for the king.

Why else would Thalmus be here?

But when he saw there were none, he was surprised.

"What, no legs?" Culinary said, disappointed.

"I have not been hunting," Thalmus answered.

The children slid off Thunder's shell, petted Dallion, said goodbye to Thalmus, and scampered away.

"Has the king summoned you then, Thalmus?" the cook asked.

"No, my friend, I have come to speak to him about other matters," Thalmus replied as he waved to the children.

"Oh, well, he'll be happy to see you, I'm sure," Culinary said. "He's been very upset since the statue."

Hearing this, Boschina glanced at Thalmus with a worried look.

Thalmus raised his eyes and smiled at her.

"Who's your young friend?" Culinary asked. Looking up for the first time at Boschina on Dallion's back, he paused with surprise and gasped, "The stone cutter's daughter!"

"We've come to talk with the king about my father," Boschina said with a confident smile.

Culinary looked at Thalmus and shook his head. "Perhaps the king won't be so happy to see you."

"Perhaps," Thalmus said with a shrug. "I can always count on your honest opinion, Culinary. So, tell me, what did you think of the statue?"

The cook looked around to make sure there was no one close enough to overhear him, and then he said softly, "I liked it. It was truly beautiful, the very image of the king."

"Its true likeness to the king seems to be the problem," Thalmus replied.

"Yes, who would've thought that the king sees himself as the most handsome fighting man in all of Ameram."

Thalmus smiled. "I suppose it is not for us to know what a king thinks."

"The great Metro knows," Culinary said.

Thalmus was surprised and concerned by Culinary's reverence for the mysterious magician.

"You believe this man has magical powers?"

"Oh, yes, Thalmus. You can feel it all about him. He's powerful."

"I was scared of him," Boschina said. "I hid when he came to see my father working."

"He saw the statue before it was unveiled?" Thalmus asked.

"Yes. He came many times and sat and watched," Boschina replied. "He wanted Father to change the stone, to make it different. They argued each time, but Father wouldn't give in."

"I would like to see this statue," Thalmus said.

Culinary shook his head. "You can't. It's gone or has been destroyed, by orders of the king."

"Yes, so it is said," Thalmus replied. "Well, now I must speak with the king. Come, Boschina." He helped her down off Dallion. "You go with Culinary and get something to eat."

"Can't I go with you?"

"Not this time, Boschina."

"It would upset the king's appetite to see you," the nervous cook said, holding his big hands out as if to stop her. "We mustn't do that. He might blame it on my cooking."

"All right," Boschina said reluctantly. She looked at Thalmus with sad, but hopeful eyes and turned toward the kitchen with the cook.

"Come on Thunder, I have plenty of scraps for you," Culinary said. Then turning back to Thalmus, he called, "I'll have some eats for you, too, when you're done."

Thalmus nodded as Dallion nuzzled him and whinnied.

"Yes, Dal, would you like some eats too? Then go to the stables." He stroked Dallion's neck and smiled. "But, don't cause any trouble with the other horses."

Dallion tossed his head and snorted.

Thalmus laughed. "Go on. I will come for you."

Dallion trotted away, and for a few moments, Thalmus watched his friends heading off in different directions. Then, he turned and climbed the wide steps to the Great Hall, thinking about what to say to the king. At the top of the steps, he passed between large marble columns that supported the roof. Carved in these columns—in words and pictures—were the heroic deeds of the king and his royal ancestry. Masons, moving up and down on scaffolding, were at work chipping and carving new images. He paused to look at their work, for he was not ready to face the king. It was critical that he change the king's mind, but he was not sure of the right approach—or what to expect from the fog of untruth that had been seeping into the castle.

The new carvings in progress around the column were a series of scenes depicting the king as a tall, youthful, and strong man in combat with various foes. In one carved image, he was sword fighting with five opponents—and slaying them all. The words engraved below these pictures said: KING AHMBIN CONQUERS THE EVIL KNIGHTS. Thalmus grunted with surprise at this version of the event; for he had been at the battle, and knew that the king did not destroy the knights by himself.

Another scene showed the king stabbing a truly ugly and fierce-looking creature the likes of which Thalmus had never seen or heard. It looked something like a man-size lizard with vicious eyes and jaws full of pointed teeth. The inscription below said: KING AHMBIN RIDS THE LAND OF THE GAUK.

There were other new, glorious scenes, all of which showed King Ahmbin as a handsome, fearless conqueror. Granted, the king had won victories, and he had been a tireless warrior in his youth, but he never looked as he was portrayed in these engravings. The old pictures and carvings of the king were accurate even though they were twenty or more years old.

These new images completely distorted the truth. Thalmus shook his head. Now he saw the problem: Veracitas' statue of the king, with its stone reality, had shattered this new image, and therefore had to be destroyed—if indeed, it had been destroyed. So, what had convinced the king to believe in this masquerade?

Thalmus still wasn't sure how to change the king's mind, though he was beginning to form a strategy. At least, he felt more prepared now to speak to the all-powerful ruler. He went on through the foyer to the Great Hall's entrance. At the doors to the court, several unfamiliar guards stopped him.

"Look, it's the little one they call great," one of the men said. He was tall, had a bushy brown beard and was missing some front teeth.

"He looks like a stable boy, not a hunter," the other one said. This man had scars on his arms from sword cuts. Both of their uniforms were unkempt, dirty and ripped at the seams.

"What makes you so great, huh?" the Beard said. "Ya kill a few frogs and the king calls ya great?"

"He couldn'ta done that by hisself. He's too little," Scarred Arm said.

"What sort'a magic you got, Frog Hunter?" the Beard said, stepping closer.

"Let's put a sword in his hand and see how great he is against a man," Scarred Arm threatened.

"Is it that owl that's always flyin' around you? Is that your magic?" the Beard persisted.

Thalmus stood calmly through this but was inwardly concerned by their attitude. He had encountered jealousy from soldiers before; however, this was much more aggressive and the question of magic in Bubo implied other intentions. Without saying a word, or even acknowledging the two guards, Thalmus started toward the door. The tall bearded one stepped in front of him.

Thalmus looked up at him and calmly said, "You do not wish to delay me. The king awaits."

The Beard did not move. He stood in the way, sneering down at Thalmus. To his surprise, he looked into eyes so deep and a confidence so strong that it unnerved him. The grizzled soldier saw nothing but danger in the smaller man's stare and stance. He noticed Thalmus' hand hanging near the handle of the large knife on his hip. He had heard the stories of how quick the hunter was with his blade. Realizing that challenging him would be a deadly mistake, the Beard cautiously stepped aside.

Seeing his partner's defeat, Scarred Arm stepped forward and pushed open the large iron door. "Pardon us, oh great one," he said sarcastically. "We mustn't keep thee from our glorious king any longer."

As Thalmus passed through into the hall, the two men laughed behind him as they closed the door. The arrogance and disrespect of these guards concerned him, not for his own safety, but rather for the king's. A tall, white-haired man wearing a tan robe with a maroon sash and sleeves approached Thalmus. His once-round face displayed the collective years of time; yet, his posture remained erect and confident, his blue eyes shone clear and friendly.

"How good to see you, Thalmus," he said, clutching Thalmus' arm with affection. He had steady hands with long, strong fingers and a remarkably firm grip.

"Thank you, Lord Rundall. As always, you make me feel welcome."

"That's because you are," the old man replied.

Rundall was the head of court, and the king's uncle. He held a special position of authority because he was closer to the king than anyone; in fact, the king was like his son. Rundall had no children of his own, so he helped raise and train the boy to become king. He had been his friend, teacher, and counselor— especially after Ahmbin's father, King Ahmbin the Second, died. Rundall had always supported him, fought by his side, advised him on political and financial matters, and comforted him when his wife, Ekala's mother, died unexpectedly at an early age.

For many years, they managed the kingdom together. Now, they were old and wondering how much time they had left to resolve the problem of the throne's inheritance and to keep the kingdom safe from war. Rundall had never been ambitious, except in his protection of King Ahmbin.

The high-beamed ceiling and stone floor echoed their footsteps as Thalmus and Rundall started walking toward the far end of the hall where the king's pedestal stood. A group of men—the Council of Learned Men—were congregated there. The odd collection of advisors stood waiting in colorful clothes that denoted their lofty roles and rank. Sunlight beamed through many portals in the south wall, lighting the large room with shafts of brightness.

"I understand that you have not been hunting?" Rundall asked.

"I have come to ask the king's advice," Thalmus replied.

"The king is most curious as to what it can be," Rundall said, but Thalmus remained quiet so Rundall went on. "I believe I know why you are here, Thalmus. The stone cutter's daughter is with you?"

"Yes, she is," Thalmus confirmed, not surprised by how quickly word had spread of Boschina's presence.

Rundall nodded and took several steps before speaking again. "Life has been changing here," he said thoughtfully. "The king is losing faith in his own ability. His confidence is weak, which is something I had not expected. He worries constantly about the succession of the throne and that causes him to make poor decisions. These decisions have weakened his authority and opened the door to saboteurs. I was hopeful that Veracitas' statue would enlighten the king. Instead, it had the opposite effect. It drove him deeper into despair." Rundall stopped to look directly at Thalmus. "And now, you are here with the stone cutter's daughter, requesting to search for her father."

He grasped Thalmus' arm.

"This is the start of the prophecy," Rundall said intently, but quietly. "The journey that should bring Ekala to the throne, the first woman to rule in any land. I had seen the signs, but I did not know if it was truly the beginning until now. I must admit that this lifts my heart, yet scares me at the same time."

"I understand," Thalmus replied. "Success is not certain and there will be changes and struggles, but the time has come. How many do you think are aware of this?"

"I believe there are only a few who still believe in the prophecy," Rundall said softly. "And some of those, I fear, will fight to defeat us."

Thalmus had been thinking about this and remembering the ancient writings. "That was predicted," he said, and then looked into the eyes of the tall man. "The first part of the prophecy is to free Veracitas and to bring him back. That is why I am here. To do that, I will need your help, Rundall. You know me; you know my role in this. I am a hunter. I am not used to speaking much."

Rundall nodded and smiled at him. "You are a man of action, Thalmus, always have been—and much wiser than any I know today. You know I will help all I can, for at this moment you carry the hope for the future of our kingdom."

Walking on, without speaking further, they neared the pedestal and the cluster of Learned Men who nodded polite greetings to Thalmus. Two of them, Lord Bevie and Lord Cartridge, received him warmly, inquiring about his friends and their good health. The other men kept their distance as befit their positions—and to wait for the king's attitude toward the frog hunter. The clear tone of a bell rang through the hall, and the king appeared on a balcony high on the back wall. They all kneeled reverently as the king walked down a long ramp that descended from the balcony to his throne, a large, beautiful rosewood chair with maroon cushions. The chair stood on a circular pedestal that was raised one meter above the floor. Carved in the high back of the chair were crossed swords amongst rose trees; the emblem of the Ahmbin family. On top of the chair was a large circular crown carved from a single piece of rosewood. Stones of ruby set atop five pinnacles around its rim. Light coming from the windows behind the throne illuminated the ruby crown and shinned in the eyes of those standing before it.

Even though the king wore a large fur-lined robe with sashes of maroon and gray, it was clear that his figure did not resemble the carvings on the columns. King Ahmbin was large. His clean-shaven face was round with a double chin, his gray hair was stringy, and his skin pale. He appeared tired and moved slowly; still, he had a broad smile on his face for Thalmus. He finally reached the pedestal and sat heavily into his royal chair. They all stood and Rundall stepped forward.

"Your Majesty," Lord Rundall said. "Your Royal Frog Hunter."

He bowed and backed away as Thalmus took several steps forward and bowed. "It is an honor and a pleasure to see you again, King Ahmbin."

"Of course," the king said in a high-pitched voice that did not match his personage. "Since I will not be tasting frog legs tonight, I am full of wonder at why you have come before me. Can it be that there is finally something I can do for you?"

"Your Majesty," Thalmus said, picking his words carefully. "I am not a wise man, nor am I clever. I am merely a simple and stubborn hunter."

"You are far more than that, Thalmus. You're the best fighter and hunter in this land," the king cried in his high voice. The Learned Men nodded and mumbled their agreement.

"Thank you, Your Majesty."

"It's the truth," the king said, settling back in the cushioned chair.

There it was: truth. The understanding of which Thalmus wanted to speak—and the king had provided an opening. So, Thalmus decided to use it.

"That is why I am here," he said, "for the truth."

The king misunderstood. "Oh no, Thalmus," he said, disappointed. "You no longer want to hunt for me?"

"Your Majesty, I will always be your hunter."

"What then?" King Ahmbin looked at the Learned Men to see if they understood.

The advisers just shook their heads, confused.

"You still want to hunt," the king said slowly, trying to understand. "Then why are you here, Thalmus?"

"Don't you want truthful men around you?" Thalmus asked.

"I do, and so I have," he answered, gesturing to his Council of Learned Men—to which they all nodded in response.

Thalmus tried again.

"Do we not strive for truth in our lives?"

"Of course we do," the king replied, with a wave of his hand.

"But, Your Majesty," said Baldoff, a member of the Council, as he stepped forward from the group. "A wise man knows that total truth is not always possible, nor is it healthy. We must know how to allow...subtlety in our actions." His voice was firm, not loud, and exuded confidence.

The king nodded his head. "Subtlety," he repeated the word, as if trying to grasp its meaning. "Yes, that is also true."

So, this is Baldoff, Thalmus thought, *the man Ekala described as a devious dandy.* He stood medium height, with long blond hair and a close-cropped beard. He wore a floppy, black velvet hat, forest-green trousers gathered at the waist with a wide leather belt, a billowy long-sleeved white blouse, and a brown, quilted vest.

Thalmus returned his eyes to the king.

He decided to try a different approach.

"Should a man be punished for honesty?"

"Of course not," the king said, becoming frustrated and leaning forward. "What is this all about, Thalmus? This is more words than I've ever heard from you, and I still don't know why you're here."

"I am here because I want to help a child search for her father who is an honest man."

"That's it?" the king asked, holding out both hands with the palms up.

"Yes, Your Majesty."

"Why didn't you say so to begin with, Thalmus, instead of all this talk about truth and honesty? This is a strange request and I don't know why you feel that you need my permission, but you have it. Go with my blessing."

"Thank you, Your Majesty," Thalmus said. "But there is more to it. You must know this man I wish to search for was imprisoned by you and has escaped."

"Is this true?" the king asked turning to his Learned Men, who seemed just as surprised.

"Your Majesty," Rundall said, stepping forward. "I believe Thalmus speaks of the sculptor, Veracitas."

"No," the king shouted.

"This is true, Your Majesty," Thalmus said calmly. "The man I speak of is Veracitas."

"But why?" the king asked, perplexed.

"Because he is an honest man who does not deserve punishment," Thalmus replied bravely.

The king bit his lower lip and sat back in his chair. There was a stunned silence in the Great Hall. No one made a sound for a long time. The Learned Men, in their colorful robes, watched—glancing back and forth from the king to Thalmus, who continued to look up at King Ahmbin.

Finally, Lord Rundall spoke, "Your Majesty, you did give Thalmus your blessing."

The king looked at Rundall. "I did? Oh … I did … didn't I?"

"But, your Royal Grace," Baldoff said, stepping forward again. "That was before you knew who the hunter wanted to hunt."

"That's right," the king said. "I didn't know."

"Your Majesty," Lord Rundall said. "You have always promised Thalmus whatever he desired. He now desires to find this man and see to his safety."

"But this stone cutter has wronged and hurt the king," Baldoff said. "He must be punished."

Many of the Learned Ones nodded and mumbled that he must be punished—except Lords Bevie and Cartridge, who objected.

"That is true," the king said. "He tried to hurt me."

Thalmus took another step forward and looked directly up at the king. "How could this simple sculptor hurt the great King Ahmbin? How could he hurt our fearless king who saved us all from that terrible creature, the Gauk? How could he possibly hurt our powerful king who by himself, with no help from others, slew the Evil Knights?"

The king sat up proudly in his chair.

"You're right, Thalmus. He cannot hurt me."

"But he did, your Grace," Baldoff said, "with that terrible statue. Remember?"

"Your Majesty," Thalmus said. "I am called 'great', and fantastic stories about my skill are spread throughout the land. But look at me, I am small and not what anyone would consider handsome. It does not bother me, for I know myself. I know who I am."

"Come, come, Frog Hunter," Baldoff interrupted. "What does this have to do with the stone cutter?"

"If Veracitas were to make an honest statue of me, it would be as you see me," Thalmus said, holding his arms out from his sides. "Not as I am portrayed in stories."

The Learned Men started mumbling amongst themselves. They were worried. This situation had become dangerous. Someone was going to have to answer to the king, and none of them wanted to take that risk.

Thalmus turned and looked at them. "Can any of you deny that Veracitas' statue of the king was not honest?"

The king stared at his advisers.

They remained hushed and afraid to answer.

However, Baldoff was not intimidated. "Your Royal Grace, I fear your hunter, as did your sculptor, is trying to destroy you."

"Our king is wise enough to know that honesty will hurt him far less than deceit," Thalmus said to Baldoff.

The king seemed confused and began to stare down at his feet. Thalmus was surprised at his behavior. Never before had he seen King Ahmbin befuddled or weak.

Baldoff turned toward Thalmus. "Do you mean to imply that I am deceiving—"

"Your Majesty, if I may clear the situation," Lord Rundall said, interrupting and putting his hand on Thalmus' shoulder. "This man, who has willingly risked his life in hunting and fighting for you over the years and never once asked for a reward, has now made a request. And that is simply to allow him to search for Veracitas, the sculptor, and that this man and his daughter be allowed to live in peace. I think that in your thoughtful compassion his request should be granted, my lord."

Baldoff started to object, but the king suddenly rose from his throne and they all had to kneel.

"Yes, yes, it is granted," King Ahmbin shouted, holding his arm out to stop the conversation. "How did this get so involved? If you wish to waste your time in this manner, Thalmus, you have my permission to search for this man."

"And Veracitas' freedom?" Lord Rundall asked.

"Yes, yes, that too! Make a decree," the king said to Rundall, who nodded. Then, the king straightened his sword arm and pointed a stiff finger at Thalmus. "This man's life is yours, Thalmus, to do with as you please."

"Thank you, King Ahmbin," Thalmus said.

The king turned to the ramp. "Don't let this search keep you very long, Thalmus. I will desire some frog legs soon," he said as he moved slowly up the incline. Then, he stopped and looked back at Thalmus. "That reminds me, my daughter has been fussing about going on a frog hunt."

"Yes, Your Majesty," Thalmus said, waiting to hear his decision.

"When she asks—for I know she will, despite my wishes—you will refuse. It is too dangerous and it will not happen as long as I am king."

"As you wish," the frog hunter replied.

Satisfied, the king started up the ramp again when Baldoff spoke. "Your Majesty, perhaps Metro could help the frog hunter in his search for Veracitas."

King Ahmbin stopped and looked at Baldoff, nodded, and turned to Thalmus. "Yes, go see Metro. I'm sure he will be able to shorten your journey."

"Yes, Your Majesty," Thalmus said. Though, he could not help but think, *how could the magician save time in my search when he, or anyone else for that matter, has been unable to find Veracitas?*

After the king was gone, the bell rang and they all rose.

Baldoff glared at Thalmus. Then, slowly, a wicked smile came over his face. "I congratulate you," he said. "For a simple hunter, you are very clever. Of course, without Lord Rundall's help, your request would have been denied. I would have seen to that."

Thalmus looked at the blond man as Rundall joined them. "Do you have a reason for wanting to deny Veracitas his freedom?" he asked Baldoff.

Baldoff ignored the question. "The two of you make a formidable team. Though I am curious, Thalmus, to see if you will be as successful at hunting men as you are at hunting animals."

Baldoff lowered his head in a brief bow to Lord Rundall before turning and walking away.

"I do not remember this man being here before," Thalmus said.

"He is new, since you were here last," Rundall replied. "There are some who believe him to be very wise, and as you saw, he is influencing the king."

"Ekala told me of him," Thalmus said, watching Baldoff hurry out of the Great Hall as if he were late for an appointment.

Rundall smiled. "You have seen her recently. I am glad of that."

"We met on the road several days ago," Thalmus said, turning to Rundall. "She is very troubled."

"Yes, I know. She has told me of her frustrations," Rundall said with concern. "I have tried to help her, but she seems to be moving on her own. She spends a lot of time away from the castle. I worry about both her and the king, for our country's welfare depends on them."

"Do you think Baldoff knows of the prophecy?" Thalmus asked.

Rundall pursed his lips and nodded.

"Unfortunately, he is aware of it. That is why he speaks against her taking the throne and has the king doubting her ability to rule."

"Where did he come from?"

"No one knows, except Metro, who brought him here."

"And where did he come from?" Thalmus asked, wondering how these two outsiders got positions of authority in Ahmbin's court.

"I was gone for some time with Lords Bevie and Cartridge inspecting the farms and granaries. When I returned, Metro and Baldoff were here. I had never heard of them before. When I questioned the king, he said that they had been sent by King Dieten of Zinkila as ambassadors. They very quickly gained his confidence, especially Metro—and I have been struggling with them ever since."

"Why would our friend, King Dieten, send a magician as an ambassador?"

"That's exactly what I asked our king," Rundall said. "At first, His Majesty took Metro as a humorous gift but has since fallen under his influence."

"Sounds like sorcery to me," Thalmus replied.

"Yes," Rundall agreed. "When I realized this, I sent a messenger to King Dieten requesting information about these two men. I have heard nothing in response."

"Puzzling," Thalmus said, almost to himself, then looked up at Rundall. "I think it's a lie. Dieten did not send them."

"I have no proof of that," Rundall replied. "And unfortunately, they are entrenched here now."

Thalmus looked around. They were the only ones left in the great hall. The silence in the cavernous room was eerie. Turning both palms downward, Thalmus sensed something more beyond the emptiness. "There is a tremble in this castle that I have never felt before," he said softly, still listening to the stillness. "There is something wrong here." He lifted his gaze to Lord Rundall. "Do you feel it?"

Rundall nodded. "Yes. I have been feeling an undercurrent. The politics and games of this court have always been a tricky business, but I have never feared for the king as I do now. More and more, he believes in fantasies. Until the statue incident, I did not realize how blurred the king's vision was or what a battle I have on my hands with Baldoff and Metro. Veracitas' statue failed because it caught the king off guard. It was contrary to what he has come to believe about himself."

"What happened to the statue?" Thalmus asked.

"Currad had workmen move it to the north yard. It stood there, covered up, because I delayed its destruction while I tried to change the king's mind. Alas, he would not give in. But when they went to break it apart, it was gone. Under the cover was just a frame. And no one claims to know what happened to it."

"So, it still exists?" Thalmus asked, hopefully. "And if it were found, it might still be of use?"

"Perhaps. If not, we must find a way to clear the king's vision and to rid the castle of this deceit."

"It is more than that," Thalmus said. "It is a disease that will destroy the king and allow our enemies to steal the throne from Ekala."

"I see it, Thalmus," Rundall said sadly. Then, he took on a defiant look and seemed to strengthen himself. "I believe there is still time. I must fight the influences here while you find Veracitas. Together, we can work to heal the king of this delusion. Then, perhaps, I can truly believe in the prophecy of Queen Ekala."

Thalmus watched the old advisor and realized that he alone was holding the king in power. The great Ahmbin was faltering, doubting his daughter, grasping for his youth, while forces were building against him. Sooner or later, they both would be overcome. How much longer could Rundall endure? Long enough for Thalmus to return with Veracitas and Ekala? That was his hope and he prayed it be so while a new sense of urgency pushed him to move.

"You must be careful, Lord Rundall," Thalmus said. "For the king's guards have been infected."

"Do not worry about me. This castle is my home. I know what animals dwell here, but you will be encountering new and strange creatures. Beware and guard yourself and Boschina."

"I will. I have my friends with me," Thalmus replied, thinking that Rundall had none.

Rundall nodded and smiled. "Aren't they always with you?"

They parted as Thalmus headed for the kitchen, anxious now to leave, but knowing there was more to do before he and Boschina could be on their way. So, he changed his direction and headed for the north wing of the castle where prisoners were kept.

This side of the city was cold, dirty, and weathered.

The buildings and streets were not maintained as well as the rest of the community because the lords and ladies rarely ventured there. It was also where the army stored its supplies and practiced occasional barbaric ceremonies. There were several large piles of debris and stone from old structures that had been knocked down and not rebuilt.

Thalmus inspected the cell from which Veracitas had escaped. It was in the middle of a row of eight dark cells. Small and solid, it had thick stone walls and three narrow slits—about the width of a man's arm—for air and light. The door was heavy and tight; the rusted latch and chain that held it shut were strong. He stood inside, listening to the routine of the guards outside. Thalmus examined it all and knew now that to escape from this cell would require help from someone outside. It could not be done from within or all alone. The guards told him about the wild storm the night that Veracitas disappeared. They did not leave their shelter until morning. That is when they discovered he was gone, but the door to his cell was closed, latched, and chained. They had seen no one all night or heard anything beyond the rain and crashing thunder. When Thalmus asked what they thought happened to Veracitas, the guards shrugged.

"I think Metro got him," one of them ventured.

Word of the king's decision to rescind Veracitas' condemnation had spread quickly throughout the castle. When Boschina and Culinary heard the news in the kitchen, they were overjoyed. "I knew Thalmus could do it. I knew it," she shouted.

And when Thalmus finally joined them, she was so excited that she could not sit down—until he told her that they had to see Metro before leaving on their search for Veracitas.

"Why?" she asked, settling onto a bench at a table. "He hates my father. Why would he help us?"

"The king requested it," Thalmus answered. He was sitting across the table from Boschina and eating from a plate that Culinary had placed before him.

"He won't help us," Boschina said, hoping to convince Thalmus that it would be a waste of time to see the magician.

"The king wants to see if he can."

Boschina looked down at the table and was silent for a while. She brushed her hair back and rubbed her temples. Then, she stuck her fingers as deep as they would go in the gap between the boards of the table.

"I don't want to see him," she said.

Thalmus looked across the table at her. She did not know how important she was, what she had started in motion, or how she was going to change. He reached out and gently gripped her hand. "This journey is yours, Boschina. You have created it. Therefore, you must be prepared to face whatever it brings before you. I can help, but you are the one who must be strong. You are the one who must endure."

Boschina looked up at Thalmus. "I'm afraid of Metro."

"Yes, I know. But you must rise above that fear, Boschina, if you want to find your father, for this is only the beginning."

Chapter Five
Metro

T he magician's room was on the south side in the lowest part of the castle where the foundation clung to the edge of the black cliffs that dropped straight down from the thick stone walls into deep, dark, Cold Canyon. Thalmus and Boschina entered the room by way of a heavy wooden door and were struck by a strong wind blowing in through large window openings that overlooked the canyon. The wind whistled in their ears as it swirled freely around the room, playing with the different objects on the tables and shelves. Vials and bottles, bowls with pestles and wooden spoons vibrated, rolled, and clattered about. Large iron lamps hanging on chains from the ceiling swung in the current. Faded banners whipped and tugged at their moorings along the walls—and bits of paper swirled in the air. Boschina felt as if she had stumbled into the stomach of a wild and hungry beast. She stepped back against Thalmus and covered her ears. Thalmus put his arm around Boschina to steady her. Then, Metro entered from a dark door on the other side of the room and the wind increased in strength and speed as if it were excited by his presence. He went straight to a window and shouted above the roar, "Swind, wind! Heave and leave!"

The wind gusted and blew out the window openings, billowing Metro's robes and leaving only the sounds of the different objects slowly ceasing their dance without their partner.

Metro turned and fixed his penetrating eyes upon them. He had a short, curly, black beard and equally black, long hair that coiled about his face. His hair was tossed and wild-looking from the wind that had just blown through him on its escape to the canyon outside. He wore a long-sleeved gray robe with wide black stripes down the front that made him appear larger than he was. His hands were adorned with gem-studded jewelry. Finger-sized crystals hung around his neck. His feet were encased in elaborate leather boots with large heels that increased his already tall stature. These boots were covered by his robe, but the wind had shown them to Thalmus. The skin of his hands and face were creased and weathered. However, the dominant feature, by far, that one became aware of instantly were his eyes. Sparkling, emerald green and deep set under bushy brows. They looked like creatures coiled in the brush ready to attack.

Thalmus stepped away from Boschina. "We have come—"

"I know why you're here," Metro said—his voice deep and resonant, like an echo. "Though, I have to question why. You have Bubo and the giant shell creature. Are they not your eyes and ears?"

Thalmus looked at Metro and wondered, *is he mocking the reputation of my friends or does he truly believe in their powers? Is it just a magician's paranoia or is there more to it? Curious,* Thalmus thought, *the man is certainly full of anger.*

"It is true that my friends are most helpful to me," Thalmus said calmly. "Yet no one seems to know where Veracitas is. The king—"

"You're a hunter," Metro said, interrupting Thalmus again, "a great one, I'm told, a fearless killer of beasts and a man who can change a king's mind. Why would you need me?"

Thalmus smiled, but his eyes did not leave Metro.

He fears me, Thalmus thought. *He perceives me as a threat.*

"The king wanted me to see you," Thalmus said slowly, enunciating each word as if he were speaking to someone who did not understand the language. "His majesty thought you could help in some way."

"I know that," the magician responded with disgust.

"Yes, of course you do," Thalmus replied, speaking normally. "Perhaps you are unable or not willing to help us. Whichever it may be, we will no longer bother you."

He motioned to Boschina and they turned to go.

"Wait," Metro commanded.

Thalmus stopped and looked at Metro.

"You're clever," the magician said. He turned and looked out of the window at the vast emptiness beyond the cliffs. "The king has requested that I assist you," he said angrily. Then, he pivoted and focused his crystal eyes on Thalmus. "So, I will use my powers to help you find this…deceiver."

He is too proud, Thalmus observed. *He wants to show me his skills. He wants to scare me. So, who is the real deceiver?*

Metro went to a row of shelves on the wall that held assorted flasks and vials and surveyed them for several moments. "To find someone who does not want to be found in a land as vast as this is a test of one's skills," he said.

Metro looked over his shoulder at Boschina, then back at his bottles. He selected several vials, sniffing one, feeling the weight of another, and began pouring their contents together into a bowl. The liquids created a greenish, oily brew with a foul odor. He took a third container and checked its color as he carried it and the bowl to a table.

"Stone Daughter," Metro called abruptly, turning his eyes on Boschina.

Startled, Boschina tried to look at the magician without looking at his face, but Metro's eyes grabbed her own and held her gaze as tight as a fist on her wrist.

After several moments with no words being spoken, Boschina—with her eyes locked on Metro's and moving at his will—stepped to the table and slowly raised her arms and placed her fingertips in the bowl. Metro tipped the third flask over the bowl. Several drops fell into the mixture and the green liquid turned blood red.

Boschina trembled and her fingers shook the liquid.

"What does your blood tell you?" Metro whispered. "Does not a father's blood call out to his daughter's?"

The frightened stone cutter's daughter remained silent.

"Can you not feel him? Where is your father, daughter? From where does he call you?"

Boschina tried to speak, but could not. Her eyes stared into Metro's and she trembled uncontrollably. Images of her father passed before her eyes, visions of his weathered face and muscular arms working in new and strange places. He appeared to be calling her, to be searching for her. She wanted to shout out to him, "Here! I am here, Father!"

Still, she could not find her voice.

"Feel your blood, daughter," Metro was saying. "Feel it calling your father, calling him to you. Where is he?"

Veracitas was there in Metro's eyes. Boschina could see him. She could not hear him or tell where he was, but she could feel him calling her—reaching out to her. She tried to respond, struggled desperately to answer her father; yet, something prevented her. Deep in her thoughts, beyond the image of her father, beyond the emotion and her desire to speak, was a voice telling her, "Do not tell Metro. Do not tell Metro."

The image of Veracitas was starting to fade, slowly drifting away.

"Don't let go," Metro shouted. "Call to him, daughter, tell me where he is!"

Boschina's connection with her father was slipping, her energy waning. The liquid in the bowl, in which her fingers shook, returned to green and with it Veracitas' image disappeared before her eyes. Boschina slumped against the table as her hands fell from the bowl.

Thalmus stepped forward and held her so she would not fall. Metro continued to stare at her; then grabbing the bowl in a fit of anger, he threw it out the window. Its foul contents were picked up by the wind and dissipated into the canyon below. Without saying a word, he hurried to a shelf, grabbed a vial, and drank from it—swallowing hard and breathing heavily.

Thalmus observed all this and was now watching Metro. *His fiery anger controls him and rapidly burns his strength*, Thalmus thought. *Therein lies a weakness to his tricks and deceit.*

Metro felt Thalmus' eyes and slowly turned his head and glowered at him. He seemed to know what Thalmus was thinking. "I said it would be a test," he growled. "And so it is."

"We will go," Thalmus said.

"Wait. I'm not finished," the magician said. He was breathing normally now and once again in control of himself

Thalmus thought: *this is more than a game, more than just a challenge to him. This man wants to know where Veracitas is hiding.*

Metro took a canister from a shelf and set it in front of one of the large openings to the canyon. "Stone Daughter, rise and be observed. Let's see what visions the far-reaching power of the winds can bring us." He raised his arms above his head and spread his fingers wide. "Swind, wind, swirl and swerve, tend and bend, align and find this child's father!"

The wind suddenly filled the room, rushing through the openings, whipping Metro's hair and robes as it swept toward Boschina. She felt the wind encircle her as it roared in her ears, played in her hair, inhaled her scent, and then blew from the room.

Metro remained frozen with his arms and hands outstretched. The room became still and totally silent. Nothing moved—even their breathing seemed to stop. Boschina felt as if they all had become stone statues placed in their proper positions in a scene, like the ones she had watched her father create. As quick as it had left, the wind returned. It burst into the room like a tornado, past Metro, and swirled around and around like a mixture in a bowl.

Boschina shivered. "It's cold and damp," she said.

The wind had returned with the smell and feel of another place.

"What else do you sense?" Metro asked.

"Water. Lots of water. It smells like rain."

"Let's see the images the wind has brought us," Metro said.

He opened the canister that he had placed in the window, took out a handful of silver powder, and tossed it up into the circling wind. The cloud of powder was whipped about and formed into a glistening picture like a reflected image on the flowing surface of a river. The shining picture revealed an image of a man obscured by falling water.

"Father," Boschina exclaimed, staring up at the image in the wind. "It's my father. Where is he?"

"He's in the rain," Metro said with an insidious smile growing on his face.

"Where in the rain?"

"I know of only one place like this," Metro replied. "And there is no place worse." He began to snicker and then burst into a hideous cackle, throwing his head back like an animal.

"Where is he?" Boschina pleaded.

The magician looked at her, his eyes gleaming with triumph and laughter. "Your father is in Rainland."

Chapter Six
Rainland

Thalmus and Boschina returned through the maze of stone halls and stairs to Culinary's kitchen, which was like a laboratory itself. Cooking fires burned in numerous recesses with boiling pots hanging on iron bars and hunks of meat or birds roasting on spits. Pans and pots, stirring spoons and knives of various sizes hung from the walls and ceiling. There were rows of shelves with assorted crocks and containers each painted in a different color. Long, worn, wood tables with benches and scattered utensils stood in the middle of the stone room. Culinary was famous for experimenting with food and concocting new and exotic recipes and elixirs. He was also known for being sensitive and fussy.

Thunder was glad to see his friends, nudging them both as they came in, and the red-faced cook was anxious to hear what had happened with the magician. Boschina was still trembling from her experience in Metro's room, but was filled with excitement at knowing where her father was.

"Rainland," Culinary exclaimed when she told him of their destination. He looked at her in disbelief. "Nobody goes there."

Boschina thought about that while she rubbed her hands together, trying to stop them from shaking. "Maybe that's why father went there, because it's a good place to hide."

The cook was still incredulous and grasping for understanding. He set down a large pot of soup that he had been carrying when they came in. "But, it's a place of…well, I don't even know if people still live there. It's nothing but water."

"Father's there, I saw him," Boschina replied defensively. "We'll find him and bring him home."

Culinary shook his head. "It's a dangerous place."

She looked to Thalmus for support.

"We'll bring him back, won't we, Thalmus?"

"We'll find him," Thalmus said with a nod, "whether he is there or in some other place."

Culinary looked back and forth at his friends, shaking his head at one and then the other. Then, he sighed. "Well, you're gonna need some food. Why don't you go get Dallion, girl, while I pack some eats for ya?"

Boschina smiled at the pudgy cook.

"Thank you," she said—and she ran out to find Dallion.

Culinary watched her go, then turned and hooked a hunk of meat that was cooking over the fire, plopped it on the table, and began carving slices from it with a large knife.

"Thalmus, my friend," he said, focusing on the sharp knife cutting through the large roast. "This place you're goin', this Rainland, is dangerous."

"So I've heard," Thalmus answered as he organized their supplies on the large table.

Irritated by Thalmus' casual response, Culinary grunted and continued slicing the meat with determined strokes of the knife. "Then perhaps you've *heard* that many bad things live there?" he said sarcastically. "Perhaps you've *heard* people there are like fish, and there are giant water creatures that pull ya under and drown ya, then eat you. It's supposed to be such a tangled, dark swamp that you're easily lost and starve or get eaten by the water creatures." The cook had worked himself up emotionally and now he stopped cutting the meat and turned to Thalmus. "Boschina should not go with you."

Thalmus looked up from his packing at Culinary, who was staring him down with a dreadful look. "I have no choice in this," Thalmus said gently, but firmly. "She has to go."

Culinary pointed his knife at Thalmus.

"Then I'm puttin' her life on your back."

Thalmus smiled, for he knew that there was a lot more riding on his shoulders than the weight of one life. "I accept the responsibility," he said.

Culinary snorted and shook his head in frustration. He took a deep breath and blew it out, then laid the knife down. "Well, if she has'ta go, I can't think of anyone better than you to protect her. I still don't like it, mind ya."

"I understand," Thalmus replied. "It will be a difficult journey, but I believe she is up to it. In the little time I have known her, I've learned that Boschina is stronger than she looks. And," Thalmus added for the benefit of the cook, "it should ease your mind to know that I will be teaching her how to use the tools to defend herself."

The cook, satisfied with Thalmus' answer, wiped his greasy hands on his already dirty apron. "Well, how about some bread? I just baked a batch of loaves."

When Boschina returned, racing Dallion through the streets, the cook was ready with canvas bags full of food. He helped them tie the supplies on Dallion, who was not thrilled about becoming a pack horse. The worried Culinary looked at all of them, shaking his head slowly. Then, he quickly hugged Thalmus and whispered, "Be careful." He turned to Boschina, hugged her a little longer, and then stepped back. "Find your father and bring him back."

"We will," she said with a smile and returned his hug. "Thank you for the food."

Culinary nodded, holding back tears. Thunder pressed against him and snapped his jaw. The cook rubbed the giant's head. "You're welcome, Thunder. Now go on, the lot of ya," he said waving his hands as if shooing them away.

Thalmus, Boschina, Thunder, and Dallion left Ambermal quietly with much less fanfare than when they arrived. After they had passed through the gates and were in the open land beyond the walls, Boschina felt a sudden chill, like the cold that had gripped her in Metro's room. She glanced over her shoulder and saw Metro watching them from atop the castle wall.

Baldoff was standing beside him.

"They're watching us," she said in a worried soft voice to Thalmus, as if the two distant men could hear her.

"Yes, I know," Thalmus said without looking back. He smiled at her. "I doubt that they will miss us."

*

Owl joined them at dusk as they camped near the south fork of the Camotop River whose origin flowed from Rainland. In the morning, they waded across the river at this shallow spot and for twelve days they followed the wide, slow-flowing Camotop as it curved northeast into the bright interior of the country. The days were hot and the sky was clear and blue. They rested in the shade of trees along the water's edge and ate the food Culinary had made for them. Each day as they walked, Bubo flew great circles around their route to scout the land and reported to Thalmus that they were always being followed by a small column of troops that stayed just out of sight. Dallion stomped and snorted about these troops spying on them. Thalmus tried to calm his friend; still, the stallion could not ignore this threat. So, when the supplies had been shifted to Thunder, Dallion galloped back and around the troops to let them know that he knew they were there. Whenever he did this, the soldier's horses became agitated, bucked, and pulled at their reins— wanting to run with him. The riders had to work very hard to hold tight and keep their mounts from bolting from under them.

At night, Thalmus and Boschina slept comfortably and undisturbed with the knowledge that the ever-watchful eyes and keen senses of their three animal friends would detect any intruder.

On the very first evening of the journey, Boschina's education of weaponry had begun under the patient and steady tutelage of the wise frog hunter. He was not convinced that Veracitas was hiding in Rainland—and he was even more suspicious of Metro's motivation, let alone his magic. With the troops following them, the reputation of Rainland, and the deviousness of the magician, Thalmus expected trouble. From his experience in many campaigns, he knew that their journey would not avoid conflict. Thalmus was not sure when they would be in a fight in which Boschina would have to defend herself, but he knew it could be soon.

It was inevitable.

There was not enough time for Boschina to study and become proficient at each tool, or to build up the muscles required to handle them properly. On that first night of training, Thalmus un-wrapped the tools from their canvas and leather covers and presented a sword to Boschina that he had brought for her.

"This is yours," he said, pulling the blade from the scabbard and holding it out to her in his upturned palms. "It is like the one I gave to Ekala when she began her lessons. This one has been waiting for you."

Boschina grasped the leather-wrapped handle and slowly lifted the sword from Thalmus' hands. She felt an immediate connection and comfort with the weapon, as if it had once belonged to her.

"There are engravings on the blade," she commented as she studied the tool in her hands. "Why, it's the images of Thunder and Bubo," she exclaimed and turned the blade over. "And Dallion is on this side."

"So that you know that they will always be with you," Thalmus said. "This crossbar at the handle will serve to protect your hand. The steel of the blade is unmatched in strength but light and not too long; it is a good fit for you. The tip is quite sharp, so be careful where you point it."

"It's beautiful," she said. "Is this my own?"

"Yes, it has your initials engraved here in the pommel, SCD."

"SCD?" she questioned, looking rather puzzled at the letters that did not match her name.

"Stone Cutter's Daughter," Thalmus replied.

Boschina laughed. "That's who I am," she said and laughed again.

Thalmus smiled at seeing her wonder and joy.

"Now," he said. "Let's begin."

He taught her the basic skills of each weapon, beginning with the short sword or long knife and progressing through the sword, bow and, finally, the short and long spears. Boschina was an eager student and quick learner and practiced with Thalmus each night until she was exhausted. Mostly though, Thalmus had her work with the sword and knife, as he felt those tools would be needed more frequently to protect herself in close combat.

Archery was second: bracing the bow, drawing and releasing an arrow, understanding distances, flight of the arrow, sight line, choosing location in a target, when to nock, draw and release an arrow. During the day, he had her wear the sword and knife to get used to their weight and occasionally carry the bow slung over her shoulder. Practice continued each night with the bladess and every day along the trail with archery, choosing a target in the distanceand shooting arrows for accuracy. At Thunder's slow-but steady pace, they were able to shoot and retrieve arrows and still proceed toward their destination.

Rainland was not the sort of place that was easily visible; it was not a place that could be recognized in the distance, so you could change your direction to avoid entering its dark realm. No, it came upon travelers without their knowledge, ever so slowly, as it did to Thalmus and Boschina.

An entire day passed before they realized that the sharp blue sky had softened into a constant gray—that there was no longer a bright sun or shadows beneath the trees or warmth in the meadows, but only a constant cool gray light that existed everywhere.

The rain began gradually, almost without their noticing. At first, it was a dampness that caused them only to be aware of a temperature change. Then, it slowly moistened like dew in the morning. It became a mist that obscured the horizon, then a faint wisp of drops that was not unpleasant, but increased ever so slowly until they were finally aware of being wet. And all the time, the distance they could see lessened and the grayness closed in around them.

Thalmus stopped to let Thunder catch up and to prepare for whatever might lie ahead. He pulled two frog-skin coats with hoods from the pack on Dallion and gave one to Boschina. She shivered as she buttoned the coat.

"It's not very warm," she said.

"No, but it will keep you dry," Thalmus responded. Then, feeling his own wet clothes against his skin, he added: "Well, it's too late for dryness. It will protect you, though."

"Is this what you wear when you hunt the frogs?"

"Yes," Thalmus said as he untied his sword from the packs on Dallion and strapped it on his waist. Boschina watched him and noticed that Thalmus' appearance changed. He was poised now, with a serious bearing. She checked and adjusted her own belt with the knife and sword scabbards and wondered if these tools changed her looks as well.

"Do you think there are frogs here?" she asked.

"Perhaps." Realizing her concern, he said, "In this coat, you have no fear of frogs."

Led by Owl, Thunder finally joined them. Thalmus and Boschina climbed onto Dallion and they started again, this time moving slower so Thunder could keep up. The rain continued to increase as they slogged deeper into the mysterious realm of water. Owl could no longer fly very high, for he would enter the grayness of the sky and lose sight of his companions on the ground. He was forced to fly just above their heads, and this he did not like, for it was not a position of advantage. There was no road or trail to follow because the entire surface was covered with water or a mucky bog. Besides, there was no traffic traveling into or out of Rainland to establish a road. The ground was so soggy that Dallion's hooves sank into the mud, sometimes so deep that he became stuck. Thalmus would slide down off the frustrated stallion to help him pull his legs from the sucking mud.

Finally, it was too deep for Dallion to continue.

Thunder would have to carry them from here. Adjustments had to be made though, for there was not enough space on Thunder's shell for the two of them, the supplies, and tools. Thalmus helped Boschina dismount. They removed the packs and hung them in a tree, thinking that they would pick up the supplies on their way out. Thalmus left the bow, quiver, and spears wrapped in their leather cases secured to Dallion so that he would have less weight on him. Dallion nuzzled into Thalmus, who stroked his nose and put his forehead against the stallion's head. Boschina rubbed Dallion's neck and hugged him. Thunder moaned and nudged Dallion's leg. They touched noses and snorted. Owl, perched in the tree by the packs, hooted and Dal bobbed his head at him. Dallion reluctantly left his friends and headed back to the edge of Rainland to await their return.

Thalmus stuffed some food from the supplies into his satchel and adjusted it under his frog coat. They continued on, riding atop Thunder as he splashed through the mire. Thalmus and Boschina peered through the rain, looking for the city that stood somewhere in this wet land. All they could see was a dripping forest of sagging, bent, trees—their green colors dulled by the gray light—and water. There was murky water everywhere, completely covering the ground. The surface was splattered and churned from the constant rain; worst of all, it was getting deeper.

Suddenly, Thunder stopped with a jerk. Thalmus and Boschina slid off his back into the water. Something had caught Thunder's back leg, and he was struggling to free himself. Thalmus lifted Boschina from the muck and was helping her onto Thunder when Owl began squawking wildly. A giant worm was rising from the mud. Thunder turned and snapped at the creature, biting out a chunk of its flesh. Slime oozed from the wound and the worm, learning a quick lesson, leaned away. It hung onto Thunder's legs with its other end and stayed behind him, just out of reach of his powerful jaws. The swivel-snapping move by Thunder had caused Boschina and Thalmus to slip off his shell again. Seeing its prey floundering in the water, the creature swung around and came in after them. Thalmus quickly pulled his sword and slashed at it, but his blade bounced off the worm, barely cutting its thick skin. Still, the impact caused the worm to retreat, and they scrambled out of the muddy water back onto Thunder.

The monster worm had no discernible head or eyes in which they could plunge a sword. On its tubular end was a large gaping mouth with roots and vines dangling from it. Mud spilled from the mouth and splattered as the creature stretched over them. The worm swerved back and forth, in and out, attempting with each pass to knock them into the water. And each time it came near, Thalmus struck it, but with little effect. Boschina followed suit, using her sword for the first time. She hacked at the worm, doing even less damage than Thalmus.

Thunder kept turning and snapping, but the worm avoided him and held fast to his legs. Owl swept down and clawed at the worm with his talons. Thalmus and Boschina kept dodging the swinging roots, and chopping at the beast with their swords. Then, with a sudden sweeping motion, the monster knocked Thalmus from his feet. It was about to grab Boschina in its mouth when a great flood plunged down on the creature. A sheer wall of water—as powerful as a waterfall— caught Boschina and Thalmus, along with the worm, in a raging current. Thalmus grabbed Boschina by the frog-skin coat as she swept by him. He plunged his sword into the muck hoping to anchor it into the ground. The worm had been flattened out by the deluge and was now being stretched and pulled away by the intense torrent of water. Boschina fought to keep her head above the swift current as Thalmus held onto her by the hood of the coat. The sword that he had given her was still in her left hand and she wasn't about to let go of it.

Thalmus felt his sword pulling loose from the mud. It could not hold the weight of both of them. If he did not find something to latch onto, they would be swept away in the flood. The nearest tree was out of reach and he quickly searched for something else, something near. Just as the blade slipped out of the muck, he let go of it and grasped for his last hope, the only stable object available.— Thunder's tail. He caught it and held on as tightly as he could, fighting against the current and hanging onto Boschina with his other hand.

The worm was not as strong; it could not maintain its grip on Thunder. The pressure was too great. It finally let go and was washed away through the trees in a gushing flood. Then, as quickly as it had begun, the downpour stopped. Thalmus cautiously loosened his grip on Thunder's tail and the great tortoise turned to check on them. They both stroked his head, thanking him.

Thalmus looked around for more worms or creatures in the rain splattered water. Finding no threats, he began to search for his sword. "Boschina, hand me your sword," he said, holding out his hand.

Boschina turned quickly. "Is the worm back?"

"No, I need to find my sword."

"I don't understand," she said, handing Thalmus her sword.

He grasped the handle and began waving the blade slowly over the water as he moved away from Thunder. Boschina watched and started to question what he was doing when the sword began to vibrate. Thalmus stopped, stuck his free hand into the muddy water and pulled up his own sword that was also vibrating.

"How'd you do that?" Boschina asked, as they climbed from the water onto Thunder's great shell.

Thalmus returned her sword. "The blades have a common—"

Suddenly a voice, sounding like the roar of a waterfall, spoke to them through the rain. "What are you, half frog and man?"

"What...did you hear that, Thalmus?" Boschina said, turning to look around.

"Yes," Thalmus replied and spoke into the rain. "We are not frogs, but we wear their skin as coats."

Again, the unseen watery voice questioned them. "Who are you that travels atop such a creature, the likes of which I have never seen?"

Thalmus shielded his eyes with a hand and looked around. "I am Thalmus. This girl is Boschina. We are looking for her father. And as for Thunder, upon whom we ride, he is no stranger than that worm that has since been washed away—nor you who seem to speak from the very rain itself."

"I am the Shower Knight," called the voice. "I am the faithful protector of my lord and his kingdom. I am the controller of floods, the cleanser of evil. It is I who saved you from the mud worm by washing him away."

"And very nearly us as well," Boschina said.

Thalmus put his hand on her shoulder to quiet her response.

"We owe you our gratitude, as well as our lives," Thalmus said as he searched the grayness for the Knight. "Won't you come forward and make yourself seen?"

"It is better that I am left unseen," the voice replied.

"But why?" Boschina asked, understanding now Thalmus' approach to this situation. "You're so powerful. How can we appreciate you if we can't see you?"

"It is not necessary," said the Knight.

He was either very cautious or very shy, Thalmus thought. Whatever the reason, he wanted to see the owner of the voice and the source of such a unique and forceful power. Perhaps he could draw the Knight out in the open.

"Be as you must be then," said Thalmus. "We still thank you. But, it is getting late and we must be on our way."

There was a pause in which they heard only the rain splattering the surface of the water. Finally, Thalmus tapped Thunder's shell indicating it was time to move on.

Then, the voice said: "There is not much to see."

Thalmus smiled at Boschina.

"Without seeing you, we have no way of judging that."

The Shower Knight did not reply. They stood on Thunder's back waiting in the rain. After several moments, Thalmus said: "As you wish then," and turned to Thunder's great head that had been up, alert, all this time. "Let's move, Thunder."

"If it will ease you," the voice suddenly said. "I will show what there is to see, at this moment."

Out of the dripping grayness a small cloud, emitting its own rain, drifted up to them. The cloud was the shape of an egg and as it came closer, they could make out the image of a man floating within it. The cloud itself was not much larger than the man, but he seemed to fade in and out as if it had tremendous depth and he was trying to stay toward the surface.

Boschina and Thalmus, shielding their eyes from the rain, stared in wonder; however, Owl fluttered away from the strange sight.

"The bird need not be afraid," the Shower Knight said. "I will not harm him. He is a rare and beautiful sight in this land, for all of our birds left long ago."

"That's a shame," Boschina said, "a land with no birds."

"It is sad," the Shower Knight said. "But enough of this drivel. Who is it that you search for?"

"My father, Veracitas, who has fled from King Ahmbin for being an honest sculptor," Boschina replied.

"I know not of your father."

"He has not passed through your land?" Thalmus asked.

"No one enters or leaves Rainland without my knowledge," the Shower Knight said indignantly. The rain from his cloud increased momentarily.

"Of course not," Thalmus said. "We do not want to trouble you any further. The sun will be down soon. Is it very far to your lord's castle?"

"No. I will take you to the palace. Lord Luminous will be happy to receive you and see to your comfort."

Boschina shivered and crossed her arms. "I'd like to get dry and warm up."

"Then follow me," said the Shower Knight, and he started drifting ahead of them.

They tried to follow the Shower Knight to the palace. He kept disappearing, fading into the rain, and then suddenly appearing to scold them for wandering off the path.

"But I can't see any path," Boschina complained.

"It's right before your eyes, girl," the Knight replied.

"Perhaps if the rain stopped I could see it," Boschina suggested.

"It never stops. So don't think about it."

Owl gave up trying to fly around and through and under the distorted, hanging tree branches. He dropped onto Thalmus' shoulder and perched there in a rather frustrated, angry, mood. Thunder splashed through the mire, taking Thalmus' directions and watching for mud worms at the same time. Thalmus and Boschina worked to hang onto Thunder's slippery back and tried desperately to keep track of the Shower Knight, which was difficult enough in the gloom of the forest; but, their vision was blurred even more with the rain that ran off the hoods of the coats into their faces.

And so it went, on and on in the rain, while the wetness soaked through to their spirits—until finally they came to a stone bridge that rose out of the water several feet and continued for as far as one could see through the wet gray fog. Once on the bridge, Boschina and Thalmus got off Thunder and walked. It was a pleasure to be out of the muck, but the rain flowed over the stones like a stream and the slimy moss growing there was slippery and almost as difficult to traverse as the mud.

Protruding out of the water on both sides of the bridge were the crumbled ruins of the city. Some buildings still stood, though they leaned one way or another as their foundations slowly sank. Somewhere the day was ending, the sun was disappearing from the sky, but here in the dusk of Rainland the opaqueness merely grew dimmer.

Just when Thalmus was becoming concerned about the approaching darkness, they reached the end of the bridge and a large, gray, wood gate set in a thick stone wall. Several guards were there waiting along with the Shower Knight, who had disappeared at the beginning of the bridge.

"This is as far as I go," the Knight explained. "These troops will show you where to sleep. You have just enough time to get there before the Black. Once there, do not wander! You will be sent for when the Gray returns."

"Thank you," Thalmus said.

"Go quickly," the Knight replied.

Boschina looked up at the Knight. "Thank you for saving us".

The Shower Knight's cloud puffed up a little.

"Go on," he said, "or you shall be caught in the Black."

The guards—or troops, as the Shower Knight called them—had been staring at them with startled eyes; now, they moved aside for Thunder as he pushed the gate open wider. Boschina and Thalmus stepped in and the gate was quickly closed behind them. They were finally out of the rain. Bubo clinched tighter onto Thalmus' shoulder as he stared at the troopers. In an attempt to calm him, Thalmus patted his feet and stroked his breast feathers.

"Oh," Boschina sighed. "Maybe now I can get dry."

One of the guards motioned to hooks on the wall.

Bubo clicked his beak and pushed off Thalmus' shoulder. He glided onto Thunder's shell, where he stretched his wings and shook the water from them. Boschina and Thalmus took off their dripping frog skins and hung them up on the hooks. The guards examined the coats and touched them carefully, then looked curiously at Owl on Thunder—who glared back at them.

The guards wore blue and gray uniforms with a faded yellow emblem of the sun on the chest. Each man carried a short sword that was strapped at the hip. The swords were not fancy and not well cared for; the hilts and blades were battered and rusty. In the fading grayness, these men appeared gaunt and hunched. Both were shoeless, and Thalmus noticed that they had partially webbed feet.

One of the soldiers pointed at the hooks again and said, "Sword."

Thalmus did not want to give up their swords, though he was willing to leave them in a safe place where no one but he or Boschina could retrieve them.

"We shall leave the swords with him," Thalmus said, pointing at Thunder.

The two guards looked at one another and at Thunder, then at Thalmus, back to Thunder, and then at each other again. They exchanged some quick mumbled words before the one who had been doing all the speaking pointed at Thunder and said, "Must stay here."

"Yes," said Thalmus, "but the Owl comes with us."

Thalmus and Boschina took off their swords and laid them side by side on the ground under Thunder. Thalmus leaned against Thunder's shell and Bubo hopped onto his shoulder. Thalmus stroked Thunder's head. The big tortoise had brought them here safely through a terrible land. He was tired and Thalmus knew he needed to rest. Thunder could withdraw into his shell for safety; still, Thalmus wanted to make sure that no one would bother him. It was almost dark. They had to go. So, he spoke loudly for the benefit of the guards: "No one touches our swords," he said to Thunder. "And don't eat anyone!"

Chapter Seven
Lord Luminous

Thunder was more than happy to withdraw inside his shell for an overdue rest. His legs were tired from struggling through the muck and this place seemed safe for his friends, so he relaxed and settled down to sleep.

One guard stayed at the gate while Thalmus and Boschina followed the other stooped man up five steps and into a long, dark, and damp corridor. They could not see the guard in front of them, but could hear his feet slapping on the cobbled floor. The stones of the floor were uneven and Boschina stumbled along, clutching Thalmus' arm. She reached out to the wall for balance, but instead of touching solid stone, her hand felt something soft and fuzzy and she pulled away quickly.

"Don't you have a torch?" Boschina asked. Her words were quickly muffled by the tunnel and disappeared into the darkness. "Do you have a torch?" she repeated, louder. "Some light!"

The trooper mumbled something that they could not understand and continued on through the blackness. When the slapping feet finally stopped, Owl gripped Thalmus' shoulder tighter and hooted; in turn, Thalmus stopped Boschina. They could hear a door being opened. The hinges creaked and the odor of stale, dank, air engulfed them.

"Stay in here," the guard's voice came from the darkness. "Do not come out until the Gray returns."

"What about food?" Boschina asked. They had left most of their supplies hanging in the tree when they parted with Dallion.

"Food?" the guard repeated, puzzled.

"Yes. We've been traveling all day through the rain, and I'm hungry."

"No food now," he replied.

"Come, Boschina," Thalmus said. "I have something to eat in my bag."

Taking her hand, Thalmus stepped through the door slowly, feeling with his feet and senses. Owl surveyed the room and hooted that there was no danger. The guard closed the door behind them and they heard his footsteps fade in the hall.

Thalmus moved carefully along the inner wall of the room, turning at each corner and continuing until he reached the door and Boschina again. Then, with Owl's guidance, he slowly crisscrossed the room several times, finding a raised wood platform in the center of the room and nothing else. He was satisfied with his inspection and had a feel for the room.

Boschina was exhausted. She was almost asleep on her feet. Thalmus sat her on the platform and gave her a carrot and some snap beans from his bag.

"How could anyone live here?" she asked, crunching on the carrot. "It's so damp and cold. And there's no light."

"One learns to survive, Boschina, whatever the conditions are."

Boschina thought about this while she finished the carrot and then ate the beans. "No, I couldn't live here," she said, lying down. "And I don't think my father could, either." She fidgeted—trying to get comfortable—curled up in a ball for warmth and finally fell into a restless sleep.

Thalmus reclined back on the hard old wood and let his body relax. He had slept in worse places than this, and in worse situations; still, there was something unsettling about this place, this Rainland— something that he could not yet name. He thought about the timid gate guards, their weapons, large eyes, and unusual feet; about the mud worm, its strength and weakness; and about the Shower Knight in his own world with his unique power and invisibility. Thalmus wondered if Thunder felt safe enough to sleep. He did not like leaving him alone in this strange castle. Seeing the image of their parting with Dallion in the rain, he hoped his friend was now grazing on the hills beyond this wetness. He hooted softly and Owl, perched on the end of the platform nearest their heads, turned his glowing, watchful, eyes at Thalmus and hooted in return.

Then, Thalmus closed his eyes and slept.

*

In the morning—if you could call it that—the blackness merely lightened to a misty gray in the corridor, but their room was still dark. Owl hooted, waking Thalmus, when he heard footsteps outside the door.

There were no windows or openings in the stone walls of their room except the one door, behind which now many foot pattings seemed to be gathering. Thalmus could hear them over the constant hum of the rain, which permeated the walls with a cold dampness.

He woke Boschina, who was still shivering.

"Is it morning?" she asked, blinking her eyes.

"Yes."

"But it's so dark."

"It will be lighter out of this room."

Boschina closed her eyes again. "I'm cold and sore."

"And hungry, too, I imagine," Thalmus said.

"Yes."

"Then get up, and let's go find the lord of this castle. We'll get something to eat and look for your father."

The thought of her father roused her spirits. She felt for the edge of the platform, stood, and stretched. Owl suddenly flapped his wings, stretching them out to their full length. It surprised Boschina and she laughed.

"I guess he's ready to go, too."

"Bubo does not like being closed in like this, do you?" Thalmus said, stroking Owl's breast feathers.

"I'm with you, Bubo," Boschina said. "Let's get out of this cave."

Thalmus knelt by the platform they'd used as a bed and Bubo climbed onto his shoulder. He took Boschina's hand—so that Owl was on his shoulder between the two of them—and walked to the door. He knocked once, loud and sharp. The shuffling of many feet could be heard as the old door slowly swung open.

The hallway was lighter than the room; still not the full gray of day, but clear enough that as the door opened they were surprised to see the corridor packed with soldiers in their pale blue uniforms anxious to see the strangers. Word had spread during the night of their arrival. Many of the troopers had already been to see the giant shell that they were told housed a creature that sprouted a head and legs, who walked and ate people. Now, they stared at the large feathered animal with the bright eyes on the small man's shoulder. Most of them had never seen a bird; they were fascinated and wanted to see it fly.

Owl just sat still and glared a warning at them to stay away.

The Rainers, as these people were called, were sallow-looking people with large eyes that stared with a dull gaze. Thalmus could see that once they had been tall and broad-shouldered, but now were gaunt and slouched forward and silent.

"Is your lord ready to see us?" Thalmus asked.

Two troopers with yellow sun insignias on their shoulders, and wearing larger swords than the gate guards, stepped forward and motioned for Thalmus and Boschina to follow. They started walking up the corridor as the rest of the gawking troops made way for them, then closed in behind and followed.

The corridor rose in elevations of five steps at a time; on each level elevation were five doors, five rooms. This continued for some time. Up five stone steps, past five wood doors—two on the left, three on the right—then up another five steps to pass five more doors, all of which were closed. Moss and lichen grew everywhere except on the floor. The walls and ceiling looked like a bumpy multi-shaded green carpet.

As they went, the crowd following them grew larger on every elevation as it was joined by people who heard the parade pass their doors and came out to investigate the commotion. Every new addition was told, in whispers at first, about the strangers and the bird riding on the man's shoulder—and the creature in the shell. Excitement and anticipation spread through the people as they had not known in a very long time. The noise level rose as the growing throng climbed each elevation. The Rainers spoke louder and began knocking on the doors that had not yet opened, to excitedly tell the inhabitants of the event taking place: "Come and see the strangers and their creatures!"

Owl kept his head turned toward the crowd like a rear guard watching for a possible attack.

The two officers in the lead kept turning around nervously to check on the noisy crowd. The excitement was building and as the pace of the procession naturally picked up, so did Boschina's hopes—

—for she was surprised to see so many people in this cold, wet place and to hear something other than rain.

The elevations continued and the crowd and their fervor multiplied until, finally, they came to some stairs that went up fifteen steps to a round, domed, room. The procession burst into this room and filled it like water gushing from a river into an empty reservoir.

Thalmus and Boschina followed the two officers across the center of the room to the opposite side, where the lord of Rainland sat waiting. He was wrapped in a blue blanket, which was the same color as the soldier's uniforms. There was a smile on his face as he leaned from side to side trying to see past his soldiers to the approaching visitors. He waved impatiently at the men to move out of his line of sight. The two officers finally interpreted their lord's signal and moved aside as they continued forward. The lord's eyes widened and his smile grew upon seeing them clearly.

He threw off his blanket and stepped forward to greet them.

His lordship was dressed all in yellow; pants, shirt, vest, socks and shoes were all of the same material. Here and there, gold sequins or glass had been woven into the fiber. If there had been any sun rays, these trinkets would have sparkled; but in this pale light, they just looked like blemishes.

Thalmus glanced around the great room and noticed that the colors of all the banners and the clothes of the people—who now swarmed past them on both sides—were faded. Everything appeared dull and there was an overwhelming mustiness in the air.

"Welcome. Welcome. I am Lord Luminous."

Thalmus stood erect with Bubo on his shoulder while Boschina bowed; before Thalmus could speak though, Lord Luminous continued. "A pleasure to meet you, Thalmus. You are Thalmus?" he said looking him up and down. Speaking to himself, the lord muttered: "Hmm, smaller than I imagined." Turning to Boschina quickly, he said: "And a pleasure to meet you as well, child." Then, his full attention focused on Bubo. Staring intently at Owl, he stepped forward. "And this marvelous creature on your shoulder, the likes of which I have not seen in many a year."

He reached out to touch Owl. Thalmus carefully stepped back. Bubo started bobbing his head and moving it side to side, focusing on Lord Luminous. Thalmus knew that Owl was sizing up a threat and preparing to attack.

"Pardon, your lordship," Thalmus said. "He will not be touched by any man other than me."

"I merely want to feel his feathers. Surely you will not deny me that?"

"No, lord, I would not. But he does. He trusts no man. Believe me, his bite is painful and his claws are deadly." Having said this, Thalmus knew that there might be a problem. He saw great disappointment in Lord Luminous' face, so he asked, "Would you like to see him fly?"

The Lord of Rainland smiled again. "Yes, yes, we all would," he said, motioning to include his people, and they murmured in agreement.

Thalmus whispered to Bubo and then rolled his head to the side. Bubo took off from his shoulder with a great flapping of wings and flew up to the domed ceiling. The crowd gasped and watched in awe as Owl circled the room over their heads. For the Rainers it was a wonderful, memorable, and new experience. For Bubo, it was a stretch and an opportunity to survey the room for exits, for dangers, and for safe perches.

Thalmus walked toward the lord's chair, away from people, and hooted. Owl returned a hoot and on his next pass, dropped to a stone ledge rimming the room atop the tall walls, where he was unreachable. "Whoo-who-who," Bubo called to Thalmus: a thank you, and a warning.

The Rainers applauded gleefully.

Lord Luminous, however, was in a trance, staring at Owl. The large room became very quiet with anticipation as the Rainers looked at their lord, at Owl, at Thalmus, and then back to their lord. Once again, the ever-present rain could be heard. Boschina suddenly felt uneasy and very hungry and cold. She wanted to move over next to Thalmus, but was afraid to disturb the silence. Their eyes met, and he smiled as if he knew what she was thinking; and smiling in return, she felt better.

Thalmus stepped toward Boschina and spoke, breaking the silence. "We greatly appreciate your hospitality, my lord, and the kindness of your people."

Lord Luminous continued to gaze at Owl and said, as if to himself: "This is wonderful." Then he must have felt a chill, for he shivered and looked around at Thalmus and Boschina.

"Bring them blankets," he ordered and went to the chair and wrapped himself in his blanket. "We're very pleased that you have come," he said, smiling once again. "It's so seldom we get visitors that my people have become shy and, I guess, suspicious." He laughed, looked around the room at the crowd, and then back at Thalmus and Boschina. "Especially of someone like you two with your strange creatures." He chuckled to himself, as if he were enjoying a private joke, before he burst out laughing in joy.

His eyes bulged as he did so.

Thalmus thought his laugh was rather sinister—and his bulging eyes like those of a frog. "I don't know why you would be suspicious," Thalmus replied, taking a blanket that was being offered by a trooper and wrapping himself in it. "We do not pretend to be anything more than who we are: simple folk on a journey in search of Boschina's father, with full approval of the king. These creatures, as you call them, are my friends and, like most animals, are harmless, unless threatened."

"Well, we certainly do not wish to threaten them, do we?" Lord Luminous said, motioning to his people; they murmured their agreement. "And no one," he continued, "with the great King Ahmbin's approval can be called simple folk. Nor should they be treated as such. Even here, in this land that has been cut off from the rest of the kingdom, we have heard of you, Thalmus. You shall have lodgings on the upper lift to fit your position."

"My lord," Boschina said, wrapped in a blanket now but still shivering. "We wish merely to ask you about my father and—"

"Of course, child, but not now," he said with a wave of his hand. "You must be hungry and tired from your journey through the Wet. Come, sit at my table and eat."

He stood, spun around, and led them through an arched wood door to a room with a large stone table that was set with dishes. They were seated and served a green goulash from a large bowl, and a cup of cold tea. As hungry as Boschina was she gagged on the food and could not eat much. However, it was acceptable to Thalmus, who was curious as to its content.

"Tubers and leaves?" Thalmus asked.

"And a few other plants unique to our land," Lord Luminous answered. "I'm sorry it does not suit you, child. This is our daily food, grown on our farms. I've ordered some fish to be brought from the ponds for a feast and celebration tomorrow. Perhaps you will like that better?"

"A celebration? For us?" Boschina asked.

"Of course, child," Lord Luminous said. He grinned at them and leaned back in his chair. "Your unannounced visit is a glorious event."

Boschina was not overjoyed about a longer stay in this land, but felt she could not say anything against the celebration that would give these people something to look forward to in their drab lives.

"You have farms and fish ponds here?" Thalmus asked.

Lord Luminous looked at Thalmus as if an idea had just come to him. "Surprised?" He leaned forward in his chair. "Perhaps you'd like to visit them? Our farms are inside, of course. Not in this castle. The ponds were built long ago, in another time, before the Wet came."

"Yes," Thalmus said. "I would like to see how you farm in Rainland."

"Do not call this land by that name," Lord Luminous snapped. His eyes bulged even larger at Thalmus. "My realm, this land," he said, raising his voice and holding up his index finger, "is Sol Lindan! And always shall be."

"I apologize for my ignorance," Thalmus answered calmly. "I have never heard it referred to other than by that name. So, I assumed that was its proper title."

"It's not," Lord Luminous shouted. "Sol Lindan is." He leaned forward onto the table directly across from Thalmus. "How easy it is for others to condemn—to sneer. But they don't know." His eyes were getting redder and they seemed to throb as he spoke. "This land was not always as it is now. Oh no, it was once sunny and hot and dry with scarcely a drop of water falling from the sky. My grandfather, who truly was a wise man no matter what anyone says, served on the king's supreme council of lords and ruled Sol Lindan with love. He cared for his people—just as I do. And they…why… they loved him. They were devoted to him. Yes, they were. There were thousands more then and all were prosperous and happy. They did not blame him. No, not his people!"

Blame him for what? Thalmus wondered. *What was he defending his father and grandfather for?*

Lord Luminous stopped speaking and began staring at a banner hanging on the wall with images of birds flying around the sun that was bursting with a halo of light.

Boschina was surprised by Lord Luminous' outburst and stunned by his eyes—and now his silence. She glanced at Thalmus, who was studying the Lord of Sol Lindan. The silence stretched out. A trooper started to move, thought better of it, and stopped. The rain droned on.

Finally, Boschina could not hold back the question.

"What happened to cause the rain?"

Lord Luminous appeared not to hear her. His stare was glazed, his body frozen, his mind far away. Slowly, he returned to the present, but he continued staring at a distant past. "I'm very tired," he said. Turning, he motioned to one of the officers who had led them to him. "Corsair will attend you." He slowly rose from the table and walked from the room.

"Is he all right?" Boschina asked.

"Only he can answer," Corsair replied.

Corsair—though gaunt like all the other Rainers—looked healthier. He was not as stooped, and one could see in him the once proud stature of these people, for he had an air of confidence.

"But I want to know about my father," Boschina said.

"Only Lord Luminous can answer," Corsair said again.

"When will he come back?" Boschina asked. "When will he tell us?"

Corsair shook his head. Thalmus felt that the soldier knew more and wanted to speak, but would not. He was holding back, controlling his emotions, so that he would not reveal anything about his lord, this land, or himself.

"Ohh," Boschina said, frustrated—and sneezed.

"You must go to your room now," Corsair said, motioning toward the door.

Chapter Eight
The Farms

Thalmus and Boschina followed Corsair back into the domed room where the people were still standing and waiting and watching Bubo, who was glaring back with attentive eyes.

Thalmus called to Bubo with a hoot and rolled his head to one side. The owl was happy to see him and ready to leave. He returned Thalmus' call and dropped from his perch, glided silently down, and, at the last moment, flapped his wings—pulled up and landed on Thalmus' shoulder.

The Rainers were delighted, once again, as they held their breath and exhaled together with smiles and awe when Bubo settled on Thalmus. Crowding together, the people followed the visitors down the fifteen steps to the first elevation, where Corsair opened the door to one of the five rooms.

"You will stay in this room," Corsair said and led them inside.

Although Spartan, this room appeared lavish compared to their previous accommodations. There were a few worn rugs, some bare shelving, wardrobes, and four beds with blankets. There were two window openings in the wall that were covered with a hard, smooth, opaque material that blocked the rain, but allowed the dim light to illuminate the room.

"Rest now," Corsair said, smiling at them. "I'll come again, later." Corsair's smile was a soldier's smile: it was one of practice, a mask that gave no warmth.

"Is it possible to have some tubers taken to the shell creature?" Thalmus asked. "I'm sure he's hungry."

Corsair's expression did not change. He studied Thalmus for a moment. "Of course," he said carefully, his smile unchanging. "I'll see to it now." Then, he closed the door and dispersed the crowd.

"Oh, this is much better," Boschina said, getting into a bed with the blanket still wrapped around her. "Maybe I can get warm."

Thalmus and Owl surveyed the room.

"Well, Bubo, what do you think?"

Owl swiveled his head to glare at Thalmus. He chortled and rocked once, then flew to perch on one of the shelves.

"I know, Bubo, you do not like being trapped inside. I don't either. But, until we have a chance to look for Veracitas here, we don't have much of a choice."

Thalmus went to the wall and examined the strange material in the window openings. "This is unique," he said as he touched it carefully with his fingers.

"I wish we could get some answers," Boschina said. "I understand how Bubo feels. I don't like this place, either."

"It is a bit strange here."

"A bit strange?" Boschina exclaimed, shivering. "Lord Luminous is more than a bit strange. The people seem all right, but he scares me."

Thalmus turned from the window. "This is not a good place to live, Boschina. He is struggling to hold his people together. That is difficult to do even in a fair land. You can see the strain on him."

"All the more reason not to trust him," she replied and curled deeper into the blankets. "And what's all that about his father and grandfather?"

"For some reason, he felt a need to defend them."

"More questions," Boschina said and sneezed.

She was right: Lord Luminous was not to be trusted. He knew it from the moment they first met, and Bubo that wanted to attack him. He was glad to see that Boschina realized it, too.

"Will you feel all right if I leave Bubo here with you and go see Thunder?"

"Of course," she said, looking up at Owl. "I'll take care of him."

Owl glared at her. He opened his wings and shook, tucked them in again, and swiveled his head away from her.

Boschina grinned. "That got him."

"You know how to ruffle Bubo," Thalmus said, smiling. "You look so tired, Boschina. Try to sleep."

"I will. Give Thunder a pat for me."

Thalmus closed the door quietly behind him and headed down the long corridor of the now-descending elevations. The few people he met smiled and nodded politely at him. It seemed to take a long time, but he finally reached the lower level where they had spent the night. It was definitely damper and colder here. The moss was thicker on the walls, the light fainter, and the splattering of rain louder. Thalmus shivered and went down the last steps to the gate area. A group of Rainers with their children were observing Thunder, who had been poking his head out to observe them.

Thunder was so happy to see Thalmus that he stretched his great neck out, extended his feet, and lifted himself off the ground. He stepped forward and nuzzled his snout into Thalmus' chest, almost knocking him over. Thalmus laughed and hugged the big head. The onlookers laughed, too, but kept their distance. Two troopers arrived carrying a tub of food between them. Upon seeing the shell creature, the men stopped, afraid to go closer. Finally, they followed Thalmus' directions and dumped the container near Thunder, where he could watch everyone while he ate.

While Thunder chomped away, Thalmus coaxed the children into coming and touching Thunder's shell and legs. They smiled with amazement, but refused to be put up onto his shell. Then, one very small boy decided to brave it. Thalmus lifted him onto Thunder's back while the parents held their breath. Thunder rocked from side to side and took a few steps around his food pile. The little boy grinned with nervous excitement. The adults smiled and burst into applause.

After that, all the children wanted a ride.

The initial fear had left them and now it was just a matter of taking turns to ride the creature. As always, Thunder was patient and repeated the same routine for each one. When the last child finished her ride, Thalmus put all six children on the huge shell and Thunder took a longer walk around the area, and the parents reached out and touched their outstretched hands as they went by. The children did not want to stop, but Thalmus told them it was time for Thunder to eat. So, some slid off and others jumped off his back. They all turned and patted him before joining their parents.

Thunder went back to his eating and the Rainers slowly dispersed, laughing and chatting with their excited children. Thalmus felt good. The children had made him happy. Their laughter had brightened this dull spot and chased from his mind that incessant sound of rain, but the respite was brief. The monotonous patter returned to his ears, bringing with it a quiet, but desperate call from the shadows.

Thalmus looked around, but could see no one. The troops had returned to their duties and the people were fading into the gloomy corridor.

He heard the whisper again.

It was louder this time, calling his name, and beckoning him to the shadows. Thunder had lifted his head and was staring across the yard at a stone buttress near a corner of the interior walls of the castle. There, at that wide, projecting buttress was an arm sticking out of the wall and the hand on the arm was motioning to Thalmus to come. He left Thunder's side and moved carefully toward the frantic hand.

Hiding behind the buttress was a man who was obviously not a Rainer. He had a flat, round face with narrow brown eyes, black hair, and dark skin. Muscular and broad shouldered, dressed all in dark leathers, he blended into the shadows.

"You must leave right away," he said desperately. "It's not safe here for you."

Thalmus kept more than an arm's distance from the intense man and watched his eyes. "What do you know?"

"The one you seek is not here. Never was," he replied quickly, sneaking looks around the buttress. "You must get away."

"Get away? What do you mean?"

"A messenger came through the Wet before you. Luminous knew of your coming. He's a deceiver, do not trust him." Then, another desperate thought pressed him. "And the bird...the bird...take care of it."

"Who are you?" Thalmus asked, watching the man carefully.

"Once a traveler, like you...now trapped here."

"Trapped?"

"I'm not permitted to see strangers. I was...." the man stopped and listened. "Troops coming. I must go," he said urgently. "Take the girl and leave before it's too late." He squatted down. "Don't trust anyone, especially Corsair." Then, he turned and vanished through a low, narrow opening in the wall.

Thalmus knelt and peered into the hole. It was rank smelling and so dark that he could not see a thing, but he heard the last faint echo of running footsteps before they were obscured by the rain. He returned to Thunder just as five soldiers, all armed with swords, marched from a corridor. Corsair was leading the group and when he saw Thalmus, his mouth curled into that odd smile.

"So, Thalmus, you and your creature have made our people happy."

"Yes," Thalmus replied, noticing their weapons and serious attitude. "And they made me happy as well."

The troops stopped short of Thunder and stared at him. The tortoise had lifted his head from eating and turned to face the soldiers. He was still chewing, but his jaws were ready to snap and his slit eyes watched them closely.

"Lord Luminous will be glad to hear it," Corsair said, watching Thunder. "Is it harmless, as children said?"

"Yes, to the harmless," Thalmus replied.

"You should not go about the castle alone," Corsair said, his gaze now searching the area.

"Why? Is it dangerous here?"

Corsair's eyes returned to look at Thalmus. He grinned—that false smile again. "Lord Luminous wishes it so," he answered, ignoring Thalmus' question.

Thalmus nodded. "How courteous of him. I hope your lord is feeling better."

"He wishes you to see the farms now," Corsair said abruptly. "We'll take you."

Thalmus motioned toward the troops.

"It takes an escort of four?"

"To carry the cover," Corsair replied. "Come."

"Shouldn't I have my sword?" Thalmus asked.

"No need," Corsair said, noticing the handle of Thalmus' sword sticking out from under Thunder. "You won't need your sword. We are armed."

"Yes, I can see that," Thalmus said.

Corsair and the troops started across the courtyard toward a large archway in the interior wall that was the entrance to a wide corridor. When they noticed that Thalmus wasn't following, they stopped and, looking back, waited for him.

Thalmus spoke softly to Thunder, telling him to be friendly, but wary. Then, he joined Corsair and the four soldiers, who fell in behind them as they entered the tunnel.

This dingy corridor traversed the ground level of the castle where the stores and supplies were kept. It was wide enough for two teams of horses pulling wagons to pass one another. Along the sides of the passageway were hundreds of cubicles, some of which had once housed horses, but now were packed with various crates and parcels. Several of the openings were boarded up or recently filled in with stone; there were some that were guarded by troops. Vision was difficult, though possible, because of small shafts of dim light that filtered through holes in the rock ceiling every fourteen meters. Hearing was confused by vibrations that reverberated off the stone walls and echoed down the corridor, which exaggerated the origin and size of the object creating the sound.

Thalmus stayed abreast of Corsair, the two of them several paces ahead of the escorting troops—and all of them walking rapidly in step. He had felt uneasy before the warning from the stranger in the shadow; but now, Thalmus definitely was suspicious of this Corsair and his soldiers. Why did he need an armed escort to go about the castle? And why suddenly was he to see the farms? Were Boschina and Bubo safe? He tried to ignore the confusing signals his senses were receiving from the cacophony of echoes and the murky light in the tunnel as they marched on. He watched Corsair without looking directly at him, anticipating any sudden movement. Outwardly, Thalmus appeared relaxed and naïve. However, his senses were on full alert and he was prepared to move quickly if these troops tried to move against him.

After what seemed an interminable time, the passage turned to the right and lightened as an open arch to the outside appeared and the corridor finally came to an end. They had reached the other side of the castle. This area had once been open space between the perimeter wall and the main tower. It was now covered by a crude shed roof structure that diverted the rain and water run-off from the upper roof of the castle to the outside of the fortified wall. The roof was six meters above the ground. The area under its protection was long and open—except for a row of spindly, stone columns. A lone mason was working at replacing stones on one of the columns that was braced up rather precariously with wood poles.

"Aren't you finished yet?" Corsair demanded of the mason.

The man looked nervously at the officer.

"I'll be sure to finish this Gray."

"See that you do," Corsair snapped. He turned to see Thalmus watching him and his demeanor changed to that fixed smile. "One of the loads got loose and hit this support," he said casually. "Our mason will have it repaired shortly."

This was the entrance and staging area where supplies from the outside world and food from the farms were brought into the castle. Half-sized wagons, that had flat skids instead of wheels, and were completely covered with rounded, metallic tops, were being pulled in through a gate by pairs of Boogalas harnessed one in front of the other. Thalmus examined the strange looking horses that had a horse's head with a duck's bill and web feet. He had heard of this unique blend of animals but had not seen one before now. Many Rainers were working here, emptying the covered sleds and packing the food off to various parts of the castle while the rain pounded on the thin roof and blurred the air with a pale mistiness.

Corsair stopped them at a guarded supply room where, upon his orders, a warehouseman issued them gear for traveling in the Wet. Thalmus was given long boots that were covered with a smooth transparent animal skin—and a coat of the same material. The strange clothes fit him tightly, conforming to his body. A large brimmed hat was added to this apparel to complete the dress preparations for entering the Wet. Corsair and the troops dressed in like fashion, then all moved to the large gate in the perimeter wall where the four troops picked up the cover. This domed cover was like the arched metallic tops on the sleds, but had four poles with handles—one at each corner—inset from the edges so that the bearers were under its protection, as well as the honored ones who walked in the center.

Passes had to be shown to the men guarding the gate in order to exit. Thalmus was eyed curiously by the guards as Corsair presented a pass—a small, flat, chip of wood with a carving of the sun. It was obvious to Thalmus—from the reaction of all the troops and the people—that Corsair held authority and was a person of power in this castle. Everyone snapped to attention when he spoke and carried out his orders with a hurried and nervous purpose.

The guard quickly handed the pass back to Corsair and ordered the gate to be opened. Gatekeepers who had been working on one of the door's rusty hinges scurried down and pushed the tall, heavy, wooden doors open. With the four troopers under their cover, Corsair and Thalmus stepped out into the Wet, and the creaky doors of the gate were quickly closed behind them. Almost immediately, they came to what appeared to be a junction of three roads, all of which were made of cobble stone and partially covered by water. Without hesitation, the troops took the middle road as they headed into the murky gloom.

The rain pounding on the cover over their heads was not as loud as Thalmus had expected. The quality of the metallic half shell dulled the sound of the rain drops and was actually less noisy than the splattering all around them.

"Are the gates always kept closed?" Thalmus asked over the din as they splashed through the water that covered the road.

Corsair was slow to answer and kept looking straight ahead. "It's for protection." He waved his arm at the landscape. "People are safe in the castle, not out here."

"Can people leave if they so wish?"

"If Lord Luminous wishes it so."

"It must be an honor then to be able to come and go as the load drivers do."

Again, Corsair thought before answering. "They've sworn allegiance to our lord." Then, he added. "They're all family men."

"What difference should that make?" Thalmus asked innocently, already knowing the answer.

Corsair smiled. "Guarantees their loyalty. They will always return."

"And the ones working the farms?"

Corsair snorted and shook his head. "Yes, family men. They're dedicated believers in the future."

"And what is the future for Sol Linden?" Thalmus asked, being careful to use the old name.

Corsair turned and stared down at Thalmus, who was calmly gazing back at him. *Why does this small man have such a big reputation?* he wondered. *I see no great magic in him. Yet they warned us about him. Why do they fear him? I don't. He is in our control and shall remain so,* Corsair thought.

"The future," Corsair finally replied, "is a return to how our land once was."

"And when might that be?"

Corsair smiled at him. "Soon."

After thirty minutes at a steady pace, a large building slowly appeared through the gray. As they approached a pair of double doors, one of the troopers swung a small horn to his lips and blew a five-note scale, from low to high. They stopped in front of the doors and waited.

"Signal again," Corsair demanded.

The trooper repeated the five notes and in a few moments, the doors were pulled open from within. They moved quickly inside and the doors were closed immediately behind them.

Once inside, Thalmus saw a cavernous warehouse with high ceilings. The floors were furrows of earth in which small leafy plants grew in rows. Sections of the roof had been replaced with the same opaque shields that were over the windows in the castle. These squares allowed the gray light to filter in. They also leaked; the Rainers had built troughs under these leaks that caught the steady drips and dispersed it throughout the rows of plants. The excess water was funneled to the outside through pipes in the walls. A constant rattling noise from the rain pounding on the roof windows and the water dripping into the troughs beat like a snare drum throughout the building. The farmers, moving about at work, were dressed warmly as it was quite cool and damp.

The manager of the farms, an ashen-faced old man with large eyes named Oddkin, was very proud to show Thalmus his domain. Visitors were even rarer at the farms than at the castle. Oddkin kept touching Thalmus as if to verify that he was real. Oddkin tried to explain the entire operation to Thalmus: how he and another ancient Rainer, now gone, had developed the indoor growing process and the material for the windows that made it all possible.

Thalmus was very interested and asked many questions, which excited Oddkin into long and detailed explanations. He led Thalmus and the troops through connecting tunnels to other buildings where tubers and mushrooms were grown. In several buildings, large rocks of various shapes had been brought in and piled in rows to have a moss-like plant grown on them. It was something Oddkin had developed himself. He named it Rocbed and insisted it was quite good, after one acquired a taste for it, of course.

Large double doors had been built into the exterior walls of all the buildings to allow the teams of Boogalas pulling the wagons to enter. To Thalmus' surprise, the web-footed Boogalas were not permitted to spend a night at the farms. If a wagon was not loaded in time to make it back to the castle before the Black, then the team would be unhitched and returned without its load.

This rule, Corsair explained, prevented anyone at the farms from taking a Boogala for a ride to the Dry. Oddkin did not agree with this practice. He scolded Corsair for not trusting his loyal and dedicated farmers.

Oddkin's farmers worked in shifts. They lived at the farms for fifteen days and then returned home to their families, to the castle, for five days. All of them were family men. It was a requirement to be a farmer, but they were fed well and respected. Their homes were among the upper elevations of the castle.

Thalmus noticed that there was a lighter, jovial, mood amongst the farmers that did not exist in the Rainers he had seen at the castle. These men did not seem intimidated by the troops. He even heard a few of them singing to themselves as they went about their work.

When Thalmus pointed out these observations, Oddkin smiled with satisfaction. "Here, we have only the work and each other. So, often at the start of a new Gray we sing together."

"What do you sing?"

"Old songs," Oddkin replied, "Songs from before the rain, before the Gray. Then, I remind them that it is they who keep our people alive. It is they who carry the task of feeding our world until the sun returns. And this task, I tell them, is not a burden, but a pleasure. So, we go about our work with pride and a warm heart."

"When do you think the sun will return?" Thalmus asked.

"Soon, I hope," Oddkin replied. Turning to watch several farmers digging up tubers, he said in a lower, restrained voice. "I do not know. Lord Luminous says it is not for me to work on. Others have that task."

"Then there is something being done?"

"Oh yes," Oddkin answered, still watching his farmers. "Something is being done. Though it is not what I would do." He looked at Corsair with his large eyes. "But it is not my task. Mine is the farms and the food."

There was such disappointment and frustration in Oddkin's voice that Thalmus did not want to press the old man further. He could see that Oddkin was being controlled and held in obedience by the strength of his love for his people and his land.

"As you see," Corsair was saying to Thalmus, "Oddkin is most valuable here at the farms, where he's learned how to feed us.

Without him we'd all starve." He looked at them with a false smile on his face for a moment. "We'll return now."

"Before we go," Thalmus said. "I must ask you, Oddkin, if you have seen or heard of a man here by the name of Veracitas?"

"Veracitas?" Oddkin repeated the name and thought for a moment. "So few visitors come here that I remember everyone, and this name I do not know. Is that why you came, in search of this man?"

"Yes."

"Are you his friend or enemy?"

"Friend," Thalmus replied and told Oddkin Veracitas' story—and about Boschina and their journey.

"You must be a true friend," Oddkin said, touching Thalmus on the shoulder. "I wish you well."

"We must return now," Corsair said impatiently, motioning toward the cover where the troopers stood waiting.

As they walked behind Corsair, Oddkin leaned closely to Thalmus and said softly: "Be careful in this land. There are forces here at conflict."

Before Thalmus could say anything without Corsair hearing him, they reached the soldiers at the doors. Thalmus turned to the old manager. "Thank you, Oddkin. I wish the best for you and your farmers."

Oddkin started to speak, but Corsair interrupted, motioning Thalmus to the cover. "We must go now."

The cover was lifted by the four troopers; Corsair and Thalmus stepped beneath it. Two soiled farmers pulled open the doors and the entourage moved out into the Wet. Thalmus turned and held a hand up in a wave to Oddkin as the doors were closed between them.

Splashing through the water on the road back to the castle, Thalmus thought he saw the Shower Knight moving along beside them, though he couldn't be certain. There would be that extra rain—almost almost an image appearing—then nothing but rain. He was convinced something was there; he felt it or so his senses told him. His eyes were tired from straining in this dull light and his thoughts were becoming muddled from the gloom, wetness and sound of the constant rain. He decided to search the castle as best he could for Veracitas and leave this land as soon as possible.

They returned through the large gates of the outer wall, leaving the cover there with the gate guards. At the supply room, Thalmus removed the boots and protective clothing, and they were hung up along with many others. The Dry Suits, as they were called, were turned in each day by those who had worked or traveled in the Wet.

The troopers then escorted Thalmus back to his room. Boschina and Bubo were very glad to see him. He told them about the farms and Oddkin, but not of the mysterious man or of the warnings. Bubo watched and listened to Thalmus. When he was done speaking, the owl clicked his beak and swiveled his head left then right to let his friend know that he knew Thalmus had not told everything.

Thalmus just replied with a smile.

Corsair returned with word that Lord Luminous would not be able to dine with them. Besides, it was late. The Dark would be soon. Food was brought to their room and they ate slowly as the Gray faded to darkness.

Boschina, who had slept half the day, was still ill and tired but could not sleep. Thalmus was exhausted and his eyes were sore and ready to rest. Bubo wanted to fly, to leave this place. He was not happy and told Thalmus so, hooting and rocking on his shelf long after Thalmus had fallen asleep.

Chapter Nine
The Banquet and Aftermath

When the Gray returned, Thalmus roused himself from sleep to find Owl staring at him. Thalmus took a deep breath, stretched, and looked away from those bright, piercing, eyes.

"I know, Bubo, it is time for us to leave this place."

Bubo agreed with a short guttural noise, then swiveled his head to look at Boschina who was awake but still lying under the blankets.

"I don't feel good," she said with a foggy voice then sneezed.

Thalmus smiled at her.

"Neither do I, and we know Bubo is not happy."

Boschina uncovered her head and looked up at Owl. "That's not hard to figure, is it, big boy? You've been complaining since we got here."

Bubo clicked his beak at her then looked away.

Thalmus ran his fingers through his hair and rubbed his face and eyes. "Boschina."

She was clicking her teeth at Bubo.

"I feel that your father is not here."

She looked at Thalmus. "But I don't understand. The image that Metro made me see was so clear. Father was there, in the rain, standing in the water."

"He may be in water," Thalmus said. "But I don't think he is here, not in this land."

Boschina thought about this. "Our presence here is well-known."

"If he were here, wouldn't he have come to us?"

"Yes," Thalmus said, thinking of the mysterious man in the tunnel. "Unless he was being kept from us."

"Why would they do that?" Boschina asked. "I don't think they'd do that."

Thalmus stood up, putting his thoughts of the strange man away for now. "We will ask Lord Luminous again about Veracitas, thank him for his care, and request an escort to lead us out of this land."

"He never did answer us," Boschina said. "I think he's sick. I don't think he knows anything."

"Corsair is the one who would know," Thalmus said. "He is in charge of the troops. Very little goes on here that he does not know about."

"Then let's ask him."

"He is not willing to speak," Thalmus replied. "Besides, I do not trust him. He is devious and, I believe, dangerous."

Boschina looked up at Bubo. "This is a strange place, huh Bubo?" She suddenly threw back the blankets and sat up. "I'm ready, Thalmus. I won't get better lying here nor is this any way to find my father."

"Good, Boschina. You must stay strong."

"I know, in body and mind, right?" she said recalling his words from Culinary's kitchen.

Thalmus touched her forehead gently with his fingertips.

"Your spirit is rising."

"Yes, I feel it," she said. "I'm ready to leave this place."

They gathered their few belongings together and, with Owl perched on Thalmus' shoulder again, opened the door. When they entered the hallway, the Rainers were waiting for them. People were pressed together, lining the passage up the steps to the great room. The children who had ridden on Thunder were amongst the crowd. Several of them, the brave ones, took Thalmus' hand and proudly walked with him up the fifteen steps and into the domed room where, once again, it was full of Rainers. A hubbub of noise and activity filled the great space as food was being brought in and heaped in large bowls on long tables. Barrels of juice were being rolled around, set up, and spigots being driven into the ends. All this preparation stopped and people applauded when they became aware of Thalmus and Boschina's presence. Bubo was decidedly nervous. He did not like the look of this at all and he let Thalmus know by tightening his talons on his friend's shoulder.

Corsair, who had been directing the preparations, turned to Thalmus and Boschina—but his eyes focused on Owl. "Our honored guests," he said with that odd smile. "Everything's ready. Lord Luminous is on his way."

"We are...surprised by all of this," Thalmus said.

"Why? Lord Luminous said there'd be a banquet."

"Yes, he did," Thalmus answered. "I did not expect the banquet, because he was too sick to dine with us yesterday. We were just preparing to leave."

The smile dropped from Corsair's face. He stared hard at Thalmus. "No, you cannot." he said firmly. Then Lord Luminous, wearing his sparkle suit and a wide smile, swept into the room and the people cheered him. He was surprised by their cheers, and he giggled with joy as he came to Thalmus and Boschina.

"You see." He waved his hands gesturing toward the crowded room. "You've made my people happy."

"Yes, and that makes us happy," Thalmus replied.

"We...we are all happy," Lord Luminous said, with some wonder. He looked around at the people, who were watching him because they weren't sure of his mood. "This is... a happy occasion," he said, softly and stared in a trance at nothing in particular.

"Yes, your highness, it is," Corsair said, touching Luminous' arm, as if to wake him.

Lord Luminous' eyes focused. He looked at the children by Thalmus, then up at Owl on his shoulder. "Truly magnificent." he exclaimed. He crossed his hands flat on his chest. "I know. I can't touch. You told me I can't touch, but he must fly. He must fly for us," he said, motioning with outstretched arms to his subjects.

"Yes, yes. Make him fly." The crowd shouted in response.

Thalmus could see this was leading to trouble. "Thank you, Lord Luminous, for your concern for Bubo. You know that he would be more comfortable on a high perch."

Thalmus tilted his head to the side. Bubo lifted off from his shoulder and flew up, around the room, and settled on the high shelf. The people watched and then were quiet and waiting. Lord Luminous continued to stare at Bubo. Thalmus waited. He glanced at Boschina, whose head was almost lying over on her right shoulder as she watched Lord Luminous.

"Lord Luminous, Boschina and I are most hungry," Thalmus said, trying to divert attention from Bubo. "May we begin the banquet?"

Lord Luminous looked at Thalmus with a blank stare, The smile slowly came back into his eyes. "Of course, it has all been prepared. Has it not, Corsair?"

"Yes, my lord," Corsair replied and smiled at Thalmus.

Boschina and Thalmus were directed to sit on Lord Luminous' right at a wide table covered with a blue cloth streaked with faded golden sun rays. Corsair settled in a chair on his lord's left side. Shiny eating utensils with pewter plates and cups were already set before them. Thalmus noticed that the other tables were bare wood with no cloths and the forks, knives, and plates were not polished. Large bowls, each supported by two men, were carried in and servers spooned ample portions of a fish and potato casserole onto their plates. Women poured juice, tapped from the wooden kegs, into their cups from battered pitchers. Boschina tested the food with a small bite and was surprised to find it to be tastier than the tubers and vegetables they had been eating. Thalmus enjoyed it as well as he watched the Rainers who had filled all the tables and were happily consuming this special meal.

Boschina was watching Lord Luminous and waiting patiently for a time to speak while they ate. Finally, she could not hold back her question any longer. "Lord Luminous, has my father been here?"

He stopped eating and looked at her with bulged eyes.

"Your father? Here? Who's your father?"

"His name is Vericitas. He is a sculptor."

"A sculptor? A stone carver? Why do you think he'd come here?" He turned to Corsair. "Have you seen or heard of this man?"

"No, my lord," Corsair replied.

Thalmus did not trust Corsair, but he believed he was telling the truth about Vericitas.

"It was Metro, the king's magician," Boschina explained. "He thought my father might be here."

Lord Luminous and Corsair glanced at one another, but said nothing. Thalmus noticed their visual exchange. He sensed they had a mutual recognition of the magician.

He took a swallow of juice. "You know of Metro?"

"Metro, you say?" Luminous replied casually. "The name sounds oddly familiar. Corsair, have you heard of this Metro?"

"No," Corsair said flatly, not looking up from his plate.

This time, Thalmus did not believe him.

"So, my father is not here?" Boschina persisted.

"If we've not heard of him, he's not here," Luminous replied, not looking at her.

As the meal progressed, Lord Luminous kept looking up at Owl and occasionally speaking so softly to Corsair that Thalmus could not hear them.

Thalmus did not like what he sensed coming from the men. He decided it was time to say goodbye and move on. "Lord Luminous, we wish to thank you for taking us in and feeding us and treating us so well. You and your people have been very kind. We have learned much about this land. We will spread good words about you and your realm. I will also tell the king how misunderstood this place is."

"This sounds like a farewell," Lord Luminous said, still staring at Owl.

"It is time for us to continue our journey," Thalmus said. "The king requested that we not delay."

"Oh, the king requested that, did he?" Lord Luminous spat some partially chewed fish onto the floor then returned his gaze to Owl as he muttered, "the king requested it."

"Yes," Thalmus continued, watching Luminous. "Would you provide an escort to lead us out through the Wet?"

Lord Luminous did not reply for a long time. His attention stayed fixed on Owl. Boschina felt the tension rising as well. She took another swallow of juice, pushed her plate away, and looked at Thalmus apprehensively.

Lord Luminous spoke in a whisper. "He can't leave. He must stay here until the Dry returns."

Thalmus glanced up at Owl, who was glaring at them, and then spoke slowly to Luminous. "That is not possible."

"He will be our first bird," Lord Luminous said, as if in a trance. "His magic will help bring the Dry. His powers will populate our land again with flying, feathered, creatures."

"Lord Luminous," Thalmus said calmly. "When the Dry returns to your land, we will return—and Bubo will bring other birds to live here."

"No. We need his magic now," Luminous said, his voice rising. "We need his power."

"Bubo's power is not for you," Thalmus said.

"It has to be," Luminous demanded.

106

"What makes you think he has the magic to change your world?"

"I can see it. I can feel it!"

"He is truly beautiful and a wonderment," Thalmus answered. "And he *is* magical. How he chooses to use that power though is his choice, not yours."

"He must, maybe not all by himself, but combined with other powers he can change this rain."

Thalmus watched Lord Luminous intently. "What other powers?"

"The power that we are gathering, the power that will come, starting with your owl," Lord Luminous said and turned to glare with his bulging eyes at Thalmus.

"He is not mine," Thalmus replied, calmly meeting Lord Luminous' stare. "And he is not yours."

"Bubo belongs to no one," Boschina said. "He is free."

"Not now," Lord Luminous hissed.

"What are your intentions?" Thalmus asked.

An ugly sneer spread across Lord Luminous' face. "I'm glad that you are so interested in our world, Thalmus, because you're going to be staying with us for a long time."

Thalmus sighed. He was disappointed. This was the confrontation he had hoped to avoid. And now, he knew that the warnings were true and he had but one choice.

"No, you are wrong," he said calmly. "We choose not to stay. We wish to leave now."

Corsair chuckled. "That's not possible."

"You can't keep us here," Boschina blurted.

"Oh, yes, I can," Lord Luminous replied.

"You intend to hold us prisoner?" Thalmus asked.

"Call it what you wish, but you're not leaving," Lord Luminous said and began laughing.

Corsair stood, and with one hand on the hilt of his sword, joined his lord in a hearty laugh as he stepped behind Thalmus.

"You can't keep us here," Boschina repeated. "King Ahmbin will be angry."

"King Ahmbin," Lord Luminous yelled. "You dare to threaten me with that arrogant imbecile!"

Boschina was shocked, but Thalmus was observing Lord Luminous and judging Corsair's readiness.

"Your king has no power here and never will. He'll be lucky to keep what he has, including his little girl," Luminous shouted. "Take them to their new quarters," he said to Corsair. "A room more suited to their level."

Corsair shoved Thalmus to get him up from the table. Children, who were bringing Thalmus another cup of juice, jumped in front of Corsair and shouted at him to leave Thalmus alone. Corsair slapped and pushed them aside. That was enough for Thalmus. He would endure much, but he would not allow abuse of the innocent. He sprang out of his chair and struck Corsair with a sudden, solid fist to the chest, knocking him back into Lord Luminous. They fell against the table, slid off, and landed on the floor. Thalmus motioned to Boschina to head for the door, and then whistled at Bubo. The blow had stunned Corsair and knocked the wind out of him. Lord Luminous though was scrambling to his knees to call the guards. Bubo dropped from his perch and glided with a horrifying screech and talons outstretched at Lord Luminous' head. Luminous screamed and ducked under the table just below Owl's sharp black talons. Bubo swooped up, circled, and came at Luminous again as he poked his head out.

The Rainers sitting nearby had moved away when the confrontation started because they knew their lord's temper and Corsair's meanness and did not want any part of it. Everyone in the room was stunned that Thalmus had knocked Corsair down. No one had ever stood up to Corsair, much less dared to strike him. Owl's violent screech and assault on Lord Luminous had frozen them.

Thalmus and Boschina moved quickly around the tables, through the crowded but motionless room, and out the great doors into the hall. Bubo kept swooping at Luminous and now at Corsair, too, who was regaining his voice and trying to yell for the doors to be closed.

Four troopers, two on each door, started to swing them shut. Thalmus saw this, whistled for Owl, and then shouted and kicked one of the doors back at the two startled men trying to close it. Owl made one last dive along the table where Lord Luminous and Corsair hid before he flew across the room and out the one open door.

As soon as Bubo winged through the opening, Thalmus pulled on the handles, helping the men on the other side close the door between them. He turned and joined Boschina as they ran down the steps, down the various levels, down through the castle with Bubo, feeling victorious, flying in front of them. On they went, running and jumping down the curving passage, dropping level by level, passing the rooms that were all deserted, for everyone had been at the banquet. Behind them—rushing down the hall after them— came the sounds of yelling and slapping feet, as the troops gave chase.

Thalmus' hope now was to get to Thunder and their weapons, and then down that wide corridor to the Boogalas—who might be able to lead them through the Wet. Despite her illness, Boschina was moving quickly. The action and escape from the great room had energized her and she was running now as fast as she could. Still, the sound of the troops chasing them was getting louder.

When Thalmus and Boschina finally reached the bottom, Bubo was screeching and flying about while Thunder, hissing and snapping, had the two gate guards backed into a corner. Their swords were drawn, but fear was in their faces and they did not know what to do.

Thalmus quickly picked his sword off the cobblestones from where it had lain under Thunder. "Drop your swords," he yelled at the guards. "Or I will command him to eat you."

The guards did not hesitate. They threw down their swords. Thalmus snatched up the weapons and ordered the guards to open the gate. Shaking with fear, the two men hurried to obey. Still keeping a watchful eye on Thunder, they slid the heavy bars out of their latches and swung open the gate.

"Now go. Get away," Thalmus shouted. "Or the bird will claw your eyes out and the giant beast will eat you!"

The guards ran out into the rain and disappeared in the Gray. Thalmus left the gate open and grabbed their frog coats from the hooks on the wall. Boschina retrieved her sword and hurried to strap it on her belt as she followed Thalmus across the courtyard into the wide tunnel under the castle.

Thalmus glanced at her as she adjusted her belt. He knew she was not ready for combat. Her sword-handling ability was weak, and she had never faced the intensity, strength, or speed of an opponent in a fight. However, the Rainers did not know that. Perhaps just seeing her with a weapon would put them off enough to give her an advantage. Thalmus was reassured with the knowledge that she would have the presence of Thunder by her side, Bubo overhead, and the spirit of the sword in her hand.

Owl flew on ahead into the tunnel. Thunder followed as rapidly as he could, which was surprisingly fast for a big tortoise. Thunder could move quite quickly for short distances when he knew it was necessary. Still, they had not gotten very far when their pursuers, led by Corsair, finally entered the courtyard with their swords drawn, ready for action. Out of breath and expecting a fight, they were surprised to find the space empty and were confused, not knowing which way to go.

The gate was open and the guards gone.

Most of the troops thought Thalmus, the girl, and the shell creature had escaped into the Wet, but did not want to follow without the Dry Suits which were kept on the other side of the castle. To go get the suits and then give chase would take too long. There was much talk and discussion. Their mingled voices bounced down the corridor to Thalmus and he told Boschina and Thunder to stop. They stood motionless and quiet, waiting to hear what the troops decided.

Back in the courtyard Corsair got control and quieted his men. He walked to the opening of the wide corridor and listened, hoping to hear some sounds reverberating off the walls, but all he heard was the rain pelting on the roof. He rubbed his chest where Thalmus' fist had struck. The little man had surprised him, not only with his speed, but with the force of the blow. He was caught off guard and embarrassed; he vowed it would not happen again. *So, now what would Thalmus do*, he wondered. *Which way would he go?*

Corsair held the central ground. He could go either direction, but he wasn't sure which was right and there wasn't time to make a mistake. "Where did you go, Frog Hunter?" he mumbled to himself. Guessing on the tunnel, he sent two troopers running down the corridor, searching, while he and the rest listened. He expected to hear yelling—perhaps the clash of swords—but there was nothing. The echo from the padding of the men's feet faded down the tunnel. Would they run all the way to the other side and not find them? Corsair hurried across the courtyard to the open gate and looked out at the Wet: nothing but drooping, faded, trees and water everywhere. He turned and noticed the frog coats were gone from the hooks on the wall.

He had forgotten about those skins.

Now, they became the deciding factor.

Thalmus must have gone into the Wet. Corsair sent ten reluctant troopers into the Wet to search—and left two to guard the gate while he and the other eight would go get the dry suits and more troops with Boogalas.

Corsair and his men started jogging down the tunnel.

The light coming in from the shafts was dim, but he knew the corridor. He knew all the possible hiding places and one was just ahead: an old stable, deserted and dark. Just to make sure Thalmus didn't come this way he ordered four of his men to check the stable. As the troopers moved toward the dark and quiet recess, Owl suddenly flew at them, slashing at their heads with his talons; the giant shell creature snapped from the darkness. Several of the men dropped their swords with fright and ran. Thalmus sprang from the black hole to engage the other two, who were so startled that he easily knocked their swords away as they stumbled back, scrambled to their feet, and hid behind the other soldiers. Thalmus and Thunder withdrew into the darkness; but now, the surprise was over. Corsair cursed himself for sending so many of his men into the Wet; he needed them here. He was pleased at finding Thalmus and the owl; they had not escaped after all.

Thalmus knew that he could not wait.

They would have to fight their way down the corridor before more troops arrived. He hooted for Owl, and Bubo answered from the dark. The calls bounced off the stone walls and the troops, afraid of an attack from the air, began looking around because they weren't sure from where it was coming or which hoots were the real bird. Corsair started yelling orders not to harm the bird and to regroup to fight. Then, Thunder began hissing and pounding his feet; Boschina started a high-pitched scream; Thalmus began yelling and Owl screeching. The corridor had become a cacophony of terrifying and ominous waves of sound. Corsair tried to yell over the din to order his men to stand their ground. Despite his effort they began to back up—away from that frightening blackness. That created a gap, an opening by which the entrapped could escape. Owl suddenly appeared from nowhere, clawing the head of the soldier at the end of the line.

He screamed in pain and ran.

Thalmus sprang from the darkness again, swords flashing, driving the soldiers back farther. Thunder scurried out and took up a position to the right of Thalmus in the middle of the corridor, blocking anyone from getting around them. Boschina hurried out—still screaming as loud as she could and holding her sword forward at the ready—and stood to the right of Thunder. Keeping this battle line, they started backing down the tunnel, fending off the swordsmen in front of them.

Now that they were out where they could be seen, the troopers regained their confidence and, this time led by Corsair, renewed their charge. Several of them danced around in front of Thunder, staying clear of his quick jaws, while trying to stab him. Thunder was vulnerable to the sword when his head was extended in a snapping motion, so Bubo swirled over him constantly, swooping and diving at the men attempting to strike him before he could recoil. Boschina defended the passage and Thunder's right side. At first, the soldiers she confronted laughed and swung mighty overhead blows, expecting to knock her down or, at the least, the sword from her hand. However, Boschina kept her balance, stepping from side to side, forward and back, deflecting the men's swords with quick sweeping arcs—as Thalmus had taught her. With each clash, her engraved blade sent a vibration back to the attacker stinging his hands, elbows, and shoulders. Surprised by the pain and her ability, the attackers became cautious and hesitant in their thrusts at her.

At first, despite her bravado, Boschina worried about her strength and skill against these men—but she grew in confidence as the fight continued. The handle of the sword seemed to grab hold of her and become one with her wrist and arm. It almost directed itself as much as she controlled it. The sword sang as it cut the air, flashing in the haze, searching for the soldier's swords to punish. One particular man was determined to beat her and persisted in slashing and stabbing—trying to wear her down—until Boschina's sword swept his blade to the side, sticking it into Thunder's shell and forcing it from his hand.

Thalmus was fighting with a sword in each hand, staying close to the wall on his left and Thunder on his right so no one could slip by. He listened to the song of Boschina's sword and knew that it had come alive in her hand. With quick glances at her, he could tell that she was holding her own. Thunder, as always, was a menacing brute force keeping the attackers at bay, while Bubo brought fear and quick sharp assaults from the darkness. Still, there was a long distance to go, and he was not sure if they could keep up this pace, let alone, take on more soldiers that might be waiting at the tunnel's end.

Corsair was vicious. The captain's humiliation and anger were focused solely on Thalmus. He hung back, getting his breath, while two or three troopers engaged Thalmus. Then, he would charge forward and push one of his soldiers into Thalmus, hoping Thalmus would stab the trooper so that his one sword arm would be down when Corsair came over the top of the man, his sword extended, trying to impale Thalmus.

Wise from many battles, Thalmus did not fall for the trick.

He kicked the unfortunate man aside and deflected Corsair's thrust. Corsair tried this several times, until the trooper on his left fell during the assault and Thalmus' right arm was free to take an unhindered swipe at Corsair. Thalmus' reach was just short, and the sword swished so close to Corsair's throat that he felt the breeze and decided to stop that tactic. Then, Boschina yelled that there were more troops coming up the tunnel behind them.

"How many, Boschina?" Thalmus called.

"I don't know. I can't see clearly!"

Now what? Thalmus wondered. He could not divert his attention from the troops he dueled—and he surely could not take on any more. There were some rooms and side tunnels ahead, he remembered, but where they went or what advantage they might be was a question.

While deciding what to do, he noticed a shadowy figure beyond the troops he battled.

This dark image faded in and out of the light and appeared to be waving at him, trying to get his attention. Was it the stranger who had warned him to leave Rainland? Thalmus could only get glimpses of the man in between fending off the attackers who were trying to impale him. What was the man doing? Thalmus tried to decipher his signals, but the stranger was staying back. He did not want the troops to see him.

"Give up, Thalmus," Corsair shouted. "Give up or die!"

Giving up would mean sure captivity and perhaps a prolonged death. Still, there did not seem to be much hope of escape now. Then, the stranger was there again, signaling for something—and this time Thalmus understood.

"Boschina," Thalmus called. "Throw the sword that's in Thunder's shell over the troops."

"What?" she said in disbelief.

"That sword, throw it over their heads."

"Thalmus?"

"Throw it, Boschina!"

She did not understand this, but she trusted Thalmus. Boschina lifted and pried the sword free from Thunder's shell then heaved the weapon over the heads of the troops. The troops were surprised and thought this meant that Thalmus was about to surrender. They had not seen the stranger and weren't aware that he was dashing from the darkness and picking up the sword to attack them from behind. Two of the troopers never knew what hit them as they went down under his quick thrusts. By then, the others became aware of this assault from the rear and turned to face him.

"Tobazi," they shouted, recognizing the swordsman—and started after him.

Thalmus seized the opportunity and attacked. Now, the troops found themselves caught between two furious swordsmen and several more of them were wounded before Corsair and the remaining troops broke off and ran back down the corridor.

The dark man, flushed from the fight, started to chase them—but Thalmus grabbed his arm. "There are other troops coming," he told him. "Is there another way out?"

The man, breathing heavy, thought for a moment, and then shook his head. "Not big enough for the creature," he replied, pointing at Thunder with his sword.

Boschina stared at the stranger, wondering where he had come from and how Thalmus knew him. But she was glad to have an ally, for she had felt overwhelmed by the odds against them.

Thalmus smiled at the man. "Then we must scare away these new troops," he said. "Are you with us?"

"Yes, but how will we get through the Wet?"

"I know a way," Thalmus replied.

He turned to Thunder. "Lead us to battle."

Thunder lifted his head and started scampering down the tunnel as fast as he could move.

"Scream, yell, make a lot of noise," he told the stranger and Boschina.

And so they did, following Thunder toward the other side of the castle.

The troops approaching had been hearing the fight in the tunnel. Now they saw the shell creature charging them and the bird flying at their heads. There were swordsmen, too, but they could not tell how many. These troops suddenly realized that their comrades had been defeated and the animals, screams, and the unknown was about to overtake them.

Filled with panic, the troops turned and ran.

When they came out of the tunnel into the covered area, Thalmus directed Thunder and the stranger to get the gates open while he and Boschina went for a Boogala. Thalmus knew that they had very little time before the troops would regroup against them. Fortunately, there were two teams of Boogalas harnessed to sleds that were being unloaded. The covers had been removed from the sleds in order to unpack the contents.

The Rainers working there were not about to confront Thalmus with his swords and frenzied attitude. The startled people backed away when he took control of one of the teams of Boogalas and started leading it to the gate. The troops who had turned and run in the corridor had scattered. Many of them had gone to the gate to defend it. Thalmus now found his ally, the stranger, and Thunder and Owl battling these troops to get at the large gate.

"Get into the sled, Boschina," Thalmus directed. "You will drive this team."

Boschina climbed onto the sled. "I'm not sure I can, Thalmus."

"It is like your father's wagon. You can do it."

Boschina looked at the strange Boogalas. "It's a different wagon and these...these horses? I don't know what they are."

"They will follow your directions, Boschina," Thalmus told her. "You must do this. I have to get the gate open."

Thalmus left Boschina with the reins of the Boogalas and jumped on the scaffolding of one of the damaged columns that was being repaired near the exterior wall. He climbed up the scaffold, leapt across to a wall that was about ten meters high, and ran across the top of it—over the arch of the gates—to the corner where he was behind the gate guards. A guard in a watch tower there climbed out onto the wall to confront him.

Their swords clashed as Thalmus took the offensive. He had no time to waste with this foolish gate guard. Several blows, then an upswing, knocked the guard's weapon from his hand. Defenseless, the man ran back to the tower and slammed the door shut that led to the stairs.

Thalmus looked down to the ground. It was too far to risk a jump.

The battle below was raging away from the gate. The guards had not seen him run along the wall as they were occupied fighting his friends. Thalmus quickly searched for a way to get down. Where the gate keepers had been working on the hinges, he found the ropes for their ladder still hanging down the side. Grabbing hold of the rope where it was anchored at the top, he repelled his way to the bottom. The Rainers still had not seen him. There backs were to the gate. Thalmus tried to lift the iron latch that held the gates closed.

It was too heavy.

He turned to look at the ongoing fight and saw Boschina beyond, waiting with the Boogalas. He did not have to get her attention. She was watching him. Thalmus waved his arm and signaled Boschina to charge the gate with the Boogalas.

Boschina, sitting atop the metallic sled, snapped the reins and started the Boogalas running. Thalmus charged the troops, yelling at them to look out for the runaway Boogalas.

The soldiers scattered out of the way, so Thunder and the stranger were able to follow the sled up to the gates. In the confusion, before the troops could rally to attack, Thalmus and the stranger lifted the heavy iron latch, unlocking the gates. Thunder tucked his head in, and leaned his shell against the heavy wooden doors. He pushed with his powerful legs, slowly forcing the massive doors to swing apart. When the opening was big enough for the wagon, Boschina drove the team through, out into the rain. Thalmus and the stranger followed, backing out, fighting as they went with Bubo swooping back and forth. They were through the gate, out of the castle, but the sudden wet and coldness sent shivers through them, and Thalmus felt an immediate sense of doom.

Could they carry the fight into the rain?

Just then, the troops stopped fighting and hesitated at the open gate. They did not want to enter the Wet without being ordered, but there was no one present with the authority to give that order. This situation was beyond their training or command. So, they stood at the gate watching—and waiting for an order.

With Boschina and the sled on the road out in front of them, Thalmus, Thunder, and the stranger kept backing away from the confused soldiers. As the distance increased between them, Thalmus decided it was time to leave.

"Get in the sled," he told the stranger.

The stranger glanced at him and back at the motionless troops. He nodded, turned, hurried to the sled, and jumped in. When the soldiers still did not move, Thalmus ran and climbed aboard right behind him.

"Go Boschina," Thalmus shouted. She snapped the reins and the Boogalas jerked from a walk to a run. "When the road splits, take the middle one and stay on it," he told her and dropped into the bed of the sled.

Thalmus looked back at the gate. Just before it disappeared in the cold rain, he saw more troops, with swords in hand, running out of the corridor. They were led by an angry Corsair. Thalmus could not hear him, but could see that he was yelling and hitting the guards as he ran to the open gate. Corsair had gotten there just in time to see Thalmus and the dark man—riding in the back of the sled—fade into the rain. Corsair shook his fist at them, then swung around sending men scrambling to the supply room for Dry Suits, and others for the sleds and Boogalas.

Chapter Ten
Return to the Farms

"Go, go," Boschina kept yelling at the Boogalas as she shook their reins. The animals were startled by this new driver. The pair galloped frantically through the water, pulling the sled with the strangers and towing the scary shell creature. Thalmus had tossed the end of a rope used for tying the loads down on the sled to Thunder. The great tortoise had grabbed it in his jaws, tucked in his legs, and hung on when the Boogalas bolted forward. He was now plowing through the water like a dingy pulled behind a ship.

Bubo appeared out of the gray, gliding in over the scared Boogalas and calming them with his presence. The odd horse-duck-like animals settled into a steady pace, accepted Boschina's guidance, and took the middle road at the junction as she directed them.

Lord Luminous' castle faded and disappeared in the grayness behind them. Boschina still wore her frog-skin coat. Thalmus had left his behind in the dark corridor when the fight began. He had used it to distract and confuse the troops he fought when he sprang from the darkness. Holding the durable coat by the hood in his left hand, he had whipped and slapped them with it while deflecting and prodding with the sword in his right. Eventually, it had been shredded by their slashing blades. The frog coat had served to protect him many times and in various ways. He knew that he would regret its loss, even as it served a purpose at that critical moment, and would miss the coat's comfort and unique qualities, as he did now. The rain was soaking through his clothes, but Thalmus was more concerned about their immediate future and the Shower Knight—that strange force that he knew could not be avoided.

It was just a matter of time before it found them.

And then what?

Could he convince the Knight, who had saved them once, to save them again by letting them leave? If not, how could one possibly fight such a thing? And how soon was the Dark? He had lost track of time in this place where there was no real day. How much time did they have to get to the farms and beyond—and would Oddkin help them once they got there? He rarely misjudged people, so he felt sure the old man would give them directions to the Dry.

Thalmus looked at his new ally, who was slouched against the front board of the sled, intently watching the road behind them. The man was holding his left shoulder where he had been cut. The rain was washing a continuous flow of blood down his arm. In addition, his blouse on the right side was red with blood from another wound.

"You fought well," Thalmus said. "You are good with the sword."

"It's been a long time since I've had to fight so many," the man said and glanced at Thalmus. "I'm afraid I got tired."

"How deep is the cut on your arm?" Thalmus asked.

"Deep," the man grimaced and moved his hand off the cut for a moment to show Thalmus the wound. He smiled. "But, my sword arm is still good."

"What about your side?"

"It's minor."

"If not for you, we would have been captured," Thalmus said. He cut a strip from his own shirt tail, wrapped, and then tied it around the man's wounded arm as a bandage. "That is the best I can do now. Hopefully, it will stop the bleeding."

"It'll have to do then," the man replied, straightening his arm.

"What is your name?"

"I'm Tobazi."

"Tobazi," Thalmus repeated the name thoughtfully. "You saved us. We will not leave this place without you."

Tobazi smiled. "You saved me as well, but we're not free yet."

"That is true. We have a struggle ahead of us," Thalmus replied. "How did you come into this land? Do you know a way out?"

"No," Tobazi answered. "There was a hood over my head when I was brought in."

For a moment, Thalmus saw a flash of anger and terrible memories in his eyes. Then, just as quickly, his expression changed and Tobazi spoke again. "In the tunnel you said you knew a way out."

"Yes, but it is not a direct path. We are going to the farms where we can get help."

"Do you know someone there?"

"Yes," Thalmus answered, "hopefully, a new friend."

Tobazi sat up and looked past Boschina, over the backs of the Boogalas, into the rain. "Corsair will be coming soon," he said. "He'll be brutal. Is your friend willing to sacrifice for you?"

"We will see," Thalmus replied. "You said you were brought here—by whom and for what?"

Tobazi sat down facing the rear of the sled again.

"I was a gift to Lord Luminous."

"A gift?"

"I come from the land of Toubar. Far from here."

"Yes, I know of it," Thalmus said. "I once traveled there to hunt."

"Then you must know that it's a desolate place where one must fight even the land to survive."

Thalmus nodded. "It is bleak, but I found the people to be honest and fair."

"That we are," Tobazi said. "But, I was taken from my land by one who's not. By one who gave me to Lord Luminous as a gift, to be a captive—like an animal to be bargained and traded."

"Who was that?"

"It was your King Ahmbin."

"King Ahmbin did this to you?"

"He commanded it so. He sent troops to capture me and to bring me to this wretched place."

Thalmus could not believe this.

"Are you sure it was the king? Did you see him?"

"No...just his wicked messenger."

"Wicked messenger?" Thalmus repeated with a thought of recognition. "Do you remember this person?"

"I will never forget him," Tobazi said with anger. "For one day, I hope to find him. His name is Baldoff. Do you know him?"

"Yes," Thalmus said, remembering his confrontation with Baldoff before the king. "I just met him. And I believe you are right. He is wicked."

Both men were thoroughly soaked now. The constant splatter of rain on his head made Thalmus wish he had a hat. He looked forward at Boschina and even though he could only see her back and her head covered by the frog-skin hood, he could tell she was shivering. Thalmus searched the terrain around them for the small cloud that contained the Shower Knight. He rubbed his eyes trying to clear them of moisture.

"What are you looking for?" Tobazi asked, looking over the side of the sled.

"The Shower Knight."

"I heard about him at the castle, but I have never seen him. The Rainers all fear him, yet praise him. They say he rules the Wet and is very powerful."

"He could destroy us, if he desires," Thalmus said, then looked again at Tobazi. "Why did Baldoff want to bring you here?"

"I'm not sure. At first, I think it was for magic."

"Are you a sorcerer?"

"No. But they thought I had a power. In my land, water is scarce. I dug and discovered a new well with abundant water. Because of this, an untrue belief grew that I was a conjurer. Persistence and good fortune was all it was."

"And here, in Rainland, Luminous wanted you to do the opposite. Get rid of the water?"

"That's right." Tobazi laughed. "I was to be part of some wild scheme to stop the rain. Of course, I couldn't. Who could possibly stop this? When they realized I had no power, they became bitter and angry. I was only kept alive because of my uniqueness. So, I became their slave for amusement. One thing Luminous particularly enjoyed was watching Corsair pretend to behead me."

Thalmus, who was constantly looking about for the Shower Knight, made no comment. He could feel Tobazi's anger and patiently waited for the wounded man to continue his story.

"Corsair would put me on my knees before Luminous and his court. He'd slice the air around me with ceremonial swipes of his sword, then place the blade against my throat and take a long, slow backswing. The room would be totally silent; I could hear the muted rain on the roof above. Then, he'd swing forward quickly, whipping the sword just over my head or to my side. And they'd all burst out with disappointment and laughter. Occasionally, he would cut me slightly. Once, he put two pieces of old swords together so that it broke apart when it hit my neck. Oh, they liked that. The people began to think my skin was as tough as a mud worm's. Luminous was excited by this game because he never knew whether Corsair was actually going to behead me or not. My life was totally at the will of Corsair."

As he spoke, Tobazi had been watching Thunder being pulled behind the sled. "That's the biggest and strongest shell creature I've ever seen," he said, interrupting his story.

Thalmus checked on Thunder. His jaws were clamped on the taut rope and his eyes were barely open. Thalmus knew Thunder could maintain that clamped jaw for a long time. How long the rope would last was another matter. He motioned with a slight wave of his hand and the giant tortoise opened one eye in response—which meant, "I'm all right."

Thalmus nodded at his friend then turned to Tobazi.

"How did you get loose in the castle?"

"After a while, I stopped fighting. I offered no resistance. My guards thought I'd become too weak and beaten to be a threat. So, they used fewer men to watch me. I waited, acting docile. Then, one late Gray, just before the Dark, they left one lone guard to put me in my cell. I easily overpowered him and escaped to roam the castle. They searched for me, but I avoided them. I ate from the stored food supplies and waited for a chance to get out. Then you came along."

"How long were you hiding?"

"I don't remember," Tobazi said, trying to count the days. "Twenty, maybe twenty five Grays."

"Thalmus…Thalmus," Boschina was calling from the front and pointing ahead. They looked up to see a large stone building emerging out of the Gray before them.

"The farms," Thalmus said to Tobazi.

Boschina stopped the Boogalas in front of the big double doors as Thalmus searched the sled for the horn to signal the farmers inside to open the doors. He finally found it in a compartment at the side of the seat. Putting the horn to his lips, he blew it five times, duplicating the same notes that he heard the trooper blow.

They waited in the rain, watching the doors.

Tobazi got in a crouch, ready for possible combat.

Boschina looked nervously at Thalmus.

Thalmus pointed at the doors. "Drive the Boogalas in as soon as the doors open. Don't wait."

Thunder stood up on his feet and spit the rope out of his mouth.

Owl flew down and landed on Thalmus' shoulder.

The doors shook, and then swung open. Boschina hardly had to snap the reins, for the Boogalas knew what to do. They jerked forward and pulled the sled inside the building. Bubo took off from Thalmus' shoulder and flew around inspecting the huge, open space of the warehouse before finding a spot to perch near the ceiling. Thalmus stepped off the back of the sled to tell the farmers to keep the doors open for Thunder, but it wasn't necessary. The men were so shocked by these strangers—one in frog skin, another soaked in blood, and a bird winging about—that they just stood in surprise.

Thalmus and Tobazi were both holding their sword and Boschina picked up hers when the Boogalas came to a stop. The farmers had no weapons, and when Thunder plodded in, they all stepped back.

"Do not be afraid," Thalmus said. "He will not hurt you."

"Tobazi!" One of the farmers shouted, pointing at the wounded man. The others looked, and moved farther away.

"Yes," Thalmus said. "He is Tobazi, and he is hurt. You must not fear us. We came for your help. Where is Oddkin?"

One of the farmers ran to get their leader, while Thalmus put his sword down and helped another farmer to close the doors and latch them.

Soon, Oddkin came running, hobbling as best he could, with a group of men following him. He looked around at the strange scene.

"What's going on? Who is…Thalmus, is that you?"

"Yes, Oddkin."

"I didn't expect to see you so soon or in such a state," the old man said. "Though it should not surprise me." He looked at Boschina. "This girl is the friend you are helping?"

"Yes, this is Boschina."

Boschina bowed her head.

Oddkin smiled at her. He studied Thunder and looked up at Owl perched on a water trough. "This is the shell creature and magnificent bird that we heard about. They're truly beautiful. And this," he said, stepping up to Tobazi, showing no fear of him, "is not the man you're searching for, but is certainly one in need of help."

"Your help is what we are here for," Thalmus said. "We do not want to cause you or your men any harm."

"Harm?" Oddkin turned his attention from Tobazi. "Oh Thalmus, from the looks of you three, and these weapons and this load without any troops, I can imagine what's happened. Is Corsair on his way?"

"Yes. He and his troops will not be far behind. If you would just tell us how to get to the Dry, we will be gone."

"We must move quickly," Oddkin said, ignoring Thalmus' request. "Did the Knight see you come here?"

"I watched for him," Thalmus said, "and I saw no sign of him."

"Perhaps we have a chance then." Oddkin turned to his farmers. "Listen, my friends, you feeders of Sol Linden. How often we've talked about the dire condition of our land and the changes we wish to make—changes that are necessary to save our families and friends. We are now confronted with an opportunity to not only save these people, but to take action on our words for the future of our people. I tell you the decision, the responsibility, is here now. It will not be easy. Nor will it be safe. You know the anger of our leaders. We must be united, one way or the other. So, I ask, does anyone object to helping these strangers? Speak now, and we'll send them away."

No one spoke as the farmers looked furtively at one another.

Then, the man who closed the doors with Thalmus stepped forward. "I'm scared and worried for my family. Yet, I know that nothing will change unless we do something. We must start now to save our land." He looked at Thalmus and Tobazi. "We must help them."

"Yes," the others said, and one at a time they stepped forward and committed themselves to a dangerous future.

"I'm proud of you," Oddkin said. "Remember, there's strength in numbers. We must stay united in this." Then, he gave instructions and directed several of them to move the Boogalas and sled. Boschina jumped down and joined Thalmus as she undid her coat and shook off the rain.

"Oddkin," Thalmus said. "Thank you for wanting to take us in, but this will put you into great danger. All we ask is directions to the Dry and we will leave."

"There's not enough time. You cannot reach the Dry before the Black. Besides, this one needs help or he will never make it." He put his hand gently on Tobazi, who was looking quite pale and cold.

"Come."

Tobazi leaned on Thalmus and Boschina as they followed Oddkin through the enormous rooms of growing plants to another building.

Several farmers followed behind, raking the ground to obscure Thunder's tracks and were amazed when Bubo drifted silently down and landed on the back of the great shell creature.

"I'm sending the Boogalas with the sled back into the Wet without you," Oddkin said. "So I can tell Corsair that you continued on when we wouldn't help you. We'll hide you until the next Gray."

They entered a living quarter, where Oddkin handed them dry clothes from a supply room and bandages for Tobazi. The pants and long-sleeve blouses were many layers of material overlaid and sewn together; they were quilted and warm.

"I want to look at this wound later," Oddkin said to Tobazi. "These men, Latt and Tuggle, will show you where to hide. You must stay there until I come for you. Now, I have to get back to meet Corsair."

After they quickly changed into the dry clothes, Latt took their wet clothes away to bury them in the furrows. The other farmer, Tuggle—a stocky, rosy-cheeked man with hands the color of the earth—gave them blankets. "To keep you warm," he said and then led them into another building and through several immense rooms with rows of plants to an iron gate that guarded a long, dark room. Just beyond the gate were flat, trunk-like containers and oblong boxes stacked up eight or ten high and arranged in rows that extended into the darkness.

"You will not like it here. I'm sorry," Tuggle said, shrugging. "But it's the safest place."

After this apology, he pushed open the gate. Thalmus noticed that it did not make a squeak and that it was wide enough for a Boogala sled, so Thunder had no problem getting through. Owl, who was now sitting on Thalmus' shoulder, was not happy. He did not like the scent of this place. Thalmus felt this and his own senses told him immediately what lie before them.

"It smells bad in here," Boschina said as they walked into the dark chamber.

"Put the blanket up around your face and breathe through it," Thalmus said as he lifted his own blanket to his nose.

"Oh, the air's terrible!" she gagged. "What is this place?"

"This is their burial vault," Thalmus answered with a muffled voice as he spoke through his blanket.

"No," she moaned.

"You must move back, far back, so you can't be seen," Tuggle said as he closed the gate. "Please, don't make any noise," he pleaded, and then left.

With Bubo on his shoulder, acting as his eyes, Thalmus guided Boschina and Tobazi between the rows of coffins deep into the darkness—until they found a short stack of the boxes to sit on in the midst of the rotting remains of the citizens of Rainland.

"I don't like trusting these people," Tobazi whispered.

He also had wrapped the blanket around himself and over his face. Thunder found a niche in the wall of caskets in which to squeeze out of the path, and then he withdrew into his shell.

"Why should they protect us?" Tobazi continued. "I don't like this. We're trapped here."

"I think we are safe," Thalmus whispered. "It is a sanctified tomb."

"Not to Corsair," Tobazi said.

Boschina was trying not to gag by sucking air through the blanket into her mouth.

Thalmus hushed her.

"But I can't breathe," she gasped.

They heard distant voices that became louder, and then discernable, as soldiers entered the growing room adjacent to the burial chamber. All three of the escapees recognized Corsair's voice.

"I'm not doubting you, Oddkin. I'm protecting you and your farmers. Thalmus could've forced you to hide them."

"I told you, Corsair, they went on with the Boogalas."

"I know what you said." Corsair replied, irritated. "They could be holding some of the farmers hostage and you're trying to protect your people. I know you, old man."

"But all of my farmers are here. Count them. All twenty-five are here."

Corsair, and ten troopers in dry suits and ready for action with swords in hand, began to search through the huge room. Tuggle, who had obscured the visitor's tracks to the gate, was now on his knees working in the rows of plants near the center of the room. The only possible hiding place in this building was behind the iron gate—and Corsair knew what lay in there. He had been personally responsible for dispatching some of those poor souls sent to that foul resting place.

"Search as much as you like," Oddkin said. "You'll find nothing. You're just wasting valuable time."

Corsair walked to the gate and looked through the bars. The stench from the dark chamber struck his nose and he recoiled, stepping back. "What a foul, but perfect, place to hide," he muttered. "Who would want to search in there?" Corsair shook his head. "But, why would you let the Boogalas go? They're your fastest way to escape." Corsair rolled the hilt of the sword over and over in his hand as he thought. He did not want to make another mistake. He looked at his waiting troops and then around the large planting room again until his gaze fell on Tuggle, who was sneaking a look at him. That was too suspicious. He suddenly ran toward Tuggle, trampling some plants in his path.

"Corsair, the plants," Oddkin screamed. "What're you doing?"

When Corsair got to Tuggle, he kicked him in the stomach and lifted his head by his hair—putting the sword to his throat. "Where are they, dirt man?" Corsair demanded. "Where are they hiding?"

"Who?" Tuggle choked. "I've been tending plants."

"Where's that bird? Surely, you saw it."

"Corsair," Oddkin yelled as he came to the aid of his farmer. "He has been back here working. He does not know of them."

"Why were you looking at me?" Corsair hissed. "I'll cut your throat and throw you into that hole with the other carcasses. Your children will never see you again."

"I saw no one," Tuggle whispered in between gasps for air.

"What good is this?" Oddkin said to Corsair as he reached them in the furrows. "You would kill this man who has worked hard for us—for nothing? First, you cut a man at the doors for not opening them fast enough. Now, you want to kill this one? For what? What're you doing?"

Corsair kept his grip on Tuggle, but he glared at Oddkin. "I'm making sure that you are not lying to me, old man."

"Are these people so important that you'd kill your own to get them?"

"Yes, old man, they are. And this worm gave them away. They're hiding in the burial chamber."

"No," Tuggle gasped.

"There's no one in there but dead bodies," Oddkin exclaimed.

Corsair shoved Tuggle into the dirt. "For this, you will die with them." He spit out the words, turned and headed for the iron gate. He sent one trooper off with orders to count all of the farmers and ordered four more to search the burial chamber. The four soldiers hesitantly opened the gate. Holding their noses with one hand, and swords in the other, they each took an aisle between the stacks of coffins and slowly moved forward into the darkness—whipping their swords back and forth in front of them.

Corsair and the other troops waited in anxious silence as they listened to their comrades banging their swords against the coffins in the dark. Oddkin helped Tuggle to his feet. They carefully stepped between the rows and out of the room, as if they were unconcerned about the troops in the burial chamber. To the relief of the soldiers clanging about in the suffocating rank darkness, they encountered no one except each other at the end of their individual aisles. They quickly turned around and came out, gasping for sweeter air by the plants.

Corsair cursed and struck the ground with his sword. The troops moved away from him as the man who had been sent to count the farmers came running back.

"Reporting, sire."

"What?" Corsair said, turning to the trooper.

"The farmers are all accounted for," the trooper said, breathing heavily.

"All twenty-five? You're sure?"

"Yes, sire. We counted twice."

"Line them up at the doors. I'll count them myself."

The trooper nodded and ran off as Corsair slowly scanned the burial chamber. "I could have sworn...." he muttered. He shook his head, still not believing, and looked around the planting room for tracks. He scanned the roof beams and water troughs hoping to see the great bird, but there was nothing. "Where have you gone Frog Hunter?" he said. Then, suddenly swinging his sword wildly, he chopped at a row of plants—sending chunks of green vegetation and dirt flying.

When he stopped, he spun around to his troops. "We're leaving. Return to the sleds."

They ran back through the planting rooms, gathering the troops who had been searching other rooms, and loaded into the sleds.

Corsair counted the farmers lined up near the doors. They were all there: twenty five quiet men with bowed heads.

Corsair walked down the line, looking at each man in the face. "Death is the penalty for helping fugitives." He stopped in front of Tuggle and pressed the flat of his sword into the farmer's chest. "Even if I find that just one of you helped them you will all die."

Tuggle kept his gaze to the ground as Oddkin pleaded for him. "Is this really necessary?"

Corsair ignored the old manager. He stepped back, turning the sword in his hand, and stared at the farmers. "Don't be fools, speak now and I will spare you."

The farmers remained quiet, standing motionless in their line. The doors were still open, the rain splattering on the stones of the road, the damp air drifting through—engulfing them all in a cold misty scene. Corsair waited, looking up and down the row of men. Finally, he decided there would be no response and that he was wasting time. He stepped onto a sled, still watching the farmers, and waiting for one of them to speak. Pointing his sword at them, he said: "The signal to open the doors is now ten horns. Any less or more you keep them shut. Understood?"

The farmers nodded.

"We understand," Oddkin said. "It will be so."

Corsair gave the command, the drivers snapped the reins, the Boogalas lurched forward, and they charged into the Wet in search of their illusive prey.

When the doors closed behind the sleds of troops, Tuggle returned to the burial chamber gate and called for Thalmus to come out. "It's safe for now," he said. "The troops are gone."

Thalmus, Boschina, and Tobazi carefully came down from the coffin ledges where they had climbed when the troops had entered the chamber and began thrashing along the corpse corridors. Thalmus had been straddling the corridor with a foot on each side of the stacks of coffins. The trooper had blindly walked between his legs, twice.

Tobazi emerged from the darkness very carefully, looking around thoroughly before leaving the last row of coffins and coming out through the gate. Then, Boschina appeared, followed by Thalmus. As they got away from the burial chamber, they all took deep breaths of air to clear the stench from their nostrils. Owl drifted silently out and circled the planting room. Thalmus called to him and he dropped down and landed on his friend's shoulder. Thunder had decided to stay in his nook and sleep.

Tobazi gripped Tuggle's arm. "Thank you, Tuggle, for your courage. I know the fear when the sword is at your throat."

"I was very much afraid," Tuggle said.

"You were brave," Boschina said. "Corsair's such a terrible man."

Tuggle led them to the living quarters, where Oddkin was bandaging the farmer whom Corsair had cut at the main doors.

"We are grateful for what you have done for us," Thalmus said to the farmer.

The man grimaced as Oddkin tightened the bandage. "It had to be done," the man said. "Oddkin has taught us the old ways of our people. And I see now that we must return to them." For several moments, he studied Owl perched on Thalmus' shoulder as Bubo watched him with interested eyes. Then the farmer said, "He is magical. He has given us the will to stand up."

"Oddkin has given that to you," Thalmus said. "And you have done it for yourselves."

Oddkin finished with the man's bandages. "You lie down and rest now, Lawden." He turned to Tobazi, who was sprawled in a chair. "Let's have a look at you."

He began to clean Tobazi's wounds and dress them as he spoke to the group. "Corsair could return here for the Black. There are other buildings farther out that are used for such purposes, but he could come back here. So, be prepared to go into the burial chamber again."

Food was prepared and they sat down with the farmers for the last meal of the Gray. The Rainers were excited about their role in protecting these strangers. They felt a bond with them. Their normal shyness gave way to warm friendliness. They chatted and asked questions about the world outside Rainland: about Boschina's father, Vericitas, and about Bubo and Thunder. Then, they went about their routine chores, preparing for the Black.

The Gray was fading when Boschina and Tobazi bedded down and Thalmus found Oddkin sitting in a planting room by himself. "Worried about your people?" Thalmus asked, squatting beside him.

Oddkin looked thoughtfully at Thalmus. "You've made us confront ourselves and our future."

"I did not intend to cause this trouble," Thalmus replied.

"I know. But it has happened. I just don't know if we are ready. First, we must free you and your friends. Then, my farmers and I must decide what to do."

"It will not be easy," Thalmus said, watching water stream down a trough and into a row of plants. "I'm afraid that you have a dangerous future in front of you."

"As well as you," Oddkin replied. "You're not free from here yet."

"I am not worried about Corsair," Thalmus said. "It is the Shower Knight that concerns me. Tell me how I can fight him."

"There is no way. He is all-powerful; your only hope is to get out before he finds you because he cannot exist out of the rain. He will be out there. He will be looking for you, Thalmus, for I'm sure he has been alerted by Corsair."

"He must have a weakness," Thalmus persisted.

"I know of none. He's not bad like Corsair. Though, he is the protector of our land. That's his foremost duty. And he holds that charge higher than any other."

The Gray was dimming, and the Black rapidly approaching. Oddkin looked again at Thalmus. "Corsair said you killed and wounded some of our people."

Thalmus looked up to meet his eyes. "Only those who attacked us, Oddkin. Your lord would not allow us to leave. He was going to imprison us. We were forced to fight. I don't know if we killed, but we did hurt a number of the troops."

Oddkin was staring at him. "I've never met someone like you," he said, and reached out and touched Thalmus' forehead with his fingertips. He held them there for a moment while Thalmus remained still; then, Oddkin slowly withdrew his hand. "You're not just a hunter."

"No?" Thalmus said.

"No. You carry a powerful spirit like no other. I feel strength of will in you that knows no fear or defeat."

Thalmus clasped Oddkin's hand. "You have the same spirit, the same knowledge. You may not think so, but you do."

"Me? No, I'm too old and tired."

"I can assure you that you are neither, Oddkin."

The old man sighed and looked at his long rows of plants. They were so sedate, so orderly, so soothing to his eyes. These plants, these living organisms, grew and produced and fed others. If only the world were like this.

"Our land...our people," he spoke in a slow and tired voice. "It has all become so bad. I'm afraid of what must be done."

"What happened here?" Thalmus asked. "What caused the change...the rain?"

"It's too shameful to speak of," Oddkin said. He rose to his feet. "Besides, the Black is here and you must rest for your journey tomorrow."

They returned to the sleeping quarters in near blackness and went to bed. Tobazi was snoring, and Boschina was bundled under four blankets. Bubo, on the other hand, discovered the farms to be a veritable feast during the Black. Due to the lack of predators, rodents of various size and variety came out in abundance to eat on the plants. It was easy pickings for the great owl who filled his empty stomach from the previous days of no hunting.

Chapter Eleven
Bubo and the Shower Knight

When the Gray returned, Oddkin was up and rousing everyone to action. A hearty breakfast of tubers smeared with Rocbed gravy was served by the famers. Tobazi's wounded arm was sore and stiff, but Oddkin's medicinal plant paste and bandage had sealed the wounds and stopped the bleeding.

Boschina was still sniffling, still feeling the chill. Thunder trudged out from his rest in the burial chamber as Owl watched from a high perch. They said their goodbyes to the men of the farms and then were led by Tuggle and Oddkin through the buildings to a different exit that was far from the main entrance.

Before reaching the exterior door, Tuggle quietly pulled Tobazi aside. "You're hurt, but I know you're strong. I worry for Boschina, for I have daughters of my own and want to protect them. Take care of her, Tobazi."

"I will, my friend," Tobazi said and put his hand on Tuggle's shoulder. "And you care for yourself. Don't let Corsair beat you."

Tuggle shrugged. "We'll do what we can."

Oddkin gathered them at a pair of old wooden doors. "Listen to me. You all must hear this in case you get separated in the Wet. Follow the road outside this door to the second road on the left. Stay on that road and watch for a stone marker on the right side with a sun and a lizard carved on it. The marker is about knee high and might be overgrown by vines. There will be other markers, only one will have a lizard on it. Look for that lizard. You cannot mistake it. There is a narrow road behind this marker. Take that road and stay on it, even if you think you are going in circles for it winds through bogs and pits." He paused, looking at each one of them. "Be very careful in that area; mud worms are known to live there. This road is ancient and overgrown; yet, is still paved and comes out on the north side of our realm. I believe this is your best chance to escape. Corsair will not expect you to know this route."

"We are truly in debt to you," Thalmus said. "Thank you, Oddkin."

"Nonsense, it is we who must thank you."

There was a sudden thud on the doors from the outside. Tuggle lifted the latch and pulled open the left door a meter. Two farmers hurried in from the Wet and shook off.

"Well?" Oddkin asked.

"We went as far as the second road and saw no troops," one of the men said.

Oddkin patted them on their shoulders. "Thank you." He turned to the three travelers. "Boschina, I hope you find your father, and that you both may live free. Tobazi, I hope you heal in your head as well as your arm and you return home safely to be happy again. Thalmus, I do hope I'll meet you and your friends again."

"We will not forget you, Oddkin," Thalmus said. "And, you will see me again."

Oddkin nodded and smiled with tight lips. "Nor will we forget you, Thalmus. You've done more here than you know."

Thunder snorted and leaned into Thalmus. Owl, who was perched on a wall ledge, hooted and spread his wings. Thalmus put his hand on Thunder and looked up at Owl. The bright discs of Bubo's eyes glared at him, urging him to move. Thalmus smiled. "Yes," he said quietly. "We must leave."

"They're right," Oddkin agreed. "Go quickly now. Be alert out there, and don't waste time."

Boschina grasped Oddkin's hand in both of hers. "Thank you for helping us, Oddkin," she said and then turned and hugged Tuggle. "Thanks for saving us from Corsair. You're so brave."

Surprised, Tuggle did not know what to say. "Well...I, huh, did what...what was right."

Oddkin smiled at his farmer. He was proud of him, but there was no time for long goodbyes. Touching Boschina's arm, he said, "You really must go now, if you want to escape."

"I'll take the lead," Tobazi said, stepping to the doors.

Tuggle swung open the right door and Oddkin the left one. The chilling dampness surrounded them even before they stepped into the rain. The gentle Tuggle patted each one on the back as they went out—Tobazi, then Boschina, in her frog skin coat, followed by Thalmus. Bubo glided out above Thunder as he plodded into the rain. Thalmus and Boschina turned and waved farewell to Oddkin and Tuggle as they closed the doors behind them.

They slogged through the water while keeping a constant watch for troops. Owl flew ahead into the grayness, scouting the road and returning to hoot its lack of enemy. Long before the second road was reached, Tobazi and Thalmus were soaked. The farmer's thick clothing that had been so comforting inside now became heavy and suffocating.

At the junction of the second road, they paused to wait for Owl. The three of them leaned against Thunder's shell and watched the roads. The rain poured down on them and splattered the surface water as far as they could see into the dull distance.

"I wonder how far away we will be able to hear the Boogalas coming," Tobazi said.

"In this mess," Thalmus replied, "we'll see them before we hear them."

"Then they'd see us," Boschina said, concerned.

"Yes. But, hopefully, Bubo will see them first and warn us."

This was a difficult place. Because of the rain there were no tracks. One could not hear well or see far or smell anything—even Thunder's sense of feel and vibration were obscured. *The only consolation*, Thalmus thought, *was that their enemy was in the same situation.* Except one, of course, and Thalmus kept a constant watch for him.

Owl returned hooting an "all clear" and winged off in the new direction. Glad to be moving again, they followed him on the new road. Boschina walked alongside Tobazi, watching for the marker, and Thalmus followed with Thunder behind him.

Oddkin's warning about the vines was proving correct. There was plenty of plant growth encroaching on the road. Moss, vines, shrubs, and brambles growing in from the sides were narrowing the road and obscuring the edges where the markers were to be found. Tobazi and Thalmus drew their swords and began poking and slashing the overgrowth in search of the markers.

When a steel sword chinked against stone, they stopped and cleared enough to see the marker. The only problem with this was that it left evidence of their passage.

They moved slowly along like this with Owl coming and going—and Boschina and Thunder keeping watch. A number of markers were found, but not the right one. The lizard had not yet appeared when Owl suddenly returned hooting danger.

Thalmus looked up the road. "Boogalas are coming."

They looked around for a place to hide, but there was none.

"We've to get out of sight," Tobazi said, frantically.

"Over here," Thalmus called, pointing to the opposite side of the road. "The brush is thicker down here."

Hurrying to the edge, they slid down a short bank into the muck and brush off the side of the road. Thunder burrowed under the mud and water to hide his shell.

In a short time, two teams of Boogalas pulling sleds full of troops appeared out of the Gray on the road ahead. The Boogalas moved at a moderate speed, a trot, one after the other. Thalmus saw that the soldiers' heads, even though covered with hats, were turned down, protecting their faces against the rain. Only the drivers were alert and watching the road. The sleds splashed by and moved on up the road, disappearing in the rain.

"I didn't see Corsair with that bunch," Tobazi said.

Thalmus agreed. "We would have seen his face for sure."

Now, he was thankful for the rain and water that obscured their tracks and hindered their pursuer's sight. In normal conditions, they would be fighting by now. Owl appeared, drifting down out of the Gray to check on his friends. He hooted at Thalmus who answered back, "Whoo-whoo." Knowing they were all right, he flew off to scout the road ahead.

Boschina led them back onto the road, and they continued the search, but the sight of the troops had put an urgency in their pace. Several more wrong markers were found. They were beginning to worry that they had missed the right one when Tobazi's sword struck stone again. He cleared the vines away and scraped off the moss to reveal the lizard staring up at him. They all looked at it somewhat mystified, for it was ominously different than the others. There was a sun at the top shining down on the figure of a scaly beast, but its tail curved up and over the sun—capturing its power. The lizard's claws were spread and hooked as if gripping onto the stone. Its mouth was partly open, ready to bite and its large, alert eyes glared with defiance—like a beast defending its kill from scavengers.

"What a scary thing," Boschina said.

Tobazi placed the tip of his sword on the lizard's head.

"Maybe it's supposed to be a warning."

Thalmus had seen this image before, though not for many years. It was the emblem of a power he had helped to defeat in a long and bitter battle that finally ended when it was purged from the land. Seeing that symbol again brought a rush of memories to him. He shivered and looked at the growth around it.

"Let's find the trail."

Boschina and Tobazi waded in, probing the brush around the marker until they uncovered a narrow road that was obscured by the overgrowth. Thunder worked his way through the clinging vines. Thalmus followed and tried to replace the foliage to make it appear undisturbed. With the mysterious road to freedom before them, they turned back to look for Bubo. They waited, searching the grayness, expecting him to appear any moment.

"He's been gone a long time," Boschina said.

"Yes, he has," Thalmus replied as he looked in the direction he last saw Owl flying away from them. "We need to move on."

"What about Bubo?" Boschina asked. "How will he know where to look for us? There are no other birds here to tell him where we went."

"He has his ways," Thalmus said and smiled at Boschina. "He will find us."

Thunder, who had been watching Thalmus, grunted agreement and started on the new path. Remembering Oddkin's warning of the mud worms, Boschina jumped onto Thunder's shell and kept her sword ready. She did not want to be surprised. Even knowing there was little she could do to hurt the creature, she felt better with a weapon in her hand and on Thunder's back, protected by his powerful jaws.

Thalmus looked for Bubo one last time before turning and following Thunder. Tobazi, leading again, was relieved that they were off the main road. He felt some comfort in this untraveled and overgrown trail, where the Boogalas and sleds could not pass. He was starting to feel good about their chances of making it to the Dry, but was also beginning to weaken. The loss of blood was affecting him. His wounded arm was getting stiff and hard to lift up. Tobazi turned around to check on Boschina, stumbled, and almost fell.

Thalmus was feeling hungry. He often did in dangerous situations. He thought this amusing because instead of being a distraction, it actually alerted his senses and focused them on the danger at hand. He looked for Bubo in the wet Gray, but could not find him. Owl was vital to their escape. Without him, Thalmus felt blind. Tobazi's deteriorating strength had become another concern. Thalmus wondered if the wounded man could hold his own in a fight, for he definitely felt that they would not get away without a battle.

It was just a matter of time.

Staying on the paved trail, they wove in and out of the brush—all the while keeping a watch on each side. The road curved and twisted, double-backed on itself and seemed to go in circles, as Oddkin had predicted. However, the rain was getting lighter: a sure sign that they were heading out of Rainland.

A breeze suddenly blew over them.

Thalmus stopped and looked around. That was the first wind or movement of air he had felt in this land of rain. What caused it? He could see nothing in the dull Gray but drooping plants, rain, and splattered water. Where was Bubo? He had been gone well before they started on this road.

Thalmus shivered.

He was soaked through to the skin. Looking for Tobazi and Boschina, he saw that they had not stopped and now were almost gone in the mist. Thalmus hurried to close the gap and noticed something off to their left—a small building.

Perhaps an old way station or guard post, it blended in with the trees and brush—and was almost unnoticeable. Thalmus caught up with Boschina and Tobazi and pointed at the building.

"I saw it," Tobazi said. "But there's no sense in stopping. If there's anybody in it, they've seen us by now."

"It looks empty to me," Boschina said. "I don't see any troops."

They turned to continue and saw on the road ahead something very large and long and slimy slither across the stones and into the water on the other side.

"Mud worm," Boschina exclaimed.

Tobazi hesitated. "You think they travel in pairs?"

"I hope not," Thalmus replied.

They waited, watching the road and the water around it. When another mud worm did not appear, Thalmus said: "Let's hurry through here."

Trying to run, they moved as quickly as they could, splashing and sliding along the slippery road—the whole time ready for the creature to appear at any moment. It did not, nor did any others. They slowed to a walk again and Boschina jumped off Thunder and walked with Tobazi.

Farther on, the road was not as overgrown and the rain was half of what it had been. Boschina's spirits were picking up as she realized they were getting closer to the Dry. Then, Thalmus saw what he feared most—the Knight's cloud—as it appeared to the right and moved quickly across to block their path. A breeze came with it and stopped when it did. With less rain and a lighter Gray, the Shower Knight's cloud was easy to see.

Thalmus moved past Boschina and joined Tobazi. As they approached the cloud, it suddenly released a torrent of rain that would have drowned them had they been under it. The deluge stopped when Thalmus and Tobazi stopped. Then, there was silence—except for the constant splatter of the rain. Tobazi was stunned by the power of the cloud.

He looked at Thalmus. "How do we get by this?"

Thalmus did not answer. He was looking up at the ominous cloud and deciding on a course of action. The moment he had been thinking about—the confrontation he had been dreading—was here. He could not fight this thing, but maybe he could outthink it.

"Great Shower Knight," Thalmus called. "Defender of your lord's realm, cleanser of evil, all-powerful force of rain, we wish your protection and safe passage to the Dry."

No sound or movement came from the cloud.

"That's not going to work," Tobazi said, raising his sword.

Thalmus touched Tobazi's arm, calming him and lowering the sword. Then, he spoke to the Shower Knight again. "We are not evil and are not a threat to Lord Luminous and his people. We wish merely to leave peacefully. Will you let us pass?"

"You will stay," the watery voice thundered from the cloud. "You have killed."

"In defense," Thalmus replied, "just as you have. I know that you are fair and just. We fought because Lord Luminous forced us to. We came in peace. We wanted to leave in peace."

"Corsair said you killed first, so I will hold you until he comes."

"Oh, I am surprised to hear that you take orders from Corsair," Thalmus said.

"I take orders from no one but Lord Luminous," the Shower Knight replied indignantly.

"But is not Corsair the real power in this land? Does he not control your lord and therefore you?"

"No one controls me," the Knight thundered and his image appeared in the cloud, angry and threatening, and a short burst of rain emitted from the cloud.

Thalmus shrugged. "So you say. In the castle, I heard Corsair speak that you wait on his command."

The Shower Knight roared with laughter and more rain fell. "You will wait, Frog Man," he said, his image drifting about in the cloud. "Corsair will take you back to the castle and Lord Luminous will punish all of you."

Thalmus saw a brown blur emerging out of the mist beyond the Shower Knight's cloud. It was Bubo, dropping out of the gray sky, diving silently toward the Shower Knight. His feather horns were straight up and his yellow eyes glared like Thalmus had never seen them before. Bubo's black claws swung forward and stretched out in front of him for the attack as he disappeared into the cloud.

A horrible scream erupted from the Shower Knight and the cloud immediately thundered and rained. The obscure image of the Knight disappeared, and then reappeared as he tumbled about in his shrouded sphere—fighting an attacker he had never dealt with before. It was an attacker, who for the first time, had penetrated his private world and was clawing him from within.

They watched in disbelief as the unseen battle continued to rage. The cloud shook and roiled like a thunder storm. It churned back and forth across the path—until, finally, rolling away into the Gray in a great turmoil of combat.

"Quickly," Thalmus shouted. "The troops could be here any moment."

And they began running again, splashing and slipping along until

Tobazi, exhausted, dropped to his knees. "Go on," he urged, gasping for air. "Don't stop."

Out of breath themselves, Thalmus and Boschina stopped to rest and to let Thunder catch up.

"We can't leave you here," Boschina said, coming back to Tobazi.

"You must. I won't make it."

"We all go or none of us," Thalmus told him.

"Look how light the rain is," Boschina said. "We're almost out."

Thunder trudged up and touched Tobazi with his snout.

"You are coming with us," Thalmus said and knelt to lift him.

Boschina and Thalmus helped Tobazi to his feet and then onto Thunder's broad shell. Boschina and Thunder started again, this time at a walk. Thalmus looked back for Owl, but there was no sign of him or the Shower Knight.

"Thank you, Bubo," Thalmus said softly—and then turned and caught up with the others.

They were still following the paved trail. The rain had turned to mist and the water to mud when the first Boogala appeared. It came from the southeast; its powerful legs and web feet pounding across the muck, pulling a sled full of troops. It was coming on quickly and Thalmus could see that the driver intended to pass nearby and get in front of them.

Thunder also realized this.

The sled driver though was not aware of how quickly the giant tortoise could move. As the trooper drove the sled in close to cut them off, Thunder, with Tobazi riding on his back, charged out in front of the Boogala. The startled animal reared up and jumped to the side, flipping the sled and throwing the troopers into the mud.

Tobazi slid off Thunder's shell and pounced on the dazed men with Thalmus—knocking their swords away and making them submit as Thunder glowered over them. Boschina calmed the Boogala and held it steady while Thalmus cut it loose from its harness and then chased it away, back into Rainland. The defenseless soldiers cowered before Thunder and Tobazi.

"We do not want to hurt you," Thalmus told them. "We never intended to hurt any of your people. We only fought to free ourselves. Lord Luminous and Corsair tried to imprison us as he did Tobazi. Now, go back to your families and tell them that."

The men hesitated before cautiously standing up, for they had been told that these strangers and their creatures were killers and not to be trusted.

"Go on," Tobazi said. "We'll not hurt you."

Surprised and still unsure, Corsair's men slowly began walking back into Rainland—turning around to watch as Tobazi climbed onto the shell creature and the strangers hurried on toward the Dry.

The sky was almost clear; hills could be seen in the distance and there was just dampness in the air when the second and third Boogalas appeared. These two exhausted animals were pulling sleds full of troops and Thalmus knew that this time Corsair would be among them.

Thalmus looked ahead at the hills that appeared so close—yet were just out of reach beyond a veiled curtain. After days in the smothering Gray, it was comforting to be able to see at least some distance. But, they weren't there yet. Now it looked like they would never get out of this unbelievable place called Rainland.

Still walking, he turned to face the new challenge.

Out in the open, outnumbered ten to one, Thunder would be easily flanked; Boschina, try as she may, could not fight against so many; Tobazi's strength would not last long—and Bubo was gone. On the surface, their chances looked bleak. Surrender did not offer any possibilities either.

At least the rain was no longer a factor.

Thalmus looked at Boschina. She appeared ragged and tired; her hair was wet, flat, and stuck to her checks. Determination carved her face as she confidently held her sword and walked backwards while she watched the approaching troops. He smiled at her courage. *It is for her that we are here; her and truth and a story yet to be lived.*

The Boogalas split apart, one going to each side of them. This time though, they kept their distance. Thalmus, Boschina, and Thunder kept walking toward the hills until the troops unloaded from the sleds and encircled them. Tobazi slid off Thunder's shell and stood next to him. He was ready to give all he had in one last fight. Boschina stood defiantly beside Thunder's head, with her sword in one hand and the short blade in the other. No one would seriously challenge her straight on while she stood next to Thunder's snapping jaws. Thalmus, his weapons still hanging at his side, folded his arms and leaned against Thunder's giant shell on the opposite side of Tobazi.

The ring of troops kept a safe twenty meters of distance all around them. Thalmus contemplated a straight ahead thundering charge. They could probably break through the circle, but would not get very far. There were too many troopers, and they could not outrun them.

He would have to use a different strategy.

Corsair stepped into the ring of his soldiers. He tapped his leg with the broad side of his sword as he searched the sky. Then, he looked at Thalmus leaning casually on Thunder.

"Where's the owl?" Corsair asked.

"Where is the Shower Knight?" Thalmus replied.

This answer puzzled Corsair.

He looked around again for Owl.

"Call the bird in," Corsair demanded, "and you might live."

"Call the Shower Knight in, and you might live," Thalmus answered.

What did he mean by that? Corsair wondered. He had underestimated this man twice before. He did not want a third surprise. Corsair searched the area again. Where was the Shower Knight? They were probably beyond his range. Still, he had not seen the Knight's cloud since it told Corsair where to find Thalmus. How did they get past the all-powerful cloud? And where was the owl? Was his magic that strong? No. It couldn't be. *He must be trying to fool me again*, Corsair told himself.

He smiled at Thalmus. "You're very clever, little man. But you're out of tricks. I have you now." He pointed at Tobazi with his sword. "This one will die." Then, Corsair aimed the blade at Thalmus. "And you will suffer. You will submit."

"Come and get me, then, big man," Thalmus said calmly and pointed at Corsair. "You, alone, against me. Nobody else fights. This way, none of your people will get hurt. And, you can prove to them what a great and powerful swordsman you are."

Corsair was very confident in his swordsmanship. He would have liked nothing better than to humiliate Thalmus in a one-on-one duel, but this surprising man was unnerving him. There was a reason this frog hunter had lived so long and enjoyed such a big reputation. Corsair was realizing that now. He could bully his own troops, his own people, but this man was different. It was one thing to chase him; it was another to face him.

The circle of troops waited and watched their commander. Thalmus sensed that they were not eager for a fight. Tobazi turned his sword down and leaned against it as if he was tired of waiting. Boschina watched Thalmus; she could not relax knowing that at any moment the troops could charge.

"We do not want to hurt any more of your people," Thalmus said. "Let us go or come out and fight me by yourself."

Corsair could not delay any longer. He realized that his hesitation showed weakness; still, he would not fight this hunter alone. He laughed to cover his fear. "I'd like to fight you, Thalmus. But, I'm done playing with you. And we must get you back before the Dark. Lord Luminous is expecting you." Corsair gave a command to his men, and they started moving forward.

"Here we go," Tobazi said and moved closer to Boschina. "I'll protect you."

"Watch your left," Boschina said. "I'll guard Thunder's neck."

Thalmus drew one of his swords. "So, you are going to hide behind your troops again, Corsair?"

"I want him alive," Corsair shouted as he stepped behind his troops. "Attack them."

The Rainers started running forward and Thalmus drew his second sword. Then, he heard a pounding, a thunder coming from beyond the attacking troops. He looked past the rushing Rainers and saw soldiers on horseback galloping down from the hills.

As Corsair's ring of charging troops closed in on the four defenders, Tobazi screamed a battle cry so loud and frightening that it startled even Thalmus. He caught a brief glimpse of Tobazi striking out with flashing steel and heard the thump as it hit its mark. Then, came the clanging of metal on metal as swords struck one another, the clap of Thunder's jaws snapping, and then Thalmus clashed swords with two troopers in front of him. Three more attackers came up on his right. He saw Corsair coming in behind them and knew that he and his friends would not last long against these numbers.

At that moment, the soldiers on horseback galloped into the Rainers, knocking some down and slashing others with sabers.

Totally surprised, the Rainers turned and battled the mounted troops. Now, the Rainers found themselves surrounded and in the odd position of fighting and defending their prey at the same time. The mounted soldiers had pushed into the troops around Tobazi and Boschina, which forced most of the Rainers to turn and defend themselves. That relief on Tobazi was just in time, for he was fading quickly. Two of the troopers attacking Thalmus left with Corsair to help their comrades fight the horse soldiers, leaving two men on Thalmus

All three groups fought tenaciously until the mounted soldiers finally wedged between the Rainers and Tobazi, forcing the tired men from Rainland to retreat. An angry Captain Corsair looked about him and realized that they had lost the fight—and that Thalmus would get away; even worse, they were now in danger of being captured outside of Rainland.

"To the sleds," he screamed at his men. "Back to the sleds."

The Rainers hurried to the sleds, trying to help their wounded as they went. Corsair was not done though. He slashed and dropped two more of the horsemen before jumping aboard a sled as it came by to pick him up. The drivers swung the Boogalas around and they headed back into the Wet.

Thalmus watched them fade into the Gray and heard Corsair's distant voice clearly over the slapping feet of the Boogalas. "I'll get you, Thalmus."

Boschina was exhilarated. Once again, she had not seriously hurt anyone yet had managed to defend herself and Thunder's neck. She had done well and was proud. The engraved sword, still charged from combat, vibrated in her hand. Full of excitement, she turned to Tobazi. However, he could not share her enthusiasm. He was slumped against Thunder's shell.

"Tobazi!" She sheathed her swords and checked him for wounds.

"I'm so tired," he whispered. "My strength is gone."

"How is he?" Thalmus asked.

"I don't see any new wounds," Boschina answered. "He's just exhausted."

"I'm fought out," Tobazi managed to say and dropped to his knees, leaning on his sword that he had stuck in the ground before him.

Thalmus surveyed the field around them. Weapons and bloody uniformed bodies of both sides were strewn about and wounded men rolled and groaned and cried in pain. Riderless horses roamed restlessly while victorious soldiers inspected the bodies of the fallen. It was the aftermath of combat: a grotesque scene that always looked and sounded and smelled the same. Thalmus had seen it too often in years past. Each time he had hoped it would be the last, while knowing that it would not. He knelt to comfort a wounded Rainer who was lying on his back and crying for help.

The man was bleeding from cuts in the legs, chest, and neck. He grabbed Thalmus' arm as if it were a rope to a life raft. Placing his palm on the man's forehead Thalmus calmed him, telling him softly that he was not alone. The man quieted, breathed slowly, looked into Thalmus' eyes, and spoke a woman's name. Thalmus smiled at the dying man as his eyes closed.

The four tired travelers were relieved to be safe, to be alive, and, most of all, to be free of Rainland. But now, they had a new concern, as they looked uneasily at their rescuers; these soldiers were wearing the maroon and gray uniforms of King Ahmbin.

Chapter Twelve
A Second Escape

The captain of the king's soldiers waved his sword in the air at the retreating Rainers and screamed victoriously. His men joined in the shouting as their captain trotted his wild-eyed, sweating horse in front of Tobazi and Boschina. Sheathing his sword, he reined the horse to a stop, and dismounted. He paused, looked at them in a curious way, and then suddenly pushed Boschina aside and yanked the sword from under Tobazi—causing him to sprawl on the ground. In an instant, Thalmus left the dying Rainer, leapt onto Thunder's shell, and pounced on the captain— knocking him down and away from Tobazi. Nearby soldiers quickly drew their swords and ran to their captain's defense. But, they backed away from Thalmus when Thunder turned and hissed at them.

Now, Thalmus stood between Tobazi and the soldiers, and Thunder stood over the prone Tobazi, straddling him with his front legs. The tortoise's hairless ancient head protruded over the wounded man and was ready to snap at whoever might be foolish enough to attempt to grab him.

Boschina took up her position next to Thunder.

The captain scrambled to his feet. His skin was naturally red and covered with freckles. His nose was flat and wide and looked like an open sore above his beard. Long brown hair protruded from under his silver helmet. His green eyes flared. He started to draw his sword, but looking at Thalmus, he changed his mind and let go of it.

"I've got no quarrel with you, Thalmus," the captain growled. "But this man," he pointed at Tobazi, "is my prisoner."

"He is not your prisoner," Thalmus said calmly. "He is my friend."

"Friend or not, he's now ours and we," the captain waved his arms to include all the soldiers, "will collect the reward for him"

The soldiers supported their captain.

"That's right, he's ours. The reward's ours."

Thalmus was surprised. "There is a price for him?"

"Of course, why do you think we're here? We've been riding around this mud hole lookin' for you. You're lucky we found you when we did or those muck heads would've killed you and got the reward."

"You say there is a reward?" Thalmus asked. "Who do you think this man is?"

"He's the stone cutter who insulted the king."

"You are mistaken," Thalmus replied. "His name is Tobazi. He comes from Toubar."

The captain laughed. "You can't fool me, Thalmus. This girl here is his daughter."

"He is not my father," Boschina said. "But he is a friend and I will fight to defend him." She grasped her sword, angry at the captain who had shoved her and knocked Tobazi down.

"I don't believe them," a soldier yelled.

"She's tryin' to protect him," another said.

"It is true that we entered Rainland to find Vericitas," Thalmus explained. "But he was not there. Lord Luminous meant to hold us captive. Tobazi helped us fight our way out, until you arrived."

The captain was unsure now. He looked at Tobazi carefully. "I never saw the stone cutter." He looked around at his men. "Any of you seen the stone cutter at the castle?"

The men were silent and shook their heads to indicate "no." The captain pointed again at Tobazi.

"If this isn't the stone cutter, then where is he?"

"I do not know, Captain," Thalmus answered. "His whereabouts should not matter. Have you not heard that the king has pardoned Vericitas and withdrawn the reward?"

"Don't believe him, captain," a soldier yelled. "He's a hunter."

"Yeah, the best," another one said. "And he's bagged his prey."

"This is not Vericitas," Thalmus said firmly. "Even if he were, you should no longer be hunting him."

The captain paused, unsure as what to do. Thalmus was known to be a straight-talking, honest man who was in the king's favor. Still, there was a lot of money in the reward, enough to make them all comfortable. *Would that change the Frog Hunter?* the captain wondered. *Would that make him dishonest?*

"Let's take him back to the king and find out," another soldier hollered.

"A waste of time," Thalmus replied. "I am telling you the truth, Captain."

"Better to be sure than to be tricked," the soldier persisted.

The captain hesitated. He looked around for the owl and the Paint stallion. It was just the shell creature, Thalmus, and this girl. Still, it would not be easy to take the man from Thunder and the frog hunter.

"This is our chance, Captain," the soldier said. "We take him now, get the reward, and never again have to grovel or serve a master."

The others agreed. "That's right. Let's take him."

The captain made up his mind. He decided to take the risk and side with his men. There was too much at stake and he did not want to be fooled. He grasped the handle of his sword and pulled it from the sheath. "Give him up, Thalmus, or we'll take him."

Thalmus slowly shook his head. "You are making a mistake, Captain," he said. Thalmus stepped back to stand on the left side of Thunder's head and the prostrate Tobazi, while Boschina stood on the right. Thunder clicked his jaws and started hissing. The soldiers took this as preparation to fight, and they began spreading out to encircle them. However, Thalmus knew that Thunder felt something approaching from beyond the hills. He could only hope that it was not more troops. As the soldiers began to close in on them, the distant sound of galloping hooves entered their ears—becoming louder and nearer as they all turned to see Dallion appear over the crest of the hill and race toward them.

"It's Dallion," the soldiers shouted and ran in panic to grab their horses for they knew what could happen. Unfortunately for the men, their steeds had wandered a little too far from them and Dallion was too fast. The powerful Paint stallion blew into the field like a wind lifting leaves before it. All the horses were swept up by Dallion's energy of freedom and bolted away from their masters to join him in an exuberant stampede of joy. They ran with their heads high, their manes dancing as their spirits soared and they raced together, following Dallion around the field and up the hill toward freedom.

The frustrated soldiers could do nothing to stop them. All their yelling and commanding of the horses to come back had no effect.

Helpless, they stood—scattered across the field like discarded souls—
—and watched their horses gallop over the hill with Dallion.

The captain was furious.

"Make him bring our horses back," he yelled at Thalmus.

"I cannot do that," Thalmus answered.

"You must!"

Again, Thalmus slowly shook his head.

"Dallion is controlled by no one."

Two riders now appeared heading toward them from the hills
where the horses had vanished. The captain recognized them and
cursed. It was the king's soldiers, Currad and Dysaan.

King Ahmbin did not have designated knights. Though there were
a few men, like these two, who because of their loyalty were given
special rank and privilege. There was no law, written or spoken, as to
their authority over other soldiers or what rank they held. Their
power derived simply from the king's vocal praise and respect of
their independence, their fighting ability, and their continuous
support of him.

Currad and Dysaan surveyed the battle scene and the soldiers
confronting Thalmus and his friends as they rode through the field
and reigned in their horses. They stayed mounted in front of
Thalmus and the captain.

"This man's ours, Dysaan," the captain was quick to say. "I've
claimed him."

Dysaan ignored the captain. "Thalmus," he said, acknowledging
the frog hunter. He looked at Boschina standing with her sword next
to Thunder and nodded. "Stone Daughter." Dysaan glanced at
Tobazi lying under the protection of the giant tortoise, and then at
Thalmus again. "It's good to see you made it out of Rainland."

"We are glad to be free of it," Thalmus replied. "And also glad to
see the both of you."

"So I see," Dysaan said, eyeing the frustrated soldiers surrounding
them.

"I want to hear your story of this place, Thalmus," Currad said
and then turned to the captain. "But first, Captain, I want to know
who it is you claim? Certainly, it's not the King's Frog Hunter?"

"No, not Thalmus," the captain said and pointed with his sword
at Tobazi. "The stone cutter: I, we, claim him for the reward."

Dysaan laughed. "I can see from here the man's skin clearly shows he's from Toubar, not Marbala, where they cut the rock."

"You'll get nothing for this man," Currad said. "Nor will you get anything for the stone cutter, if you find him. King Ahmbin has withdrawn the reward and given his life to Thalmus."

"They're tryin' to trick us, Captain," a soldier said.

Currad turned in his saddle and stared at the soldier.

"Do you wish to challenge me?"

The man glanced at his comrades for support but got none, so remained silent.

"You made a wise choice," Dysaan told the man.

Currad turned back to Thalmus.

"Will Thunder move so we can get a better look at this man?"

Thalmus nodded and patted Thunder's head. The giant tortoise carefully stepped back. Thalmus knelt beside Tobazi and lifted his head and shoulders and rested him against his leg. The exhausted, wounded Tobazi was almost unconscious.

Currad looked at Tobazi. "Dysaan's right. I know the sculptor, Vericitas, from seeing him at the castle. That's not him. I suggest you give up your search, Captain, and return to the castle. Besides, it's not safe here. The Rainers could return with more troops."

The captain pointed his sword at Currad. "If you're lying...."

He stopped, seeing Currad's glare and decided not to finish his threat. He looked at Tobazi, then back at Dysaan and Currad. "We fought hard to save them from the Rainers. Some have died. We deserve something."

"You did save us," Thalmus replied. "We are grateful to you, but beyond that I can give you nothing."

"You've done the king a great service by saving his frog hunter," Currad said. Then, offering the captain some hope, added: "Perhaps the king will reward you."

The captain knew he was beat. He looked again at Tobazi. "You can have him. We'll find Vericitas, wherever he is." He motioned to his men, and they began to collect their things and move off to tend their wounded and dead.

Currad and Dysaan watched the soldiers until there was some distance between them, and then they dismounted.

"Thank you," Thalmus said.

"I also thank you," Boschina said.

The two grizzled soldiers looked at her standing in the frog-skin coat with a sword in each hand and saw a different person than the one they had known before. They both nodded respectfully to her.

"When we heard you were going to Rainland, we thought you might need our help," Dysaan said.

"Did Dallion guide you to us?" Thalmus asked.

Currad nodded. "Dallion found us yesterday morning and we've been following him since."

"We knew soldiers were looking for you," Dysaan added. "That was one worry. The other was if you'd get out of there." He motioned toward the gray mist of Rainland.

"We would still be there, but for this man," Thalmus said, still holding Tobazi. "He is a fighter, a good one."

Tobazi was barely conscious, but aware of the two soldiers. In between slow breaths, he asked, "Who are they?" nodding at Dysaan and Currad.

"These are friends," Thalmus said to Tobazi. "They will help us."

"We must get away from here," Tobazi whispered, struggling to stand up. "We must get away from Corsair."

Thalmus, though smaller than Tobazi, carefully lifted him and laid him on Thunder's back. Then, they started out of the field toward the hills. Dysaan and Currad walked along with Thalmus, leading their horses. Boschina had removed the frog-skin coat and put it over Tobazi to keep him warm.

As they made it over the hill away from the king's troops, away from the gray mist and into the bright sun, Thalmus and Boschina told the soldiers of their journey into Rainland: about mud worms and Boogalas; about Lord Luminous and Corsair; the mysterious Tobazi; the sad, lonely, people; about Oddkin, Tuggle, the farmers, and, of course, the Shower Knight and Owl's sacrifice. The two experienced soldiers had never been into Rainland and were now sure they never wanted to go. They also knew what a great loss Bubo was to Thalmus. They saw his sadness like a blanket that enveloped him and dragged on the ground behind his feet as he walked.

Dallion appeared on the crest of a hill ahead of them.

He was alone. The other horses were nowhere in sight.

The magnificent stallion stood, watching them from a distance. Thalmus waved to him, and he began running in a large circle around them. Dysaan and Currad hung onto their horses so they would not follow him. Dallion finally slowed to their pace and walked to his friend. The big Paint nuzzled Thalmus' shoulder and Thalmus stroked his neck and patted him.

"Thank you, my friend," Thalmus said to him. "Thank you."

Dallion blew through his lips, vibrating them, making that sound horses do when they are happy or satisfied. Then, he rubbed Boschina's shoulder with his long nose and she hugged him. He touched Thunder's head with his nose, and Thunder clicked and bobbed his head. Dallion stretched his neck over Thunder's shell and sniffed Tobazi.

He looked at Thalmus and stomped his hoof.

"Yes, Dal. Our new friend is in pain."

It was getting late in the day. Thalmus knew that the Rainers would not come out in the dark. He really didn't expect them to follow at all. Corsair was wise enough to know that he and his troops would be out of their element. And the king's captain and his soldiers would not dare come near while they were with Currad and Dysaan. Thalmus suddenly felt very weary. The comforting presence of these two burly allies was allowing his senses to relax. He was hungry and knew that Boschina must be as well. Despite looking worn out, Boschina was still walking, not complaining, and holding her own. Thalmus watched her and smiled to himself. She was getting stronger each day. Poor Tobazi, however, was fading fast. He needed food and rest more than they. It was time to stop. Rainland was far enough away now. So, Thalmus called a halt to camp for the night. Currad cooked food from their supplies, while Thalmus and Boschina cleaned and replaced Tobazi's bandages. After a filling meal, the exhausted travelers found comfortable places in the soft grass to sleep.

Boschina and Thalmus lay on their backs for a while, looking up at the stars and the vastness of the sky, trying to forget the utter darkness of Rainland.

"It's so good to see the night sky lights again," Boschina said. "In that short time, I'd forgotten how beautiful they are."

"It makes one realize how truly small we are," Thalmus said.

She soon was asleep, but Thalmus lay awake wondering why the king's troops were still looking for Vericitas. If they knew of their journey to Rainland, why did they not know of the pardon? Was this more of Metro's devious game? Vericitas had better remain hidden, for he was still in danger. Then, Thalmus thought of Oddkin and Tuggle in their troubled world, and of Corsair's viciousness. And finally Thalmus thought of Bubo, the image he had been avoiding, the last image of Owl diving out of the grayness and disappearing into the Shower Knight's cloud. Once again, and for the last time, Bubo had saved his life.

What a friend. What love. What a loss.

Thalmus closed his eyes as tears welled up. He clenched his jaw against sobbing. Slowly, silently, he controlled his grief and finally faded into unconsciousness.

Dysaan and Currad took turns on watch during the night while the three travelers slept. It took two days of rest for Boschina and Thalmus to feel recovered. Tobazi would take much longer, but he was improving.

On the afternoon of the third day, Thalmus began to feel something rising, some source of energy gaining strength and growing in presence. His senses were alert. At first, he wasn't sure if it was a force originating from within himself or an external influence. Whatever it was, it felt good.

He checked Thunder and Dallion. They were feeling it, too. By evening the sensation had become more powerful, turning his mood to one of happiness. He knew that it was coming from a distance away, yet was approaching rapidly.

After eating, they bedded down and all fell into a deep sleep— except for Thalmus. The anticipation of what was coming made him restless, anxious, and uncomfortable. He watched and listened for a long time. Finally, he shut his eyes and settled into a restless sleep. Then, sometime during the night, he suddenly awoke. Not from any noise, for there had been none, but from a strong feeling of a presence.

Someone or something was amongst them.

He sat up and looked about. There was a slight breeze blowing from the west. Dysaan, who was on watch, was sitting downwind amongst some brush at the edge of their campsite. Boschina, Tobazi, and Currad were asleep. The horses were calm, though Dallion's head was up, checking the air. Thunder was withdrawn, tucked into his shell, and appeared to be sleeping—but then he clicked softly, just once. Thalmus turned and saw floating in the dark—above Thunder's shell—two large, yellow, glowing eyes staring at him.

Thalmus smiled, and then laid back and slept soundly.

Chapter Thirteen
The Barranca

In the morning, the eyes were gone, and there was no sign of the creature to which they belonged. Thalmus said nothing to anyone about the visitor; though, he did exchange nods with Thunder when he noticed the tortoise watching him cook the morning meal over the fire. The sky was clear with no rain in sight. A gentle breeze from the north brought a chill in the air.

They sat around the fire, eating and talking about Tobazi's condition and where to go next in the search for Vericitas. Hoping to find clues to his whereabouts, Boschina tried to recall the image of her father that Metro had produced with the silver powder in the circling wind at the castle. But, she could only remember feeling the dampness and seeing the water all around him and no sign of a place.

"Perhaps, it is not rain afterall," Thalmus suggested, "maybe a waterfall?"

Boschina perked up. "Yes, it could easily be a fall. As I think on it now, the water in the vision was heavier, more solid than rain. Where would we find such a fall?"

"There're many falls at the Table," Dysaan said.

"Do you mean Table Top?" Thalmus asked.

"Yes, Table Mountain. Some know it as Table Top; others just call it the Table. There must be four or five streams that flow across the top and drop off the edge."

Currad was sitting on a boulder, casually etching figures in the dirt with a stick. "Table Top would be a likely place for Veracitas to hide," he said. Looking up, he pointed the stick at Boschina. "It would be a dangerous place for you."

"I've heard it's bad," Boschina said.

"Your father knows of it?" Thalmus asked.

"Yes, he wanted to go there once to try to carve the cliffs, but friends convinced him that it was not safe for us."

"Even I've heard of Table Top," Tobazi said from his bed. "Some of the prisoners Corsair killed had been there and told me of it. It's a fortress, a keep safe from soldiers—and a place of no law."

Currad scratched out his dirt drawing with the stick. "Tobazi's right. The people there are only united in one cause and that's control of the two narrow paths that wind through the rock to the top. Otherwise, they're lawless; the strongest rule."

"It's an island," Dysaan said, "an island that's like a prison. That's how the king views it. Why waste troops trying to control it when the undesirables go there willingly and stay there, for fear of capture."

Currad laughed. "The king sends troops occasionally to make a showing around the base just to keep the people on the Top. We haven't tried to attack for many years."

"It sounds like a place that my father would've gone to hide."

"And a place where he would not hear of the pardon," Thalmus added.

"If you go there, we cannot go with you," Dysaan said, "for we're known by the people there. If they see you with us, they might kill you as spies."

Tobazi sat up slowly. "I'll go with you."

Thalmus looked at him and smiled. "Your spirit is strong, my good friend, and I am glad of it. But you are too weak. We must return you to your people, so that your body will grow strong again like your heart."

"Thalmus," Boschina said. "I think we must look for my father at this Table Top."

"I agree, Boschina. I will go alone with Thunder and Dallion."

"Without me?"

"It is too dangerous for you."

Boschina did not like that answer. She turned to watch the dying fire. They sat for a while in silence. The wind was picking up enough now to lift dust into the air. Thalmus was calm, relaxed, and waiting for the response he knew would come from Boschina. Dysaan and Currad felt guilty that they could not help him at Table Top. Tobazi was frustrated with his condition—that his wounds made him unable to support his new friend. Boschina struggled with the thought of staying behind and the fear of going with Thalmus.

Finally, staring into the fire, she spoke. "Thalmus, you told me this journey was mine...that I had to be strong. If I'm to be strong, I can't let you do this for me. I must go there." She looked up at Thalmus. "Besides, it couldn't be worse than Rainland."

Currad and Dysaan glanced at one another and nodded their approval. Thalmus smiled at her courage. This was the response he had hoped for. The danger in Rainland was unexpected and their escape the result of help, timing, and circumstances.

She had stood up through it all.

Table Top was another matter. It was a known place of desperate, violent, people. Still, he could not deny her the right to continue searching for her father. The fulfillment of the prophecy depended on it.

"Well," Thalmus said, looking at her. "At least we won't have to worry about mud worms."

Boschina grinned at this acceptance. "Or that wicked Corsair," she said.

"No," Thalmus replied. "Though the king's troops following us worry me a bit."

Currad stood up and dropped his stick into the fire. "We know of a buried trail where they'll not be able to follow us."

"A buried trail?" Boschina said, curious.

"You speak of the Barranca?" Dysaan asked, a little surprised.

"Yes, what do you think?" Currad said to Dysaan. "It's a way to escape the troops and travel unseen across the Great Plain. And it comes up close to Table Top."

"I don't know," Dysaan replied. "It's been years since we've used it."

"Yes, but it should still be passable."

"What is it?" Boschina asked.

"It's a narrow, deep gorge with a stream in the bottom that cuts across the plain. It's not visible from anywhere until you walk right up to it," Currad said. "Yet, it's too wide to cross by any means. You gotta ride for days to get around it."

"The beauty of the Barranca," Dysaan said, "is that there are only a few trails in or out of it, making it impossible for anyone to follow you. The danger is that once you're in, you're confined and must travel to the other end to get out. If the troops know of the Barranca, and see us go down in it, they can just wait at the other end for us."

Boschina noticed Thalmus' silence.

"What do you think, Thalmus?"

Thalmus had been listening and remembering.

"It is a world all its own," he said, cautiously.

"You know of it then?" Boschina asked.

"Yes," Thalmus replied. "It is an ancient trail. Few people even know of it."

"So, we can get closer to Table Top without the troops following us?" Boschina asked.

"I doubt the troops have knowledge of it," Currad said. "If we use it, we'll suddenly drop from sight. The troops will think that the earth swallowed us."

"Then what are we waiting for?" Tobazi said.

They all looked at him with surprise.

"Why do you look at me so?" Tobazi asked. "Boschina needs to find her father before those troops do. I'm ready to move."

"I thank you, Tobazi," Boschina replied with concern. "But we must get you home first."

"Nonsense. You cannot take that much time."

Currad rolled a small rock into the fire with the side of his boot.

"We cannot go with you up on the Table," he said. "But, we can get Tobazi home. Right, Dysaan?"

Dysaan nodded in agreement. "Don't worry, Boschina. We'll get him home safe and well."

"There, you see," Tobazi said, motioning with both of his hands at the two soldiers. "I'm in good hands. You can continue your search."

"You saved us in Rainland," Thalmus said. "And we promised to take you home."

"Nonsense, I say." Tobazi waved his hand, as if brushing something away. "You have a more important task."

"Dysaan and I will travel the Barranca with you as far as Table Top," Currad said. "Then we'll take Tobazi home."

Tobazi clasped his hands as if the decision was made.

"I like that plan."

Thalmus smiled at the three men. "You are good friends."

Traveling through the Barranca was not Thalmus' first choice, for he knew the canyon was ever changing and held mysterious forces that were unpredictable and could challenge any man. Yet, their options were minimal and the destiny of this journey seemed to be pushing them into its fold. Despite his concerns, he realized that they would have to pass through this place to continue the search, to succeed in their mission.

It would be another test.

Thalmus looked at his four companions who were waiting to hear his answer. "It appears that our path to Table Top is determined," he said. "So, I agree with your plan."

"I agree too," Boschina said quickly. "And I thank you, all three of you." she added

The men were a little surprised by this, yet nodded with gratitude for her appreciation. With that decision made, they broke camp and packed up—putting Tobazi on Thunder—and started west toward Table Top. Currad, Dysaan, and Dallion took turns scouting. At the end of the first day, Dysaan spotted several troops following them. The troops veered away to the east though when they saw Dysaan.

Late in the morning of the third day, they came to the Barranca—a deep, sudden, unannounced cut in the docile terrain. The steep sided arroyo was about twenty meters wide and twice as deep and meandered almost unseen through the rolling landscape. It was impassable. They turned and traveled northwest along its edge for a short distance until they came to a crack in the earth that broke down into the Barranca.

Dallion circled the area, galloping far out, in search of anyone who might be watching—while the others, in single file, entered the narrow fissure and descended slowly into the earth. Dysaan trailed behind, brushing out their tracks with a branch, so no one would know to follow them. Tobazi rode on Currad's horse because it was a tight fit for Thunder, who had to tilt sideways and climb the bank of one side to squeeze through the passage. Down they went, following the jagged turns of the rift as the steep banks rose high above them and the fissure slowly widened. The sides and ground of the trail were carved out of sandstone, eroded from years of storm water racing through the fissure to the canyon below. The path was littered with gravel that rolled under their feet. Sliding down the trail, they rounded a final bend where the passage abruptly ended and dropped off into the bottom of the Barranca.

They stood at the edge of a cliff and looked across at the other side of the canyon. The top was a good twenty-five meters above them. Below them, the drainage from the fissure had deposited a steep bank of sand and gravel. The bottom of the Barranca was green with trees and brush and a stream that sparkled in the sun.

Boschina looked over the edge.

"Now what?" she asked, looking at Thalmus.

Thalmus smiled at her. To her surprise, he leapt off the precipice and plunged knee deep into the loose sand along the side and slid to the bottom. Currad and Dysaan watched Thalmus' safe trip. They looked at one another and shrugged. Helping Tobazi off the horse, they let their horses slip and lurch down the bank separately, while they jumped off with Tobazi between them and slid on their backs all the way down.

Boschina hesitated.

Thunder looked down at Thalmus, clicked his jaws once and stepped out. Boschina seized the moment, jumping on Thunder's shell just as he tipped over the edge, and hung on as he turned like a saucer spinning to the bottom. He came to a sudden stop and Boschina tumbled off into the sand, laughing uncontrollably. The men, who had watched her anxiously, broke into laughter, too.

Thunder regained his feet and plodded over to check on her.

"Thunder, that was fun," she said, still laughing.

The giant tortoise sniffed her and looked at Thalmus, who was laughing. He opened his mouth and appeared to smile, grunted, trudged over to the creek, and settled into the water.

Dallion appeared at the cliff in the fissure above them.

He snorted as he looked around.

Thalmus waved to him. "Come on, Dal."

The Paint stallion shook his mane, bent his head, eyed the slope, calculated the distance, snorted, stomped a hoof, and then jumped off and pranced across the steep bank as he slid down. He reached the bottom, trotted over to Thalmus, and nuzzled into his head and shoulder. Thalmus stroked his nose and patted his neck.

Currad and Dysaan checked the gear and helped Tobazi sit on Dysaan's horse. Dallion led off and they headed up the Barranca, picking their way through brush and around boulders. Sometimes, they had to draw their swords and cut their way through the tangled foliage. Often, the only clear path was in the water straight up the creek; rarely did the water get above their knees or the current too strong, but there were occasional deep pools that required swimming. Thunder enjoyed those pools, as did Boschina, who rode on his back.

Tobazi had to hang onto the horse's neck as it swam across and out the other side. There was very little breeze or air movement, for the wind blew right over this cut in the earth as if it did not exist. Many birds inhabited the trees and brush of the Barranca and Thalmus talked with them, whistling and chirping as he hiked.

That evening they camped near a pool. The water was clear and cool, and they all swam and relaxed. Because there was no horizon, just a narrow access to the sky, darkness came quickly to the Barranca—and with it, colder air. The light reflection from the moon illuminated the steep walls of the canyon and only briefly shone on the floor as it passed across the night sky. The air was still and the creek whispered in a current so softly that they did not hear its warning.

Dysaan stretched out on his blanket. "It's so calm, so secure down here. We don't need to post a guard tonight. We can all rest, for a change."

"You're probably right," Currad said. "The troops are gone and we know that we haven't been followed."

Thalmus felt uneasy. The canyon was too serene. Something seemed false: what it was he could not say. Still, he wasn't ready to relax. He added wood to the fire. "This place appears safe, but are we ready to trust it? We should maintain our vigilance."

No one spoke for a while. They were too relaxed and despite their reluctance, they could not refute his wisdom.

"It's always better to be careful," Tobazi said. "I'll take the first watch."

Dysaan sat up. "No, Tobazi, it's my turn. I'll do it." He picked up his sword and blanket and moved out of the glow of the fire to a tree trunk twelve meters away.

"I'll take the second watch," Currad offered, unrolling his blanket. "Just wake me when it's time."

"Then I will do the third," Thalmus said, looking around the fire to see where everyone was bedded down.

Thalmus liked this isolated, hidden world despite his memory telling him to be cautious. However, with a watch posted, and knowing that Dallion and Thunder were always sensitive to danger, he slept soundly until woken by Currad. On his watch during the night, when all the others were asleep, Thalmus sat in the quiet darkness trying to discern the message from the creek and listening to the nocturnal creatures. A pair of screech owls were conversing, calling back and forth to one another, when suddenly a louder, deeper, voice intruded. "Who—whoooo!" Thalmus knew it well.

It was a warning call—from Bubo.

The screech owls hushed. Thalmus peered into the darkness, listening intently to the quiet. Even the whisper of the creek had stopped. "Who—whooo!" Bubo called again.

Another warning! Something was wrong.

Thalmus listened and watched for movement. The glow from the moon was inching up the wall of the Barranca. The little fire in the camp had burned down to embers. It needed fuel. Thalmus eased up from his sitting position.

"What is it, Bubo?" he whispered. "What's out there?"

Thunder clicked his jaws, Dallion snorted in response, and Thalmus knew something dangerous was out there in the night. He couldn't believe troops were quiet enough to sneak down this gorge. Thalmus started moving toward the others—toward the dying fire—when he heard a noise like something being dragged across the ground.

He froze.

It was near, maybe twenty meters up the Barranca. Owl sailed past him and disappeared into the darkness as he glided toward the noise. Thalmus heard Dallion stomp his hoof, and he pulled his sword as he moved quickly to wake the others. Then, Bubo's loud screech pierced the silence and a rush of thumping, scraping noises came toward them.

Tobazi rolled over and crouched on all fours while Thunder moved along side of him. Currad and Dysaan snapped from sleep and jumped to their feet with swords ready. Thalmus pulled Boschina to her feet and thrust her sword into her hand. He was grabbing wood for the fire when four giant lizards burst into the clearing. They stopped and stood up on their hind legs, making them as tall as men. Their large tails flipped and swept the ground behind them; their jaws opened, revealing rows of teeth as they hissed at the humans. Their claws were as long as a man's fingers and their eyes glinted like black sapphire.

The beasts did not hesitate.

With piercing, growling hisses they attacked ferociously and without fear. Two of them charged, standing up, while the other two dropped down and ran on all fours. Thalmus quickly cut one and sliced another in front of Boschina, who was frozen with shock.

"Go help Thunder," Thalmus shouted as the two lizards backed off. Wounded by his sword, they growled and hissed. Nodding their heads up and down, pawing the ground, they sized up their prey.

Then, they charged again.

Fighting the other two lizards, Currad and Dysaan wounded one and were stabbing the other one when four more lizards entered the clearing. The new ones grouped with the other three and like a pack of wolves, started to circle whilehissing and spitting and snapping, dodging the men's swords. The lizards teamed up and took turns staying down or standing on their hind legs as they lunged at their prey.

The cries of the dying lizard that Dysaan had stabbed enraged the others and they charged repeatedly. One of them slapped Tobazi with its tail, knocking him to his knees, while another one dropped down and lunged at him. Thunder snapped, bit into the creature's leg, and pulled it away before it could reach Tobazi. The lizard howled, turned, and bit down on the back of Thunder's neck. Tobazi crawled forward and slashed the creature's belly while Boschina stabbed it through the throat.

Still, it did not let go. Boschina stabbed it again and again; screaming at the beast, until it finally released its jaws and flopped to the ground. Three of the lizards pulled away from their assault on the humans and started for the horses.

"They're after the horses," Currad shouted.

"Don't separate," Thalmus warned. "Stay together."

Dysaan and Currad ran to block the attack. They reached the panicked, rearing horses just in time to slash at the lizards' heads to stop their assault. Again, the snarling, bloody, beasts backed off; sizing up their prey, they waited for an opening and charged again. As Dysaan fought to keep one away from his legs, another one snapped at his head. While he was thrusting at the low one, the lizard on its hind feet struck, biting and clamping onto his arm. Dysaan yelled and plunged his sword into its belly, but the monster did not let go of him. Now, the lizard down on its four feet saw the advantage and sprang forwardto bite onto Dysaan's leg and pull him down. It threw its weight onto Dysaan's legs so he couldn't move and was going for his throat with its mouth open wide; its sharp teeth poised to bite when the hind hoofs of Dallion exploded into the creature, knocking it off the prone Dysaan.

The other lizard was still clamped onto his arm.

Dallion reared up and came down on the lizard's head with his front hoofs, smashing its skull. Dysaan got to his knees and with his good arm and hand, pulled the sword out of the beast, turned, and chopped the legs of the lizard attacking Currad. It squealed, dropped to the ground, and Currad finished it off—stabbing it in the heart. The stunned lizard Dallion had kicked, rolled up on its feet, turned, and—seeing Dysaan on his knees—roared and charged. Dysaan could not get away, so he lunged toward the creature, thrusting his sword before him. They collided with the blade plunging into the lizard's chest, but its jaws reached Dysaan's head. Currad was there instantly, slicing the beast's throat with his short blade and prying its jaws off Dysaan's face.

Meanwhile, Boschina, now filled with anger and confidence from killing one beast, leapt into the fight alongside Thalmus. She chopped at the tall lizard standing on its hind legs, but it dodged her sword and came back at her—roaring and snapping. She backed away, separating from Thalmus, as the beast went after her. The other creature was wounded and with only one to fight now, Thalmus stabbed and killed it. He turned to see the last—and largest—lizard backing Boschina into the darkness. It was snapping close to her head as she swung her sword frantically.

He rushed and chopped its leg from the back.

It howled, turned, and lunged at Thalmus. He ducked under its jaws and plunged his sword into its chest. The creature roared and fell to the ground. It wasn't finished though: the lizard rolled to its four feet and crawled toward him. Thalmus jumped over the open jaws onto its back and stuck his knife into the spine at the neck—and the animal dropped dead.

Thalmus sprang to his feet with his knife ready and looked about. The creatures were all dead. In the receding light of the moon, he saw Dallion standing over Currad as he was pulling the lizard's jaw from Dysaan's head.

"Boschina, are you hurt?"

"No, I'm all right, Thalmus."

"Good. Put wood on the fire, quickly. Build it up. And stay alert." He glanced around in the dark for the others. "Tobazi? Thunder?"

"Here, Thalmus," Tobazi responded. "Thunder's with me. He was bit, but he's all right."

"Call out if he starts clicking."

"You can count on it," Tobazi responded.

Thalmus hurried to Dysaan, who was still on his knees.

His body and face were soaked with blood.

"I can't see," Dysaan cried.

"It's no wonder," Thalmus said. "I cannot see your eyes. They are covered in blood."

Currad carried water from the stream and began gently washing Dysaan's face. Dallion was checking the creatures, pawing at them with a hoof and sniffing to make sure they were dead. Thalmus pulled Dysaan's sword from the lizard, cleaned it, and slid it back into his scabbard.

The fire began to snap and roar and brighten the area.

"I can see. I can see the fire now," Dysaan said as the blood was rinsed from his face.

Thalmus gathered everyone together. They sat up the rest of the night in the light of the fire, listening and waiting for the sunrise.

In the light of day, Thalmus and Currad examined Dysaan. There were tears and punctures on the sides of his head from the creature's teeth—and cuts and gashes on his cheeks and forehead, arm and leg. But nothing was broken and, most importantly, he could see.

"You're a mess," Currad told Dysaan. "You didn't even look this bad after the battle of Tanden."

"I feel worse, too. I ache all over. This arm's crushed, can't move it much."

"Give it some time, you'll feel better."

Dysaan pressed his palms to his forehead.

"It feels like someone's pounding on my skull."

"Well, your head has always been strange," Currad laughed. "I suppose it'll get better, too."

Thunder was all right as well. His leathery skin had prevented the lizard's teeth from penetrating very deeply. Thalmus made a paste from some leaves and roots, heated it over the fire, and then dabbed it on Thunder's and Dysaan's wounds. After this medicinal treatment, they examined the giant lizards.

Ants were already crawling over the limp bodies. Currad and Thalmus looked at the clawed feet and their tracks in the dirt; they pried open the mouths and checked the size and number of teeth—and length of the tails.

"I have never seen creatures like this that can stand up and be so agile on their hind feet," Thalmus said.

"Nor have I," Currad said. "They weren't here last time we traveled this Barranca."

"Where'd they come from?" Dysaan wondered.

"I sure hope there aren't any more," Boschina said, staring at the big lizard at her feet. She shook her head. "First mud worms, now these beasts. What's next?"

Thalmus had been studying the creatures.

"I do remember seeing these lizards before."

"Where?" Currad asked. "I'd like to know."

"In the carvings on the stone column outside the king's court," Thalmus answered. "Gauks, they were called. According to the legend, the king had destroyed them."

"I never paid attention to those carvings because I thought they were made up stories to make the king look invincible," Dysaan said.

"So did I." Thalmus replied. "But, here they are."

"I thought that I knew of everything in this land," Currad said, scratching his head. "Frogs are bad enough, but these creatures baffle me. Where could they have come from?"

Thalmus was pondering that question as well. He had some ideas, all of which seemed improbable, but not impossible—and none of them boded well for their quest. Forces that he thought were gone or dormant had awakened. *Who could have known that they would take this trail?*

He surveyed the creek: the water running over rocks and spilling into the pool. *It tried to warn me*, he thought. He glanced at Thunder sitting in the shallows of the water and at Dallion standing over a dead lizard. They were both watching him. Currad, Dysaan, and Boschina were still looking over the lizards. Tobazi was lying on his blanket near the fire. And Bubo? Well, he was nowhere to be seen. Thalmus looked up at the steep canyon walls. "How long will it take us to reach the trail out of here?"

"A day, perhaps two, depending on what we encounter," Currad answered.

"Then let's get started."

They worked their way through the Barranca, watching for tracks of the lizards or any other creatures. Dallion scouted ahead, but everyone stayed fairly close together. It was slow going now with two wounded men and Thunder struggling through the brush and rocky terrain. Currad and Thalmus took turns in the lead and helping Boschina with the others. When they stopped to rest, Thalmus motioned to Boschina to sit with him.

"Yes, Thalmus?"

"You did well last night protecting Thunder and Tobazi."

"Thank you," she replied, feeling a little pride.

"But, you must learn to control your emotions in combat."

"That big lizard almost got me," she said, shaking her head.

"Because you let your anger and excitement control your judgment," Thalmus explained.

She looked at him. "I was angry and scared at the same time."

"That is not uncommon, Boschina. You must learn to ride that power. It will expand your strength. Still, you must keep your mind clear to judge the situation and your opponent. That is the difference between survival and death."

"I'll try, Thalmus."

He smiled at her. "You are learning quickly."

"I have to," she said.

Thalmus stood up, but Boschina stopped him. "Thalmus, last night, just before the creatures came and you pulled me up, I was awakened by—I thought I heard Bubo's screech."

Thalmus nodded, knelt by the creek, cupped water to his mouth, and drank before answering. "Did you hear Dallion and Thunder's warning? They both heard the lizards coming and announced it. We were fortunate last night, Boschina. We could have been killed in our sleep."

On they went, back and forth across the creek, over rocks and through brambles. Whatever trail there might have been had eroded away and was grown over by wild plants. At times, they had to chop a path through berry thickets that covered the entire floor of the Barranca. The sun blazed down, heating the canyon walls and radiating through the still air—turning the narrow passage into an oven.

Thalmus saw no sign of the lizards—no tracks or trails or droppings. Had that been a lone pack? He thought not. They were full grown. Where are the young ones and their mothers? What would creatures that large eat to survive? He was full of questions, but had no answers.

The sheer rock walls of the canyon gradually narrowed, until the two sides finally met—closing the Barranca like the end of a box. There in the stone face was a large gaping hole—a tunnel, four meters in diameter, from which the creek flowed. The running water echoed from this dark cave. There was no other way to proceed. On the face of the rock above the tunnel was a faded, ancient, petroglyph.

They all gathered before the opening and rested.

Dysaan sat with his head down and his eyes closed; he had been limping all day. Thalmus checked his wounds and was pleased to see they were scabbing. There was no sign of infection. The root paste was working.

Currad helped Tobazi off of his horse and to a spot next to Dysaan. While Thalmus was checking his wounds, Tobazi reached out and touched Dysaan's shoulder.

"How are you, my friend?"

Dysaan opened his eyes and looked at Tobazi. "My head hurts."

"So it should," Tobazi said, and smiled. "It was almost food for the beast."

Dysaan grunted. "What a thought."

"He will heal faster than you," Thalmus said to Tobazi. "Your wounds are deeper and will take much time."

Boschina had checked Thunder's neck and was now stroking his head with her hand as she looked at the tunnel and the odd figures inscribed above it.

"It's not long," Currad said, motioning to the tunnel. "As I remember, it has several turns. That's why it appears so dark."

"Is it big enough all the way through for Thunder?" Boschina asked.

"I think so."

The sun was directly overhead, driving the heat down on them. Birds were flitting about. Some flew in and out of the tunnel. High up on the rock cliff a hawk perched on a precipice.

Boschina was drawn to the figures on the stone above the cave opening because they seemed to be moving in the heat of the sun. The first character was an odd-shaped man with his long arms stretched out before him. He had on a funny hat or crown and he was encircled by what looked like a ring of fire. Next, there were horizontal wavy lines and a bird in flight. It had something in its beak. Then, another man that appeared to be running. His head was partly detached from his body; and then there was a man with his arms stretched upward. Above him were vertical wavy lines. The last image was a prone figure with no apparent life.

Currad sat down heavily. "Uh, I'm tired."

"This ground is difficult to travel," Thalmus commented.

"I'm sorry," Currad replied. "It's changed much."

"What do you suppose those figures mean?" Boschina asked.

Currad looked up at the characters. "I've seen them before in other places, but I don't know what they mean."

"Perhaps it's a warning about the cave," Tobazi suggested.

"It is a statement of faith," Thalmus said and looked up at the hawk on the precipice.

"What? You know what it means, Thalmus?" Boschina said. "Tell us."

"It is about faith and spirit; about life and death."

"Faith in what?" Boschina asked.

"That is the question each one must answer for himself," Thalmus said, still watching the hawk.

"Then it's not a warning?" Tobazi asked.

"Oh, yes it is," Thalmus replied. "It is a warning passed on through time."

"Thalmus," Boschina said sternly. "What does it mean?"

He looked again at the figures on the stone wall. "It means: if one is not strong in faith, his spirit will fly away at the first test. That once lost, he cannot regain it—and without it, he is dead."

"How do you know this?" Currad asked, staring at the figures.

"You will find the same figures in other out-of-the-way places," Thalmus said. "This message used to be more prevalent. Sadly, it has been destroyed over time and is rarely seen now."

"How do you know what it means?" Boschina asked.

Thalmus shrugged. "This, and other knowledge, has been passed down."

"By whom?"

"Old ones," Thalmus replied, "who still know the faith."

"Who teaches this?" Dysaan asked.

"Very few, now," Thalmus answered and then looked at Boschina. "I believe your father is one who has the knowledge."

"My father? He has never taught."

"Oh, yes, he has. His carvings, his sculptures, teach truth. This knowledge is such that one expresses it in subtle ways. Rarely is it preached openly. He has been teaching the lessons of the old faith in all his work. I recognize in him one who knows."

Boschina thought about her father and this revelation of him.

"How many others are there?"

"Not many."

"Old Rundall," Currad said. "Is he one?"

"Yes, he is."

"I thought so," Currad said. "He's always impressed me as a man of great depth and--

At that moment a sudden, piercing screech echoed from the cave.

Chapter Fourteen
The Tunnel

Before the echo of the scream had faded, Currad was on his feet, grasping the handle of his sword. The rest of them had all turned toward the dark tunnel. They jumped with surprise when a cloud of sparrows suddenly burst from the opening and scattered down the Barranca.

Dysaan stood up. "I didn't like the sound or look of that."

"Was that the scream of a man or animal?" Tobazi asked.

"It sounded like a bird to me," Boschina said.

Currad started toward the tunnel. "I'll go see."

"Let's not split up, Currad," Thalmus said, stopping him. "It is better we stick together, for this is a place of uncertainty."

Boschina rose to her feet. "What's in there, Thalmus?"

"Are there Gauks in there?" Dysaan asked, gripping his sword tighter and turning his gaze from the tunnel to Thalmus.

"The warning on the rock is true," Thalmus replied, looking up at the figures above the tunnel. "You must be prepared for anything, and nothing."

"What do you mean?" Boschina asked.

He looked at each one of them before answering. "There are powerful, wicked, forces in there that can grab hold of you and keep you in the darkness if you let them. You must strengthen your thoughts. Do not be fooled by anything you may see or hear or feel that wants to control you. Stand firm on what you know to be true, and you will reenter the light on the other side."

Motionless, each one wondered in silence what awaited them.

"I cannot help you in there," Thalmus said quietly. "Most likely, no one can. You must pass through this on your own."

After a moment, Tobazi said: "All right then. Thanks for the warning, Thalmus. I guess I'm as ready as I'll ever be." He looked at the others. "How about the rest of you?"

Turning from Thalmus, they looked at Tobazi, and then at the tunnel. Thunder was already plodding toward the opening.

"I'm with you," Currad said, smiling at the prone Tobazi. "Let's go."

He helped Tobazi onto his horse and Boschina took the reins in one hand and held her sword in the other. They caught up with Thunder as he splashed into the creek. Thalmus jumped onto his back and they entered the tunnel. Boschina was right behind them, leading the mounted Tobazi. Dysaan, on his horse, followed them; and Currad, on foot, brought up the rear. Dallion walked between the other two horses to calm and steady them.

A damp chill met them upon entering the cave. The sound of the creek became louder, echoing off the stone walls and filling their ears.

Thalmus wanted Thunder to lead for three reasons. First, the slow pace at which he moved would allow their eyes to adjust to the darkness and ease the rush of panic. Second, his size would intimidate most predators. And third, he had a better sensitivity in the darkness than any of them.

The screech had probably come from Bubo—a warning call. However, the echo effect of the cave had changed it enough that Thalmus could not be sure. He heard muffled noises from deep in the tunnel that he could not discern above the running water and their own splashing in the creek.

Slowly, they moved beyond the light from the entrance and the cool darkness flowed around them. As they trudged farther into the cave, the dampness gradually seeped into their senses—making each one of them feel alone and vulnerable.

Thalmus could feel the presence of many souls, many stories murmuring in the darkness. He listened and felt the essence of the cave. Confusion, weakness, abandonment, hatred, betrayal: all wrapped up in the power of fear—swarming and buzzing around in the darkness looking for a crack, a chink-in-the-armor, an opportunity to squeeze in and wreak havoc on the unsuspecting.

This tunnel was a wicked and insidious trap.

The frog hunter decided that he would feel his way through this dangerous passage with his eyes closed. Besides, it was too dark to see anything. Attempting to see would only add to one's fear. Forces were bumping into him, crawling across his skin, prodding his senses.

He closed his mind to past worries and bad memories so that old concerns and fears could not creep into his consciousness to become food for the forces surrounding him. Taking deep slow breaths, he rode easily on Thunder as the giant tortoise plodded through the darkness.

A slight rush of air blew by his head.

He smiled. A short hoot sounded above the murmur.

Then, a sudden weight landed on his shoulder and clung to him with powerful claws. Bubo had found him. Thunder grunted and Bubo hooted back at him. With the fearless presence of Owl and his bright eyes, the spirits withdrew from Thalmus—back into the darkness.

*

Boschina, balancing her fear in the blackness with the sword in one hand and the horse's bridle in the other—straining to see and listening intently and thinking of her father—began to hear a voice.

She could not quite understand the words. They were too muddled.

What was it? she wondered.

The voice was speaking to her. She was sure of that. Who was it? She stopped thinking of her father to listen more intently, but could not grasp a word or any meaning. It was loud enough yet not understandable.

What was it? Who was it?

Suddenly, she felt a strange affection for the voice. A yearning deep within rose up from the depths of her soul and filled her mind with a desire for the voice. Her heart pounded. She wanted to see it, to touch it.

"Boschina," it called and she understood her name.

"Yes," she replied. "Speak to me."

But the words were jumbled. All she could understand was her name. All other sounds—the creek, the horses plodding and splashing—dropped away.

There was only the voice filling her ears.

"Boschina...."

"Yes, yes?"

"I have come for you."

The words were clearing. She was beginning to understand the voice; it was so soothing—so comforting—that she wanted to hear more, to reach out to it. An image began to appear in the darkness before her. It was a face, a woman's face, with long brown hair and brown eyes—a lovely face, like Boschina's.

"Mother," Boschina said in amazement.

"You have come so far, child," the voice said, gently. "I am here for you."

"Mother, is it truly you? Where have you been? I've longed for you."

"I am here, child."

"Oh Mother, Father and I needed you so. He'll be so pleased to see you when we find him."

"Forget your father."

"What?"

"Be with me, Boschina."

"But Father needs us. He's in trouble."

"Forget him. He is lost. Come with me."

Boschina felt the pull, the longing to at last be with her mother—to hold her and be held by her. Boschina's heart swelled and heaved, her whole body giving in to emotion. Still, her mind resisted. There was something wrong. She did not know this mother, this woman telling her to abandon her father.

Confusion filled her.

"Mother?"

"Come, Boschina, stay with me. You want to be with me, don't you?"

"Yes, I do. I do, Mother. What about Father? I can't forget Father."

"Boschina, Boschina," the voice pleaded.

"I know him. I don't know you," she said, fighting the longing to know her mother, to be with her.

"He is lost. I am here now for you. Stay with me."

"Mother, I can't. Father needs me. He needs you."

"He does not want you, Boschina. I do."

"No, I must find him."

"He left you. Come to me."

"Mother, why did you leave?"

"Stay with me, Boschina," the voice said, but the face was fading.

175

"Mother? Don't go. We need you."

"Stay with me," the voice softly repeated.

"Mother, stay and help me," Boschina cried. "Don't go away!" But the image was gone, leaving total blackness again.

"Boschina," the voice whispered faintly in her ear. "Boschina...."

"Mother?"

Running water and splashing hooves echoed again around her head. She reached out in the black emptiness and felt nothing.

*

Tobazi, still weak and sore but enduring in the saddle of Currad's horse, suddenly heard chilling laughter in the darkness. He sat up straight. The laughter was familiar.

Could it be?

He listened—waiting in the darkness—and then heard it again. Yes, he knew that mocking jeer and hated it, hated its owner. His fingers searched for the sword in its scabbard on the side of the horse. His hand gripped its leather handle; then, he slowly drew it out and held it before him in the darkness.

"So, you've found me," Tobazi said. "Come on then."

The laughter rolled again through his head and anger swelled in his chest.

"Come on. You think it's funny? Then come and get me!"

A broad sword flashed in the darkness.

Tobazi ducked and the blade cut the air over his head.

"Same old game, huh?" Tobazi said. "You'll have to do better."

The mysterious sword flashed again like lightning in the night. Tobazi dodged it and thrust his own sword into the darkness, and then swept the blade back and forth in an attempt to hit his attacker. But it found no resistance. The laughter echoed in his ears. His muscles tightened, his breaths were short and deep.

"Yeah, that's you," Tobazi said, "always hiding, using others— hurting the innocent, the defenseless. Where's the glory in that?"

The laughter stopped and there was only silence. Tobazi's heart pounded in his ears, he gripped tighter on the sword as he glanced about in the darkness and waited.

Suddenly, the sword came down from directly overhead. Tobazi deflected the blow, but the sword returned and pounded repeatedly at him. He blocked blow after blow and each one increased in force as he grew weaker with each effort.

Tobazi started to lose his grip on the sword as well as the horse— who seemed unaware of the battle. *This can't be happening,* he thought. He talked to his body, to his muscles: "Don't fail me. Don't quit!"

Then, the vicious attack stopped, and the laughter started. A face appeared in the darkness above him. It was the hideous countenance of Corsair.

Why was this happening? He felt weak and powerless. He had a weapon and a chance to strike back for the humiliation he had suffered by this man; instead, he was doomed by his failing strength. He saw Corsair raise his sword for a final blow. Tobazi closed his eyes, frustrated. Anger rose inside him like water filling a vessel. It boiled over and he burst forward with a scream and lashed out with his weapon. Again, the blade whiffed in the dark, cutting nothing but airas the face of Corsair appeared laughing and mocking.

Tobazi was exhausted, his energy spent; he was beaten. He raised his head to look at Corsair. This time he saw Tuggle in the background kneeling in the rows, cultivating the soil and nursing the plants. The gentle farmer looked up at him and smiled. Then Thunder appeared, straddling over him as he did in the battle against the Rainers. Tobazi felt calmness enter him and his anger subside.

He relaxed the grip on the sword and focused on Corsair.

"You're afraid of me," Tobazi said.

Corsair sneered and swung his sword. Tobazi did not flinch.

"You're scared of being weak, aren't you?" Tobazi continued. "That's what makes you mean and pitiful."

Corsair grunted and put the tip of the sword in Tobazi's face.

The man from Toubar stared into the vicious eyes glaring at him from the other end of the sword. "I won't play your game any longer," he said. "You don't control me." He slowly reached up and brushed the sword away, silencing the laughter.

The stunned Corsair dropped his sword and stared at Tobazi in disbelief before he fell into the darkness. Tobazi watched his enemy disappear. Was he truly gone? Was he finally free of him? He took a deep breath and slumped onto the horse's neck.

*

Dysaan could have sworn he heard hissing in the tunnel, something dragging through the water. Why hadn't he brought a torch? How stupid to rush into this darkness.

There was the hissing again. Or was that the creek?

The horse jerked under him and he leaned forward and patted its neck. What he touched was not the short smooth hair he expected; instead, it felt rough and scaly. Withdrawing his hand quickly, he shuddered and realized it was no longer a horse beneath him but something else.

Something he feared more than anything.

It was a Gauk!

He was astride the back of a giant lizard. How did this happen? Where did it come from and why now in this darkness? How could he possibly fight it? The creature twisted and bucked—and turned its long neck and body to bite him. He moved just in time to avoid the sharp teeth. Clamping his knees tight on the creature, he reached for the long knife on his belt to cut its throat. At that instant, the beast rolled over smashing him into the water and gravel of the creek. The weight of the creature knocked the air out of him and held him under the water.

Dysaan's arm and knife were pinned under him.

Using what breath he had left, he planted his feet against the Gauk's soft belly, pushed off, and wriggled free. Gasping for air, he scrambled to his feet, pulled his knife from its sheath, and backed away. He heard the beast roll over, hissing and snorting—its tail splashing the water. *If there's only one*, he thought, *he had a chance—even in this darkness. What if there are more and this is their den?* He tried to call out, to warn the others, but his voice was silent. Again, he tried to yell and nothing came out of his throat.

What was wrong?

The momentary silence in the cave was overwhelming. In a panic, he realized that he was alone. His friends had moved on. Taking deep breaths, he gathered his strength. *All right*, he thought, *it's up to me. I will fight this thing by myself, despite my wounds and the handicap of the darkness. I must kill the beast.* He held his knife out in front. Turning slowly, listening intently and staring blindly, he could feel it watching him—stalking him.

How close is it, he wondered, *will it come at me high or low?*

178

Then speaking out, he said, "All right lizard, come and get me!"

He looked for its eyes in the blackness, but could see nothing. Then, it charged; it was upon him in an instant. Slashing at the grotesque head, he jumped aside and stabbed at it again as it went by. Roaring with anger, the beast turned, its tail whipped around and caught Dysaan behind the knees. His legs buckled; he fell backward onto rocks hitting his head and nearly knocking him senseless. Struggling, he rolled over and got to his knees. He heard the beast thumping forward, the big tail scraping the ground.

It was coming in low for the kill.

"Not this time," he said. "You're not going to get me this time."

Standing up just as the giant lizard appeared, he jumped aside and grabbed his knife with both hands; with all his strength, he plunged it down into the creature's back, between the shoulder blades and threw all his weight onto it. The beast roared, stood up, and twisted— —trying to throw Dysaan off. He held on to the handle of the knife and hung from its back as the creature turned left and right, snapping at him; then, it stumbled to its belly and crawled—growling and hissing, carrying Dysaan—across the creek and finally collapsed. The great tail flopped back and forth several times before becoming motionless. Dysaan waited, catching his breath and making sure the beast was truly dead. He pushed off the lizard and stood up. He pressed his foot on the beast's back and yanked his knife out. Silence surrounded him. He breathed deeply, filling his lungs with the cool air and his mind with confidence.

The sound of the creek came back to him.

He heard splashing and turned with his knife ready.

"Dysaan, Dysaan," Currad called.

"Here. I'm here," Dysaan said, relieved that it was Currad in the dark and not another Gauk.

"Are you all right?" Currad asked, coming up to touch him. "Your horse came to me, did you fall off? You're all wet."

"What? You have my horse? Is he injured?"

"No, but are you?"

Dysaan gripped Currad's arm and stepped back to kick the dead beast and to tell him about the fight, but the giant lizard was gone. *Where did it go? Was it ever there?* Then, he heard a hiss fading in the distance. He smiled and felt the presence of his friend in the darkness. "Yes, I'm all right."

Currad helped Dysaan onto his horse and walked beside him in the darkness until the sound of Tobazi's horse and the welcome snort of Dallion told them that they had caught up with the others.

Currad dropped back to once again take up the rear guard.

*

Walking alone at the end of the line, Currad began to feel uneasy, as if something was watching him. Glancing back over his shoulder, he stopped several times to listen, to hear if anything was following them. He heard only the running creek and the horses' hoofs splashing in the water. Currad started forward again when suddenly the cave became silent and still. He froze—his hand on the hilt of his sword.

This is strange, he thought.

He called out to Dysaan, then to Thalmus, but his words died in the dank air—and no answer came from his friends. A bell chimed in the darkness. It sounded just like the one at the castle, the same ring that announced the king. *How could that be?* He wondered. That bell was unique. There was no other like it in all the land. Then, he heard the king's high voice.

"What is it now?" King Ahmbin said. He was obviously irritated.

"Sorry to bother you, my lord," a voice answered—a voice that Currad knew well. "However, I must report to you that your soldier, Currad, has betrayed you."

"What?" Currad said in astonishment. "Don't believe him."

"Betrayed me?" King Ahmbin asked, not even hearing Currad. "Do you have proof of this?"

Suddenly, Metro appeared from the darkness, glaring down at Currad and pointing a long, sharp, finger at him. "My magic has discovered that he, Currad, released the prisoner, Vericitas."

"Is this true, Currad?" the king demanded.

Currad was stunned.

Metro had discovered his secret. How was that possible? No one knew, except Vericitas. Had Metro captured him?

"Speak, my faithful soldier."

"He cannot," Metro scoffed. "For he and the sculptor conspired to mock you, to laugh at you behind your back. And when you demanded imprisonment of the culprit, your good soldier let him go.

I tell you now for your safety, my lord, chain him in the rock pit."

"No," Currad tried to yell. His voice failed, his words were silent.

Metro's eyes glared in the darkness and his robe blew about him as if there were a strong wind, but Currad felt not the slightest breeze in the cave.

"Speak, Currad," the king commanded.

The loyal soldier wanted to explain why he let Vericitas escape. He wanted to tell the king of the growing injustices because of the king's foolishness and the evil Metro. Currad had thought about this so much, worried over this moment of discovery for so long; now, he could not speak. The king's power in the land was fading and Metro's was growing.

In the darkness Metro's eyes glared at him, piercing his thoughts and controlling his mind. Currad—the soldier, the fighter, the defender of the king—reached for his sword, but it would not release from the scabbard.

"See," Metro shouted. "He thinks only of attack. He desires your throne, my lord. If he could, he would kill us both. Only I can protect you."

"No," Currad wanted to say. "I want only to get rid of you, Metro. I want to cut out the evil that's poisoning our king." Currad felt hopeless. He could not speak and he could not move. His king was in grave danger and did not know it. He could not see the veil of evil surrounding him.

The king must be saved. How was he to do it?

Then, chains with manacles—clinking and rattling—appeared from the darkness and hung over Currad. With a sweep of his hand, Metro guided them down. Currad ducked and jumped aside. The chains swung past him and reappeared again by Metro.

"He must be shackled and bound in the rock pit to starve with the stones of despair," Metro bellowed.

"Tell me it isn't so, Currad," the king said. "Say you haven't betrayed me."

Currad still could not speak. He watched the chains dangling in the air. He did not want to be fettered in the pit like an animal—fed scraps, mocked, and slowly destroyed as a man.

"You give me no choice," the king said, disappointed. "I will reject you."

"No!"

"All these many years, I trusted you. Now, I find that you take me for a fool. You have hurt me deeply, Currad."

"No, Your Majesty. What I did was for you. I'm fighting for you."

Currad's words were not heard by King Ahmbin, who looked sad and confused. Then, the king's gaze turned to anger for his prized soldier. "You force me to turn my back on you."

"No, my lord. Can't you see?" Currad shouted. "Veracitas had to be freed. Open your eyes!"

The king was turning away, his royal cape sweeping around to cover his back.

"Can't you hear me? You are being deceived!" He reached out to his king, tried to catch his cape, but the image was fading into the darkness and he grasped only air.

The chains reappeared. Currad felt their weight upon him, felt the confinement of the shackles and the loss of his king. He shook his entire body, fighting off the chains. "No," he screamed in the darkness. "I will not surrender. I'll stay strong. I'll bear the burden for Veracitas. I will not be silenced!"

Currad swung around, stepped forward, and splashed into the creek as the chains and Metro disappeared.

*

In this tunnel, time was suspended and space knew no end. There was no telling how long the passage took from beginning to end, for each person experienced a critical enlightenment that would seem incomprehensible for some time to come. The discovery of their innermost fears was more than any one of them wanted to face again.

Thunder was twenty meters clear of the tunnel before Thalmus opened his eyes to see before him a clear path through the Barranca. Bubo pushed off Thalmus' shoulder and winged ahead up the canyon. Thalmus slid off Thunder and waited for the others. Boschina, Tobazi, Dysaan, and Currad straggled out—exhausted and numb. Thalmus checked each one as they emerged. They had made it through; yet, they were physically and emotionally drained. Thalmus suggested that they stop to rest, but the warm sun and the view of a clear path brightened their spirits. They hurried on, each one wanting to put as much distance as possible between them and that black hole.

The trail finally began to ascend by way of many switchbacks to the land above. Worn out, yet anxious to be out of this canyon, they pushed themselves up the narrow path and around the many turns— constantly climbing and struggling to the top.

Seeming to rise out of the ground, the exhausted travelers emerged from the Barranca, stood on the edge of the precipice, and looked out upon a vast rolling plain. Patches of tiny flowers— orange, yellow, blue, and white—spotted the green grass before them. Despite the relief they felt, and the pleasant change of scenery, their eyes and emotions were drawn to an ominous shape in the distance.

Chapter Fifteen
Table Top

The serene landscape before them looked like swells in the ocean. Row after row of green hills that seemed to roll with the windswept grass across the plain to the base of a flat black-rock mountain that jutted straight up out of the earth. There, the gentle swells came to a sudden stop as they crashed against the dark monolith. Two silver waterfalls streaked down the formidable cliffs, giving the appearance of a craggy stone face with white fangs—while the flat top of the mountain cut a sharp line across the blue sky. The weary travelers stared in silence at the scene spread out before them. Having just survived the horrors of the Barranca, the aspect of this new challenge was not uplifting to their spirits.

However, this ominous view did not appear to bother Dallion, who bobbed and shook his big head. After days of slow moving in the confined Barranca, he needed to run, to feel the freedom of open ground again. He burst from the group and with his hooves pounding the earth, the Paint stallion raced across the first hill and disappeared. The other horses lunged and wanted to follow, but were restrained by Dysaan and Currad.

"Easy, easy," Dysaan said to his mount. "You'll be free soon."

Thalmus pointed at a cluster of bushes in a small swale just ahead. "There appears to be a spring in that low area. Let's move away from this edge and rest there."

"Anywhere away from this hole is good with me," Tobazi said.

As the group moved off, Thalmus looked back over the edge into the Barranca. The canyon appeared lush and inviting—lined by vegetation with a shiny creek meandering along its bottom. But, it was a cruel trap to the unsuspecting. So many unanswered questions lay there.

Thalmus was glad to be out of the Barranca's control, but he was also enticed by its mystery. He knew that someday he would return.

For now though, Thalmus turned his back on that cut in the earth and joined his friends.

There was a spring with good water in the swale and they refreshed themselves, lying on the soft grass in silence. Thalmus and Currad unsaddled the horses and let them roam.

No one wanted to speak about what they had just experienced in the tunnel; neither could they shake the memory right away. Thalmus, though, had put it behind him. He was thinking about Table Top as he looked at it looming in the distance.

"This is where we must part," he said, sadly.

"I wish I could go with you, Thalmus," Tobazi said.

"I wish you could, too, my friend. It is more important that you get home, be with your family, and recover from those wounds." Thalmus looked at Boschina, who was sitting crossed-legged, watching Dallion—who had appeared on a hill and was trotting toward them. "Boschina and I will be all right."

Dysaan was lying on his back with his eyes closed.

"How are you?" Thalmus asked and knelt beside him to check his wounds.

"How do I look?" Dysaan asked.

"Better," Thalmus replied. "You are healing. Though, you will have some scars."

"I just want my head to stop hurting," Dysaan said.

"That will take a few days."

Currad stood up. "You're right, Thalmus, we need to separate from you now, before anyone from Table Top sees us together."

"But we're so far away," Boschina protested. "They can't see this far."

"No, but a hunting party could see us. Besides," Currad motioned to his right, "we need to head east, to Tobazi's homeland."

"Boschina and I will move on, then," Thalmus said. He looked at the two wounded men and Currad, who was exhausted. "I suggest you stay and rest a day before starting."

"That suits me," Dysaan said.

Tobazi, feeling the pain of his wounds, carefully stood and extended a hand to Boschina. "We'll look for your father on our way, Boschina."

"Thank you, Tobazi," she said. She gripped his hand and he pulled her up off the grass to her feet. "You're a wonderful friend." She hugged him. "I hope I can introduce you to my father one day."

"I look forward to that meeting," Tobazi said, then grabbed Thalmus and hugged him. "Thank you for freeing me from Rainland."

"Oh, Tobazi, we could not have come this far without you." Thalmus stepped back at arm's length and looked into his eyes. "Go in peace."

Tobazi smiled and felt calmness come over him.

"You've given me that, Thalmus. I'm indebted to you."

"No, my friend, there is no debt between us."

Thalmus turned to Currad, who pointed toward the south end of Table Top. "See that large outcropping of rocks there at the base of the mountain?"

"Yes," Thalmus answered, "where the cliffs step toward us?"

"That's right. You'll find the trail that leads to the Top there, behind that cropping," Currad said. "It'll be guarded."

"I would expect that," Thalmus replied. He looked at Currad. "Take care of Tobazi."

"We'll get him home safely," Dysaan said, rising to his feet.

Thalmus looked at Dysaan, and then Currad. "You are true friends to me, and to the king."

Both men smiled warmly at him. They were appreciative and a bit embarrassed.

Currad motioned toward Table Top. "Be careful up there."

"We will," Thalmus replied. "You do the same."

"Thank you," Boschina said to the two soldiers. "Thank you for saving us from the troops at Rainland and the Gauks. I hope...ah, well, I...." She wasn't quite sure what else to say to these two men who were obviously friends, but did not seem to be the huggable type.

Currad handed Boschina her sword and belt.

"It was our honor to help you."

She smiled and grasped the sword as Dysaan clasped her other hand. "We'll see you back at the castle with your father."

"Yes," she said, enjoying that thought. "Yes, we'll see you there."

The men helped Thalmus and Boschina gather their gear and tie it on Dallion, and then watched as they followed Thunder—who was already plodding toward the mountain.

The four travelers left an odd-looking trail in the tall grass as they trekked over the rolling ground toward Table Top. At first, Boschina felt uneasy about leaving the security of the three men behind them. She had become comfortable in their presence. She looked back several times and waved—and all three of them waved to her until she finally lost sight of them in the uneven terrain. Thalmus was thirty or more paces ahead, and although lost in thought, he was alert to the country and possible dangers. Boschina walked in silence for a while, and then moved closer to Thunder and talked to him about the hills and grass and clear blue sky—anything but Table Top or the tunnel. Dallion, who had been grazing along with Thunder's plodding pace, came up and nuzzled Boschina. She stroked his nose and patted his shoulder. And slowly, her spirits brightened as she talked and walked with Thunder and Dallion in the warm open land of the plain.

That night, they camped by a creek that flowed from the waterfalls spilling off Table Top. Despite her fatigue, Thalmus had Boschina practice sword fighting techniques and exercises with him before bedding down.

"You must maintain a discipline of practice if you are to grow strong and knowledgeable in the use of the tools," he told her.

"Then I'll keep practicing," she replied.

In the morning, Boschina awoke to see Thalmus standing on the high ground above the creek, staring at Table Top. Behind him, the sun was rising above the horizon and shining brightly on the cliffs. Thalmus was scanning those cliffs around the area of the waterfalls. Boschina cleared the sleep from her eyes as she joined him on the rise.

She did not speak, but followed his gaze to the falls.

The two waterfalls were about three hundred meters apart and both fell the same distance—about seventy-five meters. The fall on the left, or south side, was about five meters wide at the top where the creek dropped over the table's edge. The fall on the right, to the north, was twice as wide—spilling a larger volume of water to the rocks below.

"Did you sleep well?" Thalmus asked.

"Yes. I feel much better."

"Good. You will need your strength today. We will start our search for your father at the bottom of those falls."

"The water looks promising, don't you think?" Boschina asked.

"Yes, it does," Thalmus replied. "I cannot see any carvings in the cliffs, but we are too far away."

Boschina stared at the dark wall of Table Top. "I'm not sure, but from here the stone does not look like the right kind for Father's work, and it appears or feels...menacing."

"From a distance, things can look deceiving," Thalmus said. "We will soon have the advantage of a closer look."

Boschina looked at Thalmus and smiled. "Yes, we will."

They ate a meal of fish that Thalmus had speared in the creek and cooked over the fire. Then, instead of following the winding stream, they took a direct line toward the northern waterfall.

It was impossible to approach Table Mountain without being seen by the people on the top. The ground sloped upward toward the mountain. A cluster of small dark-green trees grew along the base of the cliffs where the slope was the steepest. There was some brush in the low areas along the streams, but the rest of the land was clear and open. Occasionally, as they walked, Thalmus noticed a glint of sun reflecting off something metallic along the top of the cliffs and he knew that they were being observed. Excitement had been building in Boschina all morning. As they got closer to the waterfall, Boschina could not contain herself and she ran ahead with Dallion. She bounded up the last knoll to find a dark pool in turmoil from the constant onslaught of the water fall.

Boschina ran around the pool to the base of the falls. Searching the cliff walls for carvings, she climbed over boulders and roots of trees where the soil had been washed awaygoing as far as she could before being blocked by the waterfall. Then, she ran back and around to the other side of the pond. Thalmus came up to the pond and watched Boschina for a moment, and then searched the area. At the end of the pond where the water breeched the edge and flowed away in a gully, debris was washed up on the sand—entangled in the broken branches and caught in the rocks.

Thalmus examined the various items: planks of wood from a chest, mangled baskets, pieces of animal hides, and various clothes— some of which were torn and bloody. He looked up to the top of the falls and wondered how much of this had come from the people up there, tossed into the creek and washed over the edge. Nearby, charred logs and burnt ground marked the site where a campfire had been. There were animal, as well as human, tracks all around the pond area.

Thunder plodded into the water and cooled off. Dallion was standing knee deep, drinking and watching Thalmus. Boschina, having finished her examination of the waterfall and cliffs in the area, found Thalmus examining the ashes of the fire pit.

"I don't see any carvings," she said. "I don't think Father has been here."

"If he was, he didn't stay long," Thalmus replied as he studied some broken, burnt bones from the ashes.

"Can we go to the other waterfall now?"

"Yes," Thalmus answered. He stood and tossed the bones aside.

"What animal was that?" Boschina asked.

"I'm not sure, could have been a couple of different creatures."

He smiled at her. "But it wasn't human."

"Oh...." she said. "I'm glad to hear that."

A winding, up-and-down trail led across the rocky slope along the base of the cliff to the southern falls. This trail was well-worn from much use. According to Currad's directions, it led to the main pathway to the gate of Table Top. It was not far to the second waterfall, about a half hour's walk.

Here was more debris and trash. The pool was smaller and deeper.

Boschina and Thalmus searched the area for any signs that Veracitas had been there. Thalmus had been watching for carving in the rock along the trail. Boschina had been right about the cliffs: they were not the right kind stone for carving.

Boschina stared at the water falling from the ledge high above. "These falls are beautiful," she said. "But they're not the image I saw from Metro. They're not right."

Thalmus looked back at the trail leading to the pond. "Veracitas would not have stayed here," he said. "He could be captured too easily. Too many people pass along this trail—probably because it is a watering hole for animals and therefore easy hunting."

Boschina was leaning back, looking up at the cliffs. "Let's go to the Top."

Thalmus gestured toward the trail with an open hand. "Lead on, Boschina of Marbala."

Boschina was surprised and honored with such an adult title. She smiled at Thalmus and took a deep breath. "Onward," she said and started up the trail.

The path was about three meters wide and steep as it rose through a narrow cut in the rocks. Near the top, the trail narrowed to two meters and the shear walls on either side were more than seven meters high.

"Boschina," Thalmus said. "Do you see how narrow this passage is? How easy it would be for a small number of fighters to stop invaders coming up here?"

"Yes," she replied. "And with the cliffs so tall, this place is safer than the castle."

Throughout the climb, their pace gradually slowed and the rest stops became more frequent. Boschina's legs were getting tired and she stopped again to rest. "I do believe the trail is getting steeper," she said, taking deep breaths.

Thalmus agreed. "It has been getting more difficult as we approach the Top. That is another challenge for attackers."

"I don't want to attack," Boschina said. "I just want to get to the Top." Dallion stepped up and nudged Boschina, and then threw his head back. "Thank you, Dal," Boschina said. She climbed upon a boulder and jumped onto his back with their gear.

Thalmus took the lead and they continued as the trail made a sharp turn and continued up. It turned again and again, each time getting steeper until finally they were stopped by a gruff voice.

"Stop there! Who are you?"

Thalmus looked up and scanned the rocks until he saw the face of a man peering over a ledge. "I am Thalmus. This is Boschina."

The man was staring at Thunder.

"Does that giant belong to you?" he asked.

"He is a friend of ours," Thalmus replied.

Another face appeared next to the first one. This one looked them over, too. "You're Thalmus, the King's Frog Hunter?"

"Yes."

Two more heads popped up from behind the rocks on the other side of the trail. One man was older with a graying beard and short hair under a floppy hat. The younger man had curly black hair and a scar across his left cheek.

"Did you say, Thalmus the Frog Hunter?" asked the older man.

"That's what I said, Camp," the second man answered.

The gray-bearded Camp, with the floppy hat, looked them over. "The King's Frog Hunter? Huh," he said, looking at Thalmus. "You look small for a frog hunter. That must be Thunder then and the Paint stallion."

"Well, this is something," the second man said.

The men stared with wonder at the travelers until the first man asked, "What do ya want here?"

"We are looking for Boschina's father, Vericitas," Thalmus said, looking up at them.

The first man grunted. "Don't know him. Do you know him?" he asked the men on the other side.

"No. Don't know that name," the two men replied.

"Why are ya lookin' for him?" the second man asked.

"Don't make any difference why," the first man said. "He can't pass."

"Why not?" Camp asked.

"Because, he's the king's man."

"It is true that I hunt frogs for the king," Thalmus explained. "But now, I am searching for a man who the king wronged. This man, Vericitas, fled from prison and is hiding. We thought that he might be here."

"There are many here who are hiding from the king," the first man said. "That's why we can't let ya pass."

"I search only for Vericitas."

"I don't believe that," the second man sneered.

"Even if he were here, we wouldn't let you take him," Camp said.

"I don't want to take him," Thalmus answered. "I want to reunite him with his daughter and to tell him that he has been pardoned by the king."

"Oh, isn't that nice," the first man mocked.

"Well, I think it's nice," the curly haired young man said, speaking for the first time. He looked down at Thalmus and Boschina. "We should let them pass."

Thalmus had the immediate impression that this scarred-face young man was more than just a wayward criminal. His confident tone and inflection indicated so; plus, his style of speech marked him as being from another land.

"No. He's probably a spy," the second man said.

"He is a frog hunter," the young man countered. "His intentions are true."

The first man nodded.

"All right, let him in for twelve pieces, then."

"Let's just let them in," Camp said, becoming frustrated with the first man.

"I agree with twelve pieces," the second one said.

"We have no money," Thalmus replied, "only a little food."

"What? Doesn't the king pay ya?"

"I have never received money from the king."

"That can't be true," the second man responded, "someone of your fame with no money?"

"It's true," Thalmus said.

"Look at them," the young man pointed. "They don't look like they have any wealth."

"I agree with Maz," Camp said, siding with his cohort—the scarred-face young man. "Let's let them pass."

"For free? Gorga won't like that," the first man warned.

"They have nothing," Camp replied.

"I promise that we will not be a burden to you," Thalmus said. "We will simply look for Vericitas, then leave."

"I just want to find my father," Boschina implored.

"I believe her," Maz said, looking sympathetically at her. "I say, we let them pass."

"Me too," the second one said, finally agreeing with Camp and Maz.

"Gorga won't like this," the first man grumbled, shaking his head. "No fee and he's a king's man."

"He comes despite the king," Maz replied.

"This feels like trouble to me," the first man said, still shaking his head.

"Ah, let 'em pass," the second one said.

The first man exhaled loudly. He was outvoted three to one. He groaned and looked down at Thalmus. "If ya pass to the Top, you must never reveal who ya see here."

"I promise," Thalmus said.

"What about you, girl?"

"I want only to find my father," Boschina said. "I don't care who else is here."

The first man took a deep breath, blew it out, and groaned again.

"All right then, c'mon," he said and waved them forward.

They continued up the trail, around several more turns, and then a straight climb through the narrow passage and a stone archway to finally stand on the Table Top.

At first glance, the Top looked deserted. Wind gusted across the open land, shaking the scattered oak trees and brush that dotted the terrain. There was no sign of people or structures.

Boschina swung her leg over and dropped down from Dallion.

"Where are all the people?"

"I think there is more to this place than we see from here," Thalmus said.

Two of the guards, the friendly ones—Camp and Maz—walked up from the rocks overlooking the trail. As they did so, Thunder stepped alongside Boschina, ready to protect her. Dallion snorted and pawed the ground with a hoof, but Thalmus calmed him with a few strokes on his neck. The stallion moved back, ready to rear or charge if need be.

"Thank you for letting us through," Thalmus said to the men.

"Of course," Camp replied.

Up close now, Thalmus saw that Camp was quite a bit older than the young man and that he was a battle-scarred warrior. Broad shouldered and stout, he had a short sword at his side and carried a bow. A quiver with arrows hung on his back. He wore tan trousers, black boots, and a brown short-sleeved shirt with a wide collar open at the neck—all of which could have been the remnants of a uniform.

"It is an honor to meet you, Thalmus," the young man said.

He was medium height and square-shouldered; and though not as thick as Camp, he was solid. The scar on his cheek gave him a rugged look, but the curly black hair and green eyes that smiled along with his mouth signaled his true demeanor. He was dressed in a white shirt and gray trousers with similar black boots to Camp's. He carried a long sword on one side and a short blade on the other.

"I am known as Maz," the curly haired young man said. "This is Camp," motioning at the older man.

"This is Boschina of Marbala," Thalmus replied, formally introducing Boschina. "It is her father, Vericitas, for whom we search."

Maz and Camp nodded politely at her and then turned their attention to Thalmus. "There are so many stories," Maz said. "One never knows what to believe. I can see that the one about you being short is true."

Thalmus smiled. "I have never tried to be more than I am."

"The giant shell creature's true," Camp said, studying Thunder. "I've never seen one even half his size."

"He is the largest in the land," Thalmus said.

"I hear this horse can fly," Maz said, admiring Dallion.

"That is not true," Thalmus replied, patting Dallion's shoulder.

"But he is fast?" Maz persisted.

"Oh, yes," Thalmus answered. "I doubt you will find one faster."

"And the big brown owl?" Maz asked, looking up—as if Bubo might be hovering overhead. "Where is he?"

"I do not know. He is away right now," Thalmus responded cautiously and then changing the topic, he said: "You seem to know a lot about me and my friends, Maz."

Maz smiled, a little embarrassed. "Well, as I said, one hears so many stories that to finally discover—to see for myself the truth…well, now I know that…I can believe in you."

Thalmus nodded, realizing that Maz was searching for something as well. "What land do you come from?" Thalmus asked.

Maz and Camp glanced at one another. Camp answered. "We've taken refuge here. Where we are from doesn't matter."

Maz quickly added: "One's name and history are not required on the Top."

This was a polite way to say, "It's none of your business."

Thalmus nodded and changed the subject. "Do either of you know of a man here who carves stone?"

"A stone cutter?" Maz said and thought for a moment. "No, but that doesn't mean he isn't here."

"He may not be carving," Camp offered.

"He could not live without carving," Boschina replied.

Maz adjusted the sword on his side and glanced at Camp before he spoke. "Larma is who you want to see."

"I know Larma," Thalmus said, a bit surprised to hear the name from Maz—and suddenly this place took on more importance than just Vericitas. If Larma was here, then something new and powerful was brewing—something that surely had to do with the prophecy. "Larma is here on Table Top?" Thalmus asked carefully.

"Yes. If the person you seek is here, Larma will know," Maz said. "Then again, so will Oleen, who's here now."

"Oleen," Thalmus repeated. There was some familiarity with that name, but he could not recall why.

"Yeah, so will Gorga," Camp was saying. "But, you don't want to talk to him."

"Why not?" Boschina asked.

"He's the self-appointed lord of Table Top and behaves so. I suggest you stay clear of him."

"You don't follow him?"

"No, no. Maz and I are not part of his gang. We just do our turn guarding the gate."

Maz pointed across the Top. "Head for that big oak tree, the big one beyond the scragglies. You see it?"

"Yes."

"If you keep going toward it, the fourth trail on the left will take you to Larma Hollow."

"Thank you," Thalmus said.

Thunder, as usual, was already plodding off, but Dallion stayed near Boschina, walking alongside her.

"Good hunting, Thalmus," Camp said.

"I hope you find your father," Maz called to Boschina.

Boschina looked back and waved.

Maz and Camp watched them walking off across the Top. Then, Maz turned to Camp and said: "I have a feeling that we will be seeing them again."

Camp looked at his friend and nodded. "Thalmus did not show his thoughts, but he has questions about us."

Looking back to watch Thalmus, Maz smiled. "We just met the Frog Hunter, Dallion, and Thunder, here, at Table Top! I tell you, something will come of this; whether it affects our future or not, we will remember this day."

*

Sparse, short grass grew across the rocky ground. Tiny flowers of various colors were scattered amongst the grass: little white ones that looked like popcorn, miniature yellow and purple daisies, and pink roses. Boschina bent down to get a better look.

"These little flowers are so beautiful." She picked several and showed them to Dallion and then to Thalmus. "They're so small, you hardly notice them. But when you look close, you see how pretty they are."

Thalmus smiled. "It is a matter of truly looking, isn't it?"

"Thalmus," Boschina said, examining the flowers as they walked, "who is Larma?"

"Larma is…." he thought for a moment. "Larma is a mystic, a teacher. Larma has ancient and powerful knowledge."

"Is he one of the old ones you told us about at the tunnel in the Barranca?"

"Yes. Larma is the oldest and wisest."

"I hope we get to meet him."

"I believe we will," Thalmus answered and paused before adding, "Larma is not a *he*, Boschina. Larma is a woman."

Surprised, Boschina looked up from the flowers in her hand.

"A woman?"

The wind was whipping across the Top—not strong, but gusting enough to lift small dust clouds here and there. The ground rolled down to a creek where black, lumpy, lava rock lined the edge of the streambed. The trail crossed the creek. Dallion smelled the slow moving water and tested it for taste. It was all right and they all drank.

Downstream two men were filling water pouches. The men watched them for a moment, and then hurried away.

Dallion waded through the knee-deep creek to the other side. Thalmus and Boschina followed with Thunder coming behind. Ahead of them on the trail, they saw a man run across the path. He was gripping a canvas bag and was being chased by a woman who screamed after him. The man suddenly stopped, dropped the bag, and grabbed the woman. He threw her to the ground, and then picked up the bag and hurried off.

"Did you see that?" Boschina asked.

Thalmus was already running to the woman.

"Can I help you?" Thalmus asked as he stopped at the crying woman's side.

"He stole my food," she cried.

Thalmus turned and ran after the thief, though Dallion had already caught up to him. The stallion had blown past the man, reared up, and stomped his hoofs in front of him. The man stopped and backed up, surprised by the sudden appearance of this wild and threatening horse. Determined to escape, the thief drew a dagger and lunged at Dallion.

"Get away, you demon," the man screamed.

Thalmus ran up from behind and kicked the legs out from under the man. Before the man could recover, Thalmus stepped on his wrist that held the knife. The man's hand was forced open and Thalmus took the dagger and threw it away.

Laying on his back in the grass—his right arm pinned to the ground and Dallion stomping the grass on his left—the man stopped fighting. He stared up at them in panic. Dallion calmed his hooves, but his flared nostrils kept snorting at the man.

"Please don't hurt me."

Thalmus took the bag of food from him.

"You should not steal—and you should never hurt a woman."

"I won't do it again, I promise. Just don't hurt me," he pleaded

Thalmus lifted his foot from the thief's arm. The man hesitated and then rolled over, got up, and slowly backed away. When he cleared ten meters between them, he turned and ran off—looking back over his shoulder to see if they were following. Dallion and Thalmus watched the man until he was out of sight.

Thalmus patted Dallion on the shoulder. "That's a troubled man, who is trouble." Dallion snorted in agreement and they returned to the woman who was cowering on the ground.

Her dress was shabby, her face and hair dirty—and her hands worn. Boschina was standing beside her and Thunder was next to Boschina. Thalmus set the bag down next to the stunned woman.

She looked at it and up at Thalmus, not sure what to expect.

"What else can we do to help you?" he asked.

She was suspicious of these strangers, not knowing what to think. She looked at Dallion and Thunder, then at Boschina, and finally at Thalmus again. "You're a strange lot," she said.

Boschina laughed.

"I suppose we are. We would like to help you though."

"Why? I've nothing to give you."

"We don't want anything," Boschina replied.

"I am Thalmus. This is Boschina, Thunder, and Dallion," Thalmus said, motioning to each one of them.

The woman got to her feet, moved away from Thunder, and looked them over from a new perspective. "My name's Vie. You must want something." She paused and reluctantly said, "All I can give you for your kindness is some food."

"Thank you, but no," Thalmus replied. "Keep your food."

"We are looking for my father, Vericitas," Boschina said. "He is a sculptor. Do you know of him?"

"I don't know anyone by that name, nor a man who carves stone." She thought of something and looked at Boschina. "Oleen would know." Vie looked away, in the direction she had come. "Now, I must go back to my place."

"May we walk with you?" Thalmus asked.

She hesitated and then pointed at Dallion and Thunder.

"Keep them away from my plants."

They walked back across the main trail and down a side path. This narrow path went over a rise, and then curved down into a hollow through which a little creek flowed. Here was a small garden with rows of various plants terraced into the slope. A lava ledge that jutted out along one side of the hollow created a natural cover. There was enough clearance under it for a child to stand and deep enough for about three adults to lie down. Rocks had been stacked at both ends to close it in and deflect the wind. A straw bed and the woman's things were spread on the ground. The remains of a campfire smoldered at the outer edge.

"What a nice place," Thalmus remarked.

"I work hard to grow the food," Vie said. "The ground is bad up here."

"Too shallow?" Thalmus asked.

"Yes. And too hard," she said, looking at her garden. "There are better places, but they're taken."

"You must trade your food?" Thalmus asked.

"It's how I live. I don't have much. When the scoundrels, the lazy ones, steal it, then I have nothing."

"Why do you stay here?" Boschina asked.

Vie looked over the little rows of plants. "My husband and I had a farm at Seena. The king's collectors kept taking more and more of our crop. It was not fair. My husband finally resisted. Soldiers came and beat him and chased us off the land. He tried to fight back, for the land had belonged to his family for as long as anyone could remember. The other farmers were afraid and wouldn't help. So, we stood alone. Finally, we were chased here. By then, my poor husband was sick. His body was broken from the beatings. His spirit was gone. He didn't last long. Now, I survive as best I can."

Thalmus was saddened to hear her story and to learn of the soldiers' behavior. "I can't believe that the king approves of this," he said. "This must be the work of others."

Thunder had been standing to the side, eyeing the rows of plants; now, he shifted and turned his head to the south. Thalmus noticed the move and watched his friend for a signal. It wasn't long before Thunder clicked his jaws. Dallion lifted his head, sniffing the wind.

"Someone is coming," Thalmus said.

Boschina looked at Thunder, who stood watching the high ground.

"It had better not be that thief," Vie said.

Thunder clicked twice more and Thalmus said: "It is many more than one."

A man appeared on the ground above the hollow. Thalmus recognized him as the guard who had not wanted to let them pass. He looked down at them and hollered: "There they are!" In a few moments, more men joined him; Thalmus counted a dozen. As that group started down the slope toward them, more people appeared and followed.

"Oh no," Vie said. "It's Gorga and his gang."

"What do they want?" Boschina asked.

"Trouble, that's what they want."

Leading the group was a tall man with blond hair and a short-cropped beard. He was not muscular, but walked with long strides and a fluid movement that announced confidence and authority. He stopped three meters in front of Thalmus, who stood beside

Thunder's outstretched head. Boschina took her position on the other side of Thunder and Dallion stood alongside her. The crowd fell into a semi-circle behind the blond man. Boschina looked for Camp and Maz, but they were not there. Thalmus, Boschina, Thunder and Dallion watched and waited.

What a ragtag gang, Thalmus thought.

Still, he would not underestimate a possible foe—for he, of all people, knew that looks can be deceiving. Vie was not sure whether to stand with her new friends or to stay clear; so, she backed away toward her garden to protect her plants.

The blond-haired leader looked them over.

"I'm Gorga," he said in a loud, forceful tone.

Thalmus looked up at Gorga and said calmly: "I am Thalmus. This is Boschina and our friends, Thunder and Dallion. We are looking for--"

"I've heard of you and your friends," Gorga interrupted and then turned to the guard. "You're right. He is short." The crowd—which was growing steadily, laughed.

"I told you," the guard said.

"I find it hard to believe that you can kill frogs," Gorga said.

"I can understand your doubt," Thalmus replied. "But size really has nothing to do with it."

"I believe it does," Gorga said aggressively. "I control this mountain and everything and everyone here. You should not have been allowed up." He glanced at the guard. "But, you're here. That's bad enough. What's worse, you lied and assaulted one of my people."

"I have done neither," Thalmus said.

"Razzi," Gorga called.

The thief emerged from the crowd.

"Is this the man that attacked you?"

"That's him, Gorga, and the horse. It almost stomped me."

Dallion snorted and pawed the ground.

"That thief stole my crops," Vie shouted, pointing from her garden at the man. "He knocked me down. This Thalmus stopped him and got my crops back."

Gorga sneered at the woman.

"He says he paid you. Then Thalmus and this horse beat him and took the food from him."

"That's not true. He stole them," Vie insisted.

Gorga ignored her and turned to Thalmus. "The way I see it, Thalmus, you owe Razzi a sack of food or money. Which I'm sure the king must be paying you."

"You are mistaken four times, Gorga," Thalmus said.

"Four? What do you mean?"

"That man did not pay for Vie's food. I did not attack him. I owe him nothing. And the king has never paid me."

"Yes, I know that you claim to have no money. Then you'll just have to trade something for your debt. I'm thinking this beautiful horse would do. What do you call him?"

Thalmus smiled. "Your man should be punished for thievery and striking this woman. I'm wondering what kind of leader cannot control his people."

Gorga took a step forward. "I'll show you what control I have. If you cannot pay, we'll throw you out of here—the shortest way to the bottom—over the falls."

Some in the crowd shouted: "Over the falls."

"You are not interested in the truth, are you?" Thalmus asked.

"Only the truth as I see it," Gorga replied.

There was a sudden commotion at the back of the crowd. People were being pushed aside like stalks of corn. "Move over! Get outta my way!" a voice demanded.

Boschina stretched, leaning one way and then another, trying to see who it was. Then, the men in the front row were violently shoved apart as the person came through them. The assaulted men complained, but fell silent when they saw who it was. A sturdy woman wearing a short-brimmed leather hat, a leather vest, short sleeve blouse, and a sword at her side stepped out to face Gorga.

When Thalmus saw her, he smiled and crossed his arms.

"What are you doing?" the woman demanded of Gorga.

Surprised, Gorga stepped back.

"Oleen. Why I'm…I'm dealing out justice."

She blurted a short laugh. "You? Giving justice? That'll be the day."

"What, uh, why, why are you here?" Gorga stammered. "This is no concern of yours."

"These are friends of mine," the warrior woman said. "I've been expecting them."

Now, Boschina recognized the brazen woman.

Her mouth dropped open in total surprise. It was Princess Ekala.

"These…they are your friends?" Gorga stuttered.

"You do not believe me?"

Gorga looked at her suspiciously. He was recovering from the surprise of her sudden appearance. "I'm not sure I do." He looked around at the crowd, to see if any of her followers were with her, and then turned back to Oleen. "You're alone? We have you greatly outnumbered here, Oleen."

"Outnumbered?" She laughed again and motioned at Thalmus. "This man could take out half of your people by himself." She pointed a finger at Gorga. "Thunder would chomp you in one bite. And Dallion would stomp and kick the insides out of the rest of you," she said, glaring at the crowd. "I wouldn't even have to draw my sword. But," looking back at Gorga, "I wouldn't ask my friends to do that. Because," she grasped her sword handle, "I can take you myself."

The men near her backed up, stumbling and falling over the people behind them. Gorga took a step back, grasped the handle of the sword at his side, but hesitated.

She was staring at him, standing ready to pull her sword. He was not ready for this challenge, especially now with the frog hunter here. The time was not right. He removed his hand from the sword and motioned toward Thalmus and Boschina. "So, they're under your and Larma's protection?"

"What do you think?" Oleen scoffed. "I'm not here to greet *you*."

Gorga wanted a confrontation with Oleen, but knew that he had to bide his time for he did not have the man power yet to take on Oleen and Larma. Reluctantly, he had to appease her for now.

"I want no quarrel with you and your followers, Oleen," he said.

"Then you'd best turn your tail around and leave."

Embarrassed in front of the crowd, he took a step forward and pointed at her. "Someday, Oleen, you will suffer. I'll see to it."

"Thanks for the warning," she said and waved her hand, dismissing him. "You can go now."

The crowd began to disperse.

Gorga wanted the last word. "You and Larma will not always have it your way. A day is coming when there will be a stronger power here."

"Maybe, but not in your lifetime, Gorga," Oleen responded. "By the way, I'm concerned about this farmer woman's safety. You will see that she's not bothered anymore."

Gorga stared at Oleen while he tried to control his anger. Finally, he said, "I'll spread the word."

"Good. Now go."

Gorga backed away, glaring at Oleen. Then, he turned and strode off, the crowd trailing behind him.

Chapter Sixteen
Larma Hollow

Oleen slapped Thalmus on the shoulder. "Surprised to see me?"

"Yes," Thalmus said. "I must say that I am."

She rubbed Thunder's bald head. "Still dragging that shell around, hey, Thunder?"

Dallion came up and nudged her. She hugged him and rubbed noses. "Yeah, me too, big Dal," she said and patted his neck. Turning, she stood with her fisted hands on her hips in front of Boschina. "Look at you, girl. Carrying a sword and looking like you know how to use it."

"Oh, Princess Ekala, you surprised me," Boschina said. "I didn't recognize you at first."

Ekala shushed her.

"The people here know me as Oleen, the warrior woman."

"Oh, I'm sorry," Boschina said, covering her mouth. "I didn't know."

Oleen pointed at the sword hanging from Boschina's waist.

"Do you know how to use that tool?"

"A little…I'm learning."

Oleen glanced at Thalmus. "Well, you're learning from the best. You do know that?"

"Oh, yes."

Oleen opened her hand in request. "May I see your sword?"

"Of course," Boschina replied, drawing the weapon from the scabbard. "Thalmus said it was made for me. My initials are on it."

Oleen took the sword by the handle and cut several figure eights in the air—listening to the blade hum and feeling a slight tingle in her hand. "It has a nice balance."

"It's just right for me," Boschina said. "And the grip holds my hand."

Looking at the initials etched in the metal Oleen asked: "SCD?"

Boschina smiled. "That's me, Stone Cutter's Daughter."

Oleen nodded as she examined the engravings on each side of the blade and smiled in recognition. She pulled her own sword from its scabbard hanging at her belt and held the two blades side by side.

She looked at Thalmus. "It's just like mine."

"Yes, it is," Thalmus replied. "There were only three swords made in that style. They are unique and, as you know, have special qualities."

Oleen handed the sword back to Boschina. "You're fortunate to have this tool because it's fitted to you alone. In your hand, it can be a powerful weapon; I know mine is."

Boschina carefully slid the blade into its scabbard.

"It has already protected me in four battles," she said proudly.

"Four," Oleen responded, impressed. She glanced at Thalmus. "You've been getting into more trouble than I thought." She looked again at the Stone Cutter's Daughter. "Maybe I'll be able to help you, too. Every woman should know how to protect herself."

Thalmus smiled. "Protecting yourself is one thing," he said. "Challenging someone to a fight is another matter."

"You're right, Thalmus. But I've learned that strength is the only thing they understand around here. So, that's what I give them."

"Just be careful to not push that too far. It could get you into trouble."

Oleen smiled back at Thalmus. "They would not have been a match for us."

"No," he replied. "Not with Boschina on our side."

Oleen blurted a laugh and bear-hugged Thalmus.

"It's good to see you, Thalmus."

"I am glad to see you, too," Thalmus said, then added with a whisper, "Ekala."

"Well, come on," she said, stepping back. "I'll take you to Larma Hollow."

"Oleen," Vie, the farmer woman, called from her garden. "May I come with you? You've offered before and I refused because I wanted to live on my own. But I want to come now."

"Of course," Oleen responded, walking to her. "You were strong to live on your own. I believe you will be even stronger joining with us."

They helped Vie gather up her things and harvest the plants that were ready. Then, they walked up out of the hollow, into the breeze, and headed across the Top as the sun settled toward the horizon. There were people living in the ravines, crevices, and hollows that creased the surface of the hard earth. Some had built shelters; others had set up camp under rock ledges or in shallow caves. Many of them had fires burning and were cooking the evening meal. Upon seeing Oleen, most of the people waved and called out her name. She returned their greeting with an outstretched arm and open hand—a sign of friendship.

"Most of the people here are not dangerous," Oleen said to Thalmus and Boschina. "But it's an unruly place."

Oleen struck out away from the trail and they followed her to the outer rim of the Top. Standing close to the edge of the precipice, they could look straight down at the land far below and out as far as the eye could see. Thalmus scanned the distance for the Barranca, wondering if it was visible—wondering about Tobazi, Dysaan, and Currad. Were they still there? Or had they moved eastward? Would he be able to see them? Finally, he spotted a slithering brown line in the green plain. But, it was too far to see something the size of people.

"I think I see the Barranca," Boschina said. "It seems to be moving. Do you see it, Thalmus?"

It did look like it was sliding one way and then another, getting wider then disappearing all together—only to reappear again in a slightly different form.

"Yes, it does look as if it is moving," Thalmus replied. "It must be the distance and the wind in the grass that makes it appear so."

"It looks like it's moving to me," Boschina said.

To their left was one of the creeks that flowed smooth and helpless over the edge, falling free and widening until plunging into the pool at the bottom. The pulsing roar from the constant crashing of water echoed off the cliffs. Occasional cool drifts of mist from the waterfall were caught in the updraft, lifted to the top and blew over them.

"Isn't this beautiful?" Oleen said to no one in particular. "This is the highest place in the land, where you can see the farthest and feel the freest. And few know of it or even care. Don't you find it odd for this to be here, in this place where people come to hide, to confine themselves?"

"I like it," Boschina said.

Oleen looked at Thalmus. "This morning I saw you from here and knew you would come to the Top. I thought of going down to meet you. To save you the trip up, because I know that Veracitas is not here."

"Are you sure?" Boschina asked.

"Yes, I have checked every hollow for him, Boschina. He is not here. There's something I want you to see, Thalmus."

"This?" Thalmus said, indicating the view.

"This is only part of it." She glanced at the sun. "It's getting late. We must go on."

They doubled back, crossed the creek, and then skirted the rim for a distance before leaving it and joining the trail. Once again, they were heading for the oak tree. The tiny yellow flowers were abundant here, growing in a wide path to the oak that hovered like an umbrella. As they approached the tree, Oleen turned to the left on a path that descended into a hollow. At the beginning was an outcropping of rock with the name LARMA clearly formed in the natural flow of the stone.

The trail passed through a stone arch as it continued to sink below the flat ground of the Top. The opening in the arch was symmetrical—about four meters in diameter and about two meters thick. On the other side of the arch, a spring bubbled out of the bank and into a flume that had been dug along the right side of the hollow. Thus directed, the water flowed down the flume to a pond. The pond had been created by a small earth-and-rock dam. There was a spillway where the pond overflowed into another flume and continued on. The trail went around the pool, but the group stopped to drink. Shadows grew in the hollow as the sun reached the horizon. Beyond the pond were several stone huts.

Two horses were tied to one of the huts where four guards, all women dressed like Oleen, stood talking. The moment they saw the strangers though, the guards began to nock arrows and move toward them until Oleen waved them off with a call that it was all right.

When the horses saw Dallion, they whinnied—pulling at their moorings and stomping. The guards had to calm the horses and secure their attachments; for his part, Dallion stayed with Boschina rather than stirring more emotions in the other horses.

The banks of the ravine here had been terraced. Plants were growing in rows on each level. Attached to the second hut was a water wheel that spun in the flume and lifted buckets of water to a trough above the roof. The buckets dumped into the wooden trough that extended across to the highest terrace, where the water poured out into the rows of plants. From there, the water was channeled to the lower levels.

Thalmus saw that, like the farms in Rainland, these people had designed and built a system to bring water to a large crop to feed many people in a difficult land. Workers were making their way off the terraces, down the bank, and along the trail. They were all women, and they stopped to look at the approaching strangers with the giant shell creature. The women relaxed when Oleen greeted them. They were happy to see her and to meet the newcomers. Oleen introduced Vie and the women welcomed her and gathered her things from Thalmus and Boschina, and then continued down the trail, for the day was ending.

When the trail descended into a cave, Boschina hesitated at the entrance. She was looking at the rock above the cave opening for warnings when Thalmus noticed she had fallen behind and came back to her.

"It is all right, Boschina," he said. "This is not like the tunnel in the Barranca."

"Are you sure?"

"Yes. This is a safe passage way to their camp."

As Thalmus started into the tunnel with Boschina, several of the women watched him and confronted Oleen.

"Is he coming in? Is he allowed to come in?"

"Yes. He's coming in," Oleen replied. "It's all right. He's a friend of mine and Larma's."

This satisfied the women and they went on.

Thalmus heard this and was concerned about offending. When he and Boschina reached Oleen, who had waited for them, he asked: "Is there something wrong?"

"No, Thalmus. It's rare for a man to be allowed in here, but you are an exception. You must come in," Oleen said. "Larma is expecting you. Besides, this is what I wanted you to see."

"All right, but you must tell me if I should leave."

"Don't worry, I'll tell you. Come on."

This tunnel was about three meters wide and fifty meters long. The ceiling was high enough for a rider on a horse and it was lit with torches. Two more guards, armed with swords and spears, were stationed at the other end of the tunnel. They greeted Oleen with respect as their leader, but eyed Thalmus suspiciously.

The group came out of the tunnel into a large open area that was well below the Table Top and extended out, like a shelf, about one hundred meters—then dropped off again to the plain far below. It was about two hundred meters wide with a sudden drop at both ends as well. Thalmus looked back at the tunnel where the wall of sheer cliffs rose to the Top above them. There were caves in the cliffs and stone huts built all along the base.

The shelf was a natural fortress.

At one end of the shelf was a large cooking area: stone-wrapped fire pits with meat roasting on grills, large pots with bubbling soups, a rounded stone bread oven, and rows of rough-hewn wooden tables. The site was busy with many women preparing, cooking, and serving food to other women.

"We'll eat and then go see Larma," Oleen told them.

"Oh, good," Boschina said. "I'm so hungry and that food smells wonderful."

"Dal," Oleen patted Dallion's neck. "Shadahn is in the stables." Dallion whinnied and nudged Thalmus with his nose.

"Yes, Dal," Thalmus said. "Let's get all this off you."

Boschina and Thalmus untied the gear and removed it from Dallion. Oleen told a woman to show Dallion to the stables; then, they went to the eating area.

Vie was already eating with the workers she had come in with. Oleen, Boschina, and Thalmus stood in the food line. They were each served a plate of mutton and vegetables—and sat down together at a table with Oleen between them. She had greens brought and placed on the ground for Thunder. The women who brought the greens stood for a moment, watching him eat, and then returned to their duties.

Thalmus spoke quietly to Oleen as he ate.

"Your life is quite different here."

Oleen smiled. "You noticed."

"Standing in line for food," he said. "Sitting at a common table, dressed like a soldier; yes, quite different from your life at the castle."

"It's not the same here," Oleen answered. "I'm not the same."

"I can see that," Thalmus replied.

"You disapprove?"

"Not at all," he said looking at her. "It is good."

Ninety women were in the cooking and eating area. They had all fallen silent when Thalmus had entered the area. Some were staring at him, but most of the women pretended to ignore his presence.

"I can't believe this," Oleen grumbled. "Normally, supper is so noisy you can't hear yourself." She stood up and looked around at the women. "All right, listen to me," she said sternly.

They all stopped what they were doing and turned toward her.

"This is Thalmus," She said, pointing at the only man there. "I know you've heard of him. He's the King's Frog Hunter. But, more important than that, he is my friend. He's helping this girl, Boschina, to find her father. Today, he protected this farmer woman, Vie, from Gorga. We can learn much from him, for he's an old ally of Larma's.

Now, be yourselves—act normal!"

She sat down and went back to eating.

Gradually, the women began talking amongst themselves and the noise rose to a level that suited Oleen. It was dark now, but the area was lit by the cooking fires and torches on poles. Thalmus could see candles burning in the various caves and huts. Smoke from the fires wafted above the ground, reflecting the light and giving an eerie fluorescence to the shelf.

"Thalmus, I know that you've been observing," Oleen said. "What do you think of Larma Hollow?"

"This is what you wanted me to see?"

"Yes. I've been working here for a long time."

"It is a very organized village," Thalmus said.

"There are one hundred and eighty three women here," Oleen said.

"Where'd they all come from?" Boschina asked.

"From throughout the land," Oleen replied. "Each one of them, for one reason or another, was alone and struggling. I brought them here for safety and to teach them how to survive on their own. We've taught them how to farm, how to hunt, how to use a bow and sword and spear. We grow and hunt our own food."

"They appear to work in groups," Thalmus observed.

"It was Larma's idea to arrange them in groups, called forces, of ten to twelve. That's how the work is assigned and done. Each force has a leader. We've trained each group how to fight together and in unison with all the forces."

"Have they been tested?" Thalmus asked.

"We've had two fights with Gorga."

Thalmus grinned. "I could tell by Gorga's reaction today that he was not the victor of those fights."

"Hah," Oleen laughed. "We routed them. But, they're a band of scoundrels, not well-trained. What I'm really proud of, Thalmus, is just recently, about the time I left the castle and saw you two on the road, two of our forces were returning from a hunt in the flat land when they were attacked by regular troops."

"Why did the troops attack them?" Boschina asked.

"Those troops not only wanted the fresh meat we had, but wanted to get to the Top. You see, we control the only other trail from the plain to Table Top." She pointed across the shelf. "It comes up over there."

"What happened?"

Oleen leaned in closer to Thalmus and Boschina. "Our forces were outnumbered; still they fought the troops at the trail head and beat back each charge. We hurt them so badly that the rabble finally limped away. And I wasn't even here. I'm so proud of them."

"Were any of the women hurt?" Boschina asked.

Oleen sighed. "Three died and five more were wounded. They're recovering. The men though, had twice those numbers. It gave our people strength. They're wary, but much more confident now."

"Do you think the troops wanted up here to look for Veracitas?" Thalmus asked, pushing his empty plate away.

"I believe so, Thalmus. The troops kept yelling about fighting for the reward."

Thalmus shook his head. "This was before I spoke to the king and he retracted the reward."

"We know the troops are still looking for him," Boschina said, "They've been following us."

"They haven't given up," Oleen confirmed, as a woman took their empty plates and utensils away. "Our hunting forces that returned this morning reported troops still roaming the area."

"You are staying alert?" Thalmus asked.

"Oh, yes. Since that fight, we've doubled the guards at the lower trail and increased the size of the hunting forces."

"What about the Top trail, at the farm?"

"I'm not worried about Gorga," Oleen said, standing up. "He doesn't want to fight us. Those guards are mainly to keep his scoundrels from stealing food. Come. We must go see Larma."

Thunder picked his head up from his food and started to turn with them.

"You can't come, Thunder," Oleen told him and looked at Thalmus. "The trail is too narrow."

Thunder bumped his head against Thalmus. Thalmus placed his hand on the leathery head. "He does not feel safe here by the fires. Can we move his food away, into the darkness?"

"Of course," Oleen answered. "I'm sorry, Thunder."

The three of them scooped up his food and moved it away. Boschina stroked Thunder's head as he trod after them.

"Don't worry, Thunder. We're safe here," she told him. The giant tortoise bobbed his head and clicked.

Oleen led them through the dark, without a torch, across the open shelf to the wall of cliffs. They walked by some of the stone huts that were lit by candles. Women inside were softly singing lyrical songs that drifted on the night air. Beyond the huts, it was quite dark. Boschina could barely see Oleen in front of her as they moved along next to the mountain. When they came to the end of the shelf, Boschina gasped as she thought Oleen was stepping over the edge; but, there was a narrow rock ledge—no more than a half of a meter wide—across the face of the cliff.

"Hold my hand," Oleen said. Boschina's hand searched in the darkness until she found Oleen's open hand. "I can't have you falling, Boschina. Lean against the rock with your other hand and feel the path with your feet. Are you with us, Thalmus?"

"I am right behind Boschina," Thalmus answered. He was thinking of Bubo and how he could use the owl's help right now.

They shuffled along the ledge as a quarter-moon appeared over the Top. The trail rose and descended—and went in and out of the crevices of the cliff. Finally, the ledge followed the rock into a crevice and kept going inward, widening into the floor of a cave. Boschina breathed a sigh of relief. There was an orange glow emanating from the bowels of the cave. Thalmus whiffed a sweet fragrance that slapped him with memories he had not recalled in a long time. Oleen led them deeper, toward the glow as laughter echoed in the cave.

"Well, somebody's having a good time," Boschina said.

Rounding a bend, they entered a large room with a fire burning in a pit to one side. The flames bounced light and warmth off the walls. The smoke rose to the high ceiling and went out through a chimney hole. The room was filled with a pleasant fragrance that was instantly soothing. Five women were seated in wooden chairs, while a sixth woman was doing an awkward dance—imitating a bird. The dancer had bandages wrapped around her midsection and over her right shoulder. Four of the seated women also had bandages. All six were laughing.

"Oleen," one of the women said, upon seeing her enter the light. "You should've seen Thoe."

"I see her now," Oleen responded and then addressed the dancer. "You must be feeling better, Thoe."

"Oh, yes. Larma has made us laugh."

"It looks like you were the cause of that," Oleen replied, smiling at her. "I'm glad to see all of you are feeling better."

"How could we not heal in Larma's presence?"

Oleen turned her attention to the woman without bandages. "I have brought the ones you wanted to see."

Thalmus stepped forward. "It is a great pleasure to see you once again, Larma."

The woman glowed with happiness. She looked young and strong like the women around her. In the next instant, seeing her from another angle as she stood, her face appeared aged and ancient. Then, just as quickly, her countenance changed again to that of a middle-aged woman. No matter how her face appeared though, there was always brightness in her eyes; and at this moment, they were focused on Thalmus. He felt those eyes envelope him and her smile caress him.

"Thalmus, the pleasure is mine," she said. "It has been so long. Welcome." She extended both hands with her palms up.

Laying his hands slowly, carefully, into hers, they stared into one another's eyes. Time and memories passed between them. The others waited while the fire crackled and popped and danced in the silence of the cave. Finally, Larma and Thalmus started laughing, as if they had just shared a joke together.

"You, above all the others, I miss the most," Larma said.

"I had not heard anything about you for so long," Thalmus said, "that I wondered where you were."

"I have been here for some time. I must admit, I like it."

"Then it is a good place for you," Thalmus replied.

"And you, Thalmus, once again, are on a very important mission. Let me meet this girl, this Boschina."

Thalmus stepped back and motioned to Boschina.

Larma turned her gaze on the girl. "Come, child, take my hands."

Boschina was entranced. She moved forward and placed her hands in Larma's.

Larma peered into her eyes. "Let me see where you have been in search of your father. Oh my, you were in the grasp of Metro. That must have been frightening." Larma said, her eyes glistening. "I see that you have been to Rainland. You escaped, but some grayness still hangs in your mind. I'm sorry to tell you, that will always be with you." Larma probed deeper. "The Barranca, you have traveled that sunken trail, fought the Gauks, and you have passed through the tunnel?" Larma gripped her hands. "Oh child, you have grown much in a short time."

"Because of my father," Boschina said. "I need to find him."

"Yes, you must find him. It is just as important for the rest of us, as it is for you."

Larma lit a candle from the fire, and led Boschina, Thalmus, and Oleen out of the room—through a passageway—and into a smaller room. There, she lit more candles in the recesses of the walls. A balmy haze hung in the room from incense smoldering in a bowl.

Larma looked at Boschina. "I brought you away from the others because I did not want them to hear what I'm going to tell you. Thalmus knows much of this story and now you will learn it."

She put a gentle hand on Oleen's arm and smiled at her. "Long ago, when Oleen, Ekala as you know her, was a baby, I was called to oversee her life. I became her nanny. Beginning when she was a small child, her mother, the queen, and I started bringing her to Table Top. While we were here, Ekala called herself Oleen, an ancient name I had told her. It was my sister's name, a great teacher and spiritual leader." Larma paused, stirred the bowl of incense, and inhaled the aroma.

Then, she continued. "After Oleen's mother died, the king put me in charge of raising her. So, I would bring her here to teach and to train. It was different then. The people who came here were not running or hiding. They were not being chased by the king's troops. I never dreamed that one day Oleen would turn this into a refuge and bring me back to teach other women. I also never dreamed that the king would start behaving as he is. We were hopeful that your father's statue could change that."

"It only made the king so mad that he had Father thrown into a cell to die."

"That was the sorcerer's spell at work," Larma said. "Metro knows that the power of truth will expose him and destroy his magic."

"That is why Veracitas' statue is so powerful," Thalmus said to Boschina.

"It is powerful," Larma continued. "Unfortunately, the king—in his anger at growing old and his doubt of his daughter's strength to lead—has become an easy mark for wicked ones, like Metro."

"You know Metro?" Boschina asked.

"No. But, there have always been, and always will be, people like him. We fight them constantly. This one, though, this sorcerer, is very clever. He has spread his influence everywhere, including Table Top."

"Here?" Boschina questioned. "Even here?"

"Gorga," Thalmus said.

"Yes. Gorga is an agent of Metro's."

"Do not underestimate him, Ekala," Thalmus warned. "I see in him a strong desire for power. He will do anything for it; therefore, he will be controlled by it. That makes him very dangerous."

"His followers are not warmed by the same fire," Ekala replied.

"He may not have the men now who have the will, but he could get them," Thalmus answered. "The renegade troops, perhaps."

"What about Corsair?" Boschina asked. "He's terrible, even to his own people."

Thalmus agreed. "Corsair is probably controlled by Metro. It is good that you realized that, Boschina."

"It will take all of us to defeat this plague," Larma said. "Most important, though, is Veracitas. We must find him and return him and his statue to the castle."

"My father, the king, must see the stone truth, and change." Ekala said. "I don't know how much longer he can rule under Metro's spell. Rundall is barely hanging onto control in the court."

Larma reached out and gently held Boschina's hands. "Show me the image of your father that the wind brought back for Metro." Boschina closed her eyes to visualize the falling water.

"Keep your eyes open, Boschina," Larma told her. "Look into my eyes. Do you see yourself?"

"Yes. Yes, I do."

"Now, look past your image, deeper into me."

Boschina stared into Larma's eyes. Her own reflection was there for a moment and then it dissolved. The waterfalls from Table Top appeared and ran out. The tunnel in the Barranca with her mother's hand in the darkness drifted by—followed by the giant lizard trying to bite her and Dallion rearing and stomping the beast. Next, the grimacing face of Corsair came as he attacked them and Tobazi flailing with his sword; then, Bubo diving from the grayness into the Shower Knight's cloud and it jumping and thundering in the rain. Blackness came and slowly the squeezing and crawling amongst the coffins at the farm, following the serious faces of Tuggle and Oddkin. Suddenly, the mud worm reared up and was washed away by the Shower Knight. And finally, the image of Metro's room evolved with the wind swirling the silver powder that showed the sparkling falling water appearing over Veracitas.

"Hold on to that image, Boschina," Larma said. "Let me study it."

They were locked together, eye to eye, for several moments. Then, Larma slowly pulled back and clasped Boschina's hands together in hers. She smiled. "I know what the image is. More importantly, I know where it is."

Chapter Seventeen
New Allies

"You know where my father is?" Boschina asked, surprised. She blinked. "You saw where he is in my eyes?"

"Well, I know where the image in your head came from," Larma replied. "You will have to find out if he is still there."

"Where is this place, Larma? So, we can go find him."

"It is where this land meets the Great Water."

Boschina was puzzled by this.

"The Great Water?" she asked. "Why would my father go there?"

"There is a place in the cliffs of a stone cove where a spring of hot water boils out of the rock and spills over the edge to fall on the shore of the Great Water. It is a beautiful sight."

Boschina looked at her, still not convinced. "Are you sure the image you saw in my eyes and this hot spring at the Great Water are the same?"

Larma smiled at her. "Yes, I am, Boschina. I have been there many times. It is unique. You can stand in the shallows with the waves of the cold Great Water hitting your legs as the shower of hot water falls on you from above. Trees grow out of the rocks. Birds land on your shoulders. Fish walk on the sand. The stone can be carved. And, it is a place Veracitas has been before."

Boschina was surprised. "He has? I don't remember such a place. I've never been to the Great Water."

"It was before you, child. It is one of the places where I taught your father."

Boschina was stunned to hear that Larma not only knew her father, but was his teacher. "I thought my grandfather taught him how to carve stone," she said. "What did you teach him?"

"Oh, he knew how to work the stone," Larma said, lighting another candle. "He had that skill from his father, but his statues

were cold and lifeless. I showed him how to make them come alive—
to take what he saw with his eyes, pass that through his heart and
create it with the tools of his hands. I taught him to build the power
of truth in everything he did."

"He learned from you how to make the statues seem real?"
Boschina asked.

"He had it in him, Boschina. He just didn't know how to express
it"

"And you did this at the Great Water?"

"Mostly, yes."

"Then I must go there," Boschina said. "How far away is it? How
long will it take to get there?"

"I know how long it would take me," Larma answered. "But, I
have never traveled with Thunder, so I don't know how many days it
will take from this place to there. What is your estimate, Thalmus?"

"It is a long way to the Great Water, Boschina," Thalmus replied.
"It will take many days."

"Well then," Boschina said, looking at Thalmus. "How soon can
we leave?"

Thalmus smiled at her. "If you are ready, tomorrow."

"I'm ready, Thalmus."

"I thought you would be."

"Come on then," Oleen said to Boschina and headed into another
tunnel. "We better get some sleep."

Boschina followed her. "I don't think I can sleep."

"You must if we're going to get an early start."

"What?" Boschina said. "Are you coming with us?"

"I have to," Oleen said and put her arm on Boschina's shoulder.
"You two keep getting into too much trouble by yourselves. I think
you need my help."

"Did you hear, Thalmus?" Boschina said, turning around.
"Ekala—I mean Oleen—is coming with us."

"Yes, I heard," Thalmus said, happy to have Ekala's company on
the journey.

Larma held Thalmus back while Oleen and Boschina left. "There
is someone here who has been waiting for you," she said softly.

She picked up a candle and led Thalmus down another corridor
that wound through several rooms and finally ended near the face of
the cliff. There was a small opening through the wall, a window to

the outside, and on a ledge by that window sat Bubo. His large yellow eyes and black pupils were glaring at them.

Upon seeing Thalmus, he hooted.

Thalmus smiled and hooted back. He rubbed the owl's head and chest feathers while Bubo nibbled at his fingers.

"So, this is where you have been hiding," Thalmus said.

"Bubo's arrival was a wonderful surprise," Larma said. "Scouting Table Top for you, he saw us. He flew in to tell me that you were coming. I thought you might have trouble with Gorga. That's why Oleen was watching for you."

"Aren't you the smart one," Thalmus said to Bubo. "Getting help for me before I knew I needed it."

Bubo hooted softly.

Thalmus turned to Larma. "Two men, soldiers really, helped us gain passage through the gate today. Maz and Camp, do you know them?"

"Yes, I have spoken with them several times. They even asked to join us, but Oleen and I refused. Still, I have a curiosity about them as they not only come from a foreign land, Toulon, but I can tell that they are enmeshed in a dangerous conspiracy."

"Toulon?" Thalmus said. "Ekala told me that they are enlarging their army."

"Yes," Larma replied. "That's why Maz and Camp have drawn my interest."

"I was intrigued by them also," Thalmus said. "The young Maz has an attitude about him that speaks of one who had authority, while Camp has that bearing of military leadership."

"I wonder what the flame might show me about them?" Larma asked herself. She lifted the candle up to eye level and stared into the flickering flame. There, deep in the orange-red dancing heat of the flare, she saw fighting and destruction—and the faces of Oleen and Maz in the midst of battle, fighting side by side. "I foresee Maz and Camp will be important to us," she said slowly. "Their destiny is intertwined with Oleen's." Then, returning from her meditation in the flame, she looked at Thalmus. "I want you to talk with them tomorrow before you leave and tell me if you think they can be trusted."

Bubo hooted and Thalmus looked at the owl, who looked back at him. "Yes, it is late, my friend, and we have a long road ahead us."

"Long and dangerous," Larma added.

"So it appears," Thalmus replied. "It is hard to believe what we have already been through, huh Bubo? I will be happy to go back to hunting frogs."

Bubo hooted in agreement to that.

"I want some of our warriors to travel with you and Boschina—and now Oleen," Larma said. "If you find Veracitas and return to the castle with him, you all will be in great danger."

"What about Larma Hollow?"

"We are secure here. Oleen has it well organized. She has been working on Larma Hollow and the women here for a long time. She is a leader, Thalmus."

"Yes, she is," Thalmus replied. "I knew that she could be, but I did not know how good until I saw this place—and how the women are devoted to her."

Larma put her hand on Thalmus' shoulder. "She is ready and the time is right to take over the throne from her father. She struggles with the thought of it because she is so devoted to him."

Thalmus looked at Larma. She looked so old and yet so young, so strong—and ever so wise. In her touch he felt the compassion, wisdom, and power that showed in her eyes.

"Her father stands on tradition," Thalmus said. "He does not think the people will accept a woman ruler. Therein lies the whole problem. That is why Metro has been able to get a foothold."

"Well," Larma said, "then we must loosen the ground from under his boots."

Thalmus laughed. "It is good to be here with you, Larma."

"And I with you," she answered. "When I learned that you had accepted the call to guide Boschina on this journey, I was quite pleased and felt the possibility of success increase a hundred-fold."

This praise from the great Larma made him feel good, but at the same time embarrassed. "You place too much confidence in me," he said.

"No, Thalmus," she replied, "There really is no one else who could do this. I've always had, and always will have, great faith in you."

*

In the morning, Oleen organized the gathering of supplies and three forces of eleven women each to accompany them. Thalmus made some suggestions as to the quantity of weaponry and when he had Thunder prepared to travel, he spoke with Oleen.

"I want to talk with Maz and Camp before we leave."

Oleen looked at him curiously. "What for?"

"Larma asked me to see them. We think they can be helpful to her."

"I like them," Oleen said. "But, I'm not sure I trust them."

"That's why I want to talk with them: to know if they can be trusted."

Oleen thought about this. A smile grew on her face. "That curly haired Maz is an interesting fellow, he's got a story that he's not willing to talk about. I'd like to know how he got that scar on his face; I think it adds to his good looks." She glanced at Thalmus, who was watching her with a curious expression. "Well," she added, embarrassed. "I guess they both have a secret past."

Thalmus left it at that and rode Dallion out of Larma Hollow onto the Top. He found Camp and Maz preparing breakfast where Ekala had told him they lived, a small ravine with a couple scrubby oaks and a shallow cave. Two horses, tied to a rope line between the oaks, picked up their heads when they sensed Dallion. As Thalmus approached, the two men instinctively stood and held their weapons in hand until they recognized him. They were surprised and glad to see Thalmus. He slid off of Dallion, who did not like getting close to strangers, and walked the last twenty paces to their cooking fire.

"Thalmus, ya want to eat?" Camp asked. "I've got plenty."

"No thank you, Camp."

"We hear you met Gorga," Maz said with a big smile on his face.

"Yes, I did."

"I wish I'd had seen that meeting," Camp said, "Gorga against Oleen and Thalmus the Frog Hunter."

"I hear he left with his tail between his legs," Maz said, still smiling.

"Where were you two?" Thalmus asked.

"They left us guarding the pass by ourselves when they went looking for you," Camp replied.

"Gorga did that on purpose," Maz explained, stirring a steaming pot. "That way we couldn't leave and maybe side with you."

"Did ya find your man?" Camp asked.

"No," Thalmus replied. "Veracitas is not here."

"Are ya leaving the Top then?"

"Yes. We must continue our search," Thalmus said and sat on a rock outcropping near the fire. "Before we leave, I wanted to know what brought you to Table Top, if you are willing to tell me."

Camp laughed.

"You mean what law did we break to have to hide here?"

Thalmus hesitated and then continued with a serious tone. "Pardon my curiosity, Camp, but neither one of you gives me the sense of being bad men."

"Well, I don't think we are," Maz responded.

"In fact," Thalmus continued, "I believe that you are soldiers."

Neither man spoke for a moment, avoiding Thalmus by focusing on their cooking. Then, Camp looked up and said: "That we are."

"But not from King Ahmbin's troops," Thalmus stated.

"No," Maz replied. "I think you know we're from a different land."

"Yes. Toulon," Thalmus said. "What drove you here, so far away from home?"

"That's a legitimate question," Maz said and tasted his soup with a carved wooden spoon.

Camp pulled a short knife from his belt and started cutting meat from a carcass he was cooking over the fire. "We got run out," he said finally.

Thalmus nodded and waited for more of their story.

"There are dire troubles in our land, somewhat like here," Maz said carefully. "You probably haven't heard about it because it's too far away and why would people here care what goes on in a distant land?"

"It's a struggle for control of power, isn't it?" Thalmus said. "A fight for control of the kingdom."

Maz looked surprised.

"Yes, that's what it is," he said. "Do you know about it?"

"Just that it eventually happens in every kingdom."

Maz nodded. "Well, we got on the wrong side of the wrong people and had to leave for our own sake."

"Were you in the king's army?"

Maz glanced at Camp. "You could say that."

Thalmus looked at the two of them. "Perhaps you can tell me then. We hear that Toulon is growing their army, preparing for war."

Maz looked up quickly. "That's why we had to leave, Thalmus. We opposed this action and their authority to do so."

"That's when they came after us and we had to run for our lives," Camp added.

"Our kingdom is not threatened from outside or, for that matter, from inside our realm," Maz continued. "The buildup of the army is solely intended for conquest, which will cost many lives and much destruction."

Thalmus did not need to ask what country Toulon intended to attack nor question if these two men were spies. Advanced scouts would not be hiding at a remote location like Table Top, unless there was a plan with Gorga to gather a force here to attack from the plain.

"So you found your way to the refuge of Table Top," Thalmus said. "How long will you have to stay here?"

Maz shrugged. "Until something changes or we figure out how to return without losing our heads." Then, trying to change the direction of the conversation, he asked: "Why didn't you tell us that you are friends with both Larma and Oleen?"

"I did not know who Oleen was until I saw her," Thalmus answered "Because I know her by a different name."

"There are many here who use different names," Maz replied. "Like us."

"Yes, so I've learned," Thalmus said. "How did you meet Oleen and Larma?"

"We've run across them a few times," Maz said. "Nothing combative, of course, just talk. I've seen Oleen standing on the edge, looking out over the land for long periods. She seems to have something troubling on her mind."

"That Oleen is a good fighter, though," Camp said. "We saw her scrap with some of the roughs here. They took a beating and decided not to mess with her anymore. She's a tough one and an honest leader. We'd follow her, but they won't let us in to Larma Hollow."

"You can still be on their side, if it comes to a fight."

"Oh, there's going to be a fight," Maz said, "you can bet on it. Gorga's been talking about it since we got here—claims he's got soldiers on the way to help."

Camp looked at Maz. "We wouldn't fight for Gorga, that's for sure."

"No, we only help him guard the pass for our safety and everybody else up here. That's all," Maz said and then sipped some hot soup from the steaming pot.

Camp nodded. "We've got no loyalty to him and his gang."

"Then you can help by watching Gorga and telling Larma what he's up to."

"Larma," Maz said, shaking his head in wonder. "There's no one else like her."

"We don't need to tell her anything," Camp added. "She knows what you're going to say before you say it."

"She still needs to be warned of any tricks that Gorga is planning. And if there is a battle, fight alongside her."

"We'd be honored," Maz said.

"Good." Thalmus stood up to leave. "Then I will depend on you."

Maz set his spoon down and moved around the fire to Thalmus. "I'm glad we met you, and I hope we will meet again."

"We wish you and the girl luck finding her father," Camp said.

"Thank you," Thalmus answered. He looked at the two of them and knew that they could be trusted. Circumstances of their exile seemed clear now, but their true identities were still unknown. There was a sincerity to them that had a ring of honesty and loyalty to the one they served. He thought about telling them the purpose for finding Veracitas, but decided to leave that to Larma.

When Thalmus and Dallion rode back through Larma Hollow, there were ten guards, instead of four, at the stone huts by the farms. Ekala was acting on his advice by reinforcing the hollow's security.

The guards gave him a friendly greeting and wished him luck. Thalmus thanked them for their hospitality. Dallion trotted on through the tunnel and they came out onto the shelf where Oleen and Boschina were waiting. Thunder had already left, getting a head start down the trail. The three forces of women were gathered around Larma, saying goodbye. Thalmus dropped off Dallion and walked up to Boschina and Oleen, who were standing to the side of the group.

"We're ready to go," Boschina said, trying to be patient.

Thalmus nodded. "So am I."

"What did you learn from Maz and Camp?" Oleen asked.

"They're outcasts," Thalmus replied. "They were chased out of Toulon for opposing the military build-up."

"Must be serious," Oleen said. "Do you believe them?"

"I do. They will be good allies."

Oleen smiled at him. "That's good enough for me." Then, she turned to the group of women around Larma. "All right, let's go," she commanded. "Form up."

While the women lined up in columns of two, Larma turned her attention to Boschina. She touched the girl's cheek. "You are strong, Boschina. You will always be strong because you have been given the power here." She pressed her fingertips against Boschina's forehead and then moved them to her chest. "And here," Larma said, staring into her eyes. "Believe and never relinquish it, for you are never alone."

"May I come back to see you, Larma?"

"Yes, child, you may, but first—your mission."

Larma held her hands out to Thalmus. Once again, he placed his hands in hers. She did not speak, but he heard the words she spoke the night before: "I have faith in you, Thalmus. There is no one better for this task than you."

Thalmus took a deep breath and exhaled. "I believe Maz and Camp can be trusted. They will inform you of Gorga's plans and, if you so desire, they will fight alongside you."

"Thank you, Thalmus. I'm sure I can put them to use."

They grasped hands for a moment and gazed into one another's eyes. When they let go Thalmus said: "We will send you word when we reach the Great Water."

Larma nodded. Oleen stepped up and hugged her. They held onto one another like a daughter and mother—each giving strength to the other.

"Your destiny awaits you," Larma said to Oleen. "It is time to tell everyone who you are."

She held up her arms and turned around. Everywhere on the shelf women stopped what they were doing to look at Larma. The farmers and guards came in through the tunnel, gathered around, and waited in silence. When she had everyone's attention, she lowered her arms and nodded to Oleen.

Ekala looked at the women standing all around the shelf waiting to hear her words. "I am Oleen," she shouted. "I am also Princess Ekala, the king's daughter."

There was silence as the women waited—waited to hear more.

Ekala looked at Larma and continued. "Today, I leave to start the journey to claim my right to the throne of this land. I cannot do that without your help. You know me and I will always know you. I now declare my name, for all time, to be Ekala Oleen.

A shout went up from the women. "Ekala Oleen!"

The shout bounced off the cliffs and echoed back.

"Ekala Oleen! Ekala Oleen! Ekala Oleen!"

Oleen raised her right arm straight up with an open hand and looked around the shelf. All the women raised an arm with the hand open in a salute to her. She looked at Larma, standing tall with her eyes closed and a smile on her face. After a few silent moments, Oleen dropped her arm. She turned to Thalmus. "Let's go."

Single file, they led their horses off the shelf and down the narrow trail that weaved through the rocks to the land below. They caught up with Thunder at the bottom. The guards at the trailhead cheered them as they passed by and headed out onto the plain.

Bubo, who had been watching from the cliffs, dropped from his perch and glided silently down. He passed over the forces, sailed close by Thalmus and Boschina, and winged out ahead of them.

"It's Bubo," Boschina yelled, pointing up at the large brown owl. "I knew he'd come back."

Thalmus smiled, for he knew now that by showing himself in daylight, Bubo had truly recovered and was once again with him.

Chapter Eighteen
Ello

So it began: the long trek to the Great Water with Thunder setting the pace. Oleen's forces took turns scouting, hunting and trailing behind the giant tortoise. Cadres of troops roamed the plain like packs of wolves. The first day, one such group tangled with an Oleen patrol. The women dismounted, formed a battle line, and using their bows, dropped several of the attackers from their horses. Only one swordfight ensued and that was between Captain Ritzs and a blusterous man who ran as soon as she thwarted his blow and cut his arm. The men were surprised by the women's unity and strength. The soldiers broke off the fight and retreated after a short skirmish. After that they stayed clear, but continued following at a distance.

The women were well-trained and organized. Oleen directed them with an ease and confidence of one much more experienced. She was a natural leader and the women were devoted to her.

Days passed as they plodded along at Thunder's pace, which was too slow for Oleen. She would walk awhile with Thalmus and Boschina, and then jump on Shadahn and ride out with a patrol or on her own. Returning, she would walk for a distance only to mount up again and ride ahead with one of the forces to secure a campsite for the night. Dallion, as usual, was on his own—scouting or grazing, but always keeping track of Thalmus.

Boschina was in training.

Oleen had given her a roan mare named Radise and was teaching her to ride aggressively and how to take care of the animal that took care of her. In camp, in the evenings, Thalmus and Oleen—or some of the women—worked with Boschina on sword fighting technique and archery. These lessons often drew a crowd, who watched and learned, and then practiced what they had seen.

Thalmus approved. He could not think of a better situation for Boschina. He observed quietly and helped with the cooking and chores. Dallion came into camp at night to be by Thalmus, who slept alongside Thunder with Owl perched nearby or on the great tortoise's shell. The women gradually became accustomed to Thalmus and his gentle demeanor; though, they were still in awe of him, his animal friends, and their bond to one another.

On the sixth day, Oleen took Boschina out to scout with her and continue her training. Usually, they had done this with one of the forces or other scouts, but on this day the pair rode alone through the swales and mounds of the plain. Boschina on Radise chased after Oleen and Shadahn as they galloped for short distances and then stopped abruptly in a gulley or low area to act as if hiding. Soon after, they trotted down the gulley before charging out again across the open land. Radise instinctively knew how to react, when to charge or canter or stand still, not making a sound. Boschina followed her horse's lead, riding high or low in the saddle depending on the situation or Radise's speed and quick cutting. She had learned to trust this experienced animal and talked to her like a friend and advisor. Boschina started calling her Lady: "What is it Lady?"; "I'm with you, Lady"; "Let's go, Lady!" The proud mare responded with a joy and energy she had not shown in years.

Oleen finally stopped for a rest in a brushy ravine with a narrow creek. Checking the area before dismounting, they saw no sign of troops or danger. All four of them drank from the running water, humans and animals side by side.

"Let them rest a while," Oleen said, patting Shadahn on the neck.

Lady Radise turned her head to look at Boschina as if to say, "You rest too," and then went back to drinking from the creek.

Oleen walked up to where she could look over the plain and sat down. Boschina pulled some smoked meat from the saddlebag on Radise and joined her. The temperature was getting hotter as there were few clouds to block the sun. On the distant horizon, they could see the hills they would have to cross to reach the Great Water.

"This has been a fun ride," Boschina said. "I'm learning a lot, from Lady...Radise."

Oleen turned her attention from the plain to look at her.

"That's why I gave her to you. And you are learning quickly."

"How many more days until we reach the Great Water?" Boschina asked, taking a bite of the meat and offering a chunk of it to Oleen.

"You'll be happy to find your father, won't you?" Oleen said, accepting the meat.

"Of course, I've been so worried about him. And I miss him."

Oleen nodded and nibbled on the meat as she returned her gaze to the plain.

Boschina watched her as she finished her own portion. "Don't you feel the same about your father, the king, I mean?"

Oleen kept looking out at the land. "Like you, I'm worried, very worried, about my father and this dangerous mess he's gotten us into. I'm afraid to see what's going to happen to him."

"You're afraid?" Boschina asked, surprised.

"Yes," Oleen said, looking directly at Boschina. "I'm afraid of the decisions I will have to make and what I must do, when we return with your father. You understand, don't you, that I'll have to remove him from the throne? I'll have to seize power from him if we're to save Ameram from Metro and his forces."

Boschina shook her head. "I hadn't thought of the king and you in that way." She paused, thinking what anguish that would cause and how her own concerns with her father paled in comparison. For the first time, she understood Oleen's plight and saw the pain in her heart. "I want to help you," she said. "I know you are so strong, Ekala, but if I can help in any way you must tell me and I'll do it."

Oleen smiled at her. "You're a good friend, Boschina." She paused and thought a moment. "No, I think you are more than that. You're the sister I never had."

"And you're the big sister that I never had," Boschina replied.

"Thank you," Oleen said and laughed. She slapped Boschina's leg. "We need to return to the column."

She whistled for Shadahn and both horses came to them.

They mounted up and started to ride side by side.

"Oleen," Boschina said. "Do you miss your mother?"

Oleen paused, remembering the image and love of the woman who had held her so close, taught her to be strong, before leaving when she was still young. "Yes, I still miss her."

"Even though you have Larma?"

"I've been blessed to have Larma as a teacher and friend. Without her, I don't know what would have happened to me. Still, she's not my mother."

"At least you knew your mother, right?" Boschina asked. "I mean, you have memories of her?"

"Yes, I have good memories. I guess that's why I miss her."

They rode in silence for a while as both were in their own thoughts. Finally Oleen asked, "Boschina, what is it you want to know?"

"I never knew my mother," Boschina answered. "I have no memories of her because she left when I was still a baby. I imagine what she must have been like and wonder why she left and where she is now. I would just like to have one good remembrance of my mother."

"You have your father," Oleen said.

"Yes," Boschina replied. "But he is not my mother."

Oleen laughed. "I understand. We still have our fathers though, who have taken care of us; and for that, we can be grateful."

"Yes," Boschina said. "And they both need our help."

"Indeed they do," Oleen said as she kicked Shadahn into a gallop.

Radise reacted immediately and charged after them. With hoofs pounding the earth, kicking up dirt, Boschina scrunched low, leaned forward, and hung on. "Go Lady, go!" Radise finally caught Shadahn on a hill, where Oleen had pulled up to look over the land. Breathing hard and snorting, the horses nuzzled one another.

"That was good, Boschina," Oleen said and reached over and patted Radise's neck. "Your Lady is quick and determined, as are you."

"She knows what to do," Boschina said proudly, stroking Radise's neck.

Oleen pointed at a faint cloud of dust in the distance.

"What do you think that is?"

Boschina knew that this was a test and stood up in the stirrups to look. "That should be our people, still heading west. I think I can see Thunder."

"Should be," Oleen said. "Thunder doesn't kick up dust, but our horses do."

They both scanned the entire area, looking for any troops that might be lurking about.

"Dallion should be around somewhere," Boschina said, shading her eyes with her hand.

Oleen smiled. "I think Dal might be a bit jealous of Radise. You haven't been spending any time with him."

"You think so?" Boschina said, concerned.

Oleen laughed. "I'm sure he's glad that you have your own dependable ride, but you might want to give him a little attention now and then."

"I will," Boschina said, then thought about the man who had brought her this far. "What about Thalmus? He is such a mystery to me."

Oleen looked at her, a bit surprised. "How many days have you been traveling with him? Haven't you learned by now who Thalmus is?"

"You mean besides being a frog hunter...and my protector and teacher...and guide...and..."

"He's all of that and much more," Oleen said. "How can I explain it? For not everyone sees or knows him the same." She thought a moment. "We were talking earlier about our mothers and fathers; well, for me, Thalmus is like a brother—that mysterious, all-knowing, big brother who we look up to and trust because he believes in us. And he always seems to be there when we need him, especially when our parents or friends are not." She looked again at Boschina. "He has wisdom and confidence embedded deep within him and strength of heart that is unbeatable. You do not need to worry about Thalmus, just trust him."

"Well, I certainly trust him," Boschina replied, "as well as Thunder, Dallion, and Bubo."

"That's because they are part of him," Oleen said and started Shadahn into a trot. "Let's rejoin our force."

They rode side by side back to the column as Dallion ran out to meet them.

*

Each evening, Thalmus and Oleen would watch where the sun set and pick a landmark for the direction of the next day's march. On the eve of the ninth day, they stood together on a rise looking across the land. Oleen called for Boschina. The princess' new sister walked up with a smile on her face and took a position between them.

"Tomorrow, we should reach the village of Ello," Thalmus said. "It is the last place to get good water before crossing the hills to the Great Water."

"I know it well," Ekala said. "As a young girl, I stayed there with my mother several times when we traveled to Table Top—and then on my own when I was grown and became restless. The people have always been kind to me. It will be good to see them again."

"I know it, too," Boschina said, proudly. "Father started a statue there, but he left it unfinished when he was called to do the king's image. The villagers were very good to us and were sorry to see us leave."

Thalmus agreed. "They are a welcoming people. Ello has a good market, so we can replenish our supplies."

Turning away from their observation and toward camp, Ekala paused. "Wait," she said, remembering something. "Ello? Aren't troops posted there now?"

"I did not see any troops when I last passed through that village," Thalmus answered. "But that was a long time ago."

"There weren't any when I was there with my father," Boschina said.

"I remember some argument in court between Rundall and Baldoff about putting troops in Ello," Ekala said. "It went on for several days with Baldoff insisting it be done. My father became irritated. I was out of the castle when the final decision was made, so I don't know who won."

Thalmus thought about this. "It does sit on the crossroads of four directions. If Baldoff was trying to control this area, Ello would be the key village."

"That means a larger force could be there," Ekala said.

"Maybe," Thalmus replied. "The troops could be spread out over the area, like the ones we've seen."

Ekala was worried. "I hope we do not encounter troops there," She shook her head. "I should've brought a larger force. I was concerned about the defense of the hollow."

Thalmus looked at her. He knew that these sorts of decisions were never easy for a leader. "Do not second guess yourself, Ekala," he said. "We're all right. We have enough."

Ekala stood with her fists on her hips as she looked across the land. "I'll ride there first thing in the morning."

"Dallion and I would like to join you," Thalmus said and waited for Ekala's response.

Ekala smiled at Thalmus. "It'll be a fast ride."

"It will be even faster with Dallion along," Thalmus replied.

Ekala laughed and slapped Thalmus on the shoulder.

"Can Lady and I go with you?" Boschina asked.

Ekala looked at Thalmus for his preference.

"I want you to stay with Thunder," Thalmus said. "I don't want him to feel abandoned."

"But he has all of the Oleens around him," Boschina protested.

"Yes, but he is much more comfortable with one of us nearby."

"You're right, Thalmus, he does get nervous. I'll stay with him."

They gave instructions to the others—Ekala to her force leaders and Thalmus to Thunder and Boschina. At the first light of dawn, Ekala, on Shadahn, and Thalmus, riding Dallion, galloped off. The two horses raced each other across the land with Thalmus and Ekala tucked down against their necks. Weaving through brush and jumping over ravines, they played tag—pushing each other faster and faster.

It was a joyful ride, a playful ride, until they approached Ello.

Dallion instinctively slowed to a trot; Shadahn, carrying Ekala came alongside, and they stopped outside the village. Ekala lifted herself off Shadahn's back to get a better look.

"I don't see any people."

Thalmus was listening. The air was still. There was no wind or sound at all. It was as if a blanket of silence was smothering the village.

Ekala shifted on Shadahn. "This doesn't look good."

Thalmus pursed his lips. "Whoo–whoo," he hooted.

From the village came a return: "Whooo-who-whooo."

"You sent Bubo ahead of us?" Ekala said, surprised.

Thalmus smiled at her and urged Dallion forward. The horses were breathing heavily from the run; still, they walked with cautious steps into the village. Small, rock-walled homes were arranged in circles around a plaza with a well at the center. This was the market and meeting place of the town. Owl was perched there on a beam that supported an awning over a farmer's produce stand. Its shelves and table were broken and one end had fallen to the ground.

Bubo hooted and clucked at Thalmus when they rode in. Thalmus answered with a hoot, slid down off Dallion, and began looking into the homes.

"I don't like this," Ekala said.

She dismounted and pulled her sword.

"You won't need that," Thalmus said. "There's nobody here."

"How can you be sure?"

"Bubo says so."

Ekala looked up at Bubo on the beam.

His black pupils in the large yellow eyes were glaring at her.

"All right, I believe you, Bubo," Ekala said and sheathed her sword.

Bubo turned to watch Thalmus. Then, his head swiveled as he looked away to the west.

The village of Ello had always been a busy community and a pleasant, comfortable, resting place on the trade route along the western side of the kingdom.

Now, it was deserted.

After looking through some houses, Ekala returned to the plaza to find Thalmus moving cantaloupe-sized stones from a mound where they had been piled.

"These people haven't been gone long," Ekala said. "There's still some fresh food around and...what are you doing?"

"Help me move these stones," Thalmus said.

"Why?"

"There might be something under them."

"What?"

Thalmus motioned around at the plaza. "Don't you think this is an odd place for a rock pile? The whole area is clean and orderly, except this."

Ekala looked around the plaza and then started tossing stones off the pile. "Maybe they were going to build something."

"No. There is something different about this."

Dallion and Shadahn scouted the perimeter of the village while Thalmus and Ekala worked on the rock pile. Gradually, they uncovered rocks that were a different kind of stone and were odd shapes and sizes.

"Some of these stones have been carved," Ekala said as she examined a large chunk.

Thalmus rolled over several pieces of stone.

"It looks like an unfinished statue that has been broken up."

"That's odd. Why would someone shatter a statue and then cover it up?"

Thalmus looked at the rubble and at the empty plaza. "So no one would see it. And those who did see it are not here to tell of it."

"Let's put it back together," Ekala suggested. "Let's see what it is."

They began gathering the different parts and piecing them together on the ground: the torso, the legs, a scarred head, a hand with a sword, and an arm with a shield.

"It's a warrior," Ekala said, joining two parts of an arm.

The statue had not been finished. There was still some fine chipping and polishing to be done, but the image was complete enough to tell what and who it was—especially when Thalmus found a chunk of the face that had been broken off and laid it in place.

They both stared at it in amazement.

"That's me," Ekala whispered.

Chapter Nineteen
The Great Water

Ekala was stunned, staring at herself in stone.

Thalmus looked at her. "Someone made a carving of you. You did not know this?"

Ekala did not respond. She just continued staring at the broken statue.

"Ekala?" Thalmus persisted.

"No," she said, shaking her head slowly. "I've never seen this, nor heard of it."

Thalmus studied the statue lying in pieces arranged together on the ground. It was accurate and truthful, even to the size of Ekala's muscular arms, broad shoulders, and hips.

"Is this what I look like?" she asked.

"Yes," Thalmus answered. "That is you."

"I didn't know I was...." she stopped and pointed at her stone head. "Look at my head. Something has been broken off the top of my head."

Ekala knelt and felt with her fingertips the chips in the stone around the top of the statue's head. "I wonder what it was?" she said. "A hat, maybe?"

"Or something else," Thalmus replied, having an idea of what the missing pieces might be. "Let's try to find them."

They searched in the rubble, found the broken pieces, and put them together. "It's a crown," Ekala said, surprised again.

Thalmus took a deep breath and exhaled. "That must be why it was broken up," he said, "Shattered by those who do not see you as a queen."

Ekala stood up, her anger rising. "I have a good idea who destroyed it."

"Could Veracitas have made this statue?" Thalmus wondered. "And how long has it been here?"

Ekala was looking at the water well in the forlorn plaza. "We won't know that until we find the villagers."

Thalmus was suddenly aware of a breeze blowing in from the east. He turned and looked around at the empty square and deserted buildings. "We need to go. We have to find Veracitas right away."

"What about these people?"

"The best way to help them is to find Veracitas," he replied.

Ekala looked again at her statue, and then quickly gathered the pieces of the stone crown and put them in a leather pouch. They called in Dallion and Shadahn and rode back to meet the others. Owl stayed in the village until Thalmus returned with Boschina and one of the forces of women to fill water pouches. The rest of the column, with Thunder, bypassed the village of Ello and headed straight for the trail to the Great Water.

Boschina stood in the plaza, looking over the statue pieced together on the ground. "You're right, Thalmus. My father made this statue."

"Are you sure?"

"Yes, I'm sure," Boschina said and knelt by the statue. "See this small mark on the shield, this V laid on top of an A? That is his sign, his signature." She ran her hands over the statue, feeling the carved pieces—the etching, curves, and smoothness of the stone. "It's beautiful," she said, admiring her father's work.

"Did he ever tell you about this statue?" Thalmus asked.

Boschina nodded, remembering, "This must be the one he started before we left for the castle. He said it would be a warrior, but I did not know it would be Ekala." She looked up at Thalmus. "He must have worked on it after his escape. It is still unfinished, rough in parts. So, he was here, but where is he now? And where are the people?"

Thalmus offered a hand to help her up.

"We must follow Larma's vision to the Great Water. When we find Veracitas, he will tell us."

When the women had completed filling the pouches from the well and strapping them onto the horses, they all rode out of Ello and joined the others. The crusty trail to the Great Water wove through the hills, crossing several milky creeks. The water was hot; it was foul and smelled like rotten eggs.

On the second night, they camped by a very large pond that was dead. There was no life in the water. Thunder would not even enter it to cool off. All around the grasses were dry and the earth dusty. Ekala sent out fewer patrols and she ordered her soldiers to dismount and walk the horses to conserve water. The king's troops had not been seen since the day before reaching Ello. Ekala was glad for that. But, Thalmus wondered why the soldiers had abandoned their pursuit.

On the fourth day, with their water pouches now empty, very little food left, and everyone parched, they entered into grayness—a fog that at times was so thick they could not see ten paces. Thalmus and Ekala roped the horses together in a line with Dallion at the lead and Thunder in front of him, guiding them all through the murk.

Boschina and Thalmus walked on each side of Dallion.

The earth had turned gray and damp. Grass grew in thick, lumpy clumps. Tall trees, with needles for leaves, appeared—and then disappeared—into the fog.

When they stopped for a rest, and to check that no one had been lost, Thalmus became aware of a sound in the fog. He listened intently to the faint noise as Ekala came along the line of horses, counting heads.

"Looks like we got everybody," she said.

"Shhh," Thalmus whispered.

Ekala and Boschina stood still, listening.

"What?" Ekala said softly. "I don't hear anything."

Boschina had learned to watch the animals for signs. Owl was not around, but Dallion had stomped his hoof once. Thunder was barely visible ahead of them in the fog and she listened to hear any warning from him.

"What is it, Thalmus?" Boschina whispered.

"I hear water."

"A stream?" Ekala asked quietly.

"Yes." Thalmus was watching Thunder while he listened. "Look, Thunder smells it. He is moving. It's bound to be good water."

Thalmus smiled and slapped Ekala on the shoulder. "Let's go."

Thunder guided them through the mist and before too long, the gurgle of a stream became apparent. However, they still could not see through the fog and the sound of running water seemed to come from various locations. They were not sure from which direction it came. Different opinions were expressed as to which way to go and how far it might be; but Thunder knew. While the humans debated, he never slowed his pace and he charged ahead across soft, slippery ground—pulling everyone with him until he splashed into a creek. Gathering along the bank, animals and humans in one line, all drank; and those who had them, filled the water pouches.

"This water flows to the Great Water," Thalmus explained. "We'll follow it."

And so they did.

The little creek was joined by other runs and swelled into a river, which made it much more difficult to ford. The fog had not lifted. If anything, it had become worse.

"This reminds me too much of Rainland," Boschina said. "Is it always like this, Thalmus?"

"No, but it can be—"

Thunder had stopped and they almost bumped into him before they realized it. He stood still glaring into the fog. Thalmus stepped alongside of him. One click from Thunder and Thalmus drew his sword. Boschina immediately pulled her sword. Ekala whispered to her first captain, Ritzs, sending an order down the line to be ready to battle, and then pulled out her sword while she and Boschina moved to Thunder's other side. They still could not see or hear anything, but the hiss of the river flowing nearby. Thalmus released the rope that tied the tortoise to everyone so he would not be restricted. He tapped Thunder's shell and the giant tortoise quietly stepped forward.

A figure appeared ahead of them for a brief moment, and then disappeared in the drifting mist. Several more steps forward and the figure was there again in the same place as before. It looked to be a man, or woman, and stood motionless—waiting. As they approached it, another shape appeared in the fog beyond the first one. Ekala pointed toward it and Thalmus nodded.

The first figure still had not budged.

Moving closer, the fog thinned and they could finally see it a little clearer now. It was a man wrapped in a cape; his head covered by a floppy hat. He seemed to be unaware of them. His attention was focused on the river about thirty meters away.

Thalmus picked up a small stone and threw it at the feet of the person. He did not move. "Hello," Thalmus called.

Still no movement.

Thalmus looked at Boschina and Ekala and smiled.

"Come on," he said to them and motioned toward the man.

With their swords ready, Ekala and Boschina followed Thalmus through the fog to the mysterious man and discovered who he was.

"It's a statue," Ekala exclaimed.

She went to the next figure and tapped it with her sword. A dull clink resounded in the fog. She sheathed her weapon. "They sure had me fooled."

Boschina was staring at the face of the first statue.

"This is your father's work?" Thalmus asked her.

"This is my father," she replied.

"What?" Ekala said, coming back. "Let me see. Yep, that's Veracitas." She put her arm around Boschina. "It looks just like him."

"Yes," Boschina said. "Though, his face looks thinner."

Thalmus was pondering the intent of the statues and how they got there. "He did a carving of himself, hiding in a cape and hat—looking out on the river, waiting."

"He's waiting for us, Thalmus," Boschina replied. "This is to let us know we're on the right trail—that he's near."

"Look at the emblem on the cape," Princess Ekala said, pointing at the backside of the statue. "It's my father's monogram, the seal of King Ahmbin. Veracitas is showing his loyalty."

"Who's the other figure?" Boschina asked.

They walked to the marble image as the others began filing in from the fog. When Thalmus saw this statue, he smiled but said nothing. It was a broad shouldered man covered by a cloak and hood that hid half of his face. The tip of a sword protruded below the cloak by his left leg.

"It looks like Currad," Boschina said.

"You're right," Ekala agreed with amazement. "It is Currad. Why would Veracitas do a carving of him?"

Thalmus put his hand on the statue.

"Because he is the one who helped Veracitas escape."

"What?" Both Ekala and Boschina said together.

"How do you know this?" Ekala demanded.

"I just know," Thalmus said. "This statue is in tribute to him."

"Who else knows this?" Ekala asked.

"I hope just you two," Thalmus replied softly.

"Currad," Ekala murmured, looking at the statue. "I never would have thought it of him. He was so loyal to my father."

"He still is, Ekala. He is doing what he can, what he thinks is right to help the king."

"He's with us then?"

"Yes. We can rely on Currad and Dysaan to help us. They already have aided Boschina and me at Rainland and the Barranca. We could not have gotten through without them."

"Let's go find my father," Boschina said, who was excited by the discovery of the statues.

Thalmus looked at Boschina. "I know that you are anxious to find your father, but it is getting late. It will be dark soon. Trying to find him in this fog will be hard enough."

"But he must be close."

Ekala agreed with Thalmus. "We'll camp here tonight and move on tomorrow."

Just then, they heard something out in the fog splash into the river.

Ekala grabbed her sword. "That was close by."

Some of the women ran to the edge of the river, looking for the cause of the noise. "That sounded like a tree falling," one said.

"Whatever it was, it was big," another one commented.

"That was a frog," Thalmus shouted. "Get away from the water!"

"Frog?" Boschina exclaimed. "Here?"

Thalmus glanced at her. "Get your arrows ready," he ordered and ran to pull the women away from the water.

Ekala followed Thalmus, yelling, "Get back. Get back, quickly!"

Water suddenly burst up from the river and two bulging black eyes appeared on a gnarled brown head as the red streak of a tongue lashed out from its mouth, latched onto the leg of an Oleen soldier and began dragging her to the edge.

"Shoot for the eyes," Thalmus shouted at the Oleens and ran toward the woman as he pulled his sword.

The Oleens were stunned by the sudden appearance of the giant beast. They kept moving away, fumbling with their bows while staring at the vicious attacker. Thalmus swung his sword and slashed at the frog's tongue wrapped on the woman's leg. The sticky appendage loosened. He struck it again. The tongue let go and withdrew just as Ekala bounded in to help. They lifted the startled soldier to her feet and started to run away when Ekala was slapped down.

"Thalmus," she screamed.

Thalmus turned. The frog had not backed away, but instead had jumped forward to snap onto Ekala. She was caught by the waist and was kicking and trying to stab the tongue as the creature pulled her toward it. Now arrows from the Oleens began smacking into the thick skin of the frog. Boschina kept shooting, moving her bow, adjusting her aim at the eye of the beast. But the creature was moving too much. By the time she released, her arrows missed entirely or plunked against its tough skin.

"Let go. Let go of her!" she kept shouting.

Thalmus looked for an advantage but Ekala was almost at its gaping mouth, and the frog was pulling away into the river. Despite the incoming arrows, Thalmus leapt at the beast's throat, thrusting with his sword point. But he barely stabbed it as the frog jerked to the side, knocking him down. Ekala's sword began to vibrate in her hand. It clung to her fingers, swung to her side and plunged into the frog's tongue. Still, the beast did not let go.

Boschina, frustrated from not hitting the eye, kept moving closer. Then she felt her sword vibrating at her side. It was calling her to battle – calling to help Ekala. She dropped the bow, gripped the sword's handle, pulled out the pulsing blade and ran at the frog.

The fierce brown beast was slipping into the river with Ekala when the snap of Thunder's jaws clamped onto the side of its throat. The frog roared in agony and kicked violently, splashing the water. The giant tortoise bit deeper into the frog's skin and backed up, pulling the creature onto land again. Boschina rushed up beside Thunder and plunged her sword into the beast's soft under-throat. Thalmus stabbed the frog on its other side, and this time, the tormented creature dropped Ekala. She scrambled to her feet and angrily slashed at her attacker. Boschina pulled her sword out of the frog as both blades vibrated.

Thalmus grabbed Ekala's arm. "Ekala, get everyone away from the water. There are more frogs here. Boschina get back to the statues."

Ekala glared at Thalmus. "He almost killed me!" Then she turned and ordered the Oleens, who were starting toward her, to pull back to the statues. "Form a circle around the statues," she commanded. "String the horses on the other side. Everyone stay alert!"

Thalmus slapped Thunder's shell twice. "Let him go."

Thunder, who was being yanked back and forth by the frantic creature, pushed it forward toward the water and released his hold. The frog flopped into the river and disappeared in the current and fog. The frog hunters, Thalmus and Thunder, then cautiously backed away from the edge and joined the others.

Thunder clicked his jaws and nudged into Ekala's stomach.

Ekala stroked the giant tortoise's head and hugged him. "Thanks for saving me, Thunder. You're jaws are a powerful weapon." Then she hugged Boschina. "You came to my rescue. You could have been killed."

Boschina was shaking. "I couldn't let that frog get you. I...I couldn't hit its eye...then my sword...it—it moved me."

"I felt it too...mine was moving," Ekala responded.

They held up their swords, now quiet, side by side. They looked at Thalmus. His sword was still in his hand. He held it up next to theirs. The engravings of the animals were the same on each blade. "These tools served us well today," he said. The blade appeared to gleam for a moment; then he slipped it into its sheath at his side.

"That monster was something, huh?" Ekala said, still exhilarated from the struggle. "Is it always like that?"

"No," Thalmus replied. "He caught us by surprise, and that is never good."

"He was so big," Boschina said.

"They have not been hunted much," Thalmus explained. "There are very few people here, so the frogs have grown quite large, and fearless."

They camped that night between the statues, well away from the water's edge, and inside the perimeter line of Oleen guards. Boschina laid out her blankets next to the stone figure of her father and Thunder settled down next to her. Dallion had decided to stand guard outside the ring away from the other horses. The Stone Cutter's Daughter was tired but lying at the foot of her father's statue she began to think about him and his stone images. When Thalmus checked on her, she had questions for him.

"How do you think my father moved this stone here? It's much too heavy for him or even two men to move."

"The Insurphs helped him," Thalmus said.

Hearing the name, Ekala turned to them. "Insurphs. I thought they were just legend and not real."

"They are very real," Thalmus answered. "But you will not see them unless they want to be seen. They are a very shy and cautious people, and extraordinary hunters. They live in the forests along the Great Water. It appears Veracitas has befriended them. I can think of no other way he was able to move the stone here."

"Are we close to the Great Water?" Boschina asked.

"Very close," Thalmus answered. "We will see it tomorrow."

"I wish tomorrow were here," Boschina replied and pulled the blankets over her head.

Boschina awoke in the morning to feel the damp fog still clouding the land. She groaned and rolled over to look up at her father's statue. To her surprise, Bubo was perched on his head. The owl's large yellow eyes glared down at her.

"Bubo, where have you been?"

The great owl bobbed his head several times and glided silently down and landed on Thunder's back. He hopped around on his shell, hooting, until Thunder woke and stuck out his big head. Dallion came over to see what the commotion was about. Bubo fluffed up his feathers and nibbled on the horse's nose when he nuzzled him. Then, he sprang from Thunder's shell back to the statue and started hooting again.

"Well, aren't you impatient this morning?" Boschina said, standing up, but keeping the blankets wrapped around her.

By now, everyone had been awakened by Bubo. Ekala, who had given herself the last watch of the night, came over with Shadahn. She patted Dallion on the neck. "Bubo is anxious to be going, I think."

"So am I, "Boschina said, looking around. "Where's Thalmus?"

"He left early to scout ahead. Bubo was with him, but he just came back. I suppose to get us up and moving. We'll move out when Thalmus returns."

They ate what food was left and packed up. When Thalmus returned, he approached the camp with caution. He called out and announced his entrance from the fog. He did not want to be shot with an arrow from a jittery guard. Bubo hooted at him and he hooted back.

In a single file, this time with Thalmus at the lead, they followed the river through forests and across meadows. As they went, the fog lifted and moved away from the land to reveal a lush countryside. They walked through a valley of giant ferns, where vines with leaves the size of shields hung from the trees. Mushrooms, the diameter of a coin to the size of a dinner plate, sprouted everywhere under the ferns; the ground under their feet was soft and mushy.

The river descended; hissing and swirling through the forest, it slowed and spread into a marsh, obscuring the trail. Thalmus sent Thunder splashing ahead to scare off any frogs that might be hiding there. The gnarly monsters could not easily be intimidated, but they feared the snapping bite of shell creatures. The terrain fell away again and the current sped over rocks and sand bars as the column continued on.

Finally, the river banked against a canyon wall, turned, and cut its way through a long sand bar to flow into the Great Water. The weary travelers gathered on the bank to gaze at the scene before them. The expanse of blue water stretched to the distant horizon, where the gray sky came down to meet the water. Waves were rolling across the surface and crashing on the sandy shore that extended as far north and south as they could see. Two large black birds with angled wings glided side by side over the breaking waves on their way down the coast.

"I could never imagine such a place as this," Boschina said, mesmerized.

"I've seen the Great Water before," Ekala said, "but I feel like I'm seeing it for the first time."

"Where does it end?" Boschina asked, shading her eyes and staring into the distance.

"No one knows for sure," Thalmus answered. "There are other lands out there, for strangers have come from across the Great Water. But, I have never had the desire to explore beyond this shore."

"I've heard that Metro was banished from a land of magicians across the water," Ekala said. "They say his experiments almost destroyed that land and they forced him out."

"Do you believe that?" Thalmus asked, looking at her closely.

"Well," she said, "he didn't come from Ameram. That's for sure."

Thalmus smiled at Ekala, and then pointed south. "The waterfall that Larma spoke about is that way."

"Let's go," Boschina said and started to move.

"Only the three of us should go on," Thalmus said to Ekala. "The rest should stay here. If Veracitas sees this large force, he might run away."

"You're right, Thalmus," Ekala replied and turned to her soldiers. "Guard this trail. Don't let anyone come up behind us. There's plenty of game here. I want you to hunt and gather food until we return. Stay away from the river and watch for frogs"

"Frogs do not live this close to the Great Water," Thalmus said. "You will be safe from them, but stay in your forces and be alert."

Ekala pointed at the first captain. "Ritzs, you're in command."

Ritzs nodded. "Upon your orders, Oleen," she said and began organizing the women into groups and assigning tasks.

Thunder started down the beach with Dallion, followed by Thalmus, Boschina, and Ekala. Owl was still sitting in a tree back at the bend of the river. After a short distance in the sand, Thalmus sat down and took off his boots.

"Why are you doing that?" Ekala asked.

"Why?" Thalmus replied. "To feel the sand and water."

Boschina and Ekala looked at one another and then plopped down and removed their boots. They started again, this time carrying their boots hanging over their shoulders. The sand was warm and felt good under their feet. Driftwood of all shapes and sizes littered the beach at the high-water line. They stepped through debris and followed Thalmus into the wet sand, where the water rushed up and around their ankles. It was chilling at first, but they got used to it. Dallion galloped through the shallow water, splashing them as he went by. Thunder just kept plodding forward as the waves rolled in and swirled around and through his legs. Thalmus was deliberate about having them all walk in the shallow surf so that their tracks disappeared in the wet sand.

Around shallow bays and over rock outcroppings they continued, until they came into a cove surrounded by high cliffs. On the south side of the cove, the beach ended against the cliffs that extended like a wall into the water where the waves crashed against its craggy rocks. At the point where the beach ended, a stream of water gushed out of the face of the cliff high above and fell in a widening stream to splatter in the sand and surf.

Boschina ran up to the waterfall.

"This is it," she shouted. "This is what I saw in the vision."

"Look," Ekala said, pointing at the cliff wall. "The stone in the cliff has been carved."

And truly, it had. Faces of all kinds—men and women, animals and children, of varied sizes and shapes—emerged from the stone.

"There are so many," Boschina said.

"This is where Larma taught your father," Thalmus said.

"Where is he?" Boschina asked looking around. "This is it. This is the place. He should be here."

"He is," Thalmus replied. "Look, this face here is not complete and there are fresh chips and rubble below it."

"He's around here somewhere," Ekala said.

"Whoo! Whoo! Whoo!"

They all heard Owl's deep hoot and looked up to see Bubo coming right at them. He flew over their heads, hooted, turned, and headed back toward the cliffs in the cove.

"He wants us to follow him," Boschina exclaimed and took off running after Bubo.

Leaving the water's edge, they ran into the recess of the cove, where thick brush grew down the rocks to the sand. There, Bubo disappeared into the trees. The three barefoot travelers dropped to the sand and put on their boots. Boschina stood first and pushed her way through the branches where Bubo had entered and discovered a trail. It was narrow and hidden by the foliage of the trees and bushes, but it was well worn. Ekala and Thalmus came through the thick branches after her.

"Look," Boschina said, smiling and pointing at the trail.

Then she turned and ran up the path.

Thalmus started to stop her, but decided to let her go. He and Ekala followed as the trail weaved through the foliage and climbed up the cliff. Thunder and Dallion remained on the sand in the cove because the trail was too narrow and the foliage too thick for them.

Boschina was out of breath and had slowed to a walk by the time the trail topped the cliff and headed down into the next canyon. Here, trees taller than she had ever seen before, stretched high overhead. The upper branches overlapped one another, creating a canopy that shaded the entire canyon like a blanket with thousands of small tears and holes. Sunrays filtered through in sparkling beams of light.

Thalmus and Ekala caught up with Boschina as she recovered her breath. Boschina smiled at them and started again. They walked slowly, in a row, along the path—looking up in amazement at the trees. Somewhere high up on a branch, for they could not see it, a bird pounded its beak on a hollow trunk and it echoed, like a drum, through the forest.

The trail crisscrossed a creek and continued over fallen logs as it meandered back toward the Great Water. The canyon walls closed in and became steeper as the creek funneled down the center. Then, the trail came to the edge of a cliff. Straight down, forty meters below, waves from the Great Water crashed against the rocks. The narrow path turned south, flirted with the cliff's edge, and then came to a foot bridge of small logs that were lashed together and spanned across the canyon to the other side. The creek had turned into a waterfall as it dropped over the cliff ten meters above the bridge and fell past it to the sand and waves below.

On one side of the bridge was the waterfall that was so close they could have stuck their arms into it. On the other side, far below, was the open cove with its waves and the Great Water beyond. Across the bridge, nestled into a flat spot on the canyon wall, was an old, weathered cottage. Sitting erect upon its thatched roof was Bubo. When the great-horned owl saw Thalmus, he spread his wings and hooted.

Standing in front of the small cottage was a tall man; although he was thin, he looked strong. He stood firm and straight as he watched them come down the path to the bridge. So still was he that Ekala thought he was another statue. Then, he raised a sinewy arm and pointed at Boschina. The roar of the waterfall filled the air between them, but his voice pierced this vale like a knife cutting through cloth.

"Daughter."

Boschina stopped at the bridge, staring at him in disbelief. "Father," she whispered. Then shouted, "Father!" And she ran across the logs and crashed into him, hugging and squeezing him as tightly as she could.

Chapter Twenty
Safedor

"Oh, Father. I was so worried that we wouldn't find you."

Veracitas wrapped his arms around her. "And I've been worried about you, Daughter. When I fled from the castle, my escape was suddenin the midst of the storm—and there was no time to get you. The troops were everywhere, and I had to hide and travel in disguise. I thought of you all the time, fretting for your safety."

"I'm all right, Father, see." Boschina stood back so he could look at her.

"You've grown so much," Veracitas said. "You're taller and you carry weapons!"

"Yes," Boschina said with some pride. "And I know how to use these tools."

Veracitas nodded. "Well, you certainly look as if you'd know," he said, smiling. "At first sight, I didn't recognize you on the trail. I thought, who is this warrior?"

"When did you know it was me?" Boschina asked, smiling.

He crossed his arms and thought about it.

"At the bridge...yes, when you stood at the bridge."

Thalmus and Ekala had waited before crossing the bridge to give father and daughter a moment together. Now, as the princess and the frog hunter approached, Boschina moved to stand happily at her father's side while grasping his hand.

"Princess Ekala," Veracitas said and bowed at the waist. Ekala took his other hand in greeting.

"You've certainly hidden yourself well."

"Hiding away was not my choice, princess, as you know."

"Yes, well, we've come to change that."

"Father," Boschina said, looking up at him. "This is Thalmus. He has guided me here to you."

"Thalmus, the King's Frog Hunter, friend of the owl," he said, motioning at Bubo. "He told me you would be coming. I have wonderful memories of you with my father when I was a novice. I'm honored that you would help my daughter and involve yourself in my problem."

"The honor is mine," Thalmus replied. "And the problem is not yours alone."

"Thalmus convinced the king to pardon you," Boschina said.

"He did?" Veracitas was surprised. "How did you manage that? The king was very angry with me."

"It was more Rundall's words than mine," Thalmus said. "The result is that you no longer have to hide."

"What about Metro?" Veracitas asked. "He's wicked. He's the dangerous one, not the king."

"You see nothing but the truth, Veracitas," Thalmus replied. "And you carve what you see. Armed with that power, we will defeat Metro and free the true prisoner, the king."

"You mean, return to the castle?"

"You must come back to the castle with us," Ekala said.

"I'm sorry, Princess Ekala," Veracitas said, "but I don't think I can face that again." He turned and looked at the falls and out at the Great Water. "It's so peaceful here."

Ekala glanced at Thalmus, who was studying Veracitas' face. No one spoke for a while. Boschina looked nervously at her friends and broke the silence by telling her father about their journey. Gradually, Ekala and Thalmus joined in to tell what they had seen of the forces building against the king. How, even though the king had pardoned Veracitas, the troops were out of control and still looking for him.

But now, with Ekala, the king's daughter, and her forces combating the troops, Veracitas would have protection.

Veracitas thought for a moment. "I've seen boats leave men on the shore by the big river. Each time, these foreigners were met and led away by the same man. He was not a soldier—at least he was not in uniform. They followed him inland."

"What sort of men?" Ekala asked. "Farmers, workers?"

"Soldiers," Veracitas answered. "They wore no insignias, but they were armed with swords, shields, and bows."

"Soldiers from across the Great Water," Ekala said with disgust. "Metro is raising his own army." She slapped her fist into the other hand. "I should have realized that it wasn't just some of our rogue troops attacking the people and chasing after you."

"Metro can't trust the king's soldiers to do what he wants," Veracitas said. "But these men would answer only to him."

Thalmus had been listening. He thought about these new troops and Metro's grand scheme to rule the land. "Veracitas," he said. "When you came here, did you come by way of Ello?"

"Not directly. I hid in the hills outside of Ello for a while. The villagers know me; they are kind, caring people. They supplied me with food and even brought tools and the statue I had started and asked me to finish it. Working on that stone image gave me hope. But the king's troops were constantly on the prowl. I decided that, for the safety of the villagers, I should leave. The statue was not complete, but it was too dangerous to stay. I did not want anyone to know where I was going, so I went back toward Ambermal, then into the hills, and I came here by way of a southern route that Larma showed me. I don't think anyone else knows of it, except you," Veracitas said, looking at Thalmus.

That's when he saw the concern in the frog hunter's eyes.

"What is it? Why do you ask this?"

"I am sorry to tell you," Thalmus said. "When we came through Ello, seven days ago, it was deserted. All the people are gone."

"Gone?"

Ekala untied the straps of the leather pouch and emptied its contents into Veracitas' cupped hands. The sculptor recognized the pieces immediately. He carefully moved the chunks of the stone crown around in his palms. Sighing, he looked up at her and asked: "Does it still stand?"

Ekala shook her head. "My statue is in pieces in the village of Ello."

Veracitas' shoulders slumped and he looked at the ground with sadness, as if he had just learned that a loved one had died. Boschina wrapped her arms around her father and hugged him.

"They must have moved you—your image into the village after I left," Veracitas said and lifted his head to look at Ekala with tears in his eyes. "I started your statue before I came to the castle to work for the king. I should have told you about it. I'm sorry."

"It looked...beautiful," Ekala said, trying to console him.

251

Veracitas nodded, accepting the compliment. "I'm sorry the people of Ello have been hurt for my selfish indulgence." He carefully dropped the stones pieces back into Ekala's pouch. He tied the straps and gave it back to her. "Save these. Someday you'll wear the real crown as queen."

Ekala held the pouch for a moment then said, "No."

She took his hand and placed the leather pouch in his palm and closed his fingers over it. "I want you to use them when you make another image of me."

Surprised, Veracitas hesitated. He smiled, looked at Boschina, and then back at Ekala. "It will be a joyful work," he said.

Ekala slowly let go of his hand. "Before you can start that work," she said. "We have another task ahead of us. Will you join us?"

"Please," Boschina pleaded. "Return to the castle with us."

"You're going back?" Veracitas asked, surprised once again.

"Yes, Father. I set out to find you, to save you from the troops, and to be with you." She looked at Ekala and Thalmus. "With their help, I found you. But, the journey's not over. There are so many people who need help. I cannot stop now."

Thalmus and Ekala looked at each other and smiled.

Veracitas put his arm around his daughter. "You're so brave," he said. "You always have been." Turning, he looked again at the Great Water. "I...I don't know if I can go back to the castle. You don't know how I was tortured there."

"Oh, Father," Boschina said, hugging him again.

"Was it Metro?" Ekala asked.

"Yes. If it had not been for Currad, I—" He paused and did not continue.

Ekala put her hand on Veracitas' shoulder. "I'm going back to confront Metro and free my father. I could use your help. It's your statue of the king and the power of truth that Metro fears."

Veracitas shook his head. "He fears you, Ekala."

Ekala laughed. "Not yet, but, he will."

"I don't know—"

Ekala held up a hand stopping him.

"Sleep on it. When you're ready, we will talk again."

The light was growing amber as the sun was beginning to sink into the Great Water. Thalmus sent Bubo to tell Thunder and Dallion that they were safe and would return to them on the morrow. They spent that night in the shelter of Veracitas' cottage and arose the next morning, refreshed. The day was clear, though the question still hung in the air.

"Veracitas," Ekala said to the tall stone cutter. "I will not force you to go with us. If I did, your lack of will would be of no help to you or our cause. You know what lies before us, what must be done, so you must be totally committed to the end." She grasped his arm with her hand. "I believe in you, Veracitas. I believe that you can finish this."

Ekala paused, giving him a chance to speak.

When he did not respond, she let go of his arm and continued. "We must return to my soldiers at the river and start back. We can delay no longer."

The princess hesitated again, looking up at Veracitas.

Boschina stood beside her father, waiting for him to answer; Thalmus watched, realizing that the artist of stone had not yet conquered his fear. Finally Veracitas said, putting his arm around his daughter: "I will go with you as far as the river—to see you all off."

Boschina hugged him and started to cry, but pulled away and led them down the trail to the beach where Dallion and Thunder waited. After introductions of Thunder and Dallion, Ekala took the lead to start them back toward her soldier's camp—except Veracitas, who went the opposite direction to the waterfall and viewed his carved cliff. Thalmus, Ekala, and Boschina watched from a distance as Veracitas reached up and touched the figures, running his fingertips along the stone. It looked to Thalmus that Veracitas was saying goodbye to his creations. The sculptor stood back, standing in the surf, and looked at the entire wall before turning to catch up with the others as they retraced their route along the beach.

As they walked, sea birds drawn by the presence of Veracitas circled around them; some landed on Thunder and pecked curiously at his shell. A stark white bird with a black beak and stick legs landed on Veracitas' shoulder and rode there for a while. Several fish with small wings suddenly broke out of a wave and flew into their path.

Veracitas pointed at them.

"Throw them back to the water, Boschina."

Boschina hurried to scoop up the little fish flopping on the sand before the birds got them and tossed the slippery silver fish back toward the water, where they flew again until they splashed down beyond the surf.

"Flying fish," Boschina exclaimed. "Just like Larma described."

As the group finally approached the big river, Ritzs rode out to meet them and the birds scattered. The women had hunted, gathered food, fished and washed in the river. They were relieved to see their leader, Oleen, and pleased to meet Veracitas, their little sister's father, the object of their quest. They gathered at the camp for the mid-meal of fish, and for discussion.

Now, a decision had to be made. Should they take the southern route and head directly to Ambermal and the castle? Or go back the way they had come to search for the people of Ello before going to the castle?

"We need to find those villagers," Ekala said. "I'm concerned for their safety."

"I don't like that trail," Boschina said. "But, I agree with Ekala, those people need our help."

Veracitas looked at Ekala. "I'm responsible for what has happened to them," he said. "They had the courage to place my statue of you in the square."

Thalmus was examining shells he had picked up along the beach. He threw a round, flat one onto the water and watched it skip across the surface, and then turned to the group. "What do you think happened to the villagers?"

"The troops ran them off before we got there," Ekala said, putting her fists on her hips.

"You think troops took them away?" Thalmus asked.

"Who else would have the power to do that?"

Thalmus nodded. "That would account for the sudden disappearance of the troops who were following us."

Boschina could tell that Thalmus had been thinking about this. She looked around for Bubo. The owl had not returned with them. That usually meant that Thalmus had sent him somewhere. This raised her suspicions that there was a plan in the works. So, she sat down in the sand to listen.

Thalmus leaned against Thunder's shell. "Why did they move the people out of the village?"

"Because of the statue," Veracitas replied. "The troops knew those villagers would support Ekala."

"Then why not just kill them. Why move them?"

"Oh, Thalmus," Boschina exclaimed. "Are you saying that they're not alive—that the troops killed them?"

"No, Boschina. I believe the villagers are alive."

"Alive, the villagers have value," Veracitas explained to Boschina. "Dead, they are worthless."

"Yes," Thalmus added. "Alive, they become a weapon—a bargaining weapon."

Ekala was starting to get frustrated.

"Bargaining for what?" she asked.

"For you, Ekala," Thalmus said pointing at her. "To control you."

"Me! Why those scoundrels! They think they can control me? They'd better think again. Let's go get those people."

Thalmus smiled at her. "Where do you think the troops took them?"

"Some hiding place where they can guard them," Ekala said. "They should be easy enough to find. We'll just follow the tracks."

"That's what the troops would expect us to do," Thalmus replied and skipped another shell over the water.

"All right, Thalmus," Boschina said. She could not wait this out any longer. "Where do you think they are and how do we get there?"

Thalmus smiled at Boschina. She was getting to know him pretty well.

"There is a canyon named Safedor several days south of the village that has a spring and only one entrance. It is a natural fort, an easy place to defend. It would be a logical place to keep the villagers."

They all waited for more information from Thalmus, who leaned again on Thunder and stroked the tortoise's big head.

Finally, Boschina said: "So, Thalmus, how do we get there?"

He smiled again at Boschina and addressed Ekala. "We do not want to approach at the entrance. That would be futile. We take the western route through the hills at the edge of the Barrier Forest and cut across to come in behind the canyon. They would not expect that and probably do not have it defended. This is, of course, if they are there at all."

"I like it," Ekala replied. "You'll guide us?"

Thalmus nodded. "Thunder and Dallion know the way as well."

"Let's go then," she said and slapped Thalmus on his shoulder.

She turned and started giving orders to her soldiers.

While Ekala readied the Oleens to leave, Veracitas and Thalmus stood together on the bank of sand where the river flowed into the waves of the Great Water. Neither one spoke. Each man scanned the scene, taking in the sound, smell, sight and feel of the place—putting it all away in memory. Sea birds fluttered around them and walked in the sand at their feet. With all of this came Larma's presence flowing in and around them like incense. Both men felt it, heard her voice in their ears, but neither expressed it to the other.

While watching waves crash onto the rocky shore to the north, Veracitas spoke in a soft, calm voice. "Ekala's time has come."

"Yes," Thalmus replied. "We must do what we can to help her."

"I know the prophecy, Thalmus, and my role in it. Larma told me this time would come and what I must do."

"Then you know your part is critical for Ekala's success."

Thalmus waited for Veracitas to continue while they both took deep breaths of the clean salt air.

"After what happened at the castle, I did not think I could fulfill this call, this responsibility," Veracitas said. "I knew the king's statue would start this all in motion; yet, I did not know the pain it would cause. Not just to me, but to all the people." He paused and took in more of the salt air. "You and Ekala have lifted my spirits—and Boschina's courage has inspired me."

Thalmus looked at Veracitas. "Will you join us?"

Veracitas turned to face Thalmus. His demeanor had changed. He almost looked like a different man. He appeared confident and strong. "Yes," the stone cutter said in a firm voice. "For Ekala to rule, Metro must be destroyed. Besides that, I do not want to abandon my daughter again."

Thalmus nodded and motioned eastward with his hand.

"Show us the route home."

It didn't take long for the Oleens to outfit Veracitas with a horse and saddle that they had brought specifically for this purpose. She was a tall chestnut mare with a white stripe down her nose and confident eyes. Her name was Robon, and she was immediately comfortable with the stone cutter when he introduced himself, standing in front of her, speaking gently and petting her nose, head and neck. With Boschina riding Radise by his side, Veracitas and Robon led Ekala and the Oleens inland over a ridge—and away from the river and the Great Water. There was no trail for no one traveled this way. It was knowledge of the land and a sense of direction that guided him. The landscape was lush and green and they crossed many small creeks. They moved more quickly than before with Thunder and Thalmus trailing behind as the rear guard—and Dallion circling farther out to watch for troops.

They traveled the rest of that day then camped and moved on early the next morning. Veracitas kept up the pace for the next two days. By the third night, they had covered a long distance through the hills and forest. Thalmus, Thunder, and Dallion trailed in long after the group had stopped and set up camp. Boschina was waiting and glad to see them arrive each evening—hugging Thunder's head and scratching Dallion's nose. Thus far, they had not encountered another traveler nor met any resistance except the terrain.

On the fourth morning, Thalmus and Dallion joined Ekala, Boschina, and Veracitas at the head of the column. Two of the Oleens dropped back to take their place as the rear guard with Thunder. The group continued on through the morning. In the early afternoon, as they came up out of a gully into another grove of trees with spreading limbs, Bubo was waiting for them. He was perched on a branch and stared calmly at the column as it came to a halt in front of the tree.

"It's about time you showed up," Ekala said to the owl.

Bubo grunted at her and turned his head to focus on Thalmus. The frog hunter smiled at Bubo and hooted. Bubo snapped his bill, chattered, hissed, and fluttered his wings.

"What does that mean?" Boschina asked.

"It means that he saw people at Safedor and that some of them are troops with weapons."

Ekala shifted in her saddle. "How far away is it?"

Thalmus pointed east. "A short ride that way."

"Let's go see what we can see," Ekala said, and urged Shadahn forward.

The Oleens moved into the shade of the trees, dismounted, and settled down to wait for the return of their leader. Boschina and Veracitas decided to ride back to walk with Thunder.

Ekala and Thalmus rode east for a while. Reaching a short plain, they slowed the horses to a walk and finally dismounted. Leaving the mounts behind, they walked up a slope. As they approached the summit, Thalmus motioned to get down. They crawled on their hands and knees the last ten meters through tall grass to peek over the edge of a cliff into Safedor.

Spread out below them was a canyon about twice the depth of the Barranca, but shaped like a long rectangular box and closed at both ends. All the sides were steep and jagged with crevices running the full height of the walls. At the far end was a narrow passage through the canyon wall that was the only way in or out. On one side of the canyon was a spring that bubbled into a small pond. Some troops were sitting there around the water.

The rest of them were positioned on each side of the passage coming into the canyon. In this placement, the troops could defend and easily destroy anyone trying to enter through the narrow entrance. Scattered across the canyon floor and up against the opposite side were the villagers. Most of them were doing nothing— just sitting. Some were working on baskets or blankets. Except for the spot of blue water, the canyon was dry and dusty brown. The sun was behind Ekala and Thalmus, shining into the eyes of anyone who might look up in their direction.

"You're right," Ekala said, assessing the situation. "It would be certain failure to attack through that little opening."

Thalmus rested his chin on his hand, looking down at the people. "I wonder if the villagers are strong enough to fight?" He continued to watch them. "You should not expect their help."

Ekala was studying the cliff walls and the distance to the troops at the entrance. "Some of these cracks in the cliffs are deep with good foot holds. I think we could use them to climb to the bottom."

Thalmus thought about that idea as he examined the crevices in the canyon walls. "That will take time to do," he said. "You would have to go carefully so as not to fall or break off rock that would draw attention. The troops will see you."

"Not if we keep their attention at the entrance. I'll send a force around to the front to keep them busy so we can climb down. They won't expect to be attacked from within. The troops will have to turn to fight us. Then, the force outside can come through."

"They have you outnumbered, at least double," Thalmus countered. "You will have to get all your people to the bottom before the troops are aware, or they will pick you off the wall."

Ekala turned to Thalmus with a hard glare.

"What's this *you* and *your*? Aren't you fighting with us?"

"Of course," Thalmus replied. "But it is your command. You must be sure of your plan."

She continued to stare at Thalmus for a moment as his words settled on her. She looked back at the troops in the canyon. "It is my command," she said quietly, suddenly feeling the weight of leadership. "It is my responsibility."

This would be Ekala's first planned battle as a leader. She was making a decision to send her soldiers into a risky fight. She was not worried about herself, but would they share her enthusiasm and confidence? Would they be up to the task? The Oleens were disciplined and well—trained. Still, how would her women do against experienced male soldiers? She realized that success of her plan would be determined by surprise and the timing of the two-pronged attack. Any delay or mistake could be disastrous.

"I remember my father telling me, more than once, that to lead I must assess my options, make a decision, and believe in it – then others will, too."

"I agree,"Thalmus said. "You should never take counsel of your fears."

Ekala looked again at Thalmus, who was watching the villagers in the canyon. "I've made my decision. Will you assault from the cliffs with us?"

Thalmus looked at her face and into her eyes to see if she believed in her plan. He saw the determined confidence he was hoping for. "If that is what you wish," he replied.

"It is."

"Then I am with you," he said with a smile. "I like the plan. It is bold."

They both turned back to the canyon to look it over one more time—to study the distances, the location of the people, and the number of troops.

"I will keep watch while you get the others ready," Thalmus suggested.

Ekala backhanded Thalmus' shoulder with a fist and backed away from the canyon edge on her hands and knees. She got up and returned to the horses. Dallion and Shadahn sped her back to the grove where she gathered everyone together.

Bubo sat on a branch and watched from above, while Thunder nudged his head in next to Boschina. Ekala described the canyon and the placement of the troops and the captive villagers before she explained her plan. The women nodded and voiced their approval.

Captain Ritzs spoke for them all when she said, "We follow you, Oleen, whatever you command." After that Ekala was quick about assigning duties and was thorough with each one about the details of the plan. Force Three would assault the entrance and distract the troops while Forces One and Two scaled down the walls to attack from the rear.

"Boschina," Ekala said, pointing a finger at her. "I want you to ride with Ritzs and Force Three to the front. Stay back when they attack. You'll be the lookout in case there are more troops on the plain."

"I want to ride in with them," Boschina said, motioning at the women warriors.

"No, Boschina. It's important that you stay outside the canyon and watch. Once we're all inside, we could easily be trapped by more troops. We would be hostages as well. Your job is very important. We cannot be surprised. Do you understand?"

"Yes, as you wish."

Ekala looked at Thunder, his big head protruding next to Boschina and his narrow eyes focused on her. "When Thunder gets to the front, he can help you watch. He'll feel any approaching troops, so keep an eye on him. Bubo," she said, looking up at the owl in the tree. "We need your eyes and your claws wherever you see a need."

Bubo briefly fluffed his wings in response as Ekala turned to the horses. "Dallion and Shadahn will lead the free horses of those who are climbing into the canyon. The horses support Force Three when they attack."

She turned to the stone cutter, "Now, Veracitas."

"Yes, Princess?"

Ekala smiled at him. "What is your choice?"

Veracitas held up both hands with the palms open and the fingers extended. "These hands know stone and rock," he said. "We'll join you climbing down the wall." He untied the leather pouch from his belt and offered it to Ekala.

She took the bag and nodded with approval. As the whole group silently watched her, Princess Ekala—known to her soldiers as Oleen—looked back at them. "Today," she said, grasping in her clenched fist the leather pouch containing the pieces of her stone crown, "we start to make a difference…to change our land!"

The women held up their open right hands over their heads and shouted, "Oleen."

Then, they broke into action.

*

Thalmus lay on his belly peeking over the edge watching the troops in Safedor Canyon. Behind him Ekala directed the Oleens into position along the rim where rock formations spiraled to the floor below. The women had adjusted their weapons, bows and swords, to their backs for the climb.

Veracitas crawled up next to Thalmus. "Force Three should be at the entrance soon," he said quietly.

"I can hear the horses from here," Thalmus answered.

The troops in Safedor could not hear the rumble of the galloping horses outside the canyon and continued casually lying about. Then Thalmus saw the scouts from outside run in through the entrance shouting and gesturing frantically. The relaxed troops at the spring grabbed their weapons and hurried to the narrow gate. Now shouting could be heard as dust rose from the attacking Force Three. The troops had poured into the funnel of the entrance and formed another line just inside with their backs to the canyon.

Ekala waved at Thalmus and he signaled back "okay."

The princess swung her legs over the edge, secured a foot and finger hold and started climbing down. The Oleens, spread out along the rim of the canyon on their bellies, carefully stretched their legs over the edge feeling for ledges and edges to grasp. Thalmus and Veracitas ran around helping the women get started then went over the edge themselves. The force looked like spiders inching their way down the rock walls. The climbers kept glancing anxiously toward the troops. Moving cautiously, but as quickly as they could for fear of being discovered, they finally reached the bottom with just scrapes and minor cuts.

The dangerous climb was finished. Now, the fight would begin.

"Form a battle line," Ekala ordered. "Hurry, we must cross the open ground before they see us."

The Oleens with Thalmus and Veracitas on each side of Ekala started walking rapidly across the open space toward the entrance. The villagers who had been focused on the fight at the gate were shocked when Ekala and the Oleens appeared seemingly out of the rock wall. The people recognized the princess, Veracitas and Thalmus and began to cheer.

Some of the troops in the narrow passage turned to see what the commotion was and were surprised to see strange soldiers rushing toward them. They yelled an alarm to their comrades and began shooting arrows at their attackers. The Oleen archers returned fire, dropping some troopers. Ekala's advantage quickly faded, however when the bulk of the troops swarmed out of the passage to confront this assault to their rear. The two lines crashed into one another in a melee of swords, spears, arrows and dust. By sheer numbers the troops were pushing the Oleens back and beginning to take control.

The few troops in the passage still holding off the Oleen force from the outside were suddenly thrown back when Bubo appeared flying in front of the charging Dallion leading the rider-less horses in a thundering charge into the narrow opening. The men ran from the stampede right into the fight inside the canyon. Force Three followed the horses through the passage to join the battle.

Ekala saw a brief advantage and felt her sword vibrating, coming alive in her hand. She glanced at Thalmus who was watching her. "Now is the time," he told her. With the stone cutter on her left and the frog hunter on her right she stunned the troops by leading a charge screaming into their midst. The Oleens joined in with piercing high screams of their own as they engaged the fight again. The women's battle cries bounced off the canyon walls and filled the air.

Trapped in the middle, the men, still with superior numbers, were overwhelmed by these wild and strange forces. The frog hunter, the princess and the stone cutter were leading the force slashing through them while the owl swooped at their heads, the horses stomped on them and the women archers fired into their ranks. The men began dropping their weapons.

The women soldiers pushed the defeated troopers through the dust and confusion to a corner of the canyon as the villagers cheered: "Ekala! Veracitas! Thalmus!"

They had no time to celebrate because Boschina rode in through the passage shouting: "Troops are coming."

Ekala turned, still keyed up from the fight. She was breathing heavily with short gasping breaths. Sweat, mixed with dust, ran down her face and arms—the swords still gripped tightly in her hands. "How many?" she demanded.

"I counted about thirty," Boschina said excitedly. "I don't think they know we're here because they're riding slowly. But, they'll be here soon."

Ekala looked around at her soldiers. Eight to ten were hurt and could not fight. The villagers were already helping the wounded. Ten more of her fighters would be needed to guard the prisoners and the entrance. That left about twelve, including Thalmus and Veracitas.

Would that be enough?

Thalmus knew what she was thinking. He grasped her shoulder and looked into her eyes—the fire was still there. "We have enough fighters to surprise these new troops, too, if we ride out now."

Ekala stared back at him for a moment, a wild look in her eyes. She smiled and held up her sword—shining and pulsating in the sun.

She turned and ordered, "Mount up!"

The women ran to their horses. Thalmus jumped onto a horse that belonged to one of the wounded Oleens. Robon trotted up to Veracitas and he climbed onto her back. Ekala gave quick directions to Ritzs, leaving her in command of the Oleens and the villagers to round up all the weapons and guard the troops. She also ordered them to help the wounded troopers.

Thalmus, Veracitas and Boschina were first out of Safedor, followed by Ekala with ten of the Oleens and Dallion leading the loose horses.

Boschina and Radise led them east to where they could see the column of troops on the plain. Hidden in a ravine, the princess' small force stopped and discussed strategy. Ekala and Thalmus decided on a plan that she remembered from one of her father's stories. Splitting into three groups, they galloped to new positions—except for Ekala and Veracitas, who rode out to meet the troops. The princess and stone cutter stopped their horses about thirty meters short of the approaching column.

"I'm the Crown Princess Ekala," she shouted.

The troops stopped and looked at her in disbelief. Sitting atop the dark menacing Shadahn—and wearing a helmet, leather vest, and a sword at her side—she was not the princess they knew.

"I am the daughter of King Ahmbin," she shouted.

The troops waited.

"This is Veracitas, the sculptor. And I am Ekala Oleen, the future ruler of this land. Throw down your weapons and submit to me!"

This had the immediate reaction she expected.

"No, you're not our ruler," the captain of the troops shouted. "Get Veracitas!" He commanded as they spurred their horses toward them.

Veracitas nodded at Ekala—as if to say "good job"—and then they turned their mounts and galloped away as the troops chased after them. Now Ekala and Veracitas just had to keep the troops frantically pursuing them long enough for the plan to work. Shadahn enjoyed the race as she led them over hills and through ravines. In their pursuit, the troops with slower horses fell behind, and the ones in the rear became easy prey.

Thalmus and the Oleens would ride up from behind or attack the lone man suddenly from the side and knock him from his horse. Two other Oleens would pounce on him, take his weapon, bind his ankles and hands with leather straps, leave him there, and move on to get another one—while Dallion swept in and took away the stray horses into his growing herd. Radise was particularly good at this quick cutting maneuver that knocked into the soldier's mount, jarring the man loose from his saddle—especially when Boschina got used to the sudden move and contact and participated in the bumping and sword play.

In this way, the Oleens were taking down one to two troopers at a time. Before long, the odds had turned in Ekala's favor. The lead troops, who had not looked back, still thought they were chasing only two people—one of whom had a reward on his head; so, they continued their rabid pursuit. Now, realizing her advantage, Ekala led their pursuers into a sunken swell. As she and Veracitas galloped up out of the swell, they reined their horses to a stop and turned to face the troops. Thalmus and Boschina rode up to join them. The troops, which now numbered fifteen, slowed and came to a stop in the swell because the Oleens had ridden up on the crest around them. Dallion appeared on the other ridge with the rider-less horses. On seeing them, the troops' horses stammered and bucked, and the men struggled to keep their mounts under control.

Thalmus recognized the leader of the troops.

It was the same captain who had attacked them outside of Rainland. He was red with anger and frustration as he looked around to see that his troops had been cut in half and he was surrounded. No one spoke as they exchanged glares. For a while, the only sounds were the stomping, snorting, and heavy breathing of the sweating horses.

Then Ekala spoke. "I tell you again, I am Princess Ekala—"

"I know who you are and your little friend, the hunter," the captain interrupted. He looked around at the Oleens and his men. "She will never rule."

Thalmus shook his head with disappointment. "You have not changed, Captain, since we met outside of Rainland."

The red-faced captain chuckled. "You think you have me beat?"

He laughed again and said, "Not this time, Thalmus." He pointed at Ekala. "You have no power." Pointing at Veracitas, he spoke. "I tell you now, give me this man or all of the villagers of Ello will die."

A smile appeared and then quickly disappeared from Ekala's face. Thalmus had predicted this. They had saved the people of Ello and taken away some power from Metro. She stared hard at the captain. "Safedor is now in my control. Your troops are beaten. The villagers are free."

"What? That cannot be," the captain scoffed. "No one can take Safedor. My best troops hold it."

Ekala revealed a bloody uniform cloak from one of his soldiers at Safedor. She held it out to her side as the troops murmured with surprise.

"Most of them are dead," she said. "The rest are prisoners—and you are in violation of the king's orders. Throw down your weapons."

"Another trick," the captain snorted and drew his sword. Several of the troopers followed his lead and held up their swords.

"It is not a trick, Captain," Thalmus said. "Your men are defeated. Put down your swords and save yourself."

"We'll never submit to you," the captain yelled. "You no longer hold the power in this land and you are the ones who will suffer."

"Don't be a fool," Veracitas appealed to the captain. "You have already lost half of your men. Look around you." He motioned to the Oleens, who were poised on their horses with bows ready—waiting to release arrows.

265

"You will not win this fight, Captain."

Ekala called to them: "Surrender now and I will let you live."

The troops looked around at the Oleens and the foursome of Boschina, Thalmus, Veracitas, and Ekala—then at Dallion with the small herd of horses standing behind him—and realized their dire situation. At that moment of indecision, Bubo suddenly appeared from nowhere, flew over their heads and right up to Ekala—where he landed on her shoulder. She was surprised, but did not show it as his claws grasped onto her. The great-horned owl settled his wings, snapped his beak, and glared down at the men. That did it. The troops who had drawn their swords dropped them to the ground.

"What're you doing?" the captain yelled. "Pick up your swords." The men refused and all but the captain dismounted, tossing their swords and bows aside.

"Traitors," the captain shouted.

"Give up, Captain," the troops told him. "She's been chosen. She has the power."

"No. You will never be ruler," he screamed.

The angry captain spurred his horse and charged toward her with his sword raised for attack. He was halfway to Ekala when three arrows from the bows of the Oleens ripped into his chest. His body jolted with each hit and he toppled from the galloping horse. Silence prevailed as the dust settled, and they all looked from the dead captain to the princess.

"This man was one of Metro's," Ekala said, looking at the captain sprawled on the ground with broken arrow shafts protruding from his torso. She looked at the troops. "Do you really believe in your hearts that Metro is the man you want to serve? Will your life be better following him?" Ekala paused as Shadahn snorted and stamped the ground. "We're on our way to the castle to destroy Metro. I'd like you to follow me, to join us." She spread her arms to indicate everyone there. "And help save the king to whom you once pledged your life and allegiance."

The women stood up in their stirrups, raised their right hands in the air and shouted, "Oleen!"

The troops on the ground, standing next to their horses, bent their right arms across their chests and knelt on one knee.

Princess Ekala Oleen looked at the troops kneeling before her, and then up at the Oleens. She glanced past Bubo on her shoulder to see Thalmus sitting on the horse beside her. He inclined his head slightly, acknowledging her success and authority. On her other side, Veracitas and Boschina watched and waited. Ekala felt the strange weight of Bubo and his claws gripping on her shoulder that seemed to be sending a new feeling of power pulsating through her.

She turned back to the Oleens.

They were still holding their hands up as a salute to her. Responding, she raised her arm straight up over her head with her hand open, paused, lowered it slowly, and turned Shadahn toward Safedor.

Chapter Twenty-One
Wind and Smoke

Gusts of wind began to blow across the plain as Ekala rode back to Safedor. However, there was something different about this wind. It was warmer and had a strange smell. Thalmus felt the change. He stopped his horse on top of a small hill as Dallion ran up and joined him. They both lifted their heads and sniffed the air. There was an odor in the wind that Thalmus did not like. Bubo glided down and landed on Thalmus' shoulder. Dallion bobbed and shook his head, and then snorted as if he was trying to clear his nostrils.

Veracitas sensed something, too. He had been helping the Oleens gather the troopers who they had tied up and left behind in the chase. Now, he looked all around, searching the terrain, but he saw nothing unusual. He rode up alongside Thalmus and Dallion. "Something has changed, the wind is different." He saw Bubo hissing and pulling at Thalmus' hair. "Bubo must feel it, too," he observed as he steadied the anxious Robon with pats on the neck.

"Yes," Thalmus replied as he stroked Owl's breast feathers to calm him. "The wind has a different smell and I can't tell which direction it is coming from."

"This is not good, Thalmus," Veracitas said, still scanning the horizon and patting Robon, who was clearly agitated.

Thalmus was thinking about the scent in the wind.

What is that odor? Where have I smelled it before?

"The wind has turned foul," Veracitas continued. "It feels dark, like the prison cell at the castle."

"That's it," Thalmus exclaimed. "The odor in the wind is from Metro's room."

"You're right," Veracitas agreed. "The wind is filled with the scent of everything wrong at the castle. We must warn Ekala."

Bubo snapped his beak and flew off as Thalmus and Veracitas urged their horses into a gallop to catch up with Ekala.

∗

Far away, on the other side of the great plain from Safedor, Larma stood on the ledge of the cliff in front of her cave at Table Top. Her eyes were closed, her arms at her sides, as she breathed deeply of the air and felt the wind press against her. The wind may blow for Metro, but it spoke to Larma. She heard the screams and battle at Safedor, smelled the blood and fear and death of the fighters, and the excitement of the Oleens. She felt the tense muscles from the cliff climb and tight clenching of weapons, the heat and sweat of the humans and the horses as they raced and fought—snorting and stomping. She saw the Oleens with Thalmus and Veracitas fighting on each side of Ekala, and then Ekala Oleen rising above the fray, above them all with the bright white light of victory radiating from her sword. Lastly, there was Bubo, wings spread, eyes glowing, as he hovered over Ekala.

Larma opened her eyes and looked to the sky, and then out over the land spread below her. In the distance, a cloud of brown dust rose from the hooves of an approaching column of soldiers. Closing her eyes again, she could hear the pounding hooves of horses and the clanking, chinking sound of sabers and shields. These were not the renegade troops from the king's army. Their red shields and jerseys bore an emblem of a hissing lizard coiled in a circle. It was a symbol she had not seen in a very long time. They were large men who moved with a purpose and strength known to experienced soldiers. Larma could feel their intent, and she knew what had to be done. She called the captain of the Oleens, Kali, to her and ordered a call to arms.

The women assembled quickly on the shelf in their assigned forces and with their weapons—bows, arrows, and medium-length swords. A few carried long, thick-shanked spears for large aggressive creatures. No one was left out. Even the farmers and cooks were trained and ready to fight.

One hundred forty-five in all stood ready for orders.

Most were wearing the tan pants and the gray shirt with the maroon "O" over the heart that had become the Oleen uniform.

Many wore small-brim straw hats with blue bands. The leader's hats were wrapped with a maroon band and silver buckle in the front.

While the women assembled, a guard came running in through the tunnel with a message. Larma listened quietly as the guard breathlessly reported that Maz had come to the hollow to tell her that Gorga had sent word to his gang to gather at the North Gate.

Larma nodded and thanked the guard. Having her suspicions confirmed—and determining the course of action—she stood before her soldiers on the shelf. She wore a silvery blouse with the maroon letter "O" over her left breast. A silver belt at the waist supported baggy gray trousers. Her shiny gray hair blew in the wind, but she looked tall, young and powerful.

"The time has come," she said in a calm, quiet, voice. "Ekala Oleen needs us—every one of us. Feel the strength and rise to the power instilled in you."

Every woman raised an arm straight up with an open hand and they shouted together, "Oleen!"

And the echo replied, "Oleen...Oleen...Oleen."

A beautiful gray horse trotted up to Larma. She rubbed its nose and stroked its neck. "Yes, I'm ready, Eidolon," Larma said and jumped up on the horse's back and took the reins. Eidolon bobbed her head as Larma motioned to Captain Kali, who started shouting orders, and the women broke into action. Additional guards were quickly posted at the narrow path to the low land. The rest of the women soldiers, some riding and some marching, passed through the tunnel into Larma Hollow and out onto Table Top. They swept across the rocky, flat ground, checking the ravines and hollows as they headed toward the North Gate.

Gorga's men, who normally were spread out in small groups, were absent from their usual places. The Oleens found only the inhabitants who were not Gorga's followers; these poor people were scared, as they feared an approaching calamity. Larma consoled them as she passed by, now knowing for sure that the enemy was gathering at the gate Gorga controlled. The Oleens hurried on, still checking, though focused more now on reaching the only other entrance to Table Top.

Larma was right.

For at this moment, Gorga and his followers were meeting at the trailhead. The assorted men were outfitting themselves for battle and preparing to welcome the troops who were riding toward Table Top.

Being so involved, the men at first did not see the line of warrior women coming toward them. The wind blew away any noise of their approach. When several of the men saw the women, they hesitated— for they weren't sure who these soldiers were. Finally, one of men realized the approaching danger and shouted, "It's the Oleens!" They all scrambled to form a battle line.

Larma slowed the Oleens down as they approached the North Gate. She stopped them fifty meters from the men's line. The women had hurried all the way across the Top and she wanted them to rest. The leaders quickly formed their forces opposing the men's line and got their weapons out so they were ready for battle. Larma motioned to the women to rest and they all knelt on a knee.

Then, Larma rode alone toward the men.

The wind was blowing her clothes and hair. Gorga was stunned. He had never seen her this way. She had always seemed so old to him. Now, she looked ominous with her eyes glaring at him as she walked the horse closer and closer, until coming to a stop ten meters away. He was also surprised by the number of women; there were many more than he had expected.

"Lay down your weapons and no harm will come to you," Larma said to all of the men, but her eyes stayed focused on Gorga.

Gorga stared at her. She wore no weapon, but he could feel her power. It was as if a stiff hand were pressing against his chest. *This was not good*, he thought. He could not let her control them. He had a job to do here and in order to complete it, she had to be defeated. The women had them outnumbered two to one, but that did not worry him—yet.

Gorga waved his arm across his body, as if trying to knock away the unseen hand on his chest. "That's not possible," he said.

"Then march down the trail and leave the Top," Larma replied.

"No," Gorga said, and looked around nervously at his men. "We hold the Gate. It's ours." And he drew his sword.

The silver Eidolon snorted and stomped her front hoof on the ground. Larma continued to stare at Gorga and spoke calmly. "You choose to oppose me?"

Gorga stepped back, trying to relieve the pressure on his chest, and took a deep breath. "Aren't you a long way from your hollow?" he said, trying to mock her.

"I am never too far from anywhere," Larma replied.

Gorga looked at her. "I don't know what that means," he said. "I do know that in a little while you'll no longer control Table Top."

Just then, Maz and Camp stepped out from behind the line of men and stood alongside Larma.

"You fight Larma, you fight us," Maz said, clenching his fist.

The line of men stirred with muttering at this surprise. Gorga looked at them in disbelief. Two of the best and most well-trained fighters on the Top had just deserted him. He pointed his sword at them. "You join her?" he yelled. "You side with the women against me?"

"Does that scare you, Gorga?" Camp mocked.

Gorga laughed and tried to regain his confidence. "Nothing scares me." But, the strange force was pushing against his chest and he wished Metro's soldiers would get here quickly.

"Your cause is futile," Larma said in her calm voice. "You must leave and return to wherever you came from. This land is not your land."

Stepping back again, trying to ease the pressure he felt, Gorga turned to his men—who were nervous and growing restless. "Is this not what you've heard before?" he hollered. "That this is not your land? You were chased off your farms and out of your homes by a king who took all that you had and forced you to live here as outcasts. Now's your chance to share in a new land, to get what you deserve."

The men cheered Gorga with shouts of "we're with you" and "down with the king!"

Gorga took another step back, inhaled a deep breath, and shouted: "We'll join the army that's coming and take this kingdom for a new ruler, a true ruler with wisdom and power."

The wind gusted and blew dust across the Top and into their faces. It brought a foul odor and a shiver to all who stood there, except Gorga. In that putrid air, Larma detected the sound of the troops entering the trail at the bottom of Table Top. She could feel the weight of them starting to climb up through the narrow passage.

She could delay no longer.

Larma spoke to Maz and Camp at her side. "Soldiers have entered the trail to the Top. We must secure the Gate." She lifted her head and spoke to all on Table Top in her normal voice, but each person could hear her clearly through the wind and across distance. "There is much wrong throughout the land. Join us to make a change—for this land will be ruled by the only rightful heir to the throne. One who will be fair and open to all. It is one who you know, Ekala Oleen."

The women stood and shouted, "Oleen!"

Larma extended her arm with an open hand toward the men. "You have three choices: join us, stand aside, or perish with the intruders." She motioned to Captain Kali, who raised her sword and pointed at the men.

The Oleens sent a flight of arrows at the men, and then screamed and charged forward. The men were taken aback by the pressure from Larma and now the hail of arrows and the frightful battle cry of the warrior women charging at them. Gorga ran along the line of his men, shouting to be heard over the women's battle screams: "Hold your ground, men. They're only women. We must hold the Gate; the troops will be here soon."

Not many men had the fighting spirit in them.

Some ran while others gave up right away, dropping their weapons and kneeling. As the Oleens ran past Larma in their battle line, Maz and Camp joined them and they all crashed into the fighters who were left and quickly pushed them back to the edge of the cliff.

Gorga saw that failure was imminent.

As his men fell about him and the numbers and power of the women bore down on him, he felt the strange pressure pushing him——pushing against his chest; yet, it held him in place, keeping him from moving.

"No," he screamed. "Leave me!"

He twisted and tugged against himself and swung his sword in the air trying to cut free from what held him. Suddenly, he seemed to break loose and stumbled to the ground.

Another man tripped over him as he tried to get up.

"I can't be taken," he muttered. "I can't be captured."

He pushed the man off him and crawled away. Glancing back at the melee, he saw that he was free for the moment. He stood and ran as fast as he could through the Gate and down the narrow trail.

Larma watched Gorga break, run through the Gate, and disappear down the winding path. She had focused her attention on him and was disappointed he had escaped. *His fear had served him well*, she thought. Now, he will warn the soldiers on the trail so that they will be prepared when coming to the Gate. Larma sighed. "It is not done yet."

The battle did not last long.

The Oleens overwhelmed Gorga's ragtag army and took control of the North Gate. Maz and Camp were quick to show the Oleens where to position along the heights on each side of the trail and they readied themselves for the approaching troops. Some women, and many men, had been injured in the fight. No matter who they were, the Oleens tended to all of the wounded. Larma and the Oleens were now in possession of both the South and North Gates; thereby, controlling who entered or left Table Top, for the moment.

Gorga, still carrying his sword, stumbled down the steep trail until he met the soldiers hiking up. "Hurry! You must hurry to the Top," he said excitedly, pointing up the path with his free hand.

A burly captain named Blayon looked curiously at him. "Gorga?"

Gorga recognized the captain. "Blayon, I'm glad you're here. The Oleens have attacked. We're fighting to hold the Gate."

"I thought you had it secured?"

"We did, but we were just attacked by a large force."

"What large force?" Blayon asked.

"Who are the Oleens?" another man asked.

Gorga ignored the questions. He knew that by now the Oleens had control of the Gate. His only hope was to convince Blayon that they could still break through before the women were organized and in position.

"We have to hurry," Gorga said, urging him with a wave and started up the path. "Come on, Table Top is ours."

The men pulled their swords, readied their shields, and followed him up the narrow path. They were a long file of one hundred and fifty men who had come expecting easy access to the strange Table Top—and to fight a few women in order to capture it.

Blayon's orders from Metro were clear: once at the Top, Gorga would lead them in destroying the mysterious Larma and her band. Blayon had thought the size of his force was too large for such an easy task, but now the captain was troubled by the situation. Here was Gorga, though he was not on the Top, and he appeared to have lost control of the Gate.

By the time they neared the Gate, the soldiers were exhausted and had been dropping the heavy chest armor and shoulder protection to lighten their load. Gorga had been watching the rocks and cliffs above the trail. He had not seen anyone.

His hopes rose. Could it be that the Oleens had only posted a few guards, not expecting an attack? Gorga stopped the troops just short of what he knew was the final run to the Gate.

"Is this it?" Blayon asked between heavy breaths.

Gorga, gulping air, stepped aside and pointed up the trail. "The Gate to the Top is just around the bend. Go take it!"

The captain looked at him with surprise. "Don't you want to lead?"

"No, Blayon. The victory of Table Top should be yours."

Captain Blayon looked at the narrow trail that disappeared around a boulder. He looked up at the ledge of rocks high above them and finally glanced at Gorga suspiciously. Blayon did not like this; it felt like a trap. Still, he had plenty of men to risk an assault and his orders were to follow Gorga. So, he ordered his men forward, but stepped aside with Gorga as the tired soldiers charged two abreast up the path.

The lead soldiers were just five meters from the Gate when the Oleens suddenly popped up on the rocks above both sides of the trail, their bows already drawn, and released a shower of arrows into the troops. The men tried to cover themselves with their shields, but the attack was too quick and the arrows struck them down. Acting independently, several soldiers held up their shields and tried to continue the charge around and over the dead and wounded, but were shot in the legs and stumbled to the ground. Taking a new approach, a wave of troops grouped tightly, held their shields together over their heads, and ran forward over their comrades. This bunch got through the barrage of arrows, only to be stopped by Maz and Camp—who stepped into the Gate and blocked them. Vicious hand-to-hand sword fighting ensued, but the advantage went to Maz and Camp.

In that narrow Gate only two men could get abreast of one another, so the soldier's superior numbers and size did not help them. Exhausted from the hike up the steep trail, the soldiers were no match for Maz and Camp who slashed and stabbed—or for the Oleen archers who stepped into the Gate and shot into the ranks of the soldiers whose bodies were exposed with their shields held over their heads.

Gorga kept urging more men forward as the ones before them fell. Soon, the path was blocked with bodies, so the soldiers had to withdraw. Gorga knew it was hopeless. He had failed. Table Top was lost and Larma was still a threat. Metro would be angry and surely punish someone. He started thinking how to blame the defeat on Blayon.

"You've lost Table Top," Gorga said.

Blayon was furious. He had followed orders and trusted Gorga against his better judgment. "You're blaming this on me?" he yelled. "No, Gorga, you were in charge here. You will take the blame. I'm leaving at once to report this failure."

Gorga knew he was in trouble and quickly changed his approach. "Blayon, we can still win this. We can wait on the plain and attack them when they come down off the Top. They will be in the open then and no match for us."

The captain had listened enough to Gorga. "I've lost half of my men because of you. We're leaving." He gathered his soldiers and headed back down the trail. Gorga could do nothing now but leave Table Top and flee to save his life.

Larma stood on the edge of the Top, near the first waterfall, and watched the soldiers as they rested and tended to their wounded around the pool at the bottom of the falls. She waited until she saw the red-uniformed soldiers mount up and start the ride across the wide plain.

The Oleens now controlled Table Top.

It was a wonderful victory.

If they had not taken the Gate when they did, and the soldiers had all reached the Top, the fight could have gone against them. At the least, she would have lost many women. She knew the next fight would not be as easy. The wind was still blowing and the odor was just as foul as before. There was much to be done and not much time. Larma turned away from the precipice and called Kali, Maz, and Camp.

*

The wind beat against the walls of Safedor and blew over the top. Inside the box canyon the air was calm—though emotions were not. The aftermath of battle was on full display: picking up and caring for the wounded, burying the dead, gathering and repairing weapons, guarding the prisoners, and the relaxing of muscles after long hours of tension. Thalmus and Veracitas had informed Ekala of the source of danger blowing in the wind and what clues it gave for events at the castle. They discussed the loss of soldiers from the fight and the strength of their small force. Ekala wanted to send a messenger to Larma to inform her of their victory, until Thalmus assured her that Larma already knew. Ekala had the prisoner troops gathered together and with Thalmus and Veracitas at her side, she addressed the men.

"I know there's been much injustice across the land. Some of you have been part of that. You may think that my father, the king, has allowed it, or does not care about the people. You're wrong. He has been sick and men who want to rule over our land have taken advantage of him. These men have told you lies and convinced you to work for them with promises of position or wealth or some authority that you desire. I tell you now, once they come to power you'll be tossed aside—thrown in with the rest of the people to suffer under their control. As you know, Metro and Baldoff have brought soldiers here from across the Great Water; soldiers who answer only to them. They are the ones who will rule over you, and as you have seen for yourselves, they don't care about our people or you. Maybe some of you are Metro's men."

Ekala slowly scanned the troops, looking for reactions. Most of the men were watching and taking in her words; others were sitting with their heads down, not looking at her.

"You know me. I am not my father. I am the one and only heir to the throne," she said, still watching the men. "I cannot allow our land to fall into the hands of this terrible enemy. You saw today how we can fight. Did you think we were weak? Did I prove my strength to you today?"

She looked around again.

Most of the troops were nodding.

"I ask you now to join me. I give you the chance to fight with us, to save the king and our land. I will be grateful if you choose to do so. I leave it to you. It's your choice, for the task ahead of us will not be easy, yet, it's worth our lives." Ekala looked the troops over again. "Give me your decision in the morning," she said, then turned and walked away.

Next, Ekala spoke with the villagers who wanted to go with her to the castle and she set them to work making preparations to leave in the morning. The freed people from the village of Ello cooked up a feast from the food that the Oleens had brought with them from the shore of the Great Water. It was a night to celebrate a great victory, to rejoice in their freedom and to honor Ekala. They sang songs and danced and told stories of the old days gone. And there, around the fires in the enclosed canyon, the legend of Safedor began to grow as they talked about the events of the day. Boschina and Veracitas were in the center of it all as the villagers honored both of them for their courage and for the stone cutter's great craftsmanship.

Ekala left the revelers to check on the wounded and then on the posted guards. As she left the women watching the narrow entrance, she found Thalmus nearby in the darkness—lying atop Thunder who was resting along the side wall of the canyon. His other two companions were not present.

"Is Bubo out hunting?" She asked.

"Yes."

"And Dal?"

"Dallion is roaming outside, watching for troops."

She leaned against Thunder's shell. "We'll be ready to leave in the morning."

"Good," Thalmus replied. "I fear there is serious trouble at the castle."

"We could move faster if the wind dies down."

"The wind will not stop," Thalmus told her. "It is being driven. We'll just have to work through it."

"You think it's from Metro, don't you?" Ekala asked.

"It is devious and reeks of his malicious odor."

"Maybe I'll take a small force and ride on ahead to check on Father."

Thalmus shook his head. "Now is not the time to divide. It is a time to gather forces."

"I wish we could get the rest of the Oleens to join us," Ekala said. "But, they have the Top to defend." She sighed. "I'm a bit worried about them and Larma."

Thalmus sat up and looked at her. "Larma will be all right and the forces with her. It is you I worry about."

"Me?" Ekala said with a surprised laugh. She turned away from Thalmus' steady gaze and watched the guards at the entrance. After a while, she said "There is much to fear in this world."

"Everyone has their doubts and fears," Thalmus replied.

Ekala continued. "I used to worry all the time whether I could be a leader—if I had the strength and the will to stand alone—if I could inspire men to follow me, to respect me." She looked at Thalmus. "I don't think about it anymore. I know it is for me to do. I have learned who I am and what I can do. The rest will follow."

Thalmus put his hand on her shoulder.

"You are ready, Ekala Oleen. Your father will be proud of you."

She felt his hand on her shoulder, the same shoulder Bubo had landed and grabbed onto in front of the troops. "Thalmus, today, when Bubo was on this shoulder, I felt a strange power come into me. I can still feel his claws and it still pulses within."

Thalmus nodded with recognition of what she was saying. "That does not always happen," he said and slowly removed his hand from her shoulder. "Do you understand that it is something more than Bubo? He is just the messenger. You have been entrusted with a gift that you must use wisely."

She smiled. "I shall endeavor to be worthy of the gift."

Before the light of early morning, Ekala gave the order to rise and prepare. Most of the troops, especially those of the king's old guard, swore their loyalty to Ekala and formed up behind the Oleens. Some of the villagers joined as cooks and helpers. By sunrise, Ekala was leading her expanding army out the door of Safedor and in the direction of the castle.

The foul wind was still blowing. It assaulted them as they entered the plain. Boschina rode alongside Ekala in the lead, while Veracitas and Thalmus rode back and forth along the flanks of the column—keeping the formation tight and watching for stragglers. By noon, the wind was stronger. Dust was rising in great clouds and swirling across the land. The brown tempest blew in circles and roared like a giant beast hungry for prey. As the column struggled forward, the angry furor caught and enveloped them in a blinding cloud of dust. Visibility became difficult and keeping direction was almost impossible. Thalmus and Veracitas strung the horses and people together with rope so that no one would get separated.

Ekala tried to keep her bearing, watching for familiar landmarks, but it was impossible to see through the dust storm. She could not be sure if she was heading straight or going in circles. All day long they continued, leaning into the wind, trying to keep their heads and eyes covered from the blasting dust and sand.

*

At Castle Ambermal, Rundall had been looking for the king. The old counselor had checked all of the king's favorite places in the castle: at the pond in the royal courtyard, where his majesty liked to sit and watch the fish; in the kitchen, where Culinary fixed him snacks at all hours of the night and day; on the parapet of the tower, where he gazed over his land; and in his bed chambers, where he napped. He was not at any of these places and Rundall was becoming worried; though, there was more to it than that. In place of the normal guards were new, unfamiliar, guards and there were many more than usual.

"Have you seen the king?" Rundall asked the two husky guards who were at the door to the king's chambers.

"No," they replied gruffly.

"Aren't you new?" he asked them.

"No," they replied again.

"I don't recall seeing you before. Surely, you are new to the Royal Guard?"

"No," they insisted. "We've been here."

Rundall looked at them suspiciously. "Where is the Captain of the Guard?"

The men shrugged.

Rundall gave up. He moved away slowly and continued his search. He decided to ask some of the king's advisors, who were supposed to be doing research in the library. When he entered the room, he discovered a meeting in progress. It appeared that all eight of the counselors and advisors were in the middle of a discussion with Baldoff. They stopped when he entered and stared at him with guilty faces.

Baldoff quickly regained his composure.

"Lord Rundall, welcome."

"What is this?" Rundall demanded.

"This? Oh, well it's—an impromptu meeting," Baldoff replied.

"About what? Rundall asked, looking at the counselors and then back at Baldoff. "And where is the king?"

"The king?" Baldoff said innocently.

"Yes, the king," Rundall said impatiently. "I cannot find him anywhere."

"Well," Baldoff said looking at the counselors, "that's what we were just talking about."

The Learned Men, the king's advisors and counselors, sat quietly around an old wooden table in their colored robes. Most were old gray bearded men, who over the years had ingratiated themselves with the king and become comfortable in the allowance of their offices. Two were younger men who had only been on the council for a short time. These men were more ambitious; therefore, they were more willing to consider new ideas or changes, which Rundall found refreshing—but also dangerous. Though Rundall had often found the Learned Men to be a nuisance, and an unnecessary influence on the king's decisions, they had always been loyal to the king.

Rundall eyed each member of the group. They all shied from looking at him except one, Cartridge—a young brown-haired man in charge of the royal granary. He had a stern look on his face and was slowly shaking his head back and forth.

Rundall did not like the feel of this at all.

He turned to Baldoff.

"Tell me what you have been talking about."

"We were going to tell you soon enough; but now that you're here, you might as well know." With a sweep of his hand, Baldoff indicated everyone in the room. "We think that the king is no longer capable of ruling."

Here it is, Rundall thought, *Baldoff is making his move.*

"You all feel this way?" he asked the men at the table.

Cartridge started to protest, but Baldoff shushed him with a sudden motion of his raised hand. "It's everyone's opinion that, for the good of the kingdom, the king must be replaced."

Rundall stared at Baldoff. "This is a very serious charge against the king. Princess Ekala will not take it kindly."

Baldoff laughed. "The princess has no authority."

"She is the heir to the throne," Rundall said calmly. He turned to the advisors. "You dare to deny Princess Ekala her birthright?"

"Well, the king has not been well for so long now," one of the men said.

"That's right," another said. "How long do we wait? And she is...not a man."

Rundall glared at them. "I have told you, it does not matter. Son or daughter, it is the law of our land. You know it is her right, and you all know Ekala. Most of you have had to deal with her. How can you tell me she is not strong?"

"Hah," an old counselor laughed. "You call being difficult strong."

"She is strong," Cartridge said, looking at the others. "It's not right that we try—"

Baldoff interrupted him. "She may be the king's daughter, but that is all she is." He looked to the Learned Men with a question. "Besides, where is she?" Baldoff turned again to Rundall. "I rather doubt we'll see her again."

Rundall had had enough of this.

"This will not stand. I will see to it. Where is the king?"

Baldoff smiled. "He's with Metro."

"Metro," Rundall gasped. A dreadful feeling stabbed him in the chest. He turned and hurried out of the room. He closed the door behind him and started shaking uncontrollably. Leaning against the wall for support, he tried to gather his thoughts. This could not be happening; it was too soon. Where was Ekala and what did Baldoff know of her? Was she all right? Where were Thalmus and Bubo? Had they found Veracitas? He needed them all here, right now.

The old man calmed himself, taking slow deep breaths until the shaking stopped. He had to hang on until Ekala and Thalmus returned. He straightened up, pulled his shoulders back, put his head up, and started down the hall to Metro's chambers.

Black smoke seeped out from around the edges of the closed door to Metro's room. The smoke drifted up the wall and gathered itself like a willowy beast against the stone ceiling, hovering there, waiting to descend on unsuspecting prey. Rundall hurried down the corridor, glancing up at the smoke. It smelled of burnt sweetness. He stopped in front of the door, hesitating a moment before slapping his chest with his fist and pounding on the thick wooden door.

"Who's that?" a voice from within asked.

Rundall pushed open the door.

Smoke billowed out.

He stepped back and waited for it to clear. When the smoke thinned out enough to see, he stepped through the portal and looked around. Despite the window openings, the room was thick with smoke that oozed from various bowls sitting on tables around the room. Metro was nowhere to be seen. The king sat on a chair mounted on a platform that was very similar to his throne in the Great Hall.

"Who is it?" the king asked, peering through the haze.

"It is your servant, Rundall, Your Majesty." Rundall pulled the neck of his blouse up over his nose and mouth in an attempt to filter out the smoke.

"Rundall? Is that you? Isn't the incense wonderful?"

"It is foul, Your Majesty."

"What's that you say?"

"I have come to help you back to your chambers."

"What chambers?" the king replied. "This is my throne."

"No, Your Majesty," Rundall said through his shirt. "This is not your throne."

King Ahmbin looked around at the chair he was sitting in. "Quit talking foolishness, old man. I am sitting on my throne."

Rundall shook his head. The smoke was burning his eyes, blurring his vision and muddling his thoughts. He looked at the king. "What is happening here? That is not your throne."

"Of course, it is. Where else would I sit?"

Rundall leaned against a table.

"Your Majesty, we must go from this place."

"Where are my counselors?"

"Come with me, Your Majesty," Rundall said and stretched out a hand. "I will take you to them."

The king started to rise and then sat down again. "No, I am the king. Bring them to me. And, by the way, where is Thalmus? I am hungry for frog legs. How soon can he get some?"

"Your Majesty, you sent Thalmus to find the stone cutter, remember?"

"The stone cutter?" the king said confused, looking around the room. "Here?"

"No, Your Majesty, not here. Thalmus is searching for him."

"Oh, yes, now I remember," the king said holding his head in both hands. "Metro and I were discussing this sculptor, Veracitas. He must be punished. He must be found and punished."

Rundall shook his head.

"You pardoned him, Your Majesty. You gave him to Thalmus."

"I did? Well, then, I've changed my mind." The king gripped the handles of the chair. "Send for Thalmus. I want him here."

Rundall rubbed his eyes and squeezed his head with both hands. He looked around the room at the smoking ooze rising from the pots. One of the pots was at the end of the table he was leaning on. He shuffled to the smoldering container and shoved it off the table. The clay pot smashed on the floor and the cinders scattered on the stone. Now, the smoke rose from each cinder and was worse than before. He heard footsteps and turned to see Metro standing in the doorway. The magician was wearing a red robe with an insignia on the chest that Rundall immediately recognized: a hissing lizard coiled in a circle. The creature's vicious eyes blazed. Rundall looked from those eyes to Metro's fierce eyes glaring at him.

The men stared at each other for a moment.

As foggy as Rundall felt, he knew what was taking place. The king was now totally under Metro's control. Still, he could not give up. He must break the spell. Rundall braced himself against the table and turned back to the king.

"Come, Your Majesty. Princess Ekala is on her way. She wants to see you."

"Ekala, my daughter?" The king asked. "Are the flags up?"

"Yes, Your Majesty," Rundall said, reaching out his hand. "The flags have been raised in Ekala's honor. We must hurry to the wall to greet her when she arrives. Take my hand."

"Oh yes," the king said, rising from the chair. "She has been gone for so long. I have missed her so. Ekala my—"

"King Ahmbin," Metro bellowed from the doorway. "Sit down!" The king obeyed as if hypnotized.

"Lord Rundall," Metro said. "You can leave now."

The magician smiled and stepped aside for the two burly guards from the king's chamber. The men came in and took Rundall by the arms and dragged him out. He was confused and weak and could not resist. They pushed him along the smoky corridor, through the castle, and out to the holding cells, where the guards shoved him into a small dark cell and locked the door.

Chapter Twenty-Two
A New King

Baldoff herded the Council of Learned Men into the Great Hall and in front of the king's chair on the raised platform, where they milled around and spoke in hushed voices.

"Why did Baldoff insist we come here?" one asked of the others.

"I don't know," another one answered. "The throne's empty. We agreed to remove the king and rule by council."

"Then why are we here? We should be meeting to take care of business."

"Yes, there's so much to be done," a third man said.

"Where's Lord Rundall?" Cartridge asked looking around the Great Hall.

"Perhaps we're waiting for him to arrive," one of the old men said. "I do wish he were part of this; I mean I wish he'd agree with us."

"I do, too," Cartridge replied. "His participation is vital for our success. The people will be more likely go along with removing the king if Lord Rundall leads our endeavor."

"If he chooses not to, we have Baldoff," a younger man said and motioned toward the blond-haired Baldoff standing away from them as he waited impatiently.

"No," Cartridge whispered. "He's too ambitious."

The Learned Men were interrupted at that moment by six armed guards who marched into the hall and up to Baldoff, who directed them to stand three each on either side of the throne. This was highly unusual, for the king was not present. The surprised Council of Learned Men stared at these strange guards who were wearing a uniform they had never seen before: black trousers tucked into high leather boots and red shirts emblazoned with a vicious-looking lizard. Besides swords sheathed on their belts, the guards carried long-shafted spears with large arrowhead points. Suddenly, a strong wind blew into the room and pulled at their robes and hair. The men shielded their faces with their hands and grabbed at their clothes.

Just as quickly as it had appeared, the strange gale was gone.

When the men looked around, they were surprised to see Metro sitting in the king's chair. He glared at them for a moment, and then burst out laughing. The Learned Men were not sure what to do. The magician's laugh was so deep and ghastly that they recoiled and stepped back.

"I am now the lord and master of this land," Metro bellowed.

Baldoff pointed to the floor in front of the throne. "Bow before the great Metro."

The men stared in disbelief and confusion. They were not accustomed to bowing before the magician.

"I said, bow before your king," Baldoff shouted and he motioned the guards into action. The soldiers encircled the advisors, lowered their spears, and began poking and prodding the men with the points until they fearfully stumbled forward and kneeled before the throne.

Even that wasn't good enough for Metro.

"On your bellies," he demanded.

The eight men, with spears at their backs, dropped to their stomachs with their colored robes and scarves in disarray on the floor.

Metro smiled. "That's right. You all look better to me now." The magician leaned back in the large-cushioned chair and gripped the armrests with his hands. "I'm so glad that you supported me in my rise to king."

Cartridge raised his head.

"We only spoke about removing King Ahmbin."

"And you agreed to do so," Metro countered. "So, I ask you, who else but I could be king?"

"We didn't speak of a new king," Cartridge replied. "Baldoff said the council would rule in his place."

"And you believed him?" Metro laughed again. "The Learned Men," he mocked. "You are nothing but learned fools." He leaned forward in the chair as his eyes grew darker and he thumped his chest with a fist and held it there. "Now hear this: I'm the new king! Ahmbin will no longer be a problem."

"What about Princess Ekala?" Cartridge asked.

"We won't be seeing the princess again," Metro sneered.

"Even if she survives, she has no power," Baldoff joined in. "She is a woman, and therefore not fit to rule."

"What about Lord Rundall?" another man asked.

"Lord Rundall?" Metro smirked. "He is rat food."

The Learned Men glanced at one another. They had gone along with deposing the king because he had become incompetent and they had assumed he would be cared for. Now, they wondered what Metro had done with him—and old Rundall, faithful Rundall, he did not deserve death.

"Now," Metro said, leaning back in the massive chair. "My first command to you is to change into new clothing with my royal crest." He pointed to the circular lizard embroidered on his chest. "This symbol and color red will replace all of Ahmbin's emblems. Your new clothes are waiting for you in the foyer. You will always wear my crest to show your loyalty. I want you to go out in the land, amongst the people, and declare to them my authority and title. You'll tell all the lords and elders to come and pay homage to me."

"But we are counselors, not messengers," a short gray-haired old man said.

Metro almost jumped out of the chair, but he stopped, settled on the edge, and glared at them. "I don't need counselors or advisors or learned men. I know all there is to know. No one can tell me anything that I don't know."

"But Metro—"

"Your Majesty," Baldoff corrected the man.

"Yes, I…I mean, Your Majesty," the man continued, "You see, we help to govern the country. We have certain duties."

"Not anymore," Metro replied, sitting back and motioning with his hand toward Baldoff. "Lord Baldoff will be my one and only assistant. In fact, he is second-in-command. You will obey him above all others except me. Understood?"

The prone men on the floor mumbled amongst themselves.

"You will announce this to all the people. You will demand their loyalty to me, King Metro. And you'll report to Baldoff anyone who will not submit, anyone who speaks against me."

Metro waited for a response, but the Learned Men said nothing, for they didn't know what to say. This turn of events left them feeling guilty, betrayed, and helpless.

"If you choose not to follow me," Metro said casually, "then you'll starve to death in the dark cells, never to be heard from again." He paused, watching the prostrate men on the floor before him. "So, do you understand my instructions?"

"Yes, yes," the men said, nodding their heads. Though Cartridge was thinking, *I must pretend to follow and say what he wants to hear in order to escape and warn Ekala.*

Metro smiled and waved with the back of his hand, dismissing them. "Then go and do not come back until you have told all the people in every village." He pointed his finger at them and said with a menacing glare, "Do not try to trick me. I'll know of any deception."

The Learned Men cautiously rose, looking around at the guards who were lifting their spears.

"Go to the foyer and change your clothes now before you leave," Baldoff commanded.

The once-proud men began slinking from the room.

"By the way," King Metro said, "if I were you, I'd stay clear of the Northern Bushy Plain for awhile. It seems that a terrible dust storm has been raging there and will not be going away for some time." He started snickering, and then burst into another deep and horrible laugh.

*

Larma could smell the dust in the air and could see the great brown storm blurring the distant horizon. She was sitting on her horse, Eidolon, who was nibbling on the sparse grass of a knoll. A strong breeze was blowing at her from across the plain, tugging at her clothes and hair. Closing her eyes, Larma leaned into the wind and felt its complaints and listened to its secrets.

The wind might dance for Metro, but it sang for Larma.

Knowing the land and the wind, she learned how large the storm was and that Ekala was bogged down in its midst—so, too, were the defeated soldiers that had just left Table Top. The wind chuckled about that. This meant that Metro's soldiers would not be able to return directly to the castle to report their failure or the numbers of the Oleens. Larma pressed her crossed open hands over her heart, closed her eyes again, and drifted into a realm that very few could travel. She heard and felt many things, but continued searching for the elusive spirit that could bring them success.

"Where are you, Bubo?" she whispered. "What are you doing?"

Going deeper and farther into the vibrations and senses of this world, she hunted for his presence, but could only discover that the great owl was not in the storm.

Larma opened her eyes, stretched, and glanced back at the column marching toward her. The Oleens, led by Captain Kali, were in front, followed by the men from the Top who had joined them. Farther back, almost out of sight, rode the rear guards, Maz and Camp. Flanking riders, Oleen scouts were on the left and right.

After the victory at Table Top, Larma and Captain Kali had met with the two foreign soldiers to get to know them and confirm their allegiance. With the horses standing nearby, they sat alongside the creek in a gully to avoid the wind as much as possible. Maz and Camp were still exhilarated from the fight at the gate as was Kali, who was proud of her soldiers for their performance in battle.

"Your women fought well today," Maz said to Kali. "You have them well-trained for their strengths."

Kali looked at him, judging his sincerity. "Thank you, but it's not my credit to take. It's Oleen and Larma who have taught and inspired us."

"It looked to me like you did a pretty fine job yourself," Camp responded.

Kali nodded, accepting the complement. "As did you."

Larma took a small stone, a little larger than a coin, from the creek and, holding it in her hand, settled next to Kali. Her presence suddenly enveloped them with a sense of importance.

"You have done us a great service today," Larma said, looking into Maz and Camp's eyes.

"It was our pleasure to help chase that no-good Gorga out of here," Maz said, feeling a little uncomfortable under the mysterious woman's gaze.

"You have done more than that," Larma replied. "You have helped thwart the scheme of a much more dangerous enemy."

Camp shifted his legs and stretched his lower back. "The way Gorga talked, so big and mighty, we figured he was working for somebody with more power than himself."

"You are correct," Larma said. "This was an important victory, securing Table Top; yet, it is small in comparison to what lies ahead."

She stopped speaking, though her eyes never left Maz as she rolled the stone on her fingertips. He wanted to look away, but was fascinated by her gaze that held him and a curiosity to know what was to come next.

"I thought you were just hiding here," Larma said slowly. "I see now that you are searching, yearning for truth and understanding."

She paused. "Do you know who Oleen is?"

"I know she's important to you all," Maz said. "I also have a sense that she has significance beyond this place."

"As do you," Larma said quickly.

"What?"

"Your own land, Toulon, is waiting for your return, but the time is not right, is it? For you, there is more danger there than here."

Maz looked back at her in wonder at her perception. "You're right. We're biding our time here. Through no fault of our own, we are outcasts."

"You have a long road home, Maz," Larma said. "The curious thing to me is that your fate is intertwined with Oleen's."

Maz was surprised by this realization, but understood it to be true.

"I did feel a strange connection when I first met her. Who is she?"

Larma nodded at Kali, who said, "She is Ekala Oleen, the only child of King Ahmbin, heir to the throne of Ameram."

Maz and Camp reacted with surprise.

"Oleen is a Princess?" Camp asked.

Maz joined in. "She will be the Queen?"

"Yes and yes," Kali answered.

"She's not like any princess I've ever seen," Camp exclaimed.

"I think I understand the situation now," Maz said, meeting Larma's eyes.

Larma told them why Thalmus and Boschina were searching for Veracitas and of Metro and his plan—of which Gorga was part—to usurp the king and take power, where Ekala was now, and the inevitable battle to save the king and country. Then, she put the question to them and they immediately, and wholeheartedly, pledged their support to Ekala Oleen; for if their fate depended on this woman, and the success of her story, they wanted to have something to do with it. Before they stood, Larma handed Maz the stone she had been holding.

"One day, you will wear this gem in honor of your pledge."

He gently gripped the stone, studied it as Larma watched, and put it in his pocket.

Larma smiled, remembering the meeting and knowing that another piece of the prophecy was in place. Now, she returned her concentration to the land before her. *To go forward to join Ekala and get caught in the storm that lay in their path would not help, she thought. That would be falling into Metro's trap.* Then, they would all be under his control, and she could not allow that to happen.

She would have to take a different route to the castle—one that was longer, but would avoid the storm. The wind had told her that Metro's attention and power was focused on Ekala in the roaring tempest it was creating. He did not know that his army had failed at Table Top or that Larma was on her way.

Larma signaled to Captain Kali and she rode forward to join her.

"Yes, Larma?" the red-haired captain asked as she stopped her horse alongside Eidolon.

"We will turn east here and pass through the Jarbo Gap to the Laundo Ponds, and then south again to Ambermal."

Kali looked at Larma with concern.

"You want to go through the Laundo Ponds?"

"Yes, Kali, I know a solid trail by which to travel through the marshes. It will be faster and no one at the castle will expect us to approach from the ponds."

"What about the frogs?"

Larma smiled at her captain. "Be assured, Kali, I will make sure that the creatures do not bother us."

"As you wish, Larma," Kali said and turned her horse and rode back to the column.

Getting to the castle undetected was one thing; defeating Metro's army was another matter entirely. If the magician chose to close the gates and accept a siege, Larma and Oleen would be limited and could not win that fight. The castle walls had never been breached. Besides, they did not have the resources to attempt that feat. Metro could stay sheltered in Ambermal indefinitely while holding King Ahmbin hostage. Their only chance was to draw his forces out into the open, leaving the gates vulnerable.

How to do that? Larma wondered.

The man's ego and drive for power was the key to his defeat.

He wants to show his superiority, she thought, *he wants to destroy me, so I will give him that opportunity. I will challenge him and appear to be weak, and easy prey, so that he will come out after me. Then it will be up to us to take advantage of his ego.*

Larma looked to the horizon once more. The wind was blowing here and perhaps all over the land, but not like it was in that raging tempest buffeting Ekala and her followers. "Well, Oleen," Larma said. "You have Thalmus and Veracitas, and you have your own mind. I am sure you will find your way."

She paused and whispered, "I will see you at Ambermal."

*

Ekala's army was hunkered down. It was the second day of the march and she had called a halt in a ravine that was barely deep enough to provide any protection from the suffocating dust. Still, it was better than the high ground and there was a spring from which to draw water. So, they huddled there, waiting and hoping for a break in the storm. Ekala, Thalmus and Veracitas weren't sure where they were. The circling brown tempest of powdered earth and sand obscured the land and their vision; they were confused—and now motionless. The people had not complained even though they were tired. Their enthusiasm waned as they sat nestled closely together in groups.

"We can't stay here much longer," Veracitas shouted over the roar of the wind.

"Where are we supposed to go?" Ekala answered. Only her eyes showed through a slit in the scarf she had wrapped around her head. "I can't see a stone's throw in front of me."

"I can't see anything," Boschina said, holding her hands in front of her face. "My eyes are full of dirt."

"Here, Boschina," her father called. He shielded her head from the wind and rinsed her eyes with water from a pouch. "Better?"

She blinked, clearing the water from her eyes.

"Yes, it's better. Thank you."

He wrapped her scarf around her neck and face.

"Try to stay covered."

Veracitas turned back to Ekala. "This storm is not going to stop until we are all dead," he hollered. "We must try to move on."

Thalmus shook his head and shouted, "It would be futile if we don't know where we are going." He coughed and covered his mouth again. "We cannot subject the people to aimless wandering. It will exhaust them, and us."

At that moment, out of the blowing dust, Thunder plodded up to them. Thalmus had left him behind at Safedor because he thought that the giant tortoise would not keep up. Now, here he was. *Have we been going that slowly? Or are we going in circles?* Thalmus thought.

Thunder nudged Thalmus with his big head and clicked his jaws. Thalmus hugged him, and then Boschina got up and hugged him around the neck.

"He can lead us through the storm," Thalmus shouted over the wind to Ekala.

"How?"

"The same way he found us. He has earth sense. The wind cannot fool him."

Ekala shook her head in wonder at the giant tortoise. "Okay, Thunder, you beautiful creature, take us to Ambermal."

Thunder bumped Ekala with his head and started off. Thalmus quickly jumped up on his shell with the end of the rope that strung through the entire column, tying them all together. The people rose, grasped onto the rope, and followed with their heads down and their shoulders turned into the wind.

*

Metro and Baldoff stood behind the parapet atop the highest point of the castle walls. The air was warm and calm, the sky clear blue.

"How many times have I stood here dreaming of this day?" Metro said. "To be the king of Castle Ambermal and all of its land…."

"It's all ours now," Baldoff said.

Metro glared at him. "Ours? It's mine." Metro thumped his chest. "Mine! You'll get your share when I determine what it will be."

Baldoff stepped back from Metro's outburst. "I only meant that together we've conquered these people and that, once again, you're a king."

Metro smiled, calmed by the thought of being the king. "It took a little time. The old man was tougher than I expected. And that sculptor, Veracitas, almost ruined it. The power of his statue was hard to overcome, but I did." He turned and pointed a finger at Baldoff. "That statue of the old king, it must be found and destroyed."

"No matter," Baldoff replied. "There's no one to oppose you now. Ekala and the frog hunter will die in the storm. Larma is defeated at Table Top. And we have enough of our own men in control to put down any other trouble."

"The frog hunter," Metro said, thinking of Thalmus. "He's dangerous. He and his friends have a magic all their own. You can't control that wild horse and giant shell creature, and especially the owl. He is a power unto himself. We cannot let any of them survive."

Metro had been turning slowly as he spoke, surveying the landscape. He stopped when he faced the north. "Is that the windstorm on the horizon?"

Baldoff turned to look. "It appears so."

"It wasn't visible yesterday," Metro said, feeling a sudden uneasiness. "Why can we see it now?"

"The storm must have grown in size," Baldoff said, as he started down some stone steps. "Excuse me, Your Majesty, I've got to go to the library to rewrite some history."

"Good," Metro replied. "We can write ourselves into the life of this kingdom as if we have always been here." However, his eyes never wavered from staring at the distant storm as his hands gripped the stone cap on top of the wall. "What a beautiful creation that is," he said to himself. "What a natural way to extinguish one's enemies." He watched for a while longer, before stepping down the stairs to his chambers.

In the afternoon, King Metro returned to the parapet wall.

This time, he looked first to the north.

The dust storm had moved closer. There was still no wind at the castle, but the brown blur was larger and definitely closer. "What is this?" Metro muttered to himself. "Why's it moving this way?" He had directed the wind to find and to smother Ekala and Thalmus. Though he did not know exactly where they were now, he had received reports that they had left Table Top together with guards and that the column had reached Ello. That is when he sent his own army with Blayon to the mystic flat mountain to destroy Larma.

Suddenly, he realized that he had not heard a thing from Table Top.

Surely that pompous Gorga would have sent word of his victory.

"Your Majesty," Baldoff called from below.

Metro moved to the inner side of the parapet and looked down on Baldoff standing below on the next level. "What is it?"

"I've written the new laws that you wanted. They're ready for your signature."

Metro looked once more at the storm. He pointed a long bony finger at it. "Gust, hust, turn to dust, and bust to blood all that breathes thou foulest lust."

Then, he spun about and went down the stairs.

Chapter Twenty-Three
The Battle for Ambermal

Sometime in the early hours of the morning, Metro was awakened by a breeze blowing across his bed. He opened one eye and stared into the darkness. Then, his other eye awoke and looked about. The magician-king listened to the darkened silence and his nostrils flared as they sniffed the breeze. His left eye caught a blur in the night.

What was that? Not the wind? He waited.

There was only the steady breeze bringing a faint odor of earth. Yet, he felt a presence, something near, something foreign—a presage in the night. Suddenly, he saw two yellow disc-like eyes glaring at him from the darkness. He sat up quickly, but the stark vision had vanished. His eyes roamed the dark room searching, yet found nothing.

Had I imagined those eyes? he wondered. Had he fallen back to sleep? Dreams and nightmares were normal to his mind, but this image was different. A foreboding sense of trouble seeped into his soul and for the rest of the night he stayed awake, listening and sniffing. Just before dawn he rose, put on his boots and royal robe, and climbed the steps to the tower walls.

On top of the castle there was more than a breeze: it was a strong wind. Metro turned to the north and was surprised to see the swirling dust storm coming closer to the castle. He raised a fist and growled:

"What're you doing here? Have they been destroyed?"

The wind blew around him, whipped at his robe, but said nothing. He could hear troops in the streets below running to the main gate of Castle Ambermal—and Baldoff's boots hurrying up the stairs as the sun brightened the horizon in the east.

"Metro! Your Majesty," Baldoff called as he came running up the last steps, breathing hard. He was out of breath and had to rest a moment before he could speak.

"What is it, Baldoff?" Metro said impatiently. "Speak."

In between deep breaths, Baldoff was able to say: "The guards report...hostile troops approaching from the east."

"What do you mean hostile?" Metro asked. "Who is there to oppose us?"

"These troops carry the battle flag of Ahmbin," Baldoff blurted.

"What? That's not possible," Metro scoffed. "We have control of all the troops."

Baldoff was still trying to catch his breath.

He pointed to the east. "Look!"

The sky had lightened to reveal a column of troops marching toward the castle. In the forefront were rows of infantry and behind them walked several regiments of cavalry. Only half of the soldiers actually wore a uniform: tan trousers with a gray blouse and a brimmed straw hat. The others looked more like farmers and peasants, but they all carried weapons—bows, spears, swords—and moved with a military precision. The front row of soldiers carried two banners raised high on tall poles. The first banner was the gray and maroon seal of Ahmbin. The second was gray with a large maroon "O" in the center. Below Metro, the castle guard—in their new red uniforms—were pouring out of the gates and forming for battle in front of the main entrance.

Metro looked with curiosity at the odd group approaching his castle. "Who are they? Why did the guards not see them before now?"

"They came out of the Laundo Ponds," Baldoff replied. "No one travels through that bog and survives, except the frog hunter, and I don't see him in that bunch."

"Some look to be Ahmbin's troops, but who are the others?"

Baldoff shook his head. "They look like peasants. The troops surprise me; I thought we had them under control."

Metro was puzzled. "Whose banner is that with the O?"

"I don't know," Baldoff answered. "I've never seen it before."

"They are too far out," Metro said. "I can't tell...who is leading them?"

Baldoff stared, waiting for the column to get closer.

"It looks like an old woman," he said.

"What? A woman?" Metro asked, focusing more intently on the leader, riding tall on a silver horse. "Can it be--? he questioned himself as he waited to be sure. Finally, the rising sun cleared the horizon and lit up the column, shining brightly on the statuesque woman in front.

"Larma," Metro exclaimed.

"That's Larma?" Baldoff moved along the wall to get a better look. "We've been worried about an old woman?"

"That old woman is dangerous," Metro told him. "She knows many tricks. It's no wonder we did not hear from our men at Table Top."

Baldoff could not believe Larma was a threat. "She must have left Table Top before Blayon and his troops got there. That pitiful army could not have beat Blayon. She must have fooled them somehow."

"Look how few support her," Metro said. "Two hundred, two hundred and fifty at the very most—and the majority are not soldiers. We have them greatly outnumbered."

Metro tilted his head and squinted toward the Oleens. "Do my eyes deceive me: are those women on horseback? She brings a bunch of broken down troops and women to fight me?"

"That's what it looks like," Baldoff replied and shook his head. "With the frog hunter and Ekala smothered in the dust, she dares to come to us? This must be an act of desperation, their last hope." He turned to Metro. "Now is your chance to destroy her, the last obstacle to your complete control."

The magician-king looked at the small force marching toward the castle and at the mysterious woman riding calmly in the lead. He knew that she had strange, ancient powers, but she still needed an army with which to use them—and this little band was not enough to overwhelm him.

His confidence and ego began to swell. His time was now; he was the king and he had the power to defeat the great Larma once and for all. He turned to Baldoff. "Send out the rest of the guard and destroy them. I will give the men words of confidence to override any magic she throws at us."

"Yes, Your Majesty," Baldoff snapped with a smile of triumph on his face. He turned to the inside of the parapet wall and called down to the officers waiting for orders. "Send out the rest of the guard. Form your lines and attack the approaching troops. Leave no one alive!"

Metro stepped to the edge of the wall overlooking his soldiers, whose ranks were still swelling with men coming out of the castle. He spread his arms and bellowed in his deepest voice: "Do not fear. There is no one here who can defeat you. I, King Metro, give you the power to destroy all who stand before you!"

His castle guard cheered, raising their swords and spears to their king. He bathed in their applause for a moment and then pointed with both hands at Larma and shouted: "Bring me her head."

The soldiers roared like a hungry pride of lions. The officers gave orders to move and the lines of red-uniformed troops with black shields and silver-tipped lances stomped forward.

*

Larma smiled as Metro's army started marching toward them and away from the castle's gates. Eidolon stopped and so did the entire column behind them. Captain Kali sensed Larma's call and rode to her side before she spoke. "Captain," Larma said calmly looking into her eyes, "form your lines, as we planned. Let our archers shower them with attention. Have the men receive the first assault. Ready our mounted warriors for attack when the line breaks." She gripped Kali's shoulder. "For Oleen."

"It will be done," Kali said confidently. And before breaking eye contact with Larma, she said: "Give us victory today." Captain Kali turned her horse and quickly rode to the column, shouting orders to form battle lines.

Maz and Camp helped direct the fighters into position up and down the line and ready them for the assault. Then, they stood in the middle of their line of men and waited.

Looking at the large number of soldiers bearing down on them, Camp said: "What have we gotten ourselves into?"

"Have a little faith, my friend," Maz replied.

"I'm just thinking that I'm going to have a heck of a time keeping you alive today, let alone getting home again."

Maz smiled at him. "We'll get there."

Larma turned her attention to Metro and Baldoff on the castle wall. The two men were completely focused on her, their marching red army, and the imminent clash. Sitting comfortably on Eidolon, Larma closed her eyes, slipped into her spirit and felt for the grasp of time, the control of nature—the power beyond men. She latched on to the current and called to the wind with her request. "Bring them now, swift as you can, to the gates of Ambermal. Bring them now. Bring them now."

The Oleen archers stood behind the lines of men, who were kneeling in two rows as they waited for Metro's soldiers to reach them. The women had nocked and drawn the arrows on tight bow strings upon Captain Kali's orders. The captain had waited until the enemy was close enough for the bodkin points to be most effective. Then, she pointed with her sword and shouted, "Release."

Each archer loosed her arrow smoothly and calmly at the red-clad soldiers and then immediately pulled another shaft from the quiver, nocked, and released again at their moving target. The Oleens continued shooting in this fashion, delivering pointed attention on their foe. The barrage was having some effect, dropping scattered soldiers, but the combat-wise among them covered themselves with their heavy shields and kept moving forward. As they reached the Oleen battle line, Maz yelled, "stand," and the men immediately stood and took a defensive stance.

The women on horseback rode forward behind the line of men and as Metro's soldiers lowered their shields to ram into the line, the Oleens fired arrows into their ranks—dropping many in the first row. Despite this success, the second and third lines of the soldiers crashed into the men and it became a brutal battle. The size and force of the red army began pushing the Oleens back. Maz and Camp fought furiously while encouraging the men around them; but, had to start giving ground to avoided being surrounded.

Larma was still sitting on Eidolon behind the lines with her eyes closed and talking to the wind and the people in the storm. Her arms were outstretched at her side, with her hands open.

"Look at her," Metro exclaimed. "We are overwhelming her army and she doesn't know what to do. She is lost."

"I told you so," Baldoff said, gloating over their victory. "It won't be long now."

At that moment, the wind suddenly gusted, blowing dust into their faces and over the entire battle. The red army stopped, suddenly blinded by a cloud of swirling dirt. Metro and Baldoff staggered back and caught themselves against the parapet wall. They turned into the wind to get their balance and saw the dust storm rushing toward the castle. With their attention fully on Larma, no one had noticed that the storm had been moving closer with every minute.

"No," Metro shouted. "This is not what I commanded."

The massive swirling storm did not overtake the castle, but stopped short of the castle walls. To Metro, the wind seemed to have lost control of itself. *Could Larma be causing this?* he wondered.

"Why have you brought this here?" Metro yelled. The wind circled, whipping and blowing around them like a playful creature—and spinning images before him of brown, earth-coated, bodies floating in the tempest.

The magician king smiled with satisfaction.

"You are bringing me their lifeless bodies."

The wind gusted once more and then ceased; the swirling dust, from high in the sky, began to settle. That was when Metro and Baldoff saw ghosts emerge from the depths of the brown cloud. People and horses, coated with dust and strung together by a web, appeared—one after the other—as they came out of the cloud and marched toward the castle. At the lead was a giant tortoise with a man riding on its shell.

"Thalmus," Metro exclaimed.

He clenched his fist. "How did he do this?"

The dust-covered people shed blankets and coats as they lined up in front of the main entrance. This group was another odd mixture of soldiers and peasants, men and women. When the troops were settled into formation, one of the soldiers swung up on a horse and rode out in front. The black horse shook off the dust from head to tail and the rider threw off a hooded coat.

Metro did not recognize the warrior. "Who are you to come from the dust to challenge me, King Metro?"

The rider looked at the few troops still guarding the open gate, and then up at Metro waiting on the wall. "I've come to claim the throne! I am the daughter of the great King Ahmbin," she shouted and drew her sword, gleaming in the morning light. "I am Ekala Oleen."

Metro and Baldoff were stunned. They had never seen Ekala as a warrior.

Her army shouted: "Oleen!"

Larma's force repeated: "Oleen!"

Then, another cry came from the east: "Oleen!"

Metro spun around. Was that an echo?

At first, he saw nothing on the shrub-covered, eastern plain. Still, there was something strange about it. He looked again. Part of the plain seemed to be undulating, like the back of a caterpillar as it moved toward the castle.

Baldoff stared in amazement.

"The bushes are moving toward us."

"Larma," Metro said angrily under his breath.

Baldoff was confused and turned to Metro.

"Larma is doing that? Why?"

A hissing noise overhead drew their attention to the sky just as Bubo sailed over their heads. "The Owl! I knew it wasn't a dream," Metro exclaimed and grabbed Baldoff. "Quick, pull the guards back in the gate."

"But, Metro, we still have them outnumbered."

"Do as I say. Close all the gates," Metro said angrily, trying to keep his voice down. "They must not get through these walls. I will distract Ekala and Larma. We will beat them, but I must have time to prepare."

Baldoff nodded and ran down the steps as Metro turned to confront Ekala. "I am sorry to report to you, Ekala, if you are the Princess Ekala," he blared down at her, "that your father is sick, so sick that he can no longer rule."

Ekala heard Metro, but she was watching the castle guards—counting their numbers and checking their weapons. *He is not about to surrender*, she realized.

"The Council of Learned Men has appointed me king." Metro let the words settle on Ekala and all her followers before continuing. "I am now the ruler of this land. You have no authority and never will. You will disband this pitiful army of yours and submit to my power."

To Metro's surprise, a curious wave of grumbling and laughter rolled through the Oleen army. "Are they mocking me?" he asked himself in a whisper. He looked down at Ekala and her followers. "They show me no respect, no fear. What is wrong with these people? I will punish them for this," Metro said angrily to himself, but their confidence worried him.

As for Ekala, she ignored the magician on the wall—for there was activity in front of her. Someone was calling the castle guards back and the red army attacking Larma's Force was now turning and starting back to the big gate.

This was bad. If the gates were closed, they would be shut out, making it impossible to save her father and overthrow Metro. She heard Larma's voice: "Take the gate."

Turning, she saw Larma on Eidolon across the field pointing at the castle gates. Thalmus had heard Larma's message too. He jumped from Thunder onto Dallion and raced to Ekala's side. Princess Ekala waved her sword in circles over her head. Veracitas and Boschina rode forward to join them as the Oleen archers drew their bows and let fly a shower of arrows into the guards. Then, Ekala's army of women and men yelled and charged forward. The deadly arrows dropped many of the guards, while the others stumbled and recoiled in shock that they were being attacked.

Yet, the soldiers reformed with a growing anger and determination to block the gate. The red army retreating from Larma now began to run to the gate as well. The Oleen archers took advantage of their withdrawal and separation from their own troops by following and shooting arrows into their ranks. Maz and Camp rallied their force and chased after them.

Veracitas turned to his daughter, who was starting to charge the gate with him. "Boschina, stay back with the archers and use your bow."

"I want to attack with you!"

"This will be brutal, Boschina. We may get separated, and I don't want to be scared for you as well as myself. Besides, you can do more from here than in that mess." He waved at the masses piling up at the gate. "There are many targets for your arrows."

Boschina hesitated, looking around at the wild scene before them. "As you wish, Father. Radise and I will fight from here." She leaned over and hugged him. Pulling away, she said, "Go help Ekala save her father."

Then, she swung her bow around and drew an arrow.

When the battle cry of the Oleens was heard on the west side of the castle, the moving bushes stopped and were quickly thrown aside by soldiers all over the plain who had been using them as camouflage. It was Tobazi and his people, along with Currad and Dysaan. Tobazi shouted a charge and they all ran at the west gate of the castle.

Metro heard the scream and turned to see the army of dark soldiers attack the castle. "Who are those people?" he yelled at the wind. "Where did they come from?"

The wind circled, but said nothing to Metro. He shook his fist at the air and spun around to look down and see Ekala, Thalmus, and Veracitas, now dismounted.

"The Stone Cutter," Metro whispered, focusing on Veracitas. "He is here. They are all here, but he will be the first to die." He began to look around for a weapon.

Dallion and Shadahn galloped about, forming the loose horses into a thundering wedge, and charged into the melee—knocking down the guards and trampling the men under their hooves.

Metro snatched a bow and arrow from one of his guards, who was shooting at the Oleens below. He leaned over the parapet wall, aiming at Veracitas as he fought in the battle at the gate. The magician adjusted his sights down the shaft of the arrow as he followed Veracitas' movements and spoke through his clenched teeth, "Shaft of Death, strike thy mark, take this crusader to your darkness."

Just as he was about to release the arrow, the magician king was suddenly jolted and knocked off his target by another arrow striking his bow. Recovering, he turned angrily, scanning the battle for the archer who had shot the arrow that thwarted his kill.

He saw her, sitting on a horse just behind the melee, staring defiantly at him—the Stone Cutter's Daughter: the girl who would not give up the search for her father; the girl who had awakened Thalmus, Larma, and the princess to rise up against him; the girl, who had not only survived the journey, but was now threatening him, just like her father.

Metro changed his mind. "She will be the first to die and her father will suffer the agony of her death." He pointed two long fingers at her. "You will not defeat me. I am the king!" He then used those same two fingers to pull back the string of the bow and let loose an arrow at Boschina.

The arrow's flight was true, as Metro willed it; but as it reached its target, the ever-alert and quick Radise, protecting her mistress, jumped aside and the shaft with its sharp point stuck into the ground beside them.

In anger at seeing the failed arrow, Metro threw the bow off the castle wall, raised both arms into the air, and shouted: "I am Metro. I am King." Then, he spun around and ran down the steps. He had to get to his room, to his magic bowls and fluids.

Baldoff was frantically yelling at the guards to close the gates and some were trying to push them shut, but there were too many people in the way. The surge of the Oleens had pushed the castle guards and the retreating red army back into the opening. The gates were blocked open by the mass of troops fighting in the passage.

*

Tobazi and his men penetrated the lightly defended gate of the western wall. With Currad and Dysaan, they slashed through to the barracks, capturing the stock so there would be no swift escape for anyone trying to flee the castle.

*

With swords, arrows, and spears Ekala, Thalmus, Veracitas, and the Oleens fought their way through the northern gates. Once inside the main gate, at the juncture to the many streets that wove through the tall stone buildings into the bowels of the castle, Ekala quickly called her captains together. And there, off to the side of the fighting, she tried to put some order to the loud confusion.

"We don't have much time," Ekala told them. "We must maintain our advantage." She noticed Captain Kali in the group and smiled. "Kali, it's good to see you again."

The captain, who had come to the fight leading the Oleens with Larma, was out of breath from the charge to the gate and the ensuing fight. "I'm very glad to see you, Oleen."

Ekala Oleen pointed to the street on their right. "Take several forces and work your way up this street to the west gate and stables," she commanded. "Link up with Currad, who should be there with the Toubarians. Secure that side of the castle and then move toward the Great Hall."

"I know the streets and gate. I'll assist her," Veracitas said.

"Good, Veracitas. Currad may need your help. Go now."

"On your orders, Oleen," Kali said and they moved away, gathering a force of women and men to follow them.

Then, the princess turned to Captain Ritzs and pointed to streets on their left. "Ritzs, take your forces and move up those streets to the Great Hall, subduing all resistance, and secure the hall and throne."

"On your orders, Oleen," Ritzs said. She quickly called her force together and attacked the retreating soldiers in the street.

Ekala looked at those who were left, which included Thalmus—who was smiling. There was a new face next to him that she had not noticed.

"Cartridge, what are you doing here?"

"Fighting with you," he said, brandishing his sword.

"I thought the council opposed me?"

"Not any more, Princess."

Ekala laughed. "It's me or Metro, huh?"

Before he could respond, she said, "Never mind, I'll deal with the council later. The rest of us are going up this middle street to the king's rooms. Let's go."

∗

When the Oleen army pushed through the gates, Baldoff retreated up the streets, ordering soldiers and officers into fighting positions and promising rewards for killing Ekala, Thalmus, or Veracitas. He kept moving away from the fighting, while demanding loyalty to King Metro and offering gold to the victors.

Fierce fighting raged in all the streets. The Oleens dueled with speed and discipline, while the men depended on strength and weight. Ahmbin's troops, who had joined the Oleens, grew in confidence and loyalty as they fought alongside the women and Ekala. Soldiers on both sides fell in agony as the battle ebbed and flowed like surf in the Great Water.

"This is taking too long," Ekala shouted to Thalmus over the din of battle. "We must find my father. Let's get to the throne."

"He will not be there," Thalmus said. Noticing her pantleg was soaked with blood, he asked, "How bad are you cut?"

Ekala ignored his question. "You think they put him in the cells?"

"Maybe," Thalmus replied. He had already thought about this. "Culinary will know where the king is. He will be trying to feed him." He pointed at her leg. "Are you all right? I can bandage the wound."

The princess was too excited to feel any pain—or even to think about it. "Let's find the cook then," she hollered.

Ekala shoved some fighters out of her way, knocked another down that was fighting an Oleen, and headed up an alley. Thalmus followed with a sword in each hand. At almost every turn and corner, they were challenged by Metro's soldiers. She fought with strength, but also with a finesse of moves and balance that most swordsmen had not cared to learn. Thalmus was impressed, once again, by her ability, but was concerned about the loss of blood and her endurance in the long struggle.

After dueling with, and chasing off, several more of the red uniformed soldiers and heading up another cobbled street, Thalmus said: "You have become quite the fighter. The way you move reminds me of your father at this age."

Ekala's head swiveled toward Thalmus. "I look like my father?"

"Very much so—when he was young—same style, same confidence."

Ekala looked back at the street as she hurried on. After a moment, she said: "I'm proud to look like him. I just wish he was still the same man you remember."

"There they are," a soldier yelled, pointing at them. Arrows whizzed by as more red soldiers appeared in the street, drawing their bows; several more came out of a door behind them with swords ready. Ekala and Thalmus suddenly found themselves trapped between the two groups of soldiers coming toward them.

"We can charge one group and fight our way through," Ekala said over her shoulder to Thalmus.

"Not with those archers drawn on us," Thalmus replied.

"We've got to do something," Ekala said.

Thalmus glanced up toward the roof tops. "We will do something, very soon. Be patient."

"That's not my nature," the princess replied.

"It's the two biggest prizes together, men. Kill 'em now and we're rich," one of the soldiers yelled.

"Watch out for the frog hunter, he can leap far," another hollered.

"I'll shoot him before he hits the ground," a red archer replied.

Ekala raised her sword. "You're not taking us alive."

"We don't need to, Princess. We just need your heads," the archer snapped, drawing his bow and aiming at her. "And that won't take long. Now hold...ahg!"

The man suddenly screamed in pain as the weight of Bubo struck his head and the owl's sharp talons dug into his scalp. The red archer jerked forward and his arrow shot down, careening off the stone cobbles. Bubo lifted off, beating his wings frantically and landing on the next man and clawing at him until he dropped his bow. The other soldiers turned to watch in fright at the mysterious appearance of the owl and his attack. Maz and Camp suddenly appeared and turned the corner on the other side and cut down the red archers before they could react. Thalmus and Ekala slashed into the remaining soldiers as Bubo lifted off. Three more red uniforms fell to the stones before the rest turned and ran.

"Run, you pigs," Camp yelled after them.

Bubo sailed over their heads and hooted. Thalmus hooted back, and Ekala raised an open hand as Bubo flew by and brushed her fingers with the tip of his wing.

Maz enthusiastically clasped arms with Thalmus.

"This is a good fight. Bubo guided us right to you."

"Well, if it isn't the protectors of Table Top," Ekala said, happy to see them. "Thank you."

"And your servants, Your Highness," Maz said, bowing his head to her. "Larma commissioned us to be at your side."

Ekala flashed a smile toward Thalmus, and then back at her new personal guards. "You think I need a protector?"

"Well, it looks to me like we got here just in time," Maz said.

"We won't deny you that," Thalmus replied.

"It was Bubo who saved us," Ekala said, smiling. "You just trailed along."

"Larma said to find you and stick with you," Camp said. "So here we are."

"Where were you heading, Princess?" Maz asked. "We'll get you there."

"Got a cut on your leg," Camp said, pointing at her bloody pants.

"Just try to keep up with me, boys," Ekala responded as she turned and ran up the street.

With renewed energy and the added strength of Maz and Camp, they fought their way through a hastily built barrier and Metro's castle guards until they reached the kitchen. A fire was burning in the hearth. Large black pots with simmering juices hung over the flames; half-plucked ducks lay on the table.

But, Culinary was nowhere to be seen.

"Cook, where are you?" Ekala shouted, her sword still held firmly in her hand.

They hurried through the messy room to the other end.

"Culinary. Culinary!" Thalmus called.

Maz scooped a piece of meat off the grill and bit into it, and then tossed it to Camp—who tore off a bite with his teeth as they walked through the room.

Ekala threw open the storeroom door and there was Culinary, hiding with an axe ready to swing.

The princess jumped aside.

"Stop! It's me, Ekala," she said quickly.

Culinary looked at her in amazement, and then he dropped to his knees. "Princess Ekala. Forgive me, I didn't recognize you."

"Get up, Culinary," she said, bending down to help him. "Do you know where my father is?"

"Yes, Princess, I sneak food to him whenever I can—and Rundall, too."

"Sneak food to him?" she questioned. "Where is he?"

"He's in Metro's room."

"Is he all right?"

Culinary shook his head. "He is not the same man."

Ekala turned and slammed her sword into the table.

Thalmus grabbed her by the shoulders. "Don't let that anger control you. Use it to your advantage. Use it to your power."

Ekala rested against the table, taking deep breaths. She had not slowed down since the battle had begun; the intensity and exertion of fighting, and the loss of blood combined with the long trek through the dust storm, had caught up with her. She felt her strength waning, her energy nearly spent. Still, the drive to save her father and destroy the insidious force taking their land filled her with rage. *Thalmus was right*, she thought, *the power of this passionate anger will push me through to the end.*

Princess Ekala turned to Culinary.

"Have you seen Metro? Do you know where he's hiding?"

"I saw him running to his rooms when everything broke loose."

"So, those who we seek are at the same place," Ekala said. She took a deep breath and then straightened up and slapped Thalmus on the shoulder. "Let's go."

Thalmus didn't move. "We need to look at your leg," he said.

"I'm fine, we need to hurry on."

"No, Ekala," Maz said. "Thalmus is right. You are still bleeding and you will lose your strength soon. Then, you will be no good to anyone, especially your father." He touched the scar on his face. "Trust me, I know."

She looked at the two of them and gave in.

"All right, but make it quick."

Ekala swung her leg up onto the table and Thalmus took his short knife and cut back her pant leg. Culinary carried a pot of hot water from the fire, dipped a towel in it, and handed it to Thalmus—who carefully washed the wound. It was a clean cut, but deep into her calf. She winced as Thalmus worked on it. Maz and Camp watched with approval as she gritted through the pain.

"I have an ointment I made, for when I burn or cut myself," Culinary said, bringing a jar to the table. "It will help heal your wound."

"Thanks," Ekala said through clenched teeth as Thalmus rubbed on the gooey green paste, and then wrapped her leg in a towel and trussed it with twine.

"That will have to do for now," Thalmus said, looking at his work.

"Good." She dropped her leg down and tested it by taking a couple of stiff steps. "Now can we go?"

"Princess," Culinary said quickly. "Be careful. Metro is most dangerous there...where he has his poisonous potions."

Ekala stopped and looked at the old plump cook.

"Thank you, Culinary."

She turned to go and he stopped her again. "You must drink my special elixir. It will give you strength when you are vexed."

She started to refuse, but he interrupted her. "Princess, I'm ashamed."

"What are you talking about? Ashamed for what?"

"Metro came to me for herbs and root stock. He asked my advice on blending them. I did not know he was mixing other ingrediants with them, or how he was using my help, until it was too late. I'm sorry."

Culinary was tearing up and looking away from her. Ekala put her hand on his shoulder. "It's not your fault. How were you to know? Metro has fooled everyone."

He went to a shelf and pulled down a brown crock. "Please, drink my elixir before you go," he pleaded. Setting out five cups he poured some liquid from the crock into each one. "A little is all you need," he said, as if revealing a secret. He handed out the cups and then gulped his while the others sipped, testing the taste first.

"What is this," Thalmus asked. "It has a sweet honey flavor."

"I won't tell you," Culinary said. "It is my secret. I make it with my own ingredients. Now, go save our king."

They finished Culinary's brew, thanked him, set the cups down, and started out. Ekala saw that he was tearing up again. "We'll be hungry when this is done. Will you have something for us?

A large grin spread across his red face.

"For you, Princess, I always have your favorite food."

She nodded with a smile and then turned and followed Thalmus out of the kitchen.

*

When Baldoff saw the continuing advance of the Oleens—and that he could do little more to stop them—he took guards and fled to find Metro, hoping the magician's powers would stem the tide. He placed the guards in rooms and hallways to stop, or at least to slow, the invaders—for he knew that Ekala and Thalmus would be searching for Metro and King Ahmbin. When Baldoff finally reached Metro's laboratory, he found the magician frantically mixing ingredients in various bowls. The magician-king did not acknowledge him or look up from his work.

Baldoff wanted to report the dire state of the battle—it was urgent—but he knew that Metro did not like being interrupted; and this foul potion might save the day. So he waited, pacing the room. But time was short and he became impatient. Finally, he blurted, "We are losing the castle! They could be here soon. Have you come up with something?"

Metro did not look up. He continued pouring and mixing. "This is exactly where I want them to be," he said in a calm, deep, voice. "I will destroy them here."

Baldoff was surprised. "You want them to come here? We have no escape from this chamber."

Metro looked up as he stirred a bowl of red goo. His eyes glowed like a cat's in the night. "Yes, Baldoff, I want them here. The frog hunter, the princess, the stone cutter—I hope Larma will be here, too. I will exterminate them all, right here, together. Then, we will have control again." He handed Baldoff a vial with a yellow liquid. "Drink this," he said. "It will keep your mind and body clear of the poison."

✳

In the southwestern part of the castle, a fierce battle was raging between Tobazi's army and Metro's soldiers. Veracitas and Captain Kali with the Oleens and King Ahmbin's loyal troops were battling to join up with Tobazi and Currad, but Metro's castle guards had twice driven them back with axes and spears. Now, Kali and Veracitas were back in the side street deciding what to do.

"We must break through to Currad," Veracitas told Kali.

"There're too many of them," she said. "They're strong here and we've lost most of our archers."

Veracitas knew that she was right, but persisted. "We have to keep trying. The prison cells are on the other side of the red soldiers. If we can link up with Currad, we'll have them outnumbered and cornered—then they might surrender."

"That is a big *if*," Kali responded.

Veracitas and Captain Kali could see Dysaan and the leader of the dark army, Tobazi, directing his men in the fight while Currad—about fifty meters beyond—was chipping at a stone wall with a large metal spike while the battle raged. He was working on a section that was about five meters tall and was bulged wider than the rest of the wall.

"What's he doing?" Veracitas wondered.

"Is he trying to get footholds to climb the wall?" Kali suggested.

At that moment, Thunder came pounding through the western gate with scraps of red uniform hanging from his mouth and looking as if he had just devoured a soldier. Right behind him rode Boschina on Radise and Larma on Eidolon—and with her came an unseen warm wave of invincibility to the Toubarians and the Oleens. At the same time, Metro's castle guards were struck by a cold wave of fear.

Larma walked the prancing Eidolon forward around Thunder, through the Toubar fighters, and toward the lizard-emblazoned uniforms of the guard who seemed to be frozen in place—staring at the silver horse and gray-haired woman marching at them. Tobazi and Dysaan sensed her authority and followed her.

The Toubarians fell in behind her.

"Larma has them now," Kali exclaimed.

"Boschina's with her!" Veracitas said. He waved at his daughter, trying to get her attention.

Kali, Veracitas, and the Oleens came out from their cover in the streets and started walking toward the castle guard.

Metro's men had lost control of the gates, their horses were gone and their leader, who had promised them riches, was nowhere to be seen. They dropped their weapons and kneeled on bended knee.

*

Ekala and Thalmus, with Maz and Camp, were fighting their way down through the maze of corridors to Metro's chamber. When they finally reached the hallway that led to the magician's door, it was empty. There were no guards, but wisps of green smoke hugged the ceiling and snaked along like the tail of a dragon. The foursome stopped at the entrance to the stone passageway and eyed it suspiciously.

"Why aren't there guards here?" Ekala asked, looking at the smoke creeping along the ceiling.

Thalmus sniffed the odor in the hallway: it smelled like the foul wind that assaulted them outside Safedor. He sensed that in the rooms at the end of the cold, narrow corridor lived many bad things——the worst of which was not this odor.

"This place stinks," Maz said, covering his nose.

Ekala looked at Thalmus. "Where are his guards?"

Camp shrugged. "I think we just went through them."

314

Ekala continued looking at Thalmus, asking for an answer. He saw the worry in her eyes. "Perhaps Metro thinks he does not need guards."

"We'll see about that," Ekala replied.

She turned and walked down the hall to the heavy wood door.

Stopping, she studied it.

"Ekala, remember Culinary's warning," Thalmus called. "We must be careful here."

Princess Ekala Oleen was filthy from head to toe, her clothes were ripped and tattered and blood soaked, and sweat ran down her face and arms. The muscles in her right arm flexed as she squeezed the handle of the bloody sword in her hand. She looked at Thalmus for a moment, and then her good leg swung up and she kicked in the door.

Maz smiled at the others and nodded with approval.

"That's our queen."

They hurried to catch up with her as smoke billowed out of the open door. Ekala's sword led her through the doorway as the men followed and moved to either side behind her. The room was dingy and thick with the pungent smoke that hung in the air despite the large window openings. There was a fire burning in a pit in one corner of the room with bubbling and steaming pots hanging from angle irons. Different-colored bowls sat on tables and shelves around the room. Peering into the thick haze, they could barely make out Baldoff standing at the end of a table near a window opening. His mouth was ajar as he stared at Ekala. She started walking toward him through the smoke and he nervously pointed to his left.

"He is there," Baldoff said.

Ekala turned expecting to see her father, but instead saw Metro sitting in the mock throne. His sinister eyes searched for hers. Ekala looked at him and his eyes latched onto her. She felt a pang of fear, a weakness in her legs, her heart skip, and finally a faintness starting to overtake her. Then, the anger swelled up from deep within, her eyes widened, and she swung the sword back and forth—smashing bowl after bowl. Shards flew around the room and liquid splattered on the walls and floor. Baldoff ran to Metro's side as the scattered goo began emitting noxious incense that was more repulsive than the smoke.

When Ekala stopped and looked again at Metro, he calmly said, "I didn't know you had such a temper, Princess."

"I'm not here for your games, Metro. They will not work on me."

"Nor did I know what a fighter you are," Metro continued. "Where did you learn these things?"

"Where's my father?" Ekala demanded, though she was starting to feel nauseous.

"The frog hunter," Metro went on, ignoring her question. "He must be the one who taught you. Where is the little man?"

Thalmus, Maz, and Camp had held back when Ekala flailed away at the bowls. Now, they stepped forward through the smoke and odious incense.

"Oh, there you are," Metro said upon seeing Thalmus, "with new strange friends. Where's the stone cutter? Isn't he joining us?"

"Tell me," Ekala said, trying to point her sword at the magician. "Where is the king?"

"I'm right here, Ekala," Metro said. "Can't you see me?"

"You're not the king," she replied.

Her stomach was boiling and she felt her body temperature rising.

"The Learned Men appointed me," he said mockingly.

Ekala bent over with pain wrenching inside her. She forced herself to straighten up and look at Metro.

"You will never be king as long as I'm alive!"

"Well, in that case, I will be king for a long time because you won't be alive much longer," Metro scoffed and sat back in the chair. "Isn't that right, Lord Baldoff?"

Baldoff smiled, feeling confident now.

"Yes, Your Majesty. It appears the princess is very ill."

Ekala grabbed her stomach as convulsions struck her. She bent at the waist in pain and turned to Maz, Camp, and Thalmus. "Get out," she yelled with a raspy voice. It was too late, as the men were already doubled over and coughing. Thalmus dropped to his knees to get below the smoke and crawled to Ekala. She was choking. He pulled her to the floor and put a scarf over her face.

Chapter Twenty-Four
Death~Life~Freedom

T he fighting at the west gate had come to a sudden stop. The scene that had been chaotic and violent a moment before was now surprisingly quiet; the roar and intense emotion of battle had ceased. Larma's presence and mental signals to the fighters had overwhelmed them. Soldiers of both armies were stilled with the feeling that hostilities were over.

As Boschina rode on Radise behind Thunder and Larma, she heard someone calling her name. "Boschina! Boschina!" She knew the voice. It was her father. She turned and saw him coming toward her with Kali and the Oleens as the red soldiers knelt before Larma. Boschina swung her leg over, dropped from Radise's back, and ran to hug her father.

"Father, you're here," she said, holding him tightly. "You're all right!"

"Of course," he replied. "And so are you."

"Who is this warrior woman?" a deep voice demanded from behind Boschina.

She turned to see Tobazi glaring at her.

"Tobazi," Boschina said with surprise.

The man from Toubar, who had saved her in Rainland, smiled, laughed, and hugged her. He stepped back. "Look at you. You have grown much since we last fought together."

"And you're much stronger," Boschina replied.

"I don't have all my strength," Tobazi answered. "Truth be told, this fight has worn me thin. But, tell me, this man here is your father?"

Veracitas stepped forward as Boschina introduced him. "Yes, this is my father, Veracitas of Marbala," she said proudly. "This is Tobazi of Toubar, the man I told you about."

They nodded to one another and shook hands.

"It's an honor to meet you, Boschina's father," Tobazi said.

"It is my honor to meet you, Tobazi," Veracitas replied. "Thank you for helping my daughter."

"Oh, believe me when I say that she helped me more than I helped her."

Now, Currad came running toward them. "Boschina, you're here!" He also gave her a hug—although a quick one—and then a soldier's arm shake. He grabbed Veracitas by the shoulders. "Veracitas, you're back."

Veracitas was very happy to greet the man who had freed him from the prison cell and helped him escape from the castle. "Yes, my friend," he said. "I'm back."

Dysaan came up with several Toubarian fighters. "Boschina, you're looking fit," he said and put his gloved hand on her shoulder.

"As are you," she replied. "Your face is looking much better."

He smiled and nodded.

"Thanks. Where's Thalmus? I haven't seen him."

"I don't know," she responded. "The last time I saw him, he and Oleen were fighting up the street from the gate."

"Oleen?" Dysaan questioned.

"Yes, don't you know the princess, Ekala Oleen?"

Dysaan and Currad glanced at one another with a worried look. "If the princess is with Thalmus, then they must be searching for the king," Dysaan said. "We must find them as soon as we search the prison cells."

Larma silently called Kali with a wave of her hand and the captain responded promptly, leaving the reunion and going to Eidolon's side and looking up at the silver-haired woman.

"Gather these soldiers' weapons and see to their wounded."

"As you wish, Larma," Captain Kali responded.

Kali started to turn away, but Larma stopped her and looked into her captain's eyes. "You have done very well today, Kali, but we are not done yet. The victory is not complete. Evil still lurks in this castle. I can feel its presence. Gather your forces and be prepared. Send out nurses for our injured and messengers to the rest of our forces."

"It will be done," Kali said, feeling Larma's strength and confidence fill her as she began giving orders to the Oleens and Ahmbin's troops.

Larma turned to the group surrounding Boschina. "This fight is not over," she told them. "You must get to the cells to release the poor souls confined there before—"

She was suddenly struck by a jolt of grief and an image of Ekala falling into darkness. So powerful and fatal was the feeling that she nearly toppled from her horse. But Eidolon felt her mistress waiver and stepped quickly to keep her mounted. Vericitas hurried to grab Larma and steady her on Eidolon. Just about everyone there saw the change in Larma and felt a sudden shift in mood. The Oleens were stopped by the reversal, but the red soldiers no longer felt defeated. The men looked around at one another kneeling in submission and felt embarrassed for their weakness. Grabbing their weapons that they had laid down in surrender, the red soldiers stood and charged forward. Caught off guard, the Oleens and Toubarians were slow to react, but Thunder had sensed the change in the red army's demeanor before they rose with their weapons. The great tortoise lumbered forward in front of Larma and snapped back the soldiers coming at her.

"Thunder," Boschina screamed, pulling her sword from its scabbard and running to his side as she felt the handle in her grip begin to vibrate.

Veracitas grabbed his sword and joined her. Seeing Boschina in the familiar battle position alongside Thunder, Tobazi let out a frightful battle cry and ran to defend the tortoise's other side. His men, along with Currad and Dysaan, quickly fell in line. On Thunder's right side were the Oleens and Ahmbin's loyal troops, rallied by Captain Kali, forming up with Boschina and Veracitas.

With Thunder in the middle forming a wedge, the combined armies started pushing the red soldiers back. Metro's men were tenacious and tough, giving ground slowly, mainly in front of the dangerous jaws of Thunder.

*

In Metro's smoky, disheveled laboratory, time seemed to be frozen. There was no movement as Lord Baldoff and Metro stood still, looking with anticipation at the bodies of Ekala, Thalmus, Maz, and Camp lying on the floor.

"You've done it," Baldoff said with amazement as he stared at the four bodies. "You've destroyed them."

Metro was watching and waiting to see any sign of life, especially from Ekala. Finally, satisfied they were not breathing, he said: "Of course I've done it," with an arrogant shrug and sat back in the large chair of his mock throne.

"The princess and the frog hunter are dead," Baldoff said, still in disbelief.

"Of course," Metro repeated. "You doubted me?"

Baldoff shook his head. "No, I just thought that, well, if she, well, it worked. Now, we need to lure Larma and Veracitas here."

"That will be easy," the magician said. "You will go tell Larma that her precious Ekala is dying and she and the stone cutter must come save her because I, King Metro, am choking the last bit of life from the princess."

"You want me to go to Larma?" Baldoff said slowly—clearly not happy about the idea.

"Do not worry, Baldoff, she will receive you as an important messenger."

"What if she doesn't and kills me—or the owl attacks me?"

"Well," Metro replied, "they might do that, too. But, she will not be able to resist coming to help Ekala, and then I'll have them."

"What about me?" Baldoff asked, surprised at Metro's willingness to sacrifice him.

The magician fixed his sharp eyes on him. "You will have the satisfaction of knowing that you sent them to their graves. Now, go find her while I mix another batch." He stood up and walked quickly to the fireplace and the table covered with open books, mixing bowls, stirring spoons, vials, herbs, and pots of colored powders.

Baldoff hesitated, watching Metro start another mixture, and then turned and started to the door. The smoke was slowly clearing, drifting out through the window openings. The room was a mess of oozing broken pots, skewed tables, and sprawled bodies on the floor. The easiest way out was around the distorted mounds of Thalmus and Ekala. Lord Baldoff carefully stepped over the princess, noticing the scarf covering her face, and then the sword lying on the stone floor with the handle still grasped in her hand. Something caught his attention and he stopped. He bent to look closer and saw that the engraved figures on the sword blade were moving. A tortoise, a horse, and a flying owl were traveling up the blade to the point.

Baldoff couldn't believe what he was seeing. He blinked, looked again, and realized something was alive—something that the potion had not conquered. Surprised, he started to step away when a hand grabbed his ankle.

When the poisonous incense engulfed and filled her lungs, Princess Ekala Oleen fell into the shadows with pain flowing through her body. Her world became a murky, suffocating, cloud of noxious vapors. She could not see or hear anything as she was consumed with the agony of stabbing shocks in her lungs and stomach. Then, like rolling off the edge of a cliff, she fell deeper into a cold abyss—going from gray into darkness. There was no sense of time or space, just the feeling of falling deeper into the unknown. Slowly, a small light appeared in the distance and ever so gradually grew brighter as it came toward her. The light gently surrounded her, caressed her skin and wounded leg. The pain left her and was replaced by warmth and a comforting feeling of being lifted up. She heard laughter and soon recognized Culinary's distinctive chuckle. Then, she felt the strength of Thunder's solid round shell beneath her. She heard pounding hooves and the sound of strong, slow-beating wings.

When Ekala opened her eyes again, she was confused. Her mind and vision were blurred looking through the mesh of fabric covering her face. Focusing slowly, she saw someone was standing over her, bending closer, and then starting to move away. She suddenly realized that it was Baldoff. Her hand reacted without her willing; it grasped his leg and clamped on with a tight grip. Baldoff jerked with surprise and tried to pull his leg free of the hand. He screamed. Ekala felt the sudden yank in her arm and shoulder and was snapped into consciousness. In her other hand, the sword was throbbing, moving, as the wings of Bubo lifted the blade off the floor.

Baldoff screamed again.

"What is it?" Metro asked impatiently. He turned just in time to see Ekala Oleen rising from the floor and pointing her sword at Baldoff's chest.

Metro was stunned. "What is this?"

"Help, she's going to kill me," Baldoff yelled, trying to back away.

"You were dead," the magician said, staring at her.

"Maybe," Ekala said, her senses clearing. "I'm alive now, and Lord Baldoff is about to change places with me."

"No, you can't do this," Baldoff pleaded. "You're the princess."

Ekala glanced down at Thalmus, who had just rolled his head on the floor as he was starting to awaken. She lifted one foot and placed it on his shoulder and shook him. Thalmus opened his eyes and sat up, still in a daze.

"Thalmus," she called, still sticking the sword in Baldoff's robed chest.

Thalmus looked up at her, shook his head trying to clear his vision, and finally focused on what she was doing. He glanced around for his sword, found it, grabbed the handle, and stood up.

"I don't believe this," the magician said. "That potion would have killed ten horses." He was dumfounded and stood motionless, watching the dead come to life.

"We're not horses," Thalmus replied as he went to Maz and Camp and shook them. Both men groaned, opened their eyes, and rubbed their heads.

When Ekala saw that Maz and Camp were alive, she turned back to Baldoff, gripped his shoulder with her other hand, and held him against the tip of the sword. "Where's my father?"

"Your father? He's—"

"Don't tell her," Metro yelled, regaining his senses. "She won't hurt you."

Baldoff's eyes were wide with fear. "Your father, King Ahmbin, is gone—"

"That's not right, Baldoff," Metro said. "His body is still here, but his head is gone." Then, the magician threw his head back and laughed.

Maz and Camp were rising to their feet and getting their balance as Ekala glared into Baldoff's eyes. "The magician cannot save you now," she said, pushing the sword harder into his chest. "Only I can and believe this, Baldoff, I will have no problem plunging this blade through you. Tell me where my father is and I'll spare you the pain of this blade."

Taking short breaths and swallowing hard, Baldoff looked down at Ekala's sword and noticed that the creatures on the blade were no longer moving. He looked up and nodded toward a door behind the mock throne. Ekala followed his gaze to the scarred wooden door, and then threw him aside. Baldoff stumbled and looked back at Ekala, who was moving toward the door. He crouched and tried to sneak out, but Camp blocked his way.

"You will not like what you find in there, Princess," Metro warned, but he stayed by the fire and did not try to stop her. Instead, he grabbed a spoon and began stirring the liquid in the pot he was holding.

Thalmus started moving closer to the magician as Ekala reached the door. She lifted the latch and started to pull, when suddenly the door was shoved open from the other side and a sword swung at her from the darkness. She jumped back as a strange man lunged out at her. She deflected his blow and spun away, but he charged after her.

Ekala had struggled for three days through the dust storm, fought the red soldiers all morning, was wounded and drugged, and now this new challenger. She was exhausted, her strength was waning. The man was a vicious sword fighter and was driving her back as Metro yelled, "Get her."

Thalmus recognized the swordsman immediately, even though he was wearing a different uniform: a red blouse with the black lizard emblazoned on the chest. It was Corsair.

Maz, still groggy, jumped forward with his sword to defend Ekala. Metro swung the pot at him and splattered his face with its yellow liquid. Blinded, Maz stumbled over debris on the floor. Before anyone could help him, Corsair stabbed the defenseless Maz, pushed him to the floor, and continued after Ekala.

Camp screamed at seeing his friend blindsided and stabbed. He shoved Baldoff down to the stones, stepping on his back as he went to Maz's aid.

"Maz," Ekala yelled. She started to go to him, but was blocked by Corsair. He was focused intently on her as he rolled the sword in his hand and started toward her. Then, Thalmus was there, stepping between them, and looking calmly at Corsair.

Corsair stopped, surprised to see the frog hunter.

He turned the sword in his grip several times. "We meet again, little man."

"You said we would," Thalmus replied, "and here we are."

"What are you waiting for, Corsair?" Metro said angrily. "Cut him to pieces!"

Corsair hesitated. This short man had surprised him twice before and he wanted revenge. Now, here he was, standing before him and Thalmus was staring at him, not moving, not lifting his sword—just looking back at him. Corsair saw no fear or agitation or even anger in the frog hunter's eyes or body.

Who is this man? he wondered.

Ekala caught her breath and regained some strength while Thalmus confronted Corsair. She turned her attention to Metro, who was anxiously watching the odd stare down between Corsair and the frog hunter. The magician held nothing in his hands now—no pots or spoons or potions. *No more tricks*, Ekala thought. She kicked over a table that was between them and started at him.

Metro jolted and turned to look at Ekala.

He pointed at her with a stiff finger.

"Stop," he demanded with a powerful voice.

Ekala did not hesitate. She lunged forward and swung her sword at his hand. Metro jumped away with cat-like quickness to a table top. When Ekala followed, he bounded to the window sill and crouched there, glaring at her like a wild beast. Then, he burst into laughter—a deep insidious cackle. "You cannot defeat me." He stood up in the window opening and screamed in a guttural voice, "Haste thy net to receive your lord!"

Everyone watched him, and for a moment, no one moved. Then, Ekala rushed toward him and the magician jumped out of the window into the canyon. She looked over the edge and saw Metro falling into Cold Canyon, his king's cape rippling behind him.

Baldoff ran to the other opening, muttering, "Metro, Metro."

The magician fell deep into the canyon before his motion stopped. He hung, suspended for a moment—held in an updraft of air. Then, they heard his scornful laugh as the wind began lifting him up, lying on his back as if he were on a mattress. His laughter continued to echo off the walls of the chasm as he sailed on the wind, up and out of the canyon. He was almost to the top of the opposite side when suddenly Bubo appeared, diving out of the sky, cutting through the wind.

Swinging his claws forward, he struck Metro.

The great owl's talons sunk into the magician's wicked eyes. The laughter turned to screams and the two sounds of mockery and pain echoed together through the canyon. Metro tumbled and fell again as

Bubo circled above him. This time the wind did not pick him up and his scream was heard until it shattered on the rocks at the bottom.

*

While the fighting raged before her, Larma was recovering, righting her posture, and starting to feel strength return. Still, she could not shake the ugly image of Ekala, doubled up, falling into darkness.

Over the din of battle, the fighters began to hear a hideous laugh echoing from Cold Canyon, which was just beyond the low wall where the struggle raged. Even those who had not heard it before knew that the wicked sound came from Metro. The menacing laughter sent a shudder through each person, causing them to step back—to pause in their struggle.

Again, swords and spears clashed for a moment.

Then, the fighting stopped all together.

Drawn by the shrieks, and realizing something unusual was happening, both armies scrambled to the canyon edge. There, they saw Metro being lifted up by the wind and listened to his mockery. Metro's soldiers raised their weapons and cheered, confident now that their magician king was all powerful, unbeatable.

Larma closed her eyes, setting her thoughts to go deep inside— deep into her heart—to rally the strength to summon the power to rise up against Metro. When she opened her eyes again, Bubo was diving from above the wind. Everyone watched as the great-horned owl slammed into Metro with his talons and sent him tumbling to the bottom of Cold Canyon.

The sorcerer's screams turned the red soldier's cheers to silence, and their attitude to defeat, as Bubo flew up from the canyon and winged by them to Larma. Stunned, the men watched Owl pass over them and settle softly on the silver woman's shoulder. He spread his wide wings behind her head, letting the feathers flutter and ripple in the wind as he glared at the soldiers.

Larma was, once again, in control. The swagger dropped from Metro's men like iron thudding to the ground. Their cause was lost and this time, their surrender was complete.

Now, it was Ahmbin's troops and the Oleens who cheered—but not for long, as Kali and the Oleens did not waste a moment of the opportunity to gather the weapons from Metro's soldiers and corral them into submission. The way was now clear to the prison cells. Currad, Dysaan, Veracitas, and Boschina turned from the others and hurried toward the row of barred wooden doors.

Perched on Larma, his wings tucked in, Bubo silently watched the busy soldiers and troops before them and how they kept glancing up in awe at the pair.

Larma carefully reached up and stroked Owl's wing feathers. "Find Oleen, Bubo," she whispered. "Tell me she is alive."

Owl bobbed and then lifted off from her shoulder.

He flew into the canyon, for he knew where to find Ekala Oleen.

*

Upon Metro's demise on the rocks, the wind immediately swirled and roared with great volume through the canyon—as if it had just broken loose from a leash. It blew into Metro's room, knocking down shelves, tossing jars, shattering vases, ripping books apart, and flying the loose pages into a swirling vortex. The wind picked up embers and chunks of wood from the fire and spun the glowing coals around the room, igniting the whipping book pages. Finally, flames and fire were tossed out of the window. Not satisfied, the angry tornado lifted Baldoff from his feet and was carrying him screaming out the window, when Ekala grabbed his arm and pulled him back in. The wind whipped at Baldoff as Ekala held on. Then it roared and slammed into Corsair—driving him to the window and over the edge.

Thalmus lunged for Corsair, trying to save him, but the wind had its prey; cleansing the room of evil, it sent him tumbling into the canyon. Satisfied now, the wind circled once again and blew away, leaving destruction in its wake. There wasn't a pot, jar, vase, or vial that was not broken. The books were ripped apart and burned. All of the chairs, tables, shelves and curtains were strewn about like flotsam from a shipwreck. Even though various colored powders and liquids spotted the room, the air was clear.

Ekala and Thalmus knelt by the wounded Maz. Camp was washing the yellow stain from his face with a towel and was holding another one over his side, where his clothes were wet with dark red blood.

"Lost my footing," Maz whispered, looking up. "I couldn't see with that junk in my eyes. I would've had him, Ekala."

"I saw it," Ekala Oleen said. "You would have taken him."

He held up a hand to her and she gripped it with hers. "Princess Oleen," Maz said intently, staring at her. "You've earned the right to be queen, to rule this land." He grimaced and swallowed. "Don't let anyone take it from you."

"I'll make sure of that," Ekala replied and she gently touched his cheek with the scar as his eyes closed. She did not realize until now how much she liked this man and it pained her to see him lying there with a mortal wound from trying to defend her.

"This is my fault," Camp said, bowing his head in anger. "I didn't do my job. I didn't protect him."

Ekala and Thalmus looked at Camp.

"What do you mean your job?" Thalmus asked.

Camp looked up at them.

"I'm not just his friend—I'm his guard, his protector."

Ekala glanced at Thalmus and then back at Camp.

"Who are you protecting? Who is he, Camp?"

Camp hesitated. "You should know who's been fighting for you, Oleen." He looked at Maz. "This is Bolimaz, once the crown prince of Toulon."

Thalmus nodded with recognition.

"The first of three sons of King Souma."

Ekala just stared with surprise at the dying prince from Toulon.

"He's just like me. Why did he leave Toulon?"

"I'm sorry to say that his brothers convinced their father the time was right to take over Ameram. With old King Ahmbin fading and you, a woman, coming to power, they thought you'd be weak and easily overthrown. Maz objected and spoke against them until the king, his father, banished him. We had to flee quickly for his brothers tried to kill him. I was one of many who sided with Maz and vowed to protect him until we could return and throw out his brothers."

"And the scar, who gave him that?" Oleen asked.

"His youngest brother, Tamar, surprised him one night with a dagger."

Just then, Bubo glided in and landed on an upturned table. He spread his wings, clapped his bill at Thalmus, and then focused on Ekala. "Whoo–whoo."

Thalmus smiled and looked at Ekala. "You have won. We have taken Ambermal."

The princess smiled, but sensed Bubo was saying more. "What is it, Bubo?"

Owl bobbed his head, clapped, and hooted. "Whoo–hoo–whoo."

"Larma sent him," Thalmus interpreted, "looking for you."

"Tell her that I'm still on my feet, but Maz needs healing."

Bubo swiveled his head and zeroed in on Maz. He began moving his head from side to side, focusing on the wounded man. Thalmus could tell what his friend wanted to do. "Step back," he said. "Move away from Maz."

"Why?" Camp asked.

Watching Owl's behavior, Ekala touched Camp's arm and stood up. "Camp, just move away from him."

Camp, the prince's protector, looked at Bubo and felt an intense power coming from the owl. He turned back to see Thalmus holding Maz's head in his hands, so he let go of his friend's hand and stepped away. Bubo immediately lowered his head, spread his wings, and silently glided across to Maz and landed softly on his chest. He covered the man's torso with his open wings, as if he were prey, and stared into his eyes.

Bubo hooted and Maz jerked with surprise and fear, but then laid back and calmly accepted Owl's presence. Thalmus leaned closer to Maz and said in a soft, firm voice: "It is not time for you to leave, Prince of Toulon. Your story is not over."

In a few moments, Maz started breathing easier, the flow of blood stopped, and the pain from the wound subsided. A feeling of hope entered his mind and a rising strength in his body.

Bubo lifted his head, gave one short hoot, and hopped off of Maz's chest to the floor. He stood there for a moment, listening to Maz's breathing, not looking at anyone. When Owl was satisfied with what he heard from the wounded man's breath, his head and focus swiveled toward Ekala—looking into her eyes for a moment.

"Thank you, Bubo," she said.

He snapped his beak and hooted at Thalmus. Flapping his wings, he lifted himself off the floor, circled the room once, drifted by his friend Thalmus, and flew out through the window into the canyon.

*

Currad and Dysaan began unlocking the heavy wooden and iron doors, one after another down the long row of prison cells, while Boschina and Veracitas carefully brought the prisoners out into the daylight. As Currad swung open a particular weather-scarred door, Veracitas hesitated before it, staring into the gaping mouth of the cell.

"What is it, Father?" Boschina asked.

He did not respond. Currad stepped up beside him and placed a hand on his shoulder. "Are you all right?"

Veracitas nodded. "I did not think I would be so emotional here."

Boschina now understood. "This was your cell," she said, looking at the dark hole of a room with new interest.

They heard a murmur from inside, a barely audible voice of a man trying to speak.

"Who's there?" Currad called. "You can come out."

Again, they heard the muffled sound of someone trying to speak, someone too weak to move. Immediately, Veracitas' fear dropped away and he rushed into the cell to help the struggling prisoner. The Stone Cutter lifted the man to his feet and supported him as he guided him out into the light. It was Lord Rundall and they all assisted in gently setting him down. He was covering his eyes from the sun with his folded arm and a hand. Dysaan came up with a skin of water and tipped it up for him to drink. Rundall swallowed slowly, paused, and then drank some more. As he became accustomed to the light, and could focus on who was around him, he smiled and gripped Veracitas' arm and smiled at Boschina.

"This must mean Metro is defeated," he said, holding his throat, "or you would not be here."

"I'm happy to report to you, Lord Rundall, that the magician is dead," Veracitas replied.

"And the king," Rundall asked, his voice cracking, "he is well?"

"That I don't know," Veracitas answered.

"We don't know where he is," Currad added.

Rundall rubbed his eyes and held his head for a moment. "I don't know how many days have passed—how long I've been in that cell." Then, he cupped his hands together in front of him. "May I have water?"

Dysaan squirted water from the skin into Rundall's hands. The old counselor sucked the refreshing liquid from his hands. He took more water and splashed it on his face, washing and rubbing his eyes and wiping them dry with his sleeve.

"I think the last time I saw the king he was in Metro's rooms," he said slowly, trying to remember the order of events before being dragged to the prison cell. "You did not find him there?"

Currad shifted from one knee to the other as he answered, "We have been fighting Metro's army all day. Besides, I don't know where Metro's rooms are."

"Thalmus and Ekala are searching for him," Veracitas said. "But we've not heard anything from them."

"You must go straight away to search for the king," Rundall insisted, grasping Veracitas' arm. "He must still be in grave danger, if he's alive at all."

"What about Princess Ekala?" Veracitas asked.

"Ekala has Thalmus for protection, but the king has no one," Rundall replied.

"He has Ekala Oleen, his daughter," Boschina said indignantly.

Lord Rundall turned to her and saw looking back at him a different girl than the one he knew when her father carved the statue of the king. This girl exuded strength and confidence and appeared older than her years. The Stone Cutter's Daughter had fulfilled her role, her part of the prophecy—and more.

"You're right, Boschina," Rundall said, smiling at her. "King Ahmbin has always had the love and support of his daughter, Ekala. And now you, daughter of Veracitas, must go find them."

With that directive from Lord Rundall, Boschina stood up and looked at the men. "I know where Metro's room is."

"Then take us there," her father said.

Dysaan gave her a nod of confidence and Currad stood, stepped aside, and motioned with his hand for Boschina to lead. "We'll follow you," he said.

"All right," she replied, looking at the two soldiers and then her father. "Follow me."

*

Ekala and Camp knelt again beside Maz.

"Did Bubo just heal him?" Camp asked with amazement.

"Not completely," Thalmus answered. "But, Bolimaz will stay alive now, his wounds will heal, and one day his brothers will see his return."

Camp smiled with joy at seeing his friend and ward saved. "Between Larma and Bubo, this endeavor is blessed," he said.

Ekala agreed. "Larma and Bubo have given us this victory today."

"No, Princess," Camp replied, "it is your victory."

Ekala stood, not feeling victorious at all and angry for not having found her father. She looked at Baldoff lying on the floor, clutching the stone wall by the window. She walked over and grabbed him by his hair, bent his head back, and laid her sword across his throat. The edge of the blade rubbed against his skin.

"Do you have any more tricks you want to tell me about?" Ekala hissed.

"No. No more," Baldoff wheezed. "You've won."

"Do you think I have what it takes to rule this land, Baldoff, to be Queen over you?"

Baldoff tried to swallow. "Yes."

"Say, '*Your Majesty*'," she demanded.

"Yes, Your Majesty," he answered.

"I'm only going to ask this one more time," Ekala said, calmer now. "Where's my father?"

Baldoff stared at her for a moment, the question in his eyes, and then he pointed to the door behind the false throne. "He's in that room."

Ekala hesitated a moment, looking at the dark room through the open door and fearing what she might find there. She glanced at Maz and Camp, and then studied Baldoff's face again. "You scum! Why did I save you from the wind?" Her hand tensed on the handle of the sword as she rubbed the blade across his throat. Then, she felt a hand slowly grip her shoulder and heard Thalmus' voice. "Let's find your father." She took a deep breath and slowly withdrew her sword from Baldoff's throat.

"I'll watch him," Camp said, still kneeling by Maz.

Letting go of Baldoff's hair, Ekala stood and walked to the door as Thalmus joined her. They both had their swords ready, just in case.

"Father," Ekala called, standing at the threshold, peering into the darkness.

There was no response.

"Father," she called again. "It's Ekala. I'm here for you."

This time they heard a moan and movement from inside, but they were suspicious. Could it be another trap? No one knew what Metro may have hidden there and without Bubo to see for them, they were blind. Thalmus looked around for something to make a torch. He cut a piece off the curtain that had been ripped from its hooks, found a chunk of wood still glowing from the fire, lit the bundle of rolled material, and tossed it onto the floor in the dark room.

As the bundle ignited, the room was dimly illuminated. They could make out more shelves with various-shaped containers, a small dark fireplace, red draperies covering two walls, and wooden shutters sealed tight over a window. Thalmus inspected the ceiling as best he could, looking for anything dangerous that might be hanging there. Ekala decided that it was safe enough, stepped into the room, and went right to the shutters. She slid up the iron bolt latching the two sides together and swung them open as they squeaked and complained.

Light burst into the room, filling every dark corner.

The king was nowhere to be seen. Disappointed and angry, Princess Ekala slammed her sword into one of the shelves. The loud noise prompted a groan from somewhere. They stopped and listened.

"Father," Ekala called.

Another groan.

Thalmus started probing and pulling on the drapes hanging between the shelves. A stone wall was behind one drape, but the other one was covering an archway to another room. Thalmus pulled the curtain aside and kept it open by tucking the end into a shelf and weighing it down with a large bowl.

Light spread into the dark room through the archway. They could see a platform with bedding and a man lying there. It was the king, though they barely recognized him. His face was gaunt and his body withered. His wrists were tied with ropes to iron rings on the sides of the wood bed frame. He wasn't conscious, but was not asleep either––for his hands were clenching and his arms strained against the ropes.

"Father," Ekala called and started into the room.

Thalmus caught her arm.

She swung and looked at him.

"He's under a spell," Thalmus said. "Look at the walls, the floor, and the ceiling."

The walls of the chamber were painted with a mural of many scenes and creatures. Rainland was splattered there as a smeared wet scene with Corsair holding Boschina, Thalmus, and Bubo in chains. There were the Gauks that Thalmus and Boschina had fought in the Barranca. But in this depiction, the creatures were eating them as well as Tobazi, Currad, and Dysaan. Then, there was a scene at Table Top with Gorga standing proudly beside Metro and both of them standing on top of a prone, dead, Larma; next, a depiction of the destroyed statue of Ekala in the village Ello and the villagers dying in Safedor. Following that was a scene of the dust storm with the gray remains of Ekala, Thalmus, Veracitas, and Boschina being spun to dust in the wind. King Ahmbin stood in his court room, but his head was lying on the floor beside him. Metro sat on the throne with bright rays of sunshine gleaming from his body. The Learned Men were drawn as pigs, weasels, chickens, and jackasses. Lord Rundall was shown with no legs or arms and a snake coming out of his mouth.

Scattered on the floor between them and the bed were colored powders, shards of glass, and bits of iron spikes. painted on the ceiling over a red background was the crouching black lizard with its long tail circling the room, its front claws dug into the plaster, its head turned with its jaws open, and its beady eyes glaring down at them.

"That almost looks real," Ekala grimaced.

"This must have been Metro's bed chamber before he switched places with the king," Thalmus said, examining the details of the room.

"Very strange," Ekala remarked, staring at the murals on the wall. "He painted pictures of what he wanted to happen before he went to bed? And looking up at that thing on the ceiling every night? This is too strange. Let's get my father and get out of here."

"Go carefully," Thalmus warned and they began stepping between the sharp chunks of glass and iron.

"Father, I'm Ekala, your daughter. Thalmus is here. We're coming to save you!"

Walking with their swords held low, the iron scrap on the floor suddenly started flying up from the floor and sticking to the blades.

They swung and shook the swords, trying to throw off the metal, but it only attracted more pieces—clinking metal to metal. Soon, their swords were completely covered with the scraps, weighing them down and making them useless as sharp weapons.

"What is this?" Ekala exclaimed, swinging her sword and jerking it in an attempt to throw the metal from the blade.

"Stop moving your sword," Thalmus told her. "Raise it high over your shoulder and keep it still."

She followed Thalmus' advice and held her sword up—and kept moving to the bed. The metal chunks were vibrating on the floor, causing the glass shards to stand on end and dance toward them. Kicking the shards out of her way, she reached the bed. Ekala laid her sword on the covers and pulled her knife from its sheath on her belt to cut the ropes. Immediately, the metal pieces began jumping from the sword blade to her knife as she forced the edge across the rope.

"King Ahmbin," Thalmus said in his calm voice, touching Ahmbin's face. "Your frog hunter is here. Are you hungry?"

The king stirred. "Hungry," he muttered.

Thalmus felt something drip on him from the ceiling and he looked up to see that the lizard appeared to have turned, following them to the bed. Its tongue was sticking out and drooling. The beast's eyes were glaring at him.

This must be an illusion, Thalmus thought. *How could it come to life?*

Ekala cut through one rope and jumped to the other side. By now, her knife was almost covered with the iron spikes. Grabbing a handful of blanket, she tried to wipe the iron from the blade; the pieces were stuck together like one. She banged the knife on the wood bed frame and forced enough scrap off of the edge to start cutting the rope where it was tied to her father's wrist. The spikes were attaching to her knife again as she cut through the last strands. The king's reflexes pulled his arm up and Ekala threw her knife to the floor as the iron chunks covered it.

"Father," she shouted, "we must leave this place. Father!"

She rubbed his forehead and face and carefully opened his eyelids with her fingertips. Then, she took his hand and rubbed it between hers. "Wake up, Father."

"Daughter?" he mumbled.

"We must get him out of this room," Thalmus urged. "It holds the spell."

They both lifted his shoulders off the bed and pushed his legs to the side.

"I'll carry him," Thalmus offered.

"No, Thalmus, I will," Ekala responded. "Bring my sword."

She pulled her father forward, bent him over her shoulder, and lifted him up. Her wounded leg buckled under his weight; she wavered, regained her balance, and started for the door.

Thalmus sensed a movement above him and looked up to see the lizard turning toward Ekala as she carried the king. *How can this be?* He thought. He picked up his sword covered with the iron spikes. He grasped the handle firmly, swung the blade down between his legs and back up with a mighty heave— slamming the sword into the lizard. The powerful collision sent the iron spikes flying from the blade into the creature, sticking it to the ceiling. His sword fell back, clean of debris, and he caught it by the handle. He quickly looked up with his sword ready, but the lizard was not moving.

Now, the beast appeared flat and lifeless like a bad painting riddled with chunky iron darts.

Thalmus grabbed Ekala's sword from the bed and stepped in front of her. With both tools, he swept the now-motionless shards and spikes clear of her path as she carried the king from the room.

As the princess struggled into the main room, with her father draped over her shoulder, Boschina burst through the hall door, sword in hand, followed by her father, Currad, and Dysaan. They only had a moment to survey the room, to see Baldoff still sitting on the floor and Camp standing, ready to defend Maz.

"Oleen," Boschina shouted as she saw the princess coming from the inner door.

"Help me with the king," Ekala called.

Veracitas and Boschina helped Ekala lower the king from her shoulder to a table that Currad had righted to its legs. His majesty grunted and groaned, but remained unconscious.

"Is he alright?" Veracitas asked. "He looks so...shriveled."

"We must get him out of here, into good air," Thalmus told them.

Ekala leaned against the table, catching her breath and flexing her wounded leg. She started to help lift the king with the others, but Veracitas said, "Let us take him, Ekala."

She nodded. "All right. Take him to the garden with the pond. Boschina, tell Larma to meet us there." Then turning to look at Maz, she said, "We must get him out, too."

"Camp and I will carry him," Thalmus said, extending the handle of Ekala's sword to her.

Princess Ekala Oleen looked at the sweat-stained, leather-wrapped, handle and the gleaming engraving of Thunder, Dallion, and Bubo on the blade—and then at the eyes of the man holding it. She returned his smile and grasped the sword.

Chapter Twenty-Five
Resolve

Larma smiled with relief when she saw Ekala and Thalmus appear from the depths of the castle, but her mood changed to concern when she knelt beside the unconscious King Ahmbin after his bearers had laid him down. Everyone watched as Larma carefully placed her hands on each side of the king's head, gently pressed with her palms, closed her eyes, and then inhaled deeply and exhaled slowly.

The king took a sudden breath, opened his eyes for a moment, and mumbled, "Ekala...watch out...run...get away." Then, he closed his eyes again and slumbered.

Placing one hand on his chest, Larma felt his shallow breathing. She looked up at Ekala. "He will live, but the spell holds him deep. It appears this evil enchantment is going to take some time to expel."

Ekala looked around at the soothing green garden and blue pond.

"All right," she said. "This is a good place to start the healing."

Larma turned her attention to Maz, who had been placed on the ground near the king.

"Maz has a bad wound on his side, Larma," Camp explained, standing next to his prince. "He's bled a lot. I thought he was dying, but Thalmus and Bubo saved him."

"Yes, I know," Larma replied, kneeling beside Bolimaz. "Bubo told me."

The silver-haired woman placed one hand on the wound and her other hand on Maz's chest. Closing her eyes, Larma listened to his heart, the blood coursing in his veins and his lungs taking in air and exhaling. She moved her hand from his chest to his throat, just below the jaws, and listened again.

Looking up, Larma smiled at Thalmus. "You did well." She turned to Camp. "Your friend's wound is deep. I have remedies for this, though healing will be slow."

"So, he'll live?" Ekala asked.

"Oh yes, Ekala Oleen. Maz will continue to be part of your story for some time." She touched Ekala's bandaged leg. "As will the scar you will bear on this leg."

Ekala grimaced, now feeling the pain and exhaustion from the long ordeal.

"I guess I need to heal as well."

*

A great feeling of relief and joy permeated the victors of the battle for Ambermal. Their mood was tempered with sadness as well—and the understanding that there was much work and healing to be done. In the first days after the battle, hospitals were set up in various locations throughout the castle and the wounded from both armies were brought in to be attended and nursed back to good health. These were hectic and noisy sites as the stretcher-bearers came and went with bloody bodies; medical practitioners worked on wounds and broken bones; patients groaned with pain; and people cried over dying loved ones.

To remove the fallen fighters, funeral processions trudged out through the main gates to the burial grounds, which were on a small hill surrounded by rose trees a half mile from the castle. Slow and mournful, these marches and ceremonies were dreadful and emotionally for the families and friends. Ekala attended each service and wept for the Oleens, for she had trained most of them and thought of them as sisters. Larma officiated at the funerals with a soothing, graceful presence; calming hearts and souls. Songs were sung, stories told, and promises made to always hold high the memories of those who died in the great battle for Castle Ambermal.

Maz and Camp were given rooms in the castle where the prince could recover from the sword wound and relax in security. Whenever she had a chance, Ekala checked in on her "favorite prince," as she had taken to calling him.

She wasn't the only one keeping an eye on Maz. Bubo would suddenly appear, night or day, quiet and watchful and listening—and then vanish again. When they were together, the prince and princess often talked, comparing their childhoods growing up under the

338

expectations of the crown and the ever-watchful eyes of the entire kingdom.

"You've had a much more difficult road than me," the prince of Toulon would say. "Being a man, I was expected to just step in when the time came. But you have had to fight tradition, history, and doubt."

"We both have our mountains," Ekala answered. "At least I don't have sisters trying to climb over me with daggers to take the throne."

Maz laughed. "Siblings can be dangerous adversaries." He rubbed the scar on his cheek. "They will not be happy that you took me in."

Ekala shrugged. "I'm not worried about it."

*

King Ahmbin, weak and numb, rested in the garden by the pond and in his chambers after the rooms had been thoroughly washed and scrubbed to remove any scent, fiber, hair, or presence of the magician. In fact, his name could not be spoken around the king, so as not to conjure any memory of the man or his evil. Following specific orders by Princess Ekala Oleen, Currad and Dysaan stood guard to make sure that no one had access to her father, except a special few. Lord Rundall joined the king every day, but much to their surprise, Ekala forbid them to talk about any state business. They were supposed to completely relax in mind and body in order to recover from the strain and influence of the previous year.

Culinary brought his tasty delights to nourish the king and Lord Rundall. Although these morsels were filling, they were toned down in richness and quantity to help the king return to health. However, there was more to the food than just taste. Ekala, who had been saved by Culinary's antidote to Metro's smoke, instructed the pudgy, red-faced, cook to insert his special blend of elixirs, herbs, and spices into the food to cleanse the magician's spell from the king's blood. When Thalmus and Dallion appeared one day with frog legs strapped to Thunder's shell, Culinary was overjoyed and presented the king, Lord Rundall, Ekala, and Thalmus with a feast that did more to revive the old man than anything tried to that point.

It was rumored that the princess had accompanied Thalmus on the frog hunt, but much to her relief that was not true. She was too busy setting things right in Ambermal and the kingdom. There was much to be done and she took to the task with an energy and zeal that wore out the less enthusiastic.

No one questioned her authority.

Most of the former troops of Ahmbin fell in line with the Oleens and followed the commands and discipline of the princess. The people cheered Ekala Oleen because she was among them often and listened to their concerns, opinions, and was forthright with her answers.

Much to Ekala's frustration, she rarely went anywhere without an escort of Captain Ritzs or Kali and a force of Oleens. This was by the request of Thalmus, who knew that princess had more enemies now than before her success. Some of Metro's agents still lurked among the people. Renegade troops who refused to yield to the princess roamed the country and there were still rumors of attack or war coming from beyond their borders.

The magician's imported soldiers who had been captured in the battle were given the option to stay and live peacefully or return home. Many decided to stay, seeing the opportunity for a better life, and were grateful. Those who wished to carry on their mercenary ways packed up and departed by way of an armed escort to the border.

Lord Baldoff was another matter entirely.

Ekala struggled with her anger and desire for revenge toward the man. He was kept locked in Metro's rooms, after they had been carefully cleaned and emptied of the magician's things, which were burned and buried. Finally, she decided to ask Larma's and Thalmus' advice. The three of them, along with Boschina, met at the king's chair in the Great Hall. The princess included her new little sister, Boschina, for she had as much to do with this journey as any of them. There was no one else present because the throne was not being used while the king's health was in question. Deserted as it was, the Great Hall had an eerie emptiness as they gathered.

Ekala stood beside the king's chair, looking at her three friends. "Baldoff should be tortured," she exclaimed, dropping her clenched fist on the arm of the chair.

"Tortured?" Boschina responded, surprised by the idea.

"For what he and Metro did to the king, to me, and to our country, yes," she said angrily. "Many people have died or suffered because of him, including your father, Boschina."

No one spoke for a moment, letting the thought of torture sink in. Then Thalmus asked, "Did you save him from the wind so you could kill him yourself?"

"I don't know why I did that," Ekala replied. "I just saw the terror in his face and grabbed him."

"That's your nature, Oleen," Larma said. "You're a rescuer, not a killer. Whether you want to believe that or not."

Ekala looked at the empty chair where her father had sat all of her life. "Baldoff helped to destroy my father and put Metro in this chair, on this throne. He needs to be punished for that."

"Do you think torturing him would truly purge your anger?" Thalmus asked.

"I don't know, I haven't tried it," Ekala said, shrugging her shoulders.

Thalmus smiled. "Believe me, the satisfaction is temporary."

"But there must be a penalty," Ekala persisted. "Our enemies will think I'm weak if I don't do something to him."

Larma watched Ekala and felt her anger. "Your father did not use torture on his enemies. Yet, he was respected, and perhaps feared, by adversaries," she said softly. "To start using that sort of hostility is a perilous and fateful road for the kingdom, as well as yourself. Is that the way you want to rule?"

Ekala leaned on the chair with a hand on each arm of it and shook her head slowly. "I can't just forget what he did."

"You don't forget," Larma replied. "That would be foolish, but you can't let him, or anyone, control you this way."

"How do I do that?" Ekala asked, turning to look at Larma.

"Freedom from anger, and the desire for revenge, is only relieved when you decide to let go of it here," Larma said, holding her hand over her heart.

Ekala exhaled. "That will not be easy to do."

Larma smiled. "Forgiveness never is, whether giving or accepting."

The next day, when the princess was talking with Maz, she asked, "Have you thought about what you'll do to your brothers when you return?"

"Oh yes," Maz said, "many times. At first I wanted to kill them. But I realized that would just drag me down to their level and that's not how I want to live. Besides," he laughed, "if I killed them, then I would have no one around to annoy me."

Ekala laughed along with the prince.

"I'm glad I have you to talk with."

Several more busy days passed, but the question of Baldoff was never far from her thoughts. Then one morning, Ekala woke early and watched the sunrise from her window. She marveled at the joy she felt for this new day. Leaving the room, she went to Culinary's kitchen for breakfast and was surprised to find Thalmus there.

"I thought you were staying out at the ford of the Camotop with Thunder, Dal, and Bubo?"

"I was, but Bubo told me I should be here this morning."

Ekala smiled. "You've got him spying on me?"

"He does what he will, you know that."

"I can't seem to do much around here without you and Larma knowing about it."

"Stop bantering you two and eat," Culinary said, putting plates of eggs, potatoes, and bread on the table. "Your jibber-jabber is making me hungry."

After breakfast, Ekala called Ritzs to her and ordered the captain to assemble a force for travel and to meet her at the gate with the prisoner, Baldoff. When the captain and force of Oleens arrived, leading their horses and prisoner, they found Thalmus, Ekala, and Boschina waiting. The Princess and the Stone Cutter's Daughter were both wearing their swords.

Baldoff knelt, shaking, before Ekala. He could not take his eyes off of her sword. He could not stop looking at that engraved blade that had rubbed against his throat and would have killed him if it were not for the frog hunter.

"Baldoff," the princess said. "I'm done thinking about you."

"Please, Your Majesty," Baldoff begged. "I'm not worthy to be cut by your royal blade."

"You're right about that," Ekala replied. "In fact, you have no worth in our country and I'll not waste any more time on you."

Baldoff jerked about, glancing at the Oleens, men and women, standing around him until finally focusing on Boschina. "Don't let them kill me, Stone Daughter!"

"Your death is not mine to decide," Boschina said and turned to Ekala.

The once-powerful Lord Baldoff now turned to the man he had spurned and ridiculed and tried to kill. "Thalmus, Great Hunter, Friend of the Owl, you have the power to save me. I beg you to do so."

Thalmus remembered how Baldoff was when he first met him in the king's court: arrogant, controlling, and devious. "Lord Baldoff," Thalmus said. "There is always hope for those who have chosen the wrong path, but in you I see a man committed to walking in the ruts of the old road."

"No," Baldoff exclaimed and dropped his head. "I'm a dead man."

Princess Ekala Oleen looked at the sad figure before her. "Captain Ritzs will escort you to the Great Water and there you will be put on a boat, never to return again, or your life will be ended."

Baldoff could not believe what he had heard.

"What?" he said, looking up at Ekala. "You're letting me go?"

"Yes, I am. But if I ever hear of you causing trouble, then you will see this sword again."

Baldoff nodded. "Your Majesty," he said respectfully, and then rose and went willingly with a surprising happiness for his unbelievable good fortune at not being tortured or killed. That was what he had expected because that was what he would have done.

The princess had a surprise for the Learned Men as well. The self-important advisors to the king were disbanded, despite their grumbling objections, until Ekala felt there would be a need for them—except Cartridge. She appointed him to be the one and only judge to hear and settle all conflicts over the illegal taking of land and farms from their owners during the king's illness and the year of turmoil.

*

Tobazi and his people rested, nursed their wounded, and helped Veracitas prepare a surprise for the king. It seemed there was a portion of a stone wall beyond the cells that needed to be removed for a hidden treasure. Boschina also helped her father with this endeavor, but she spent just as much time in the company of Ekala, acting as her aide and sisterly confidante. Larma, always present when needed, advised Ekala when she asked for assistance. Otherwise, she mostly spent her time with the king and Lord Rundall, carefully guiding their spiritual strength and rebirth from the darkness of Metro. Although Larma's presence was vital for Ekala and the rehabilitation of the king, she longed to return to her home at Larma Hollow and her life on Table Top.

It became apparent to everyone that King Ahmbin's daughter was in charge of the kingdom. She was making decisions and issuing orders that normally would be made only by the king himself. Despite that, no one openly objected to Ekala's leadership. Perhaps it was because of her military victory over Metro that saved the people from his marching reign of terror; or that they were pleased to have order restored; or simply because they liked her. Whatever the reason, everyone wondered about the health of King Ahmbin and what was going to happen if the princess declared herself queen and sat on the throne. All but Larma and Thalmus thought that Queen Ekala Oleen was a certainty.

Ekala constantly visited her father, checking on his recovery and talking with Lord Rundall and Larma about his progress. When they determined that the king was once again thinking clearly, Ekala, the name he had given her that means "the beauty of strength," began to have conversations with her father about his desires for the kingdom and his daughter. She told him about the Oleens, Table Top, finding Veracitas, her new younger sister, Boschina. The battle of Safedor, and the dust storm, which he was most fascinated by. She informed him of the changes that she was making, like disbanding the Learned Men. His curiosity and enthusiasm began to grow as they discussed ways to improve trade with other countries.

As the discussions progressed day after day, it became apparent to Ekala that although her father was weak, he still had the ability and heart to rule. However, in the short time of being at the helm, of making decisions and guiding the country, she realized how much she liked it and how she knew it was her destiny.

As Larma had told her, Ekala Oleen was called to lead.

Then one day, Ekala found the king in a most serious mood. He was sitting in a chair by the pond, where the fish swam in slow circles. She settled in a chair next to him and he placed his hand in hers.

After a while, he said, "I feel like I have been gone for a long time."

"You have," Ekala replied. "Now, you have returned."

He looked up at the white clouds drifting across the warm blue sky. "I have given much thought to how I was so easily deceived...how I allowed power, vanity and doubt to rule me."

Ekala sat quietly and listened, wanting to hear him speak— hoping to hear the father she once knew.

"It is a danger, a temptation that I...we must constantly be aware of," he said, including her in the warning. "I have ruled for so long, so many years, that I began to think that it was all about me; that I was the most important, that I was the only one who could rule this land. And that you, my daughter, a woman, could not replace me. I thought I could go on forever because I had to. I turned a blind eye to my weaknesses and allowed others to control me." He looked at her and gripped her hand tighter. "I was wrong, Ekala."

She acknowledged his apology with a nod.

"I had forgotten the old prophecy that you, the king's only child, a woman, would be the first of your kind to rule a country. I didn't see how strong and competent you are, or how you care for the people, and how I had changed. What a fool I was." He paused. "Who am I to go against your destiny? I'm sorry that in my weakness I made you fight for it."

Ekala put her other hand over both of theirs and said softly, "It's done now, Father. But, I'm not sure you're finished."

He shook his head slowly and returned his gaze to the fish. "I allowed our people to suffer because of my foolishness. I have lost my dignity and my authority."

"Have you lost your love for our people?" she asked.

He looked at her. "No, but they've lost theirs for me."

"Don't be so sure," she replied.

The next day, after a restless night, Ekala searched out Thalmus. He was helping move the king's statue from the stone wall where it had been concealed to a shed where Veracitas could clean and polish it. When the work party saw the princess approaching, they stopped and acknowledged her by lowering their heads slightly—for the word had spread that she did not like people bowing to her.

Ekala waved at them to continue. "Don't stop on my account." Then to the frog hunter, she said, "Thalmus, a word, if you will."

Thalmus stepped away with her toward the low wall overlooking Cold Canyon. "Have you seen the statue, Ekala," Thalmus asked. "It is wonderful, even as it is, covered in dust."

Ekala kept walking as she answered. "I was there with Boschina and Veracitas when they first dug it out."

"It was very clever of Currad to hide the statue right here, where no one would think to look for it," Thalmus said.

"Yes," Ekala replied. "His willingness to risk his life and his loyalty to the king has surprised me more than once."

They stopped at the wall and Ekala leaned against it, looking into the canyon. The updraft from below blew her hair back as she looked across the expanse and into its depth. Thalmus also leaned on the wall and watched her—waiting to hear what she had to say.

Ekala held her hand out, feeling the breeze pass through her fingers. "I doubt that I will ever trust the wind," she said. "It's so fickle."

"Larma has a connection with it," Thalmus replied. "But the rest of us can only expect it to be unreliable."

"It seems so long ago now that Bubo turned this gorge into Metro's grave," she said, pulling her hand back. "Yet, my thoughts often flash with that memory as if it's happening before me at the moment. Does that ever happen to you?"

"Often," Thalmus answered. "Certain images—many powerful memories will be with you forever and will surprise you when they suddenly appear."

"Well, that pesky image of Metro keeps appearing to me, I think it's because I'm worried that his evil is still lurking about waiting for a chance to pounce again."

"Believe me, Ekala, you can rest assured that the magician and his spirit are long gone and will not be back. Bubo has seen to that."

The princess continued staring into the canyon, lost in thought.

"Are you all right?" Thalmus asked.

"Why are you hanging around here for so long?" Ekala asked, changing the subject. "I mean I'm glad you're here. I just thought you'd have left weeks ago...knowing how much you and the three miss your home and how uncomfortable you all are in the crowd of the city."

"You know why I'm still here, Ekala." Thalmus replied softly.

Princess Ekala Oleen glanced at him, inhaled deeply, and then exhaled. "Everyone is waiting for the announcement, for my decision to take the throne."

"But you are unresolved," Thalmus responded.

"I'm struggling, Thalmus. I don't mean with being in charge, with ruling and making decisions. I like it, I really like it. I was born for this. I just feel that it's not the time to take the throne from my father. He's still capable."

"Is he?" Thalmus asked.

Ekala turned to look at Thalmus. "I think he is. Oh, he knows that he stumbled terribly; he understands that now."

"Don't you think your time has come?" Thalmus questioned, watching her closely. "The people are ready for you."

"Believe me, I want to be queen, to rule our people," Ekala replied and then shook her head. "What kind of daughter would I be to steal the throne from my own father?"

"You would not be stealing it if the king stepped aside for you," Thalmus said. He felt the updraft of wind from the canyon. He turned and looked at the sun reflecting off the walls of the Great Hall where the empty throne waited. "You are not ready for the confines of the throne, are you?" Thalmus asked.

Ekala looked at this short man who had more wisdom, knowledge, and courage than she could ever imagine. "You know me too well, Thalmus," she said. "Am I ready to give up my freedom to be ruler—to no longer be able to come and go, and do as I please? I don't know. Now that the time is close, I'm not sure. Maybe that's why I hope my father is still able."

"What about the blindness that caused his downfall?"

"His eyes are open again, Thalmus. His old self has returned and I want to believe that he can still rule. But then, I wonder if Metro's evil spell is totally cleansed from his mind."

Thalmus motioned toward the statue.

"Then perhaps there should be one more test."

Ekala turned around to see the stone image Veracitas had carved of her father being rolled into a work shed. "Perhaps," she said slowly, "that statue will provide the answer I seek."

So, at their next meeting, father and daughter discussed succession and decided it was time to resolve the question as to who would sit on the throne and then present to the people their ruler.

A great feast was prepared and thousands gathered from around the kingdom to celebrate, for there had not been a royal celebration in many years. Filling the streets and grounds around the base of the steps to the Great Hall, a festive mood infected the host of villagers as they waited with anticipation the crowning of a queen. Representatives from other countries were also there to honor King Ahmbin, but also to report who would rule Ameram.

Preparing to go before the crowd, the king was nervous. He had not been in front of the people in a long time—individuals presented to him in his court, yes, but not a throng like this. Lord Rundall, Thalmus, and Larma were there, along with Currad and Dysaan, of course, still doing their duty as his guards.

"I am worried as to how I will be received," King Ahmbin said.

Ekala held his arm. "Don't worry, father, you are still the king."

He smiled and then hugged her, holding on for a long time. "My daughter," he whispered. "Your mother would be so happy to see you now—to stand beside you today."

Remembering her mother, Ekala smiled.

"I wish she was here, to be with both of us."

Her father nodded, sadness filling his eyes. "You remind me so much of her."

Ekala leaned over and kissed his cheek. "Thank you."

Lord Rundall and Larma opened the doors to the portico and walked out through the columns to the landing of the first step. The hubbub of the crowd, spread out below them, hushed as Thalmus, the King's Frog Hunter, followed Larma and turned to the side—where Thunder and Dallion had placed themselves on the veranda above the people—and stood beside his friends. Bubo was perched on a cross beam in the gable of the building, suspiciously watching the mass of people in the plaza. On the other side of the colonnade stood Maz and Camp along with Captains Kali and Ritzs, all of whom wore, along with their weaponry, the Oleen gray shirt with a maroon O over the left breast. Next through the doors came Currad and Dysaan with their large battle-worn swords held upright before them and wearing maroon and gray uniforms with a new emblem on their chests: the seal of King Ahmbin encircled by a gold O. Then, Boschina appeared in the doorway wearing her Oleen uniform, sword at her side and bow slung across her shoulders, carrying a pole with the large royal banner emblazoned with the new seal. Upon seeing the official standard, with its colorful streamers decorating the top, the people cheered and chants of "Oleen" spread through the crowd.

When Boschina reached the steps, she turned aside with the wide banner revealing Princess Ekala Oleen and King Ahmbin walking side by side, each wearing their colors. The roar from the multitude was deafening; some say it was heard all the way to Table Top. Father and daughter stood at the edge of the portico looking out at their people and letting their joy wash over them. Finally, Ekala had enough of the praise and she extended her hands for quiet.

The people responded and became still.

"My father, your king, has returned to us in good health," she said.

Cheers went up again and then quieted as the princess continued, turning to King Ahmbin: "In your honor, we present this tribute." She pointed toward a street, where a wagon with a large canvas covered object began to move forward pulled by men and women and guarded on each side by Toubarian soldiers. The content of the wagon was very heavy and the peaked canvas, the size of a man, wobbled as the procession moved forward. Riding on the wagon and holding the canvas steady were Tobazi and Veracitas.

The people shuffled out of the way making room for the pullers, while others fell in behind the large cart and pushed to help move it faster until the procession reached the steps. There it stopped while the royal father and daughter, together, moved carefully halfway down the steps.

"Your Majesty," Veracitas said loudly. "With all respect and affection, this is my homage to you."

The sculptor bowed to King Ahmbin and motioned to Tobazi. Together, they pulled the canvas away to reveal the statue that the king had ordered destroyed. There was a loud gasp from the crowd and then silence as everyone looked at the king for his reaction. People near the wagon tried to back away, but the throng was too thick and packed together.

King Ahmbin stood motionless, staring at the image. The statue seemed—almost real. The stone king was standing with his hands on his hips, his arms forming a forty-five degree angle at his sides. His right leg was straight, supporting the bulk of his weight—while the left leg was slightly bent and a step forward of the right foot. His shoulders were slightly turned with his right hip, his head was up, and his gaze looked straight ahead— unafraid of whatever confronted him.

This was a posture that King Ahmbin had been comfortable with since he was a prince; he often stood in this way. The sculptor had captured it perfectly. He also had delicately carved the weathered and wrinkled face and hands, the long gray hair, and accurately depicted the slumping shoulders and rotund waist. This is what had surprised him before, what he had not liked, and thought that he was being mocked because he had come to believe in an image of himself that was not real. But as King Ahmbin looked at this statue now, he was struck by its precision and he shook his head.

Thalmus and Currad saw the king waver and they both moved quickly down the steps to take his arm. King Ahmbin looked into the strong eyes of his frog hunter and leaned into him. Currad and Thalmus walked the king down the steps and helped him climb onto the cart. As he did so, the people knelt or bowed, but kept looking at him—to see his reaction. Veracitas waited, watching the king and glancing at Ekala, who was watching her father.

Old King Ahmbin let his hands glide over the stone image, feeling the art of the sculptor, the grooves and lines and smooth areas. In his aging life, he had known for a long time that his body was not what it once was; that his youth was over; that he was old, but he had chosen to deny it. Preferring instead to fool himself, he had been taken for a fool by Metro—who had tricked him by promising him a return to his youth.

But here, before him, in his hands, was truth. "This is what I look like. This is who I am," he whispered to himself. He looked at Veracitas, who was waiting for his reaction.

"You are truly a masterful artist, for you speak the truth in stone," the king said. "And for this, I condemned you? I am deeply sorry to you and your daughter."

"Thank you, Your Majesty," Veracitas replied with a smile growing on his face.

The king reached his hand out to the sculptor, the artist, who grasped the royal hand with his cracked, rough-skinned, hand. The people stood and cheered. Ekala smiled at Thalmus with relief. Her father had passed the test. She stepped onto the wagon and hugged him. Filled with joy and relief, Boschina rushed down and jumped into her father's arms. Tears rolled down her cheeks as she held onto him.

Before leaving the statue, the king turned to Tobazi. "You are the Toubarian who helped Thalmus and Boschina escape Rainland—and fought in this battle to save our kingdom?"

"I am he. Along with my people, we fought. My friend Thalmus called and we came."

"I have heard of your story from Thalmus. It is most interesting. I would like to hear it from you, when you're ready."

"It will be my honor," Tobazi replied.

With Currad on one side of the king and Thalmus on the other, they all went back up the steps to the top. The king looked at the people and quieted them with a wave of his hand. Turning, he looked for a moment at Larma, then Thalmus, and finally Rundall.

King Ahmbin's eyes were smiling with tears. They all nodded at him with recognition and approval. He turned back to the waiting mass of people. "Thank you," he said in his high-pitched voice. "Thank youfor your, love." Then, he bowed to the throng and slowly rose.

"Now, please listen to my daughter, who you all know as the Princess Ekala Oleen."

Again the crowd cheered, then quieted for they were anxious to hear what she was about to say.

"I know what's on your minds," she said in a strong voice. "It's been foretold that I will rule Ameram. Most of you had doubts that I was capable of this. I believe you have a different opinion of me now."

People applauded and the Oleens started to chant, "Oleen."

Ekala stopped the uproar with a raise of her hand. "Much of the fighting we just went through was because of me and my legacy. It was also because we allowed evil men to take over our kingdom. The reason we were able to defeat this enemy, the reason that we won the fight was because of you. Because you believed in me, in your country and in your king. No one should ever doubt what *we* can do together!"

She paused as the mass of people cheered. Then she continued. "I am the rightful heir to the throne and I will rule one day—but not today."

A low groan and objections rumbled from the host of people.

"No, listen to me: we have a king who is strong and wise once again, and wants only the best for our people." She moved next to her father. "I am proud to be his daughter, standing at his side, and serving him." She pointed at the people, "and serving you."

Again, cheers rose from the people.

King Ahmbin watched his daughter as she accepted the praise of the people. She was strong and confident, like he used to be. Now, he was just tired and unsure of himself. But he knew for sure that this bold woman next to him was the future of their kingdom. There was no denying it.

He touched her arm to get her attention. "Thank you for believing in me again," he whispered.

She turned to him with concern in her face. "I never stopped believing in you."

"You are so good, Ekala; just like your mother."

"And you, Father," she replied, holding his gaze. "I'm also like you,"

He smiled with her and then turned and held up his hand to still the crowd. "My people, I cannot let this be. Ekala called me strong and wise. The truth is that those words no longer describe me."

A confused muttering rumbled through the crowd.

"Those words describe your new ruler." He grasped Ekala's hand and held it up. He looked at her and she saw his love and pride for her in his eyes.

King Ahmbin turned back to the people. "After what my daughter has done to save me and our kingdom, and because of who she is, I declare now, that from this day forward, Ekala Oleen is our first Queen and the one and only ruler of Ameram!"

At that moment, Bubo dropped from his perch on high, with his wings spread wide, drifted down and landed on Ekala's shoulder. She was surprised by his sudden appearance and grip. He settled for a moment, spreading his wings behind her head and beyond her shoulders. The new queen felt a surge of confidence and affirmation. She heard Larma's voice whispering, "Blessings on you." Turning, the queen saw Thalmus smiling as he leaned against Thunder who was clicking his jaws, and Dallion bobbing his head and pawing with a hoof. Boschina and Veracitas still stood beside the statue waving and starting the chant of "Oleen! Oleen!"

Bubo hooted twice, lifted off and flew to his friends, landing on Thalmus' shoulder where he settled his wings and turned to watch the queen.

With that, the people of Ameram cheered and celebrated with the comfort and knowledge that their country would thrive for many years under Queen Ekala Oleen. The succession of the Royal House of Ahmbin was as it should be, as it was written, and was now fulfilled.

~~~

Epilogue

T he king's frog hunter lay on his back sleeping on a grassy bank of a pond. In the water floated Thunder, the giant shell creature, and grazing nearby with several other horses was Dallion. The hunter's dreams were pleasant, though searching: the soiled faces of farmers working in rows of plants, a joyful father and daughter hugging one another, a confident woman with a crown on her head, and an unflattering, but truthful, statue of a king. He heard a deep hoot from Bubo, the clack of a tortoise's jaws, and a warning whinny from the Paint. Rolling to his side, Thalmus opened his eyes to see riders coming toward him across the meadow. He sat up as the shell creature emerged from the water onto the bank beside him.

"Thalmus," one of the riders called.

He stood up, waved, and waited for them to come to him. There were twenty riders in a double column, most of whom were wearing maroon and gray uniforms with the letter O on the left breast. The lead horseman was dressed in brown and the two behind her were in green uniforms. The riders stopped their horses—snorting, stomping and nodding—before Thalmus and Thunder.

Boschina, wearing the Oleen uniform, jumped from Radise and hugged Thalmus. "When you weren't at the cabin, we knew where to find you. Right here, where I first met you."

"And here I am," Thalmus replied.

Queen Ekala Oleen swung her leg over Shadahn's back and dropped to the ground. "Hello, Thunder," she said, rubbing his head. Thunder bumped his big head into her.

"Yeah, I'm glad to see you too, big boy."

The others were dismounting as Dallion trotted up to nuzzle with Shadahn. "Careful, Dal, she's been pretty feisty," the queen said to the Paint and patted him on the shoulder. Then she turned to Thalmus, looked at him for a moment, and smiled. "Looks rather boring around here, Frog Hunter."

Thalmus shrugged. "Looks can be deceiving, as you know."

Queen Ekala blurted out a laugh and hugged Thalmus, and then slapped him on the shoulder. "We miss you at the castle. When are you coming back?"

"Not until your father wants some frog legs," Thalmus answered.

"That may be sooner than you want," she replied.

Maz and Camp, the two wearing green shirts with gray-green trousers, stepped up to greet Thalmus. "We would surely like to hunt with you sometime," Maz said.

"Oh, I would not want to be responsible for your safety, Prince Bolimaz."

"I can see to that," Camp said. "Or at least I can try."

Thalmus smiled. "It is good to see you both—and you, Maz, all healed?"

"I have a few pangs now and then, but I'm fit, thanks to you and Larma—and Bubo, of course, wherever he is," Maz said, looking toward the trees.

Motioning to their uniforms, Thalmus said, "I see you are wearing the colors of Toulon, your country."

"We want to show our support for the Queen of Ameram," Camp answered, nodding to Ekala.

"Besides," Maz added, pointing with his thumb at the force of Oleens behind him, "we feel fully protected now."

"That is always a good feeling," Thalmus replied. "What of Currad and Dysaan?"

Ekala chuckled. "Those two won't let my father out of their sight. They're stuck to him like mama bears protecting their cub."

Boschina, who had been petting Thunder and Dallion, spoke up. "Thalmus, we're going to Table Top. You should come with us."

"Table Top?" Thalmus said, glancing at Ekala.

"To visit Larma at the hollow," Boschina continued, "and to check on the other people there."

"Where is your father, Veracitas?" Thalmus asked.

"He has returned to Ello to make another statue of Oleen."

"By himself?"

Boschina grinned. "Captain Kali is with him."

"And a force of Oleens to secure the village," Queen Ekala added, giving Boschina a sideways glance.

Thalmus nodded. "Well, Table Top is several more days of travel, even without Thunder," he said, patting the tortoise's shell. "So, you must rest here. There is plenty of water and good grazing for the horses. Besides, this is a first. A royal visit to my home is a good excuse for a banquet. Did you bring Culinary?"

Queen Ekala Oleen laughed. "If I'd known that you were in such a hospitable mood, I would have brought the old cook. But then, Father wouldn't have been happy."

That evening the entire entourage enjoyed quite a feast of everything Thalmus and the Oleens could find to cook up. The only thing missing really was frog legs. They ate and talked deep into the night recalling all the previous events and what various people, good and bad, had done. At one point, Maz stood up and made a fairly long toast to Thalmus and his friends for saving Ameram from Metro and himself from death—but most important for including him, the wandering Prince of Toulon, and Camp in the great battle to put Ekala on the throne. He held his cup up for a moment until the queen seconded his toast and tipped her cup.

The two of them smiled at one another.

"Your day is coming," Ekala, said pointing at him with her cup.

And they drank again.

That night, and the night after, Bubo silently sailed past the guards to land next to Ekala. The great owl stood alongside her while she slept until the first light of day when he quietly winged away. The queen awoke feeling renewed and confident.

The royal party rested for two days at Thalmus' meadow, enjoying the relaxed atmosphere and the people of the nearby village, Tamra, who were thrilled to have the queen there. The villagers kept bringing her special food from their gardens and fish ponds. At one point, while Ekala watched children playing in the stream, she asked Thalmus, "I get the feeling that when we leave, you're not staying here. Where are you going?"

Thalmus looked at her for a moment before responding.

"You have become more perceptive."

"Really? I guess it comes with being a queen."

"No, it was always there," Thalmus replied. "You've just learned to pay attention."

"Well, that doesn't tell me where you're heading."

"To the Great Water," Thalmus answered. "We want to spend time there."

"For how long?"

"Until it's time to come back."

Ekala nodded.

"I can understand, but I no longer have that freedom."

"Do I hear regret?" Thalmus asked.

The queen smiled. "Not at all."

In the morning, Captain Ritzs and the Oleens gathered the horses and supplies and said their goodbyes before mounting up. Maz and Camp repeated their desire to hunt frogs, knowing that would never happen because Thalmus was a lone hunter. Boschina hugged him and said she would be back to ride Dallion and Thunder. Ekala patted Thalmus on the shoulder and looked him in the eyes. "Thank you. I feel so…refreshed." she said softly, and then turned and jumped up on Shadahn. Looking around at the meadow and the trees, she said, "I thought we'd see Bubo before we left, but he must be away."

"Just because you have not seen Bubo does not mean that he has not seen you," Thalmus replied.

Queen Ekala Oleen looked down at the King's Frog Hunter and smiled.

"True," she said, and paused, looking wistfully at Dallion and Thunder, then back at Thalmus. She smiled again. "We'll give your regards to Larma."

Thalmus smiled back at her. "Please do."

With that the queen turned to Boschina. "Let's go to Table Top."

Their horses started moving without a command.

Thalmus watched them ride away, and then turned to his cabin to gather his own supplies and tools.

PROFILES

Characters

Ahmbin (Ahhm-bin): Aging king of the land of Ameram. Andus Ahmbin III, grandson of the great King Ahmbin the First, was the last male in a long and continuous line of his family to rule the kingdom. His wife—and true love—died while their only child, Ekala, was still young. He never remarried.

Baldoff (Bald-off): Metro's cohort and accomplice. There is evidence of his malicious presence in other countries prior to and after the conspiracy to rule Ameram, though he was identified with different names.

Blayon (Blay-yon or Blah-yon; depending if you lived in the north or south): A famous mercenary soldier whose loyalty was devoted to the highest bidder. He was well traveled, experienced in all weaponry and tactics, and considered himself homeless.

Boschina (Bah-sheen-uh; archers referred to her as Bow-sheen-uh): Some scholars think it was Bosch-in-uh; either way, she was definitely known as "Stone Cutter's Daughter." Her story is long and intertwined with the makers of history in this kingdom. Most importantly, she is recognized as the spark that ignited the flames of the ancient prophecy for Princess Ekala.

Camp: A veteran soldier exiled from Toulon. He is Maz's companion. Together they join the Oleen forces to fight for Princess Ekala. His history and purpose is revealed through the battles and Maz's relationship with Ekala.

Cartridge (Cart-ridge): A member of the Council of Learned Men; was from a wealthy family with a long heritage as farmers and merchants. His ancestors started by building the carts and driving the horses that carried the farmer's produce to markets. Then, they expanded into farming. Their original home, and cart factory, sat on a central ridge overlooking the growing fields; hence, they took the name, Cartridge. This was the third generation of Cartridge to advise the royal family. This Cartridge took over from his ailing uncle at the age of 33 and had only been in office for six months when Metro's coup occurred.

Corsair (Core-sair): The vicious Captain of Rainland's castle guard and troops. He forced his way to the high command and to be Lord Luminous' favorite by devious and malicious means. It is unknown how he met and fell under the influence of Metro. Some historians believe that Metro had promised Corsair a lordship when he became king of Ameram.

Culinary (Kyoo-le-nair-ee): A renowned and creative cook. He managed such a unique kitchen (some might say, experimental food laboratory) that so many others imitated him to the extent that his name became synonymous with the art of cooking and kitchenware. Even today, in our world, the word is widely used.

Eidolon (Eye-doe-len): A silver-gray mare that was also known as Larma's Phantom. It seemed to appear whenever she needed to ride. The two of them together were a formidable presence.

Ekala (E-kay-la; or if you lived in the south, E-kaw-law): King Ahmbin chose the name for his daughter, after his wife, Lady Ahmbin, had died because it meant the "beauty of strength." She was his only child and heir to the throne of Ameram.

Gorga (Gor-ga; pronounced from deep in the throat, like gore, then ga with a short a): The name was originally the title for professional executioners. No previous history is known of this particular man. The first known record of him is at Table Top where he worked as an agent for Metro.

Kali (Caw-lee): A tall, strong-shouldered, woman with bushy, frizzy, red hair and freckles. She had met Veracitas when Boschina was a very young child and he carved a statue of her village elder. Kali was a struggling potter and he had admired her work, as she did his. They had a friendship that bordered on romance, but neither one pursued a deeper relationship because of Boschina's missing mother. When the statue was complete, Veracitas sadly left with his little Boschina in search of another job. Oleen met Kali at an artisan's fair and asked her to join the community at Larma Hollow to teach others the art of pottery. Once under Larma's tutelage and Oleen's training, she quickly gained confidence and became a leader.

King Dieten (Die-tin): King of Zinkila. A man about the same age and similar looks as King Ahmbin; the two of them played together as children when the families visited one another and had remained friends. Unlike Ahmbin, Dieten had four sons, all of whom wanted to succeed him. It was rumored that Dieten and Ahmbin were distant cousins.

Larma (Lar-ma): A mystic woman of undetermined age and authority with a spiritual power of truth that was beyond understanding. Her connection with Thalmus and Bubo eclipsed time. Scholars still debate the consequences and the amount of her influence in historical changes of this period.

Maz: A mysterious young man from Toulon hiding at Table Top. He and his older friend, Camp, join with Larma and the Oleens to fight for Princess Ekala's cause. His secret, and importance in Ekala's life, is revealed in a dramatic dying moment.

Metro (Met-trow): A devious, power hungry magician of unknown origin. He was able to use his extensive knowledge of alchemy and mind control methods to fool and manipulate people.

Oleens (O-leens): Devoted followers of Ekala Oleen; specifically, her army of warriors. Started by Ekala and trained by her and Larma they were initially women, who had been alone, widowed, abandoned or had no home or way to survive. Eventually, as Ekala rose in authority and the movement for her grew, men were allowed to join the Oleen Forces as separate units.

Pawndors (Pon-doors): People from the country of Pawndor far to the east who had invaded three generations previous, through Toubor, and controlled part of Ameram for a number of years until King Antell (Ahmbin's great grandfather) chased them out and destroyed their army on the fields of Touborna. It is not absolute, but many scholars believe that Thalmus fought in this campaign because of praise in the historical records for a "fearless small man with a bloody blade of death and endless strength...."

Ritzs (Writ-zz): A dedicated captain in the Oleen Forces. Her father and husband had served as officers in King Ahmbin's army. Her father died in the battle of Tanden and her husband had disappeared. Ekala found Ritzs teaching archery and horseback riding to children for food and lodging. Ekala invited her to join the growing band of women at Table Top and she became a devoted follower of Oleen.

Thalmus (Thall-mus): Commonly known as the King's Frog Hunter and guardian of the Prophecy of Ameram. He was a man of mystery to people of his day and continues to be so to researchers because he appears to have been present and influential throughout the history of the kingdom.

Tobazi (Tow-bah-zee; some recent scholars think it was pronounced Tow-bahz-eye): Helped Thalmus and Boschina escape from Rainland, where they saved his life; fought with his own small army, and the Oleens, in the battle for Ambermal, and became a devoted ally of Thalmus and Boschina.

Veracitas (Vera-see-tahs; man of truthful and accurate statement): The ancestral name of a long line of sculptors who were renowned for their artistry in making stone statues so accurate and realistic that some believed the "stone cutters" to have magical powers, turning people and animals into stone. This generation, Veracitas was the first to have no sons, only one daughter (Boschina); and he struggled with his talent under the burden of his famous paternal predecessors.

Animals

Boogala (boo-gah-lah; with a short "a" sound): A strange-looking animal that can best be described as a cross between a duck and horse. It is the size of a horse with a horse's head, but with a duck's bill and web feet instead of hooves.

Bubo (Boo-bow): A Great Horned Owl with a power and spirit to change lives. Buboas was also simply referred to by the name, Owl. He was the indomitable friend of Thalmus and steadfastly helped and defended him.

Dallion (Dal-lee-in): A striking white and brown Paint stallion who had a free spirit that influenced other horses and animals. Saved by Thalmus and Thunder from the quagmire of the Laundo Marsh he was forever devoted to his new friends.

Radise (Raw-dice): Related to Shadahn and was from the bloodline of the great warhorse Radisadan. She was a steady, experienced, horse that knew how to help a new rider with maneuvering and tactics.

Robon (Row-bon): Bred by a farmer as a racehorse to win financial stability, but he had to sell her to the army to feed his family. She understood the military training, but resisted the various soldiers who rode her until she was declared unfit and used as a pack animal. That's when Shadahn and Ekala saw her, recognized her quality and strengths, claimed her, and took her to Larma Hollow.

Salas: One of many wild or loose horses who followed Dallion. She was a gentle horse who was agreeable to people, but chose to roam free. Now in her older years, she mainly stayed near Thalmus' home where she knew she was welcome and safe.

Shadahn (Shaw-don): From a spirited bloodline of warhorses bred for the royal family. Ekala was the only person to ever ride her.

Shadahn became friends with Dallion because of Thalmus' and Ekala's friendship.

Shell creature: A mix between a tortoise and a snapping turtle, but with more dexterity. It had a broad flat shell and webbed feet that gave it the ability to move on dry land and swim in the water. Adults could be two meters in size and carry three times their weight. These unique creatures were wild and already rare in Thalmus' time.

Thunder (see shell creature for description): The giant shell creature that was Thalmus' companion and fellow frog hunter. It is not known when or how the two met but records are clear as to their loyalty and defense of one another.

Locations

Ambermal (Amber-mall): The name of the castle and walled city where the king of Ameram lived and conducted the affairs of the country. It was named for King Amberm who chose the defensive location on the cliffs of Cold Canyon and started the castle's construction.

Bevie (bev-ay): A village and its surrounding land named after its owner and noble, Lord Shawnden Bevie, who served the king on the Council of Learned Men. The community was known for growing delicious fruit and abundant vegetables.

Camotop River (Kam-ot-op): A wide and deep channel of water with a strong current that flowed from the rain and a copious spring in Rainland through Cold Canyon, below Ambermal Castle, and on to the Great Water. There were only two places where it could be crossed without a boat; but in a wet season, even these usually shallow fords were impassable. The name is derived from ancient indigenous people. It means: source of life and death.

Ello: A small, but important, village because of its water wells and its central location near a gap in the hills that held one of the few trails to the Great Water. The village enjoyed a relaxed atmosphere of trade and hospitality.

Escat Marsh (S-cat): A series of three large ponds linked together by narrow channels of water that had wooden bridges spanning the channel for travelers. But, over time, the marshes had enlarged, encroaching on the trails to the bridges resulting in making the passage more dangerous and, therefore, practically abandoned. The name is derived from the odor of the scat of the frogs.

Laundo Pond (La-un-doe): A great swampy pond in the lowlands of the mid-eastern portion of the kingdom that was named after a prince who disappeared there while hunting frogs. The pond, strangely enough, had its own tide that would rise and ebb with the phases of the moon, creating sticky mud bogs which could become fatal traps to the unknowledgeable adventurer. The ponds were inhabited by particularly aggressive frogs that were mottled brown in color with black spots.

Marbala: A village west of the Escat Marshes and nestled into the foot of the Stone Hills. Known for its unique white or blue-grey marble that was quarried there in the hills, it was the home of artists, sculptors and stone cutters. The community enjoyed a good trade in its stone, and the artistic wares produced from the famous marble. The people of Marbala had a reputation for durability, independence and for speaking the truth.

Moxfet: A picturesque and friendly community of farmers and tanners who had built and maintained the first home for orphans. It was named after the land's noble family, Steponus Moxfet.

Safedor: A box canyon in the western hills. It is also known as **Ekala's Surprise at Safedor** and is commonly accepted in the ancient annals as the turning point for the throne of Ahmbin. The princess led her small band of soldiers in a shocking victory over a larger force of renegade and mercenary troops by climbing down the craggy walls of Safedor, a feat never done before or since, to surprise the troops and save the captive villagers of Ello.

Seena (See-nah): A region of the land that had rich farming soil and had been worked by the same families for generations. It was a major food source for the realm and therefore had always been protected; but with a breakdown in authority, unscrupulous soldiers took what they wanted with few repercussions.

Tamra (Tom-raw): A village that was named after a tasty small fish that flourished in the local ponds. It was so delectable and desired that over time the local people turned it into a profitable fish-farm business. As young children, they learned to swim in the ponds while working the nets and harvesting. Once, a frog moved in to their ponds, causing havoc and horror. Thalmus endeared himself to the villagers by harvesting it for the king.

Toubar (Too-bar): A mysterious, ancient, land many leagues east of Ameram. It was a dry and desolate terrain inhabited by resilient nomadic tribes of people who fought constantly for control of the few water sources in the land.

Toulon (Too-lawn): A kingdom to the north of Ameram, across the Sol Linden River and beyond the Wilderness of Toulon. Depending on which family was in power, Toulon was either at peace or trying to conquer Ameram. At the time of our story the two countries had been at peace since Ekala's great grandfather.

Zinkila (Zin-kee-la): A small kingdom southeast of Ameram and a historical ally of doubtless support.

For more information about the book and the author visit:
www.kingsfronghunter.com

KEN YOUNG

KEN YOUNG

Made in the USA
Charleston, SC
04 December 2014